# The Regency

## LORDS & LADIES
### COLLECTION

*Two Glittering Regency
Love Affairs*

The Larkswood Legacy
*by Nicola Cornick*
&
The Neglectful Guardian
*by Anne Ashley*

# The
# *Regency*
# LORDS & LADIES
## COLLECTION

# The Regency

## LORDS & LADIES
### COLLECTION

*Nicola Cornick & Anne Ashley*

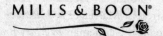

**MILLS & BOON®**

*First published in Great Britain 2005 by
Harlequin Mills & Boon Limited,
Eton House, 18-24 Paradise Road, Richmond, Surrey TW9 1SR*

THE REGENCY LORDS & LADIES COLLECTION
© Harlequin Books S.A. 2005

The publisher acknowledges the copyright holders of the
individual works as follows:

The Larkswood Legacy © Nicola Cornick 1999
The Neglectful Guardian © Anne Ashley 1997

ISBN 0 263 84570 2

138-0705

*Printed and bound in Spain
by Litografia Rosés S.A., Barcelona*

# The Larkswood Legacy
*by*
*Nicola Cornick*

**Nicola Cornick** is passionate about many things: her country cottage and its garden, her two small cats, her husband and her writing, though not necessarily in that order! She has always been fascinated by history, both as her chosen subject at university and subsequently as an engrossing hobby. Nicola Cornick became fascinated by history when she was a child and spent hours poring over historical novels and watching costume drama. She still does! She has worked in a variety of jobs, from serving refreshments on a steam railway to arranging university graduation ceremonies. Nicola loves to hear from readers and can be contacted via her website at www.nicolacornick.co.uk

# Chapter One

'Annabella! You graceless girl! Why, I declare, you are as clumsy as an elephant!' Lady St Auby brought the phrase out triumphantly, for she had seen such a creature in Lord Eaglesham's zoological collection. The words were delivered in a sibilant hiss, unlike Lady St Auby's habitual hectoring tone, but they were hurtful nevertheless. Annabella St Auby bit her lip and a flush came into her pale cheeks.

This time, her transgression had been small. She had stood aside to allow her mother-in-law to enter the Taunton Assembly Rooms first, as precedence demanded. Unfortunately, Lady St Auby had been so deeply engrossed in gossiping with her bosom-bow, Mrs Eddington-Buck, that she had not realised that Annabella had stopped and had cannoned into her back, setting her hairpiece askew and dropping her fan in the process.

It had been a disastrous way to re-enter Taunton society after a year of mourning. It seemed to Lady St Auby, in her anguish, that every head had turned in their direction and every conversation was suspended. The coiffure, which had taken her maid five-and-forty minutes to prepare, was slipping irretrievably over one ear. She knew that she had flushed an unbecoming mottled puce, and to make matters worse, her husband was gaping like a drunken fish and her daughter-in-law was hanging her head like a shy debutante. She dug Annabella viciously in the ribs.

'Well, don't stand there gawping, girl! Oh, that Francis ever chose to throw himself away on such an ill-bred little miss!' It was not the first time she had uttered such a remark. Lady St Auby made no secret of the fact that she considered her only son to have married beneath him, and Annabella had damned herself beyond redemption by failing to be the heiress she had promised to be. Hard-won self-control helped her to ignore her mother-in-law's vulgar observation, even when Mrs Eddington-Buck tittered behind her hand.

The Taunton Assembly was unlikely to be the epitome of high living, Annabella thought, as she followed Sir Frederick and Lady St Auby through the crowded ballroom to find a vantage point opposite the door. Bath would have had more society to offer, but the St Aubys were too poor to travel there. The company tonight would no doubt consist of the usual hunting and shooting set with whom Sir Frederick in particular had always mingled, and the evening would drag along with no hint of excitement. The Assembly Rooms were shabby and in sore need of a fresh coat of paint. Annabella sighed. She felt like they looked. Her evening dress might have been fashionable three years previously, but even then it had been run up by her father's housekeeper, based on a faded pattern from the *Ladies Magazine*. At the time it had been a rather pretty shade of mauve. Now it was a faded lavender, and served as the half-mourning appropriate to one who had lost her young husband so tragically a year before.

They had paused several times whilst Lady St Auby tried to find the most advantageous position in which to wait to be seen and greeted by the great and the good. Unfortunately, several early arrivals had taken the best spots and it was a while before her ladyship was satisfied, elbowing some poor unsuspecting young lady out of the way and moving a potted palm slightly to the right so that it did not obscure her field of vision. The St Auby party took up their stance, but almost immediately Lady St Auby's eye fell on Annabella with disapproval. She tugged at her evening gloves so viciously that the seam ripped.

'Smile, girl! No one will believe that you have a desire for entertainment if you stand there with such a Friday face!'

Several heads turned at the hissed undertone. Annabella flushed scarlet.

'I beg you, dear ma'am—'

'Lady Oakston! Sir Thomas!' Suddenly Lady St Auby had no time for Annabella's faults. She was fulsome, wreathed in smiles. 'A pleasure to see you again!' Now she was gushing like a mountain stream and Annabella turned to scan the ballroom again. It seemed very crowded that night, but perhaps that was because she had become unaccustomed to such bustle... Lady St Auby was simpering now as another set of acquaintances came up to greet them. It reminded Annabella of the rather unpleasant way in which her

mother-in-law would melt girlishly when Francis had
put on the charm, trading on the fact that his mother
could never refuse him anything…

'Such a sad loss to us,' Lady St Auby was saying
to Lady Oakston, wiping away a surreptitious tear.
'My dear daughter-in-law was so overcome we feared
she would become a recluse!' The insincere smile was
turned on Annabella, with Lady St Auby waiting for
her to echo her sentiments. Annabella was silent. She
had her faults, but hypocrisy was not one of them.
Lady St Auby turned her back on her.

'Simple creature!' Mrs Eddington-Buck said, with
an artificial trill of amusement, and she did not mean
it kindly.

After spending a sequestered year in the rotting
manor that the St Aubys called home, these bright
lights and loud voices were almost shocking to Annabella. As a young girl she had craved excitement,
but knew well enough now that it was not to be found
amongst the hard-drinking, hard-riding hunting set.
Before her brief marriage, her life in her father's ostentatious home had been empty and dull, and she had
briefly thought that her marriage might introduce her
to a wider society. It had done so, but she had not
been accepted into the gentry any more than her father
had been before her. And now both her husband and
father were dead, and she was stranded, a poor relation, in a county society which had once regarded her
as a curiosity and now thought of her scarcely at all.

But it seemed that the whole of Taunton society
was on show tonight and one could not but wonder
why. The hard eyes of these bejewelled women were
raking Annabella contemptuously, dismissing her old

faded lavender half-mourning with small, self-satisfied smiles. The looks of the men were more equivocal still, appraising, familiar… Annabella knew that it was Francis she had to thank for this disrespectful attitude, for when he had been in his cups he would talk loudly and unreservedly about matters which were best kept between husband and wife. His cronies, gleefully recognising this weakness, had encouraged him to the hilt until the whole of Taunton appeared to know intimate facts about Annabella that could only add to her embarrassment.

Annabella sighed again as she thought of Francis. She was guilty of the charge that she had entrapped the St Aubys' pride and joy, for she had set her cap at Francis as the only means of escape from her father. Weak and dissolute, Francis St Auby had had a penchant for women and gambling, and Annabella had gone into the marriage with her eyes open, aware of the threat to her future posed by both. She had bought Francis with the promise of her fortune, for she had known instinctively that he would have no other interest in her. Sure enough, he had set up a mistress in the town before the banns had even been read, but Bertram Broseley's wealth had been rumoured to be immense and this had at least been sufficient to prompt Francis to go through with the wedding, his mistress prominently on display at the ceremony itself. Annabella, who had known full well that Francis's character was unlikely to improve, had smiled all through her wedding day until her face ached, grimly aware of the price she had chosen to pay in order to avoid her father's alternative plan for her future.

At first, matters had not been so bad. Bertram Broseley gave them a generous, if grudgingly granted, allowance, and they lived in tolerable comfort. Annabella rarely saw Francis, who spent his time with his mistress or in the low town taverns he frequented. Then, eighteen months previously, Broseley had died unexpectedly and disaster had struck. There was no inheritance. The legendary fortune had proved illusory, swallowed up in all the debts that Broseley had left. After a few months the little, rented townhouse had had to go and they had moved back to the manor Francis's parents owned. Francis's temper, always uncertain, had become vicious in his disappointment. He joined his mother in railing at his wife for her ill-bred, rapacious nature in tricking him into marriage. Lady St Auby repeatedly bemoaned the marriage to all and sundry and Francis spent more and more time gambling and drinking. And, one night, he had become involved in a quarrel over loaded dice, had been too drunk to fight and had fallen and hit his head on a stone hearth. And that was that.

Once again, Lady St Auby regained Annabella's attention by digging her in the ribs. This time she was almost beside herself with excitement.

'Look, Annabella! Oh, Millicent!' She grabbed Mrs Eddington-Buck's arm. 'I declare, it's Mundell! And the Earl and Countess of Kilgaren! At a country assembly! How thrilling!' A shadow crossed her face as a horrid thought struck her. 'What if the Viscount does not remember us? Oh, if he cuts us, I shall die of embarrassment, positively die!'

Annabella watched the Viscount's party enter the Assembly Rooms. No wonder there was such a crush tonight if word had gone round the neighbourhood that he was to be present! Once, long ago, she remembered, she had fancied herself in love with Viscount Mundell, for he was exceptionally handsome in a rather hawkish way and, as one of the County's premier landowners, was imbued with an irresistible attraction that would still have applied had he been as ugly as sin. Tonight he was with a small party, four ladies and three other gentlemen, all graciously acknowledging the greetings of Sir Thomas Oakston as he excitedly bowed them into the room. A flutter of awareness went through the assembled ranks as ladies preened themselves and turned to show their figures and profiles to advantage. Excited whispers tried in vain to elicit the identity of the other gentlemen. Dagger glances were cast at the ladies who had the good fortune to be part of the Viscount's company.

'Let me see! Let me see!' Mrs Eddington-Buck craned her neck to look over the heads of the crowd, and trod heavily on Annabella's foot in the process. 'La, how elegant they are!' She cast a spiteful, sideways glance at Annabella. 'One can always tell *true* quality, Lady St Auby!'

Annabella smiled stiffly. Her mother-in-law and her friends never ceased to remind her that Bertram Broseley had been a Cit, a rich merchant who could never aspire to county society. His early marriage to the daughter of an Earl could be conveniently forgotten, for his wife had died giving birth to Annabella and he had never again attempted to marry above his station. It was a thorn in Lady St Auby's side that Annabella was so well-connected, with a grandmother who was the Dowager Countess of Stansfield, and a sister, the Incomparable Alicia, now a Marchioness. But Annabella was estranged from her family. Had she been close to her sister, Lady St Auby would no doubt have boasted of the connection. As it was, she used the rift to point out to Annabella that her family had cast her off as beneath their notice.

Annabella swallowed hard. Over the past few intolerable months, she had been thinking more and more of her sister and their estrangement. Probably the very desperation of her situation in the St Auby household made her long for a happier alternative. Seven years her senior, Alicia had always seemed remote, for their father had fought hard to keep them apart. If only she could think of some way of approaching Alicia, of healing the breach... But she had given her sister good reason to dislike her, and it was not so easy to undo that now.

'They are coming over! Viscount Mundell has noticed us! Oh, Millicent—' Lady St Auby was almost incoherent with joy. She planted her considerable bulk firmly in the path of the unsuspecting peer. 'My Lord! An honour! And a pleasure to see you again, is it not, Frederick?'

Sir Frederick St Auby, who had much in common with his late son, dragged his gaze away from the contemplation of a luscious blonde beauty and grunted. 'Servant, Mundell.'

The Viscount had not the first idea as to the identity of the large lady accosting him, but he nevertheless had manners equal to the occasion. His bored grey eyes moved from Lady St Auby to her spouse with indifference. 'How do you do, ma'am? Sir... I hope I find you well?' His gaze drifted past them and sharpened on Annabella. 'Mrs St Auby!' A note of genuine sincerity entered his voice. 'How do you do, ma'am? I had been hoping to see you here. I had the pleasure of speaking to your sister, Lady Mullineaux, recently. I was glad to see that both she and your new nephew are well.'

For a moment Annabella stood quite still, unsure if he was really addressing her. She was so used to slights and snubs that she could scarce believe that this deity was actually speaking to her. Then, as he waited, she realised with amazement that he was indeed awaiting a reply. Annabella smiled a little awkwardly. She was aware of nothing but surprise that Mundell had even recognised her. Though they had met on a couple of occasions in the distant past, she had made no impression on him and now she knew that only her resemblance to Alicia had helped him identify her. Although no one had ever suggested that she was an incomparable beauty, both she and Alicia had the heart-shaped faces, high cheekbones and determined chin that were the defining features of the look inherited from their grandmother. And now that Annabella had lost so much weight in the time following Francis's death, the fat that had threatened to blur her features had receded to leave her almost angular. Her hair was golden where Alicia's was auburn, and her eyes were a lighter green, and somehow she had just missed the startling beauty possessed by her sister, whilst remaining a very pretty girl.

Lady St Auby was looking furious that the Viscount's attention had been diverted to Annabella.

'La, sir,' she said, archly, 'do not speak to Annabella of Lady Mullineaux! My daughter-in-law and her sister do not see eye to eye and have not met for an age! Why, Annabella has not even been invited to visit for little Thomas's christening—'

But Annabella was not about to allow Lady St Auby to broadcast her disagreement with her sister to the assembled crowd. She had seen the faint, supercilious hint of boredom touch Mundell's handsome features at the threatened rehearsal of a tedious family quarrel, and she hurried in, with scant courtesy, 'I hope to see my sister and her family soon, my lord. It is a pleasure to hear of them going on so well.'

Mundell gave her a slight smile and made to move on, for plenty were clamouring for his attention. Annabella knew he had thought her both gauche and uninteresting, and it rankled. But any town bronze, or at least the semi-sophistication she had once achieved, had been knocked out of her by the constant criticism of her late husband, and the carping of her mother-in-law. She had never really been given the chance to sparkle.

Lady St Auby was made of sterner stuff, however. She was not about to let a Viscount out of her sights so easily. 'And your companions, sir? Will you make us known to them…?'

Fortunately for the Viscount's companions, most were in fact engaged in conversation elsewhere. The Earl and Countess of Kilgaren were still chatting with Sir Thomas Oakston, and the other ladies in the group were speaking to each other in a rather exclusive manner which suggested that they were above mingling with the *hoi polloi*. There was a pause. Annabella knew Mundell was about to snub her mother-in-law, and steeled herself.

The Viscount said with weary courtesy, 'Lady St Auby, may I present my brother-in-law, Lord Wallace? And a great friend of mine, Sir William Weston…'

Annabella, who had been admiring the elegant *ton*-nishness of Lady Kilgaren's dress, looked up, a little startled, as a shadow fell across her. Sir William Weston was bowing to her with formality. The name had meant nothing to her and she had not really been attending. Now, belatedly bestowing her attention on him, Annabella initially considered the gentleman to be nothing out of the ordinary. He was of more than average height, it was true, with a broadness of shoulder which somehow suggested strength and durability. But that was hardly a romantic attribute. Annabella, who had had little experience of true romance in her life, had always fondly imagined that her heroes would be dark and handsome, like the characters in the Minerva Press Gothics. Sir William was not particularly dark. His face was unremarkable except for a healthy tan which suggested that he had spent a long time in far hotter climes, and his thick, brown hair was bleached fair at the ends. Apart from that…

Annabella paused in her assessment as he looked directly into her eyes. Her heart skipped a beat and she caught her breath, uncertain quite what had disturbed her. Sir William's eyes, she discovered, were a rather fascinating blue, the colour of summer seas, at once sleepy and alert as they held hers for a long moment. Almost unconsciously, she started her appraisal again. Now that she was giving due consideration, she suddenly observed that Sir William Weston moved with a fluid grace that was oddly attractive when taken with his powerful physique. His face had integrity and character, and his smile was like his eyes, sleepy and disordering to the senses, hinting at all kinds of possibilities beneath the surface... Annabella felt herself blush to the roots of her hair as those very eyes scanned her face and appeared to read her mind.

'Mrs St Auby...' Sir William was smiling slightly, taking her hand in his. 'I have heard much about you. It has long been my wish to make your acquaintance.'

Lady St Auby cleared her throat noisily, bustling forward between them before Annabella could respond to this. 'A friend of Viscount Mundell!' she gushed. 'An honour, dear sir, an honour! And are you a landowner, like his lordship?' She might as well have asked his income, Annabella thought, closing her eyes in momentary despair. Her motives could not have been more transparent.

Sir William appeared unperturbed by this ill-concealed curiosity. 'Alas, no, ma'am! My estate is small. I am only a humble sailor.'

Lady St Auby's nose turned up as though the idea had reminded her of the smell of rotting fish. Unlike Annabella, she did not see the look of faintly ironic amusement which crossed Viscount Mundell's face at his friend's words. The music was starting up, but not quickly enough to cover Mrs Eddington-Buck's comments about *parvenus* who hung on the coat-tails of the nobility. Sir William's amiable smile did not waver, but his blue gaze moved from one to the other with thoughtful consideration. Annabella's blush deepened. He had said that he had heard of her, and she could easily imagine what had been said. 'The mercenary daughter of a jumped-up Cit' had been one of the more complimentary descriptions she had heard applied to herself, and here was Lady St Auby confirming just such an impression with her own behaviour!

'I am promised for this dance,' Sir William said easily, interrupting Annabella's thoughts, 'but may I hope to see you again later, Mrs St Auby? Please excuse me—'

And he was gone, leaving Annabella once again feeling oddly disturbed. She shook her head slightly to dispel the fanciful illusion. She had not been in society much, but she had met some personable men, many of them a great deal more conventionally handsome than Sir William Weston. But somehow none of them had his air of authority leavened with such good humour, and she found that powerfully attractive…

'…the lady in blue is Mundell's elder sister, Lady Wallace,' Mrs Eddington-Buck was saying, her feathered head-dress waggling with excitement. 'And the lady in pink gauze is Mundell's other sister, the unmarried one. And the other lady is a Miss Hurst, of the Hampshire Hursts, you know. There—' she pointed across the room '—dancing with that odd man, Sir William Weston.'

Annabella fanned herself vigorously, for the heat in the room was growing. No one had asked her to dance and she could only be grateful, for it would inevitably rouse Lady St Auby's ire. It was a very long time since she had attempted the country dances which were so popular, for Francis had usually been too drunk to be steady on his feet when they attended

such gatherings, and he preferred the cardroom anyway. Mrs Eddington-Buck and Lady St Auby had
moved on to discuss the dresses of the ladies in Mundell's party, and were full of extravagant praise. Annabella privately thought that Miss Mundell's rose
gauze was far too *outré* for a country assembly, and
Miss Hurst looked a cold and haughty beauty. Once
again, her gaze was peculiarly drawn to the tall figure
of Miss Hurst's partner.

'Shameless hussy!' Lady St Auby had followed her
gaze with malevolent eyes. 'Already casting out lures
to another man, and my poor, dead son scarcely cold
in his grave!'

It was not an auspicious moment for the first gentleman of the evening to approach Annabella for a
dance, and her heart sank when she saw who he was.
Glittering in his scarlet regimentals, and with a smile
easy and charming, Captain George Jeffries had managed to come upon her quite unawares. He gave Lady
St Auby a punctilious bow, acknowledged with a grin
the thin line of disapproval in which her mouth was
set, and pulled Annabella into the dance with a pro-
prietary hand she found almost intolerable.

'You must be in a fit of the dismals this evening,
my love,' he observed with cheerful informality, 'for
you have barely spoken a word all night. There!' He
gave her a grin he fondly imagined to be attractive.
'You should be flattered that I have given away the
fact that I have been watching you the whole time!'

'I did not see you come in, sir,' Annabella replied
repressively. She had no heart for idle flirtation, especially not with Jeffries. Once, perhaps, she had
found him attractive. But that had been at a time when

she was particularly lonely and vulnerable, and he had been quick to take advantage of the fact. Unfortunately, he was not now to be dismissed very easily.

'No, indeed!' Jeffries was eyeing her with objectionable familiarity. 'You were too busy fluttering your eyelashes at a Viscount to notice a mere half-pay officer!' He leant closer and she could feel his breath on her face. 'But you should not be so dismissive of my worth, my love! How much longer—?'

'Kindly stand back, sir!' Annabella said smartly, embarrassed by the licence he was taking and aware that several of the nearer couples sought to eavesdrop on their conversation. 'And refrain from addressing me in that intimate whisper!'

Jeffries recoiled as though he had been slapped. The figure of the dance separated them momentarily, but when he rejoined her he immediately took up the theme again.

'Then where and when may I address you?' The boyish charm had been replaced by a sulky, mulish expression all too reminiscent of Francis when he was in a bad mood. Annabella's heart sank. She knew that she had encouraged Jeffries's attentions during the long and boring months of incarceration at Hazeldean that had followed Francis's death. His admiration had been balm to her after Francis's black moods and Lady St Auby's constant fault-finding. Perhaps she had even allowed him more liberty than had been wise, but she had never intended that it should lead to more… And now that was what Jeffries was wanting, and the thought filled her with revulsion. She had to make it plain to him now.

'You may not, sir!' She saw him frown and added coldly, 'Your attentions are not welcome!'

At her words, Jeffries terminated his attentions in the most abrupt way possible. It was not perhaps the most desirable manner in which to draw attention at a ball, Annabella thought, to be left standing alone as one's dance partner stormed off the floor. Other couples were circulating about her, and while she hesitated, unable to disentangle herself and in grave danger of ruining the entire set, a strong hand plucked her from out of the other dancers' paths, and swept her to the side of the room.

'Forgive me my precipitate action, ma'am,' Sir William Weston said, above her head. 'I was afraid that there might be an accident if I left you there!'

Strong arms had closed about her, steadying her, drawing her so close for a moment that she could hear the beat of his heart, feel it against her cheek as it rested briefly against the crisp shirt. She felt a sudden, astounding sense of recognition and almost closed her eyes in relief. Then she was put very gently back on to her feet and Sir William stepped back, impeccably proper.

'My apologies, once again, madam.' He sketched a bow. 'I hope I have not hurt you.'

It was extraordinary, Annabella thought, completely bewildered, her feelings still in confusion. His lightest touch had caused an earthquake of sensation within her. She was not sure if she liked the feeling. She was even more uncertain of whether she could deal with it.

She took a steadying breath. 'Your actions were most timely, sir. I must thank you!' She looked up into those vivid, blue eyes and felt again the impact of his character.

Sir William's sleepy gaze dwelt on her thoughtfully, seeing she knew not what. She was aware that the faded mauve dress only served to accentuate the pallor of her face and that her hair, although a pretty honey fair, was escaping its hasty coiffure, for Lady St Auby had taken all the maid's time and Annabella had had to secure the pins herself. Yet he seemed to find no fault, and returned her smile with warmth.

'I imagine I witnessed you divesting yourself of an admirer there, Mrs St Auby,' he observed coolly. 'How very ruthless you must have been for the young man to react so! And now that I am here in his place, how may I serve you?'

Annabella had never thought of George Jeffries as a young man until that moment, but there was something in Weston's tone which made her see him suddenly as a foolish youth, for all his posturing in his pretty uniform. And in comparison with this man... Well, there was no comparison. Whilst she struggled to understand the precise nature of the difference, she realised that Lady St Auby was gesticulating at her across the floor. Annabella's heart sank. Her mother-in-law was watching her like a gaoler and she did not wish for another scene. 'Perhaps you might escort me back to Lady St Auby,' she said, a little regretfully, and saw Sir William grin down at her.

'Must I? The old dragon bullies you, yet you are eager to return to her side?' He gave her a whimsical smile. 'It seems most odd!'

Annabella tried unsuccessfully to repress her own smile. She was discovering that there were worse fates than to enjoy a mild flirtation with a man who was as attractive as the enigmatic Sir William. It had been a very long time since any man had flirted with her—except, of course, the unappealing Captain Jeffries…

'Lady St Auby can be of uncertain temperament—' she began guardedly, only to be stopped by his laughter.

'Upon my word, ma'am, that is the most astounding piece of understatement I have ever heard! You must be a veritable paragon to describe her in such terms!'

Now it was Annabella's turn to laugh. 'Oh, no, sir, that is too unkind! Her ladyship does her best with a daughter-in-law she never sought, who is left penniless to her charity! It is not easy for her!'

Sir William grimaced. 'You are all charity yourself, Mrs St Auby! But I see that Lady Bountiful is approaching us, so I may find out for myself if your words are true!'

'Oh, no!' Over his shoulder, Annabella could see the stout figure of her mother-in-law advancing on them purposefully. She wanted no interruption. Sir William's dancing blue eyes saw her dismay and he laughed aloud.

'Never fear, I will protect you! It will seem best if we are conversing on some innocuous topic,' he added in a swift undertone. 'Yes, my ship was stationed in the East Indies for two years, ma'am…' he had raised his voice for the benefit of the approaching matron '…and the weather is indeed too hot for the British temperament! Ah, Lady St Auby—' He turned swiftly. 'Your servant, ma'am! I was just telling your charming daughter-in-law how much preferable the west of England is to hotter climes!'

Lady St Auby was in a quandary. She had no wish to offend any friend of Viscount Mundell, even though it meant missing the opportunity to rail at Annabella for flirting with another man. She forced out a chilly smile.

'Indeed, sir! I should hope so too! Nothing *abroad*—' she invested the word with heavy scorn '—can stand comparison! The French are intemperate, the Russians uncivilised—although I did hear that the Czar is a charming man—and as for the Indies...' Lady St Auby paused and took a deep breath. 'Barbarous! But I believe you said you are a naval man? That would account for your sojourn in such a place, I suppose!' Her tone implied that Sir William's service in His Majesty's fleet was nothing to be proud of and her sharp gaze appraised him for signs that the wind and weather had coarsened his appearance. Sir William smiled back, not one whit discomposed.

'Just so, ma'am! I served during the recent American Wars, but am returned home now that the conflict is over.'

Lady St Auby sniffed. She was not conversant with Anglo-American diplomatic relations, but she knew a race of ungrateful upstarts when she heard of them. 'Those jumped-up Yankees! I trust our own fleet put them properly in their place, sir!'

'Indeed not, ma'am!' Sir William's smile was rueful. He looked as though he was enjoying himself immensely, Annabella thought. 'It grieves me to relate that the fledgling American navy has ships far faster than anything in His Majesty's service!'

'The *Constitution* is one of theirs, is it not?' Annabella said, suddenly. 'I read that it is a faster build of frigate than those in our own navy.' She saw Sir William's quizzical gaze upon her and flushed a little. 'I read about it in *The Times*,' she added apologetically, 'after the *Guerrière* was sunk by the Americans.'

'Most unsuitable,' Lady St Auby said frostily.

'Most commendable, ma'am,' Sir William said, blandly. 'An informed mind can never be anything but laudable.'

Lady St Auby glared at him.

'I see trouble for Britain from those big frigates from across the sea,' Sir William continued softly. Lady St Auby snorted again, glad to have the opportunity to take him to task.

'You are most unpatriotic, sir!' she declared. 'One imagines that our dear, dead Lord Nelson might have more faith in his own navy than you appear to do!'

There was a pregnant pause.

'It was Lord Nelson himself who said those words, ma'am,' Sir William said, gently. Annabella giggled, quite unable to help herself.

It was perhaps fortunate that Viscount Mundell chose that moment to come upon them, for Lady St Auby was flushing as red as a turkeycock.

'Boring the ladies with your naval tales, Will?' Mundell asked, in his lazy drawl.

Sir William grinned. 'As you see, Hugo! It is a bad habit of seafarers!'

'Then I shall feel no compunction in taking Mrs St Auby away to dance,' Mundell returned, with a smile for Annabella. 'Will you do me the honour, ma'am?'

And Annabella found herself swept into the set with

a sudden conviction that life was taking a most unexpected turn.

Once Annabella was over her initial surprise, she found dancing with the Viscount to be an entirely pleasant experience, for he was so exceptionally good that he made the whole process seem quite effortless. She soon discovered that her dance steps, though rusty, came back to her easily enough and she acquitted herself well.

'Bravo, ma'am!' Mundell said at the end, when Annabella's cheeks were pink and her eyes bright with the exertion. 'You see how good it can be for you to escape from that monster of a mother-in-law!' He ignored Annabella's half-hearted protest, taking her arm and steering her through the crowd to a quiet corner. 'We had no idea that we should find you so in need of rescue!'

'We, sir?' Annabella said, confused.

'Why, yes, my friends and I!' Mundell smiled down at her. 'Will Weston is a particular friend of your brother-in-law, James Mullineaux, you know, and when Lady Mullineaux heard that we were all to be staying at Mundell for a while, she asked that we see how you were going on! I understand that the two of you have not met for a time?' Mundell raised an eyebrow. 'She asked us especially to seek you out.' He saw her astonishment and added kindly, 'Lord and Lady Mullineaux would have been of the party were it not for the fact that they had no wish to be parted from Thomas and he is a little young to travel! But I know your sister is anxious to see you again!'

Annabella put her hand up to a head that was suddenly spinning. It seemed extraordinary that her own thoughts about seeing Alicia again should be echoed so soon and in a totally unexpected way. And it was even more amazing that her sister, who had no good reason to think of her with anything but dislike, should apparently be willing to give her another chance. Yet surely the Viscount could not be mistaken. She looked up at Mundell, a mixture of hope and disbelief in her eyes.

'Are you certain, sir? It seems most unlikely, if you will forgive me. Alicia and I...' She struggled, not wishing to go into the complicated details.

Mundell smiled again and Annabella was astounded by such unlooked-for kindness from such a man. 'Well, of course it is a matter for you to resolve with your sister, but I assure you that she is most concerned for the two of you to be friends!'

Annabella was struggling to assimilate all that she had so suddenly learned. Hope—real hope—had unexpectedly been put into her hands, and as she hesitated over it, Lady St Auby's voice rang out across the Assembly Rooms with bell-like clarity.

'...and of course, the Countess of Kilgaren is a *great* friend of Annabella's sister,' she was saying to a dowager in purple, 'and James Mullineaux and Mundell move in the same set, so it is not surprising that he should take her up...'

'Dear me,' Mundell said, with a slight shudder, 'what an overbearing woman! But I cut Will out just now for a dance with you,' he added, smiling a little mockingly at her, 'and at last I see him coming to redress the situation! Will!' He hailed his friend. 'It is unlike you to let me steal a march! I thought you were supposed to be a sound strategist!'

Sir William gave his boyish grin. 'I was engaging the enemy,' he said, with a nod in the direction of Lady St Auby. 'But I won out in the end, Hugo, for this next is the waltz, is it not? You will grant me this dance, Mrs St Auby?'

Annabella was beginning to enjoy herself a great deal. Far from lacking excitement, the ball was proving to be the event of the Taunton social calendar! Not only was she buoyed up with the hope of seeing Alicia again, but she now had the inestimable pleasure of the two most attractive men in the room vying for her attention. 'You do not take my acquiescence for granted, I hope, sir?' she asked, with just a hint of challenge.

Sir William's sleepy blue eyes widened slightly. 'Upon my word, no, ma'am! It would be a foolish thing to underestimate one's quarry! But on the other hand…' his arm was already about her waist and he had somehow drawn her into the waltz '…it is equally foolish to risk opposition! Forgive me for my lack of grace,' Sir William finished with mock apology. 'I am but a simple sailor, after all!'

Annabella cast him a look from under her lashes. 'Oh, no, sir, you are too hard on yourself! Scarcely *simple*, I feel!' And she heard him laugh in response.

Circling the floor in Sir William's arms was so exhilarating a feeling that Annabella was obliged to keep her gaze modestly lowered in order to prevent him from reading her mind. Just the proximity of his body made her feel quite light-headed and out of control. Francis had never inspired any feelings which could compare with this delightful but disturbing excitement.

'When did you start to read *The Times*, ma'am?' Sir William enquired, after one revolution of the floor.

Annabella almost jumped at the question. 'Oh!' She gathered her wits. 'Your pardon, sir, I was woolgathering! My father used to take all the papers. I read them avidly, perhaps because I travelled so little myself, and I knew his ships went all over the world, so I used to imagine them sailing to all the places I read about.'

'Yes, indeed, I came across some of Broseley's ships when I was stationed in the Indies,' Sir William said, and suddenly there was a certain grimness in his tone. Annabella felt herself blushing.

'I know…' She hesitated, constraint in her voice. 'He trafficked in slaves and arms and other unpalatable goods…he was not a pleasant man.'

'I imagine it must have been difficult for you…' Sir William's voice had softened as he looked down at her. Green eyes met blue for a moment. Annabella found herself on the verge of confiding. There was something about him that engendered a sense of kinship—that dangerous recognition again—and she knew it could be her undoing. After all, this man was a complete stranger. She knew nothing of him at all. She lowered her gaze.

'Much of the time, my father was from home, sir. I scarce knew him well. Then I married…' She shrugged a little uncomfortably, moving on quickly. 'Though we still lived in the same vicinity, I saw even less of him then. And, of course, he died some two years ago.'

'Broseley was expected to leave some considerable

fortune, was he not?' Weston said thoughtfully. 'It might have…eased…your current situation, ma'am.'

Again there was that insidious feeling of understanding, a closeness that was drawing Annabella towards disclosure. She had never had a confidant and the temptation was enormous. But it was too dangerous to allow herself to rely on Sir William. She steeled herself against him.

'When my father died it would have been pleasant to be rich, I suppose, but not on the profits of such an ill-made fortune! But tell me a little of your own plans,' she changed the subject with determination. 'How will you spend your time now that you are home from the sea?'

Weston accepted this change of direction with easy grace, but not without giving her a searching look from those very blue eyes.

'Oh, I intend to settle in the countryside,' he said, with a smile, 'and become a farmer. It sounds mundane, I know, but the delights of the capital hold little interest for me. I fear I ran through all the pleasures of the Town in my salad days!'

'But do you feel you will be able to settle in one place for long?' Annabella asked, genuinely interested. 'After all, you have spent much time in travelling and must surely find the confines of one place a little restrictive?'

Sir William looked thoughtful. 'I cannot deny that I shall always love the sea,' he said slowly, 'but I have my yacht if I take a fancy to go sailing again! Not so grand as the *Endeavour*, perhaps, but enough! And a man can tire of having no settled home!'

Annabella registered the reference to the yacht with

some surprise. There was nothing in Sir William's attire to suggest a man of great consequence, and despite his title, she had assumed that he had earned a living from the navy rather than entering it by choice over necessity. But now that she considered him further, the signs were there. The black and white of his evening dress was almost austere, but nevertheless cut by a master. A diamond tiepin nestled in the snowy folds of his cravat, and there was a heavy gold signet ring on his right hand. Annabella suddenly felt self-conscious in her old clothes. How could she be mingling with this exotic crowd, with Weston, Mundell, and their friends? She was a provincial miss with no money and no town polish. She forgot her new-found confidence and shrank.

A slight frown entered Sir William's eyes as he sensed her withdrawal. 'Whatever can I have said, ma'am, to so disturb you? I can only apologise—'

Annabella shook her head slightly, confused by both his perception and her own reaction to him. It should not have mattered that she was so far beneath his interest, but yet it did. She was in terrible danger of allowing herself to believe she could enter this world of title and privilege and escape from the existence that Lady St Auby had made unbearable for her. But suppose she tried—and failed? If Alicia had no real interest in ending their estrangement, if Mundell had only been kind and would forget her the next day, if Will Weston was only amusing himself... Her fragile composure was suddenly at breaking point.

The music was ending and she was about to ask Sir William to escort her back to the St Aubys, when Lady Kilgaren came up to them. Annabella's heart sank even further. Caroline Kilgaren was reputed to be Alicia's closest friend, and if anyone would know the sordid details of the breach between the two sisters, it would be she.

'William, I have not had the chance to meet Mrs St Auby yet!' Lady Kilgaren had a warm smile for Annabella and a beguiling look for Sir William. She was tiny, small and fair as a pocket goddess, and Annabella could not see how anyone could resist her. 'Be a kind fellow and bring us both a glass of lemonade! Please!' She saw his lips twitch and added, 'And don't hurry back!'

Sir William bowed with exaggerated deference and strolled off towards the refreshment room, stopping for a word with Viscount Mundell on the way. Caroline turned back to Annabella, her blue eyes sparkling.

'Forgive me for interfering in that ill-bred way! The truth is that I wanted to meet you and I was afraid that you would be snapped up again by Lady St Auby before I had the chance! But now I see she is enjoying a coze with that evil old gossip Millicent Eddington-Buck, so we have a little time! Will you join me?' She gestured towards two rout chairs stationed in an alcove to their left.

Annabella gave in. There was something about Caroline Kilgaren which suggested that resistance was pointless, for she was both decisive and direct. Caroline's shrewd blue eyes were appraising Annabella thoroughly, and she was suddenly very nervous.

'Forgive me for staring,' Caroline said frankly, with another of her warm smiles. 'In truth, you are very

like your sister! The gentlemen have already noticed it!'

Annabella blushed. 'Oh, ma'am, if I had a quarter
of Alicia's style!'

'It's only clothes,' Caroline said practically. 'You
have the basis of the rest already, and town polish can
always be acquired! But you looked quite apprehen-
sive when I came up, poor child,' she added consol-
ingly, making Annabella feel about seventeen. 'I only
wanted to tell you that Mundell told me he had mentioned Alicia to you, and it is quite true that she
wishes to see you again above all things!' She touched
Annabella's hand briefly. 'I know that the two of you
parted on bad terms, but Alicia has always thought
that there must be more to the case than she knew.'

Lady Kilgaren watched shrewdly as the colour
came into Annabella's face and fled as swiftly. The
Annabella St Auby she had met and of whom both
Will Weston and Hugo Mundell had spoken that evening was a far cry from the avaricious and ill-bred
girl who had so alienated Alicia Mullineaux. So Alicia
had guessed correctly when she had thought that there
was much more to the tale than the simple explanation
that Annabella had grown up in Bertram Broseley's
own image.

'I should tell you, ma'am—' Annabella drew breath
to explain.

'No.' Caroline put up a hand. 'If you wish to confide in me I should be honoured, but you need tell me
nothing you do not want! Take a little time; think
about it. I only wished you to know that Alicia is quite
anxious to see you—indeed, she will be writing to you

soon! There now—' she had seen Annabella's eyes fill with tears '—there is no need to be sad!'

'You are all kindness, ma'am,' Annabella said, brushing the tears away before anyone had time to see them. 'If you only knew how much I have wanted to make contact with my sister—'

'We will accomplish it!' Caroline said, with a smile. 'Now—'

'Caro!' Marcus Kilgaren was standing before them with two glasses of lemonade. 'Will gave me these for you, though I doubt you really wanted them!' He bowed to Annabella, a twinkle in his eye. 'How do you do, Mrs St Auby? Sir William was about to come to rescue you, but I fear he is too much in awe of Caroline to dare!'

'Stuff and nonsense!' Caroline said, getting to her feet. 'Will Weston has vanquished greater enemies than I!'

'But none more determined, my love,' Marcus said cheerfully. 'Come and dance with me, and let the poor fellow take your place here. He is languishing across the room and quite cast down!'

It was impossible to imagine Sir William in the manner Marcus described, Annabella thought, and sure enough, when she turned to scan the ballroom she saw him dancing with Charlotte Mundell. It was enough to prompt a prickle of jealousy for which Annabella took herself severely to task. She had only met Sir William that evening, after all, and hardly had a right to feel resentful if he paid attention to another woman. She herself was hardly without admirers, anyway, for as Marcus took Caroline off to dance the cotillion, Viscount Mundell took Caroline's seat and

chatted to Annabella about this and that in a manner
as entertaining as it was inconsequential.

'I fear I must oust you again, Hugo,' Sir William
said some ten minutes later, coming upon them as
Annabella was laughing at some anecdote Mundell
was telling her about Sir Frederick St Auby's exploits
on the hunting field. 'Miss Hurst assures me that she
is promised to you for this dance, and she is unlikely
to forgive you if you slight her!'

Mundell gave his friend a measuring look, but Weston was completely impassive. He got to his feet with
every evidence of reluctance.

'I do not believe you for a moment, William,' Mundell said evenly. 'Your motives are transparent! However, I will humour you this once! Your servant, Mrs
St Auby!'

He got up and Sir William took his seat with alac-
rity. Annabella considered him thoughtfully, wondering how she could ever have dismissed him as ordinary. Beneath that air of careless indolence was an
assurance and determination which were quite formidable. He was quite out of her league and she
should not tangle with him. But then, Mundell's set
were all a danger to her in their way. The glittering,
privileged world of the aristocracy was not for her and
though they might appear to see her as a new diversion, she should not depend on being part of their
circle. The misery that would be occasioned when
they dropped her and she was forced to retreat to her
circumscribed life would be quite intolerable.

'You look quite severe, Mrs St Auby,' Sir William
observed lazily. 'Can it be that you are a secret pur-

itan? Are you dismissing us all as a group of wastrels out for our own pleasure?'

Annabella smiled. 'I am sure that I derive enjoyment from a ball as much as most,' she allowed, 'but look over there, sir—why, it is well nigh disgraceful!'

Sir William followed her gaze to where no less than four hopeful young ladies had cornered Viscount Mundell and were fluttering their lashes and their fans at him, pouting prettily, hanging on his every word. Further down the room, Sir Thomas Oakston was busy flattering Miss Mundell, whilst his wife complimented Miss Hurst on her toilette.

'It is the way of the world,' Sir William said laconically. 'Everyone wishes to befriend the wealthy!'

'So you are as much a cynic as I, sir!' Annabella was still laughing as he pulled her to her feet.

'Come and dance with me, Mrs St Auby,' Sir William said, by way of reply. 'I need you to protect me from these predatory women!'

Annabella could hardly deny that she took pleasure in dancing with him. It would have been strange indeed for her to have emerged from the seclusion of the St Auby's manor to be swept up into the excitement of Mundell's orbit without enjoying it. And Sir William's evident pleasure in her company was heady as a draught of wine. She floated through the dance, which was the last of the evening, and thanked him somewhat incoherently at the end.

'It has been a pleasure, Mrs St Auby.' Sir William smiled down into her eyes. 'May I call on you tomorrow?' The words were conventional but there was something in his expression which made her shiver a little, in an entirely pleasurable way.

'If you wish, sir…'

'Thank you.' His smile was devastating, she thought weakly. He bowed and kissed her hand, and left Annabella feeling as shaken as when they had first met.

Once in the privacy of the carriage on the homeward journey, Lady St Auby was vitriolic.

'Scheming, conniving, *wicked* girl! You think that Mundell and his friends will take you up? You are deluding yourself, my girl! They'll be laughing at you now for a country dowd! And telling your precious sister what a frump you are!'

Lady St Auby knew how to wound. Withdrawing once more into herself, Annabella concluded that it was indeed unlikely that Sir William Weston was doing anything other than amusing himself at her expense. She would do best to forget the evening and her brief enjoyment, forget the heady delight of waltzing in his arms, for he would most certainly not call upon her on the morrow and to rely upon him doing so would only leave her more disappointed in the end.

## Chapter Two

'There's a gentleman to see you, ma'am.' The slovenly maid, whom Lady St Auby employed because they were too poor to have a butler, looked at Annabella with some curiosity. Mrs Francis had never had an admirer like this before—there had been Captain Jeffries, of course, but everyone knew he was no gentleman, and not averse to pinching the maids' bottoms when the mistress's back was turned as well! But this gentleman was Quality and no mistake.

Annabella pricked her finger on her needle and almost spilt a drop of blood on her embroidery. It would have made little difference had she spoilt it, for her skill was small and the uneven petals of the rose she had just completed were too poor to be displayed. Needlework was not one of her talents. She put the embroidery frame to one side and got to her feet.

So he had come after all! In the cold light of day, she had become even more convinced that Sir William had only been trifling with her, for what interest could he possibly have in furthering their acquaintance? The glittering excitement of the previous night seemed like a flimsy dream that would fade if she tried to grasp it. Yet here he was. Unless—perhaps it was only Jeffries, anxious to press her further, certain she would succumb… She turned to question the maid on the gentleman's identity, but the girl had already gone back downstairs.

Annabella ran to check her appearance in the mirror and gave a silent sigh. The dress of ruby red looked black in the dark little rooms of the St Auby town-house, and even Annabella could see the patches where the material had faded and worn. Today she had tied her hair up in a long plait, despairing of ever being able to achieve the simple elegance of the modes she saw in the old copies of *The Fashions of London and Paris*, which were passed on by one of Lady St Auby's friends. Still, she had kept him waiting long enough. Her heart beating faster, Annabella made her way down the narrow stair.

Sir William Weston was waiting in the drawing-room, his height making him appear to dominate the poky, low-ceilinged chamber. Today he was wearing a coat of navy blue superfine which appeared almost stark in its simplicity, but again, it had the simple refinement of a master's cut. He wore buff pantaloons and Hessians, both of which were elegant without being dandified, and his white cravat was once again arranged in complicated folds. He looked, Annabella thought dazedly, rather too disturbingly attractive. And when he smiled at her…

He crossed the room in two strides and took her hand in his. 'Mrs St Auby! What a pleasure to see you again, ma'am! I hope that last evening has not tired you too much?'

'Thank you, sir, I am quite well,' Annabella said, smiling a little at the thought that she might not be robust enough to survive a ball. No doubt the young ladies Sir William knew would be exhausted with the effort. But then, they could stay in bed until midday and would not be required to be up at first light to scour the scullery…

'Then I wondered if you would care to join me for a drive in the country? It is a perfect day for it and my curricle is outside. We could stop for tea at Mundell Hall on the way back.'

It sounded a tempting plan, and Annabella soon found herself donning her pelisse and going out to the curricle. Even had it not been Sir William who was inviting her, the simple pleasure of escaping from the dark house would have been enough.

She paused to admire the matched bays which Sir William had in his team, for they were prime horseflesh and suggested that he was a notable whip. The curricle, with its elegantly expensive lines, was creating quite a stir. Annabella noticed with interest that Sir William had chosen not to bring a groom and that a street urchin was eagerly holding the horses' reins for love rather than the coin Sir William now flicked to him as they set off.

'You are clearly knowledgeable about horses, ma'am,' Sir William commented when they had negotiated the busy streets of the town and were tooling along in the open country. 'Do you ride?'

'Oh, I used to!' As soon as she was out in the open air and feeling the warm sun and cooling breeze, Annabella remembered with a pang of nostalgia how she had enjoyed her rides about her father's estate. 'I rode a great deal before my marriage,' she said, 'and Sir Frederick used to keep a fine stable before the expense became prohibitive. I must confess that it is a luxury I miss!'

Sir William smiled at her enthusiasm. 'Perhaps we could go riding next time,' he said pleasantly, and the words echoed in Annabella's head: *Next time…*

So he planned to seek her out again, did he? A delicious little smile curved her lips at the thought. Having her company sought by so attractive a man was a new experience for her and one which was entirely delightful. She watched his hands, skilful on the reins, and repressed a little shiver.

'Did you enjoy the ball last night?' Sir William enquired neutrally, after a slight pause.

'Well, yes…I suppose so…' Annabella's reply sounded less certain than she had intended, and he gave her a quizzical look.

'You do not sound very sure, ma'am! Are dances and assemblies not to your taste? But surely I remember you saying that you liked them…'

'Oh, no, I enjoy them very much!' Annabella laughed. 'Not that I have been to so very many, sir! I only hesitated because I do not believe that Lady St Auby found the evening agreeable, which makes matters a little difficult…' She sighed, remembering Lady St Auby's vicious diatribe on the way home. She had managed to convince Annabella not only that Mundell and his set were laughing at her expense, but also that Alicia had never had any real intention of ending their estrangement.

'I realised last night how difficult it must be for you in such a household,' Sir William observed thoughtfully. 'Have you not considered the possibility of living elsewhere, ma'am?'

It was a rather impertinent question from a mere acquaintance, Annabella thought, but then he was a very direct man. She hesitated, conscious that almost anything she said about her current situation, her marriage, her father or her relationship with Alicia would lead her into difficult waters. She was unsure how far she could prevaricate with Sir William Weston—he seemed very determined.

'I have considered it,' she said carefully, 'but there are difficulties. It is no secret that my father left me very little money and my husband none at all. And I have no wish to impose on my sister, who, I am sure you are aware, sir, has reason to dislike me!' She gave him a defiant look. 'I have been thinking lately that the only solution is for me to earn a living!'

'Perhaps you have considered becoming a governess?' Sir William murmured, his voice completely bland. Annabella gave him a quick look, but could not tell if he was laughing at her. His gaze was fixed on the road and there was not even a telltale hint of a smile about that firm mouth. She looked away hastily.

'I have thought of it, but reluctantly discounted the idea, sir.'

'Oh, dear, why was that?'

Now she was sure that he was making fun of her. 'I am not bookish enough!' she snapped. 'I could hardly expect to be paid to teach a child those learned facts that I had not seen fit to acquire myself!'

Sir William's lips twitched. 'Was your education neglected then, Mrs St Auby?'

'No, sir, by good fortune I had a number of excellent governesses.' Annabella strove to be fair. 'It was my own attitude that was at fault. I had no patience with my teachers and what they tried to instil in me. So…'

'So, no governess post,' Sir William finished for her, one dark brow raised. 'A pity, but it would not have served. You are too young and,' he added under his breath, 'devilishly pretty besides!'

Annabella was startled. 'I beg your pardon, sir!'

Sir William grinned at her. 'I was merely pointing out that your relative youth and your appearance made it an unsuitable occupation for you! There will always be impressionable sons—or even fathers!—who would try to lead you astray!'

Annabella blushed. She hurried on to try to cover her confusion. 'But then I hit on a plan, sir!'

'Your resourcefulness is most impressive, ma'am,' Sir William commented, bland once more. Annabella shot him a darkling look.

'You are funning me, I know, sir, but I am quite in earnest! I intend to set up a circulating library!'

The horses swerved slightly as Sir William inadvertently pulled the rein, a terrible solecism for such an accomplished whip. 'You amaze me, ma'am,' he said politely. 'How do you propose to do such a thing?'

'Well, I have heard that Mr Lane, the proprietor of the Minerva Press, will set anyone up in a circulating library who wishes it,' Annabella said artlessly. 'And he is so very rich that I believe there must be a living in it! At the library in Castle Street they charge a subscription of a whole guinea to borrow the best books,' she added thoughtfully, 'but I have never been able to afford that!'

'As a business venture it would seem to have certain merits,' Sir William agreed. 'But where will you establish your library, Mrs St Auby? A seaside town or fashionable watering place might be the best. I suppose your father did not leave you any property that might be of use?'

Annabella shook her head. 'He left plenty of property, but all is sold to pay his debts,' she admitted. 'Why, the lawyers are still trying to disentangle his affairs! But I have no hope that there will be anything suitable. That is the only flaw in my plan.'

'Hmm, a pity.' Sir William had slowed the horses as they sped through a picturesque village. 'It seemed an excellent plan in all other particulars. But there are alternatives, of course! You might marry again, perhaps?'

'I doubt that, sir.' Annabella sounded subdued. They were back on dangerous ground.

Sir William allowed the curricle to slow down, and half turned towards her. 'You seem very certain, ma'am! How is it possible to tell what the future holds?'

'It is not, of course,' Annabella allowed, permitting herself to meet those perceptive blue eyes for a brief moment. 'But I do not think…'

'Perhaps,' Sir William said thoughtfully, 'when one has been married happily once, it is difficult to imagine such good fortune occurring again.'

'I imagine that might be so.' The sun went behind a cloud. Annabella shivered. 'And the reverse might also be true.'

'You mean that having been married unhappily, one might not wish to risk such a situation again?' Sir William pursued. 'Yet your sister, having been so unfortunate in the past, has now found true happiness as a result of being prepared to take that risk.'

'I am very glad that Alicia is happy now,' Annabella said sincerely, swallowing a lump in her throat and looking fixedly at the horizon.

'Yes, having been estranged from James for so long, and enduring that appalling scandal of her forced marriage, she deserves her current good fortune.' Sir William took his eyes off the road to consider Annabella's averted face thoughtfully.

'And you, Mrs St Auby, were you more fortunate than your sister in your dealings with your father? Did he not have an arranged match designed for you too?'

Annabella was taken by surprise. She had a sudden, vivid flash of memory—her father, bright red with rage, storming at her when she had refused to marry the man he had chosen for her. She had had Alicia's example to learn from, after all, and had been determined not to succumb. But though Bertram Broseley had not succeeded in marrying her off, he had managed to poison her life anyway. She pressed her hands together, suddenly distressed.

'Must we speak of such matters, sir? The circumstances surrounding my marriage cannot be of any interest to you, I am sure—'

'On the contrary, ma'am,' Sir William's tone was inflexible. 'It interests me considerably! What happens to one sister can, after all, repeat itself with another! And I have the strangest feeling that your apparent love match with Francis St Auby was no such thing!'

Annabella gasped. His effrontery in speaking of such matters was beyond anything she had experienced or knew how to deal with. No mere acquaintance should speak so, and certainly no gentleman should broach such a topic, particularly when she had shown her own disinclination to discuss the matter!

'Upon my word, sir,' she gasped, 'you are most persistent! And you presume too much! Your comments are impertinent in the extreme! Kindly stop this curricle and take me back now!' She looked around and realised that she had not the first idea where they were, for she had been quite engrossed in their conversation.

The flat country of the Somerset Levels stretched around them as far as the eye could see. Verdant green fields lined with thick hedgerows and edged with water-filled dykes stretched into the distance, empty of habitation. Her half-formed idea of stepping down and marching off in high dudgeon died a death. It would be impractical. She would look foolish. Worse, she would be lost. She looked across at Sir William, who was obeying her instruction and was bringing the curricle to a halt in the middle of the road. He did not look in the least abashed.

'My friends are always telling me that I have no decorum,' he said regretfully. 'It is a great trial to me!'

Annabella did not believe him. 'A great trial to everyone else, rather!' she snapped. 'I wonder that your friends bear with you!'

The ghost of a smile touched Sir William's mouth.

'I do believe you have a temper to rival your sister's, Mrs St Auby,' he said admiringly. 'She has always had a swift way of administering a set-down!' The amusement in his sleepy gaze only served to infuriate Annabella all the more. Despite her widowed state she was very young and inexperienced, and had no idea how to handle a man like this. And she did indeed have a temper which was slow to kindle but red-hot once aroused.

'Do I take it then, sir, that you actually require a response to your impertinent and intrusive question?' she asked coldly.

'Certainly,' Sir William responded, with equal coolness. 'That is why I asked the question! I shall not take you back otherwise!'

Bright flags of colour flew in Annabella's cheeks at this effrontery.

'Very well, sir! You will have your answer! No doubt it will give you immense gratification to know that your suspicions are well founded! I married Francis St Auby to escape my father's plans for me, for he did indeed have a suitor in mind! There was a business associate of his, a man of similar stamp to Alicia's first husband, albeit a little younger and a little less fat—and no doubt likely to live longer! Everyone thought that I loved Francis, but the truth is that I bought my husband with the promise of my fortune, and I did it simply to run away from the alternative! I had too much pride to let people see that my marriage was a sham, but I lived with that truth for the whole of my married life!' She stopped, her eyes bright with angry animation, her cheeks a vivid, becoming pink.

There was a silence. 'It was uncivil of me to push you so far, ma'am,' Sir William said, still watching her intently, 'but I find I cannot regret it. Do you wish to tell me more?'

Annabella sat staring at him. She was astonished to find that she did indeed want to tell him more: the truth about her marriage, her estrangement from Alicia, the indignities of her life in the St Auby household—words jostled with each other in her head, willing her to spill them out and tell him everything—but the conventional part of her was utterly appalled at her behaviour. One instinct was prompting her to let the whole sorry story tumble out with the artless confidence of a child, but the self-control she had learned in a hard school was asking her how she could be so foolish as to trust a complete stranger. And as she stared at him in bafflement, she heard Sir William swear under his breath and pick up the reins, making to turn the horses.

'No, wait!' Annabella put a hand on his arm, suddenly desperate not to lose the opportunity of the moment.

'There is a mail coach coming, Mrs St Auby,' Sir William said abruptly. 'I cannot leave the curricle in the middle of the road!'

Annabella's face flamed. She shrank back into the corner of her seat, trying to make herself as small as possible as Sir William turned the curricle neatly and pulled over to the side of the road as the posthorn blared. The coach thundered past, throwing up the choking dust in its path, and they were left in silence. The moment for confidences was gone. Suddenly it did not seem such a beautiful day.

'I am sorry,' Annabella said hesitantly, uncertain what the apology was for, but moved to make it anyway. She saw the tense lines of Sir William's face ease a little.

'Not at all, ma'am. You have nothing with which to reproach yourself.' He smiled reassuringly and took her hand in a warm clasp, which had a far from reassuring effect. Annabella felt her pulse rate increase. 'I forgot your relative youth,' Sir William continued, 'and I am trying to go too far, too fast, which is not a mistake I make often! Now—' his tone changed '—shall we take tea at Mundell, or do you prefer to go straight back to Taunton?'

Annabella, who had not understood his comment, was tempted to go straight home to nurse her humiliation, but then found herself torn by the wish to prolong her time in Sir William's company. She frowned.

'Tea at Mundell would be very nice,' she ventured.

'Very well.' There was nothing but a brisk agreement in his voice. Annabella's fragile confidence shrivelled a little more. Oh, how could she have acted like such a little ninny? She shuddered as she remembered her ingenuous comments about starting the circulating library. How could she have imagined that such a man, with his wide and sophisticated experience of the world, would have the slightest interest in her parochial plans? And then, how could she have overreacted so when he had asked her about her marriage to Francis? She had about as much notion of how to go on as a five-year-old!

As she sat silently beside him, Sir William Weston was also thinking about his conversation with Annabella, though perhaps in terms that would have surprised her. In common with all their friends, he had heard of Alicia Mullineaux's estrangement from her sister and the widely accepted view that Annabella had more of her grasping, materialistic father in her than was at all acceptable. He had been both surprised and intrigued to find her so inexperienced and unspoilt, when he had expected to meet a brass-faced harpy, old beyond her years. He had quickly seen the miserable torment caused by Lady St Auby, and had been determined to help Annabella if he could. That his motives sprang from something other than altruism, he was prepared to admit at once, for he had no time for self-delusion. A man of action, accustomed to rapidly sum up a situation and make a decision, he had known almost immediately that he would pursue his interest in Annabella St Auby.

He glanced sideways at her averted face, her expression unreadable in the shadow cast by her bonnet's brim. She was deliberately keeping her head tilted away from him, as though embarrassed by their recent exchange. Sir William smiled to himself a little, wondering if she had any idea how desirable she looked, how that air of innocent aloofness was at once both part innocent and part alluring. He was tempted to stop and kiss her, partly to see how she would react, but mostly just for the pleasure of feeling that sweet, pink mouth beneath his own… They had reached the gates of Mundell Hall. Will Weston gave himself a mental shake and concentrated hard on the complicated business of driving the curricle through the gateway with inch-perfect precision.

*   *   *

When Annabella saw Viscount Mundell's guests taking tea beneath a huge tented pavilion on the green lawns, she almost regretted the impulse that had led her to agree to Sir William's suggestion. Lord and Lady Wallace were not present, but the rest of Mundell's guests of the previous night were there, and looking so privileged, so immaculately *ton*nish, that Annabella felt both drab and dusty.

'Courage, Mrs St Auby!' Sir William had taken her elbow and was giving her an encouraging smile. 'You look delightful, you are charming company and—they are really quite friendly, you know!'

Annabella smiled despite herself. Strange, she thought, that her discomfort appeared to have communicated itself almost immediately to this most enigmatic of men. Even stranger to her was the fact that he was concerned enough to wish to reassure her. Her heart lightened a little.

They crossed the lawn to join the party, and Annabella immediately saw the scornful amusement in Miss Hurst's eyes as she surveyed the worn red dress and the unsophisticated plait. Miss Hurst herself was dressed in crisp pink and white candystripe, her hair an artful creation of tangled curls. Before her on the table was a sketching pad showing a water-colour drawing of the gardens and the distant church spire. It was quite beautiful. But one gift Miss Hurst lacked was the gift of generosity, and as Annabella and Sir William reached them, she drew her chair very carefully towards Miss Mundell, effectively excluding Annabella from the circle. It was Caroline Kilgaren who moved to make room for her at the table.

'Sir William!' Miss Hurst cooed, as though she had

just seen them for the first time. 'Pray come and sit by me! We have been desolate without your company!' And she gave him a melting look through her eyelashes. Sir William seemed unmoved, but he sat down next to her all the same. So that was how the land lay, Annabella thought. A small spark of rebelliousness caught in her and began to burn.

More tea was brought and poured.

'Did you enjoy your drive?' Caroline Kilgaren enquired, with a friendly smile. 'You are very favoured, you know, for Sir William is accounted a notable whip, and seldom takes anybody up! And I imagine this countryside is beautiful to drive through—'

Before Annabella could answer, Miss Hurst had intervened, yawning ostentatiously. 'Lud, but the country is so slow! Bath and Cheltenham may be tolerable, I suppose, but Taunton! Why, did you see the clothes last night?' Her malicious brown eyes dwelt on Annabella's faded red dress again. 'I declare, some of those coats last night cannot have been fashionable since my father's day! And as for country manners, did you hear the way Sir Thomas Oakston addressed us last night? Not an ounce of finesse—'

'I'm surprised you stay in the country so long if you dislike it, Ermina,' Sir William observed, in a lazy drawl. His gaze moved from Miss Hurst to Viscount Mundell and paused thoughtfully. Miss Hurst reddened unattractively. Annabella began to wonder if Sir William had in fact told the truth when he had said that his friends found it hard to bear with him.

'Oh, Sir William, how you do tease!' Miss Hurst had decided to be arch. 'But I shall punish you later! A duel at the butts, perhaps?'

The archery butts were set some distance away across the lawn, and a bow was propped up behind Miss Hurst's chair. Another of her accomplishments, Annabella thought, with a private smile, surprised to find that the evidence of Miss Hurst's achievements was starting to amuse her rather than make her feel inadequate. Sir William picked up the sketching pad and viewed it pensively.

'This is exquisite, Charlotte,' he said to Miss Mundell. 'Should Hugo ever fall on hard times, you will be able to keep him through your artist's skill!'

Miss Mundell blushed and disclaimed whilst Miss Hurst flounced, disliking the attention of the group being distracted from her. She turned to Annabella.

'Do you have any skill with the bow, Mrs St Auby?'

Annabella shook her head slowly, her mouth full of plum cake. For a moment she was tempted to speak with her mouth full and display her deplorable country manners.

'I regret I do not, Miss Hurst!'

'A pity!' The brown eyes were sharp now. 'But perhaps you have other accomplishments? Your sister, Lady Mullineaux, plays the piano exquisitely. Do you have the same talent?'

Annabella was beginning to feel like a scientific specimen, but was determined not to let this fashion-plate intimidate her. All Miss Hurst's conversation seemed aimed at disparagement.

'I fear I do not play well,' she said solemnly, ignoring the fact that she had a very pretty singing voice and could accompany herself perfectly well. 'I have no accomplishments, Miss Hurst—I have no skill with a needle and I draw very ill.'

Miss Hurst, missing the look of covert amusement Will Weston exchanged with Marcus Kilgaren, looked scandalised. 'My dear Mrs St Auby! But then I dare say such accomplishments are not regarded in your circle! More commercial pursuits—' she put just the right hint of doubt into her tone '—must be valued higher!'

'Oh, indeed, ma'am!' Annabella was all sweetness now. 'My father taught me how to barter at an early age! And I can estimate the value of a cargo of sugar cane—' She broke off, seeing Sir William's bright gaze resting upon her thoughtfully.

'Unusual talents are so much more interesting, are they not?' Marcus Kilgaren came to Annabella's rescue. 'Why, Caro is a case in point!' He smiled across the table at his wife. 'Her father was a historian who did not hold with the notion that females should be beautiful but witless. Recognising Caroline's potential and—'

'And realising her brother Charles's lack of it,' Mundell put in dryly, to general laughter.

'He taught her himself,' Marcus finished. 'Caro now has an encyclopaedic knowledge of medieval architecture which few could match!'

'Have you visited Stogursey Church, Mrs St Auby?' Caroline Kilgaren asked, leaning forward eagerly. 'It is a very fine example of—'

Miss Hurst yawned again. 'I fear my father never instilled in me anything so fascinating,' she interrupted, with a wearisome look that robbed the words of any sincerity. 'He considered that skill in music, needlework and drawing were the true measure of an educated woman!' She smiled complacently. 'I am happy to feel that I have not disappointed him!'

Annabella was startled to discover in herself a strong temptation to empty the contents of the teapot over Miss Hurst's perfectly coiffed head. She saw Marcus Kilgaren turn away to hide a grin, then Mundell said coolly,

'Surely, Miss Hurst, you would include gracious conversation and an informed mind on your list of prerequisites?'

'Oh, the art of conversation, perhaps!' Miss Hurst waved one white hand, as if to suggest that she had a natural talent that required no practice. 'And an informed mind, as long as one did not have to study too hard…such bookishness is not at all attractive! Lud, I do not believe I have picked up a book from one month end to the next!'

Annabella thought that she heard Caroline Kilgaren snort with disgust. Her gaze moved on to Miss Mundell, whose head was bent over precisely the type of embroidery that would win Miss Hurst's praise. Where Miss Hurst was surprisingly opinionated for her years, Miss Mundell was silent and in obvious awe of her friend. She had said very little, apart from a subdued greeting and her confused disclaimer over Sir William's compliment, and appeared to be a fashionable cipher. Annabella guessed that both young women were close to her own age, but seldom had she felt she had less in common with her contemporaries.

Conversation around the table became general again. Caroline Kilgaren turned back to Annabella.

'Mrs St Auby,' she said in an undertone, 'since our conversation last night I have become even more concerned to help you heal the breach with Alicia. I considered writing to her at once, but wondered whether you would prefer to do so yourself? What do you think?'

Annabella leant forward impulsively. 'Oh, Lady Kilgaren, I would so like to do so! But I do not know how to explain matters to her—there's the rub! Would you…could I tell you the story, and ask you to advise me?'

Caroline smiled. 'Of course—if you truly wish it!' She stood up. 'Have you finished your tea? Then you must come for a stroll in the gardens with me. The rose borders are accounted particularly fine, and should not be missed!'

Sir William had been watching them with a particularly intent look in those deceptively calm blue eyes. Now he turned and engaged Miss Hurst in conversation at the precise moment that she was about to invite herself to join the party. Caroline slipped her arm through Annabella's, and steered her away across the lawn.

The gardens at Mundell were indeed very fine, Annabella thought, for the rich green lawns were dotted with tall, shady trees and ornamental shrubs, whilst the flower borders were a riot of colour on this summer afternoon. They chose a bench in the shade of a huge oak tree, and Caroline turned to Annabella with a smile.

'So how can I help you, my dear? How did this sad estrangement come about?'

Annabella sighed. 'I never knew Alicia very well,'

she said. 'You are no doubt aware that she is seven years older than I, and when I was a child she was away at school, and then she went to London for her Season and…' her eyes dropped from Caroline's kind blue ones '…our father forced that hateful match with George Carberry! I know that she wrote to me several times after Carberry died, but our father would never let me see the letters. I believe he threw them away unanswered, or returned them. I once saw one on the hall table when one of the maids had accidentally left it lying there. I was about to open it when he snatched it from my hand and sent me away to my room. I would have written to her myself if I could, but I could not find her direction!'

'Alicia wondered if that was the case,' Caroline said calmly. 'I think she realised that that was none of your doing. But then you met again, did you not, a couple of years ago? I understood that your father indicated to Alicia that you would like a London Season under her aegis?'

'Yes, but it was not at all as Alicia might have imagined!' Annabella's anguished green eyes met Caroline's. 'I discovered that our father had used me to bring her to Greyrigg, spinning the tale about a Season as bait! In truth, what he really wanted was to entrap her in his business dealings again, or force her into a second marriage! But I swear that I did not know that until the very day of her visit!' She shook her head. 'He never confided in me, you see, barely spoke to me at all from one week to the next, if the truth be told! Oh, he thought he knew me, thought that I was like him because I kept quiet and always agreed with him on the rare occasions he did tell me a little of his plans! But I knew nothing of his designs for Alicia, I swear it!'

Caroline was frowning. 'I believe you, but—' She broke off and started again. 'Forgive me, but I think Alicia believed you were party to his plans because you seemed so at ease with him, so complaisant.' Caroline looked uncomfortable. 'The way she described your behaviour—'

'Oh, I can well imagine what she said!' But Annabella's bitterness was directed against herself, not her sister. 'I played a marvellous part, you see, Lady Kilgaren. I was so mercenary, so insincere! I modelled myself on Lady Grey, my future sister-in-law, and she is the most affected creature I know!' Despite herself she gave a little giggle. 'Oh, I was dreadful! My conversation was larded with 'la' and 'lud' and I am sure I gave my sister a complete disgust for me! It fooled our father, who knew me too little to realise it was all pretence! He just thought that I was jealous of her.'

She looked up and met Caroline's look directly. 'And so I was, in truth! Alicia is so elegant, so assured, so much as I would wish to be! But that's nothing to the purpose! All the time I was waiting for my chance to warn Alicia without alerting our father's suspicions, but it was hopeless! He would not leave me alone with her and he had already threatened that if I did not aid his plans he would punish me—' She broke off, closing her eyes briefly for a moment. 'In any event, Alicia did not need my help! But, of course, she left Greyrigg believing me to have connived at his plotting.'

There was a silence. A dove began to coo in the branches above their heads. It was cool in the leafy shade. 'I am so sorry,' Caroline said softly. 'It must have been intolerably frustrating for you. And at your wedding,' she prompted gently, 'no doubt you had little chance to talk to her then…'

Annabella shook her head dolefully. 'Oh, no, I could not!' This was difficult, for it entailed telling something of her reasons for marrying Francis, and after her outburst to Sir William she was disinclined to discuss the painful details again.

'There are very few opportunities for real discussion at a wedding,' she said truthfully, 'particularly one's own! Besides…' she smiled a little, remembering how James Mullineaux had made such a determined attempt to monopolise Alicia that day '…Alicia had matters of her own to divert her! James was very particular in his attentions!'

Caroline was surprised that Annabella had noticed that, for Alicia's description of her sister's behaviour at the wedding had not suggested that Annabella was anything other than a self-absorbed flirt. She eyed her more closely. As she had suspected, there was far more to this than was at first apparent, although she could understand Annabella's reluctance to tell her the whole and awaken unhappy memories.

'And when Alicia came to see you after your father had died,' Caroline said, again gently persistent, 'you still could not tell her the truth about your relationship with him? I realise that Alicia was deeply unhappy at the time because she thought that she had lost James, so that may have influenced her feelings, but she told me that…' she paused unhappily '…oh dear, this is so difficult, for I see that there must have been a grave misunderstanding here! Alicia thought that you were…that you had an interest—' It was unusual to see Caroline Kilgaren lost for words, and Annabella came to her aid.

'She thought me mercenary and vulgar, and only interested in her fortune!' she finished for her.

Caroline was so startled that she forgot to be embarrassed. 'My word! You have much of both your grandmother and Alicia in you!'

Annabella laughed. 'I do apologise if my plain speaking offends you, Lady Kilgaren, but there is no point in beating about the bush!'

But Caroline was laughing too. 'No, indeed! My dear Annabella—I may call you Annabella, may I not?—pray do not apologise! As you say, it is so much easier to sort matters out if one is frank! I was only taken aback because you sounded like old Lady Stansfield! But—' she sobered '—since a description of you as vulgar and mercenary is fair and far out, you must tell me how such a misunderstanding occurred!'

Annabella's smile faded. 'Oh, it was not so inaccurate,' she said with constraint. 'You should know, Lady Kilgaren, that Francis—my husband—married me for my money, and when my father left me virtually penniless he was not best pleased. Then Alicia came to visit us and I think he could not bear to look at her and think of all her fortune. His insulting questions about her wealth and his obvious resentment that she had so much when I had inherited so little must have given her a disgust of us both—I tried to smooth matters over, but then I only angered him.' She bit her lip. No need to tell Caroline of the unpleasant scene where Francis had threatened to beat her if she did not do as he said. 'He said that I should have a thought to secure our future so, of course, I asked Alicia a little about her plans, which made it look as though I had an eye on inheriting her money. It was all profoundly uncomfortable and I was so mortified that, when Francis died, I did not dare approach Alicia for very shame!' She shrugged her slim shoulders. 'And there it is—a sorry tale indeed!' She gave a watery smile. 'I thank you for bearing with my confessions!'

Caroline patted her hand. 'Thank you for confiding the tale in me.' Her blue eyes were very kind. 'I had no notion that your marriage was anything other than a love-match. May I be even more impertinent and ask how that came about?'

Annabella fixed her gaze on a fat bumble bee buzzing drunkenly in the rose border. Even now, it was distressing to describe the events leading up to her marriage and their painful consequences.

'My father had a suitor in mind for me, in much the same way as he had done for Alicia,' she said haltingly. 'I imagine that you, more than most, know a little of how that might be, Lady Kilgaren. I…found I could not accept his choice, so I looked around for a means of escape and Francis came to mind. I knew that he needed to marry money.' The colour had come into her cheeks and she could no longer meet Caroline's eyes. 'So I made my bargain and then pretended that it was what I had always wanted.' She shook her head. 'I was a fool. I never thought that I would live happily ever after, but I had no real notion of what marriage entailed, least of all to a man I could not respect—' She broke off.

Caroline took her hand. The knowledge of what had happened to Alicia made it easier to understand her sister's tale. 'You poor child! I had no idea! Oh, if only Alicia had known, I'm sure she would have helped you!'

Annabella's green eyes were bright with unshed tears. 'Please may we talk on other matters now, ma'am? I have no wish to succumb to a fit of the megrims!'

'Of course!' Caroline acquiesced gracefully, unwilling to press Annabella for details when she was clearly upset. 'But you asked my advice, and I can only suggest that you tell Alicia all that you have told me. She will be very sympathetic, you know, for she wants to be reconciled to you above all things!' Caroline jumped to her feet. 'Let us rejoin the rest of the party and hope for some entertaining company. One may not include Miss Hurst in that, I know, but the rest are tolerable or—' a twinkle entered her blue eyes '—more than tolerable, perhaps!'

'Miss Hurst is very beautiful, is she not?' Annabella said, a little sadly, remembering the way the haughty young woman had summoned Sir William to her side earlier.

Caroline Kilgaren smiled encouragingly. 'Oh, she has all the beauty that money can buy, certainly! But you should not repine—you are very pretty, you know, and have far more character! Miss Hurst, I am afraid, has been told from an early age that her opinions are worth more than other people's, on account of her being in possession of a fortune of eighty thousand pounds! I am a cat to say so, I know, but nevertheless it is true!'

Eighty thousand pounds sounded like a vast fortune to Annabella. She felt even more despondent. Money had a habit of attracting money, and Sir William Weston was not poor. True, he was a less eligible *parti* than a Viscount, but if Miss Hurst could not bring Mundell up to scratch, he would prove a very acceptable alternative…

Caroline's next words echoed her thoughts. 'Do not imagine that Miss Hurst dislikes you for yourself, Annabella! The truth is that she came here to catch herself a husband and is becoming annoyed by her lack of success. Mundell, her first target, is surprisingly old-fashioned and has some nice notions about being married for his title! He does not need money enough to fall for the lure. So Sir William Weston was her next thought, but—' Caroline smiled a little '—she did not know him well and understands even less what attracts him! All her overtures have met with the same bland indifference—and then, of course, you came along last night and he paid you more attention in one evening than he has given Miss Hurst in an entire fortnight! I'm afraid it has piqued her pride!'

Annabella blushed slightly at the implication that Sir William was interested in her. 'Sir William has been very kind to me,' she said guardedly, 'but I fear I cannot understand him any better than Miss Hurst does! You see,' she added naively, 'I have very little experience of the world and have never met anyone quite like him!'

'I doubt there is anyone quite like Will Weston,' Caroline said drily. 'You should know, my dear, that Will's father was very rich, but Will chose to enter the navy through inclination and rose to prominence by his own merits rather than through preferment! He has only sold out now because his estates require more attention than he felt able to give whilst away at sea so much, and I think perhaps that he is looking for a more settled life. But as a man he has a lot of attractive qualities…' she smiled at Annabella '…though I doubt you need me to tell you that! To Marcus and myself he is the best of loyal friends, and we would do a great deal for him. There now, I sound quite sentimental! But loyalty and integrity are qualities which are not always found in abundance in the superficial world of the *haut ton*!'

Annabella was not entirely sure that it was for these characteristics that Miss Hurst wished to attach Sir William's interest. There was something self-contained and a little distant about him which gave him an added mystery and must add to his attraction. And if one also considered his physical attributes… Annabella remembered the warm admiration in those bright, blue eyes and felt a little breathless. Perhaps it was not a good thing to dwell on Sir William's attractions too much. 'But surely there are plenty of titled gentlemen who would be happy to marry Miss Hurst?' she said, turning the conversation on to safer ground.

Caroline smiled with gentle malice. 'Oh, yes,' she said, with mock-sorrow, 'but she wanted a handsome one!'

They were still laughing as they crossed the lawn and heard Miss Hurst's fluting tones holding forth once more:

'La, Sir William, I insist that you join me in a game of croquet! I shall brook no refusal, sir!'

'I fear I must decline, ma'am,' Sir William's lazy drawl was as unperturbed as ever. 'I must escort Mrs St Auby back to town shortly.'

'But can you not send her back in the carriage?' Miss Hurst made her sound like an unwanted parcel, Annabella thought. 'Surely the wretched girl—' She broke off as Caroline and Annabella came into view, and bent a false, dazzling smile on them.

'La, we were just saying that the carriage must be called to take you home, Mrs St Auby—'

'But then I insisted on the pleasure of escorting you myself, ma'am!' Sir William finished, without a flicker of expression.

Miss Hurst scowled. It was not becoming.

'You are all goodness, sir,' Annabella said politely. 'Do not let me put you to any further trouble, however! It has been a delightful afternoon and I am most grateful to have the use of Viscount Mundell's carriage—'

'Lud, yes,' Miss Hurst said, brightening, 'a carriage with a crest on! What could be more exciting for Mrs St Auby?'

This time, a smile definitely touched the corners of Sir William's firm mouth as his gaze rested on Annabella. 'I insist, ma'am,' he said, gently.

'But you must not go yet,' Marcus Kilgaren said, in his amused drawl. 'Caro has monopolised you! Come and sit by me, Mrs St Auby, and tell me what you think of Sir William's team. His cattle are accounted very fine, you know.'

It was some half-hour later that the party finally broke up. Miss Hurst bore an unresisting Viscount Mundell away to play croquet with Caroline Kilgaren, whilst Marcus offered to escort Miss Mundell on a tour of the hothouses. Caroline had pressed Annabella to stay and join in the game, but Annabella had uncharitably suspected that Miss Hurst would take the opportunity to attack her ankles with the croquet mallet. She declined the offer and Caroline kissed her impulsively on the cheek, and said that she hoped they would meet again soon. Miss Hurst, by contrast, had frowned horribly as she watched Sir William's curricle set off down the lime tree drive, and had had to be gently recalled to the game by her companions.

## Chapter Three

The following day was fine and bright when Annabella set out with a long list of commissions for Lady St Auby in the town. Her ladyship always sent her daughter-in-law on errands, arguing that she could not spare the maids and that Annabella never earned her keep. It was one of the less onerous of the household duties laid at her door, and today she was particularly light of step and of heart.

She matched a ribbon successfully in the drapers and bought Lady St Auby several pairs of gloves, resisting the impulse to buy herself silk stockings. What use would she have for such fripperies? What she needed was thick woollen ones to keep out the creeping chill of winter at the St Aubys' Manor! She moved on to the butchers and the grocers, haggling for the cheapest cuts of meat and the damaged vegetables, for she knew Lady St Auby would chide her for overspending and accuse her of pocketing some of the money herself. On impulse she bought herself an apple and ate it in the street, only to regret it when she turned the corner to see Mrs Eddington-Buck watching her with malevolent eyes from the other side of the street. The apple incident would no doubt be reported to Lady St Auby. Annabella sighed. Sometimes it seemed that all possibility of spontaneity had been crushed out of her life.

A knot of people were coming down the street towards her, chattering and laughing together. With a slight shock, Annabella recognised Viscount Mundell strolling along with Caroline Kilgaren on his arm, Miss Hurst and Sir William following behind and Miss Mundell bringing up the rear. The sight of Miss Hurst's smiling face upturned to Sir William's was sufficient to keep Annabella still for a moment and then prompt her to run away. It was too late, however. With a glad cry, Caroline hailed her.

'Mrs St Auby! What a delightful surprise! We had just called in Fore Street to find you from home, and here you are!'

Mundell took her hand, a broad smile on his face. 'Delighted to see you again, ma'am! A fine day, is it not! Would you care to join us?'

'Marcus is at the gunsmith's—' Caroline was saying, when Miss Hurst's whispered aside to Miss Mundell could be heard,

'She is a novelty in the same way as people will crowd about a freakshow booth…'

Annabella blushed bright red and even Caroline's voice faltered.

Sir William spoke into the embarrassed silence, his tone expressionless but his blue eyes as cold as ice. 'And will we see you at the concert tonight, Mrs St Auby?'

'I…imagine not, sir.' Annabella pulled herself together. Lady St Auby was tone deaf and detested musical soirees. 'I believe my mother-in-law has other plans for this evening.'

'A pity.' Sir William smiled warmly at her. 'But perhaps you could join us for a while now?'

Despite the temptation of his company, there was nothing Annabella wanted less at that moment. Miss Hurst's cold gaze was resting on the bulging contents of her marketing basket and to her horror Annabella could see the oxtails she had just bought lolling out of the corner of the brown paper parcel. She switched the basket to her other arm, out of sight, and gave Sir William a flustered look.

'You are kind, sir, but I must be getting home. I have a hundred and one matters to attend to! Good day!'

She scurried down the street without a backward look, conscious only of her humiliation. They must think her nothing but a socially inept fool! Oh, Miss Hurst had been unkind, but she had been gauche! Would she never learn? And now they *certainly* would not pay her any further attention!

'Mundell and his cronies have turned your head, you foolish girl!' Lady St Auby, a malignant smile on her lips and predatory gleam in her beady eyes, was standing in the stone-flagged corridor of the Taunton house, watching with no little satisfaction as Annabella scrubbed the floor. 'There, girl—no, not there, you booby—the stain is over on this side—' and Lady St Auby deliberately smeared the mud over the piece of floor which Annabella had just cleaned.

Two days had passed since Annabella had met the

Viscount and his guests in town and in that time she had heard nothing further from them. Her excitement and confidence in the future, severely dented by the encounter, had waned further as time had passed and the inescapable facts became clear. They had dropped her. She had bored them with her awkwardness and lack of sophistication. Lady St Auby, quick to see Annabella's unhappiness, had been delighted.

'It's as I would have thought,' she continued spitefully now. 'You have no graces to recommend you to the Quality. Why, they could see you for the little nobody you are! A man of Mundell's distinction is not going to want his guests imposed upon by a fortune-hunting adventuress!'

Annabella sighed, biting back the intemperate retort which rose to her lips. Once, long ago, she had answered Lady St Auby in kind when her mother-in-law had indulged in one of her vituperative attacks. The response had been swift. She had not been given any food for several days. The same thing had happened when she had refused to perform the demeaning household tasks which Lady St Auby had demanded. Whilst her mother-in-law did not resort to physical violence as her son had sometimes done, her retribution was just as difficult to bear. And now she was angry and frustrated by the attention that had been shown to Annabella. It was there in her eyes as she looked at her daughter-in-law, a savagery that was just waiting for an opportunity to explode into life.

Annabella wrung out the dirty cloth and reached for the pail of water. At the same time, Lady St Auby leant forward and calmly tipped the bucket over so the dirty dregs soaked Annabella's skirt where she knelt on the rough floor.

It was too late for Annabella to avoid the tide of filthy liquid. She leapt to her feet, feeling the water soaking through her kerseymere skirt and the apron she wore on top of it. She lost her balance, stumbling and falling. Lady St Auby cackled with laughter.

The front door opened, although nobody had rung the bell. Lady St Auby froze. All Annabella could see, from her position on the floor in the retreating suds, was a pair of highly polished topboots.

Then: 'You appear to be in some discomfort, ma'am,' Sir William Weston said, carefully expressionless. 'Allow me to help you.'

Her elbow was taken in a very firm grip. As she stumbled to her feet, her skirt dripping and sticking to her legs, Annabella could smell the faint scent of his cologne mingled with the aroma of fresh air that she had always loved. Her gaze fixed itself on his green waistcoat and stayed there. She did not dare to look up into his face. Of all the desperately undignified situations in which to be found... She discovered that she was shaking with mortification. There was no possible way to explain...

'Sir William...' Lady St Auby had at least the grace to appear a little abashed. 'How do you do, sir. We were just—'

She was silenced by one searing flash of those blue eyes. 'There is no need to say anything, madam. The facts speak for themselves. Mrs St Auby...' his cold tone softened '...I was calling to see if you would be attending the subscription ball this evening—' He broke off. Annabella had still not been able to look him in the eye. Now she did look up as his grip tightened on her hand. He was standing, head bent, studying the raw, chapped skin of her fingers where the brush had scoured it. Then he let her go abruptly.

'Will you come for a drive with me, ma'am?'

'If you can wait whilst I change, sir—' Annabella gestured clumsily towards her drenched skirt.

'Of course…'

They were well clear of the town when Sir William reined in his horses and spoke again, and when he turned to her, Annabella realised that he was still angry. There was a tight set to his mouth and a glitter in his eyes. The butterflies in her stomach fluttered again. Whatever was he going to say to her?

'Why did you not tell us—?' he began, then broke off in frustration, slamming one fist into the palm of his other gloved hand. 'Lady St Auby is unpardonable!'

Annabella fixed her gaze on the middle distance, which consisted of a very pretty millhouse, its wheel turning.

'I have known you but a couple of days, sir,' she said carefully, 'and felt disinclined to confide my domestic arrangements to a group of strangers!'

The stormy blue gaze held her own eyes. 'That is ungenerous of you, ma'am! Have we not given you every indication that we would all stand your friends?'

Annabella looked away unhappily. 'Indeed, sir, but…' She turned back to him and said in a rush, 'Your very friendship is the goad which makes Lady St Auby worse! She cannot bear that Mundell's set recognise me when she has always been below his

notice! It has always been a thorn in her flesh that I
am Alicia's sister and the Countess of Stansfield's
granddaughter. Before you all arrived in Taunton it
did not matter, but now…'

Sir William's eyes had narrowed with concentration
and now he nodded slowly. 'I see. Then you do not
pretend that what I witnessed this morning was an
accident?'

'I collect you mean with the pail of water?' Annabella was a truthful girl and just now it was making
her uncomfortable. 'No, I cannot pretend… Oh, she
means no real harm—'

'No harm!' The words exploded from Sir William
with all the wrath he would have preferred to visit
upon Lady St Auby's head. It was extraordinary, Annabella thought, that the placid exterior she had seen
at the ball could conceal such a depth of feeling. She
managed a watery smile.

'No, truly, sir… She is unkind and malicious, but
she does me no real harm!'

'No,' Sir William said through his teeth, 'she simply makes you scrub her floors and no doubt a hundred other menial tasks besides!'

'Well, I am the poor relation—'

'Will you stop being so humble!'

They sat staring at each other. Then Sir William
seemed to shake himself out of his bad temper. He
gave her a slight smile.

'I beg your pardon, ma'am. I have been most uncivil to you.' He gave the horses the office to move
off again. 'We must—' He stopped and started again.
'If I could arrange for you to stay at Mundell until

you go to visit Alicia, would you be prepared to accept the invitation?'

It sounded like heaven to Annabella, but it also sounded dangerous. 'You have more faith in my sister's forgiveness than I dare have, sir,' she said, trying to speak lightly. 'If Alicia and I are unable to bury our differences—'

'Then we must make other arrangements.' Sir William sounded his usual cool, composed self once again. 'You cannot continue living in that household!'

'How very high-handed you sound, sir!' Annabella marvelled sweetly, and saw some expression flare in his eyes before it was replaced by reluctant amusement.

'Well?' he challenged her. 'If you wish to martyr yourself by staying there, pray do not let me interfere!'

To her amazement, Annabella found herself on the verge of giggling. How extraordinary! To be sunk in misery one minute, yet to feel this dizzy excitement the next! She cast a look at Sir William under her lashes. His stern expression had relaxed slightly; a smile still lingered around that firm mouth.

'It would be delightful to stay at Mundell,' Annabella capitulated, dismissing the fleeting thought of Miss Hurst, who would be far from delighted.

'Thank you. Are there any other dark secrets that it would be useful for me to know before I make the arrangements?' Sir William's quizzical blue gaze rested on her thoughtfully, before returning to the road.

'I think not.' Annabella spoke demurely. 'You have already provoked me into divulging far more about my marriage than was seemly, and now you know the sordid truth of my existence with the St Aubys. That only leaves my quarrel with Alicia, and I imagine that she will have told you enough of that!'

Sir William shook his head slowly. 'Your sister is remarkably loyal to you, Mrs St Auby! Oh, I believe that she told Caroline Kilgaren the whole of it, but the rest of us only know that there has been some sort of dispute between you. It would be a pity if it could not be resolved, for I imagine the two of you would get on famously. Now...' he sighed '...I suppose I must take you back to that old harridan, but if you can be prepared for a remove to Mundell tomorrow, I will come to fetch you.'

He dropped her at the door of the house in Fore Street with a reminder about the subscription ball that evening. A couple of hours later, a pair of exquisitely made evening gloves were delivered to the house. Annabella looked at her sore fingers and smiled.

Lady St Auby was nervous. Previously she had not cared how Taunton society viewed her treatment of Annabella, for the girl had no one to champion her cause. Now, unexpectedly, she had acquired powerful protection, and that had changed the whole case. She made no demur when Annabella raised the subject of the ball and even sent her own maid along to help Annabella with her toilette. Pleading a sick headache to excuse herself, Lady St Auby told her daughter-in-law that Sir Thomas and Lady Oakston were only too happy to ask her to join their party for the evening. Annabella could not wonder at it.

There was a little awkwardness to begin with. Sir

Thomas had never acknowledged Bertram Broseley as an acquaintance, and had paid scant attention to his daughter even when Francis had been alive. Now, Annabella's elevation to Mundell's social sphere suddenly made her a worthwhile connection, but Sir Thomas did at least have the manners to feel the delicacy of the situation. Fortunately the Oakstons had a very lively and unaffected son, Julius, and an equally vivacious daughter Eleanor, who was just out. Annabella, happy in her new-found friends and excited at the prospect of seeing Will Weston again, was prepared to be generous.

This time, the heads turned as she came into the ballroom, and it was a new and entirely enjoyable experience. In a determined effort to look her best, Annabella had dug an old dress of purple taffeta out of a chest, had stripped it of all frills and furbelows, had sponged it down and made it look quite acceptable. It had originally been made for her before her marriage, and the effect had been far too sophisticated for a young girl. Now it was eminently suited to a widow, albeit one of only twenty-one. Joan, Lady St Auby's maid, had cleverly turned one of the frills into a matching headband, and had arranged Annabella's honeyed curls to tumble in barely restrained profusion about her heart-shaped face. Her green eyes glowed with pleasure and for the first time she thought she might be almost beautiful.

The party from Mundell had yet to arrive, but Annabella danced with Julius Oakston and several other young men who eagerly solicited her hand, and chatted to Eleanor, who was anxious to tell her about her recent visit to the spa at Bath. There was also other,

less congenial company about. When Annabella went
out on to the balcony for some fresh air, she was
cornered by George Jeffries.

'The divine Annabella! Too far above my touch
now, are you not, my love!' He swayed a little, and
Annabella realised with apprehension that he was already drunk. Although they were within easy call of
the ballroom, it would be embarrassing in the extreme
to have to summon help. Beyond the billowing curtains, she could see dancing couples circling the floor.
They could have been several thousand miles away
for all the help it gave her. She could smell the wine
on Jeffries's breath as he came closer, put up a hand
to paw her arm. His grey eyes were narrowed with
the intentness of the very inebriated. He was having
enough difficulty just standing up.

'Go home, sir,' Annabella said wearily. 'You are
drunk and I have no wish for your company.'

'S'what I'm saying…' Jeffries caught her arm as
he lurched forwards, forcing his face close to hers.
'No time for your old friends now! Out with the old
and in with the new! But do they know the things I
could tell them, eh? Things Francis let slip…' The
cunning expression on his thin face made Annabella
feel sick.

'Francis was forever talking in his cups, just as you
are now, sir,' she said coldly.

'S'true I'm a little foxed…' Jeffries tried to smile
engagingly. 'Fra-Francis told me all about the time
he—'

'I am persuaded that the lady does not wish to hear
your squalid gossip, sir!' Sir William Weston, looking
awesomely authoritative in his immaculate evening

attire, had stepped out on to the balcony and had had the presence of mind to pull the curtain to behind him. His contemptuous gaze raked Jeffries, who had staggered backwards with an oath.

'Weston!'

'You have the advantage of me, sir,' Sir William said silkily. 'I shall not, however, press for an introduction! Now, take yourself off!'

He watched without comment as Jeffries, still swearing under his breath, slipped back into the ballroom and disappeared from view. 'Foolish young puppy,' he said without emotion, turning back to Annabella. 'I hope that he did not upset you, Mrs St Auby?'

'Oh, no.' Annabella was feeling rather foolish. First he had found her with Lady St Auby tipping dirty water over her, and now he had had to rescue her from the undignified scene with Jeffries! He was scarcely seeing her at her best!

'Then perhaps we should step inside. Your absence from the room will be missed if you spend much more time out here.'

'You always seem to be saving me from the consequences of my own folly, sir,' Annabella said, as he held the curtain aside for her to re-enter the ballroom and took her arm to guide her around the set of dancers that was just forming.

'How so?' Weston slanted a look at her. 'You can hardly blame yourself for the discourtesy of others, Mrs St Auby, be they your mother-in-law or that foolish young cub! But perhaps…' a questioning note entered his voice '…you feel you have something with which to reproach yourself over the unfortunate Captain Jeffries?'

Annabella laughed. 'I am not at all sure that you should quiz me on such a matter, sir!'

'Why? Because you have something to hide?'

'No, indeed!' Annabella looked indignant. 'I only meant that such a direct question invites a snub!'

'Ah—' a smile curled Weston's mouth '—and you have just administered one, ma'am!'

'Well, you are a most persistent man! But to answer your question, the only thing I have to reproach myself for is a certain lack of judgement, I believe! I made a mistake in choosing to marry where I did, and also in allowing Jeffries to befriend me afterwards.' Annabella put her head on one side thoughtfully. 'He was the one who sought to take advantage of my loneliness, and not for kindly motives!'

'No, I can well imagine!' Weston suppressed a smile and allowed his gaze to travel over her consideringly. What an odd mixture this girl was, half solemnity and half naïveté! It seemed to him that she was not so much lacking in judgement but lacking anyone to advise her, and that she had always been so. It gave him a strange pang to think of her so friendless in a hostile world. Her situation had been an unenviable one! But now, perhaps… He felt a sudden determination that she would not be so isolated again.

'I see that Lady St Auby is not here tonight,' he observed, as they reached the door of the refreshment room and Miss Hurst could be seen glaring at them across the rim of her glass of lemonade.

'No, she had a sudden headache.' Annabella al-

lowed herself a smile. 'She is afraid of you, sir, and
of what will be said about her in the neighbourhood!'

Sir William sighed. 'I do not seem to be making
friends for myself here in Somerset! And now I see I
shall have to share your company, for Mundell is
coming this way!' He pressed a kiss on her hand.
'You will dance with me later, perhaps?' As green
eyes met blue, Annabella knew she was unlikely to
refuse his request. She watched him go off to dance
with Miss Mundell, then turned her attention to the
Viscount. Miss Hurst was, rather improbably, dancing
with Captain Jeffries. Annabella noticed this with a
vague feeling of surprise, and almost immediately forgot about it. Later, she was to remember the incident
and wish she had paid more attention.

It was the beginning of a golden few weeks for
Annabella. The Mundell Hall house party swept her
up into its activities and entertainments, and she felt
as though she had unexpectedly stumbled into an extraordinary dream. There were outings and picnics,
evening parties and entertainments. Under Caroline
Kilgaren's benevolent patronage, Annabella found
herself overcoming her initial lack of confidence, until
she was even able to deal with Ermina Hurst with
equanimity. And throughout it all there was Sir William Weston, attentive, concerned, it seemed, only for
Annabella's enjoyment, to which he of course con-
tributed in no small measure.

Miss Hurst had not been pleased with the addition
to their party. At first Annabella had assumed this was
because of Sir William's attentions, but after a little
while, and with a sense of surprise, she realised that

Miss Hurst's antagonism was wider than that. She genuinely saw Annabella's beauty as a real challenge to her own supremacy, and although she could assert breeding and fortune, it was still irksome to her to have so pretty a rival. And, as is often the case with such things, the knowledge gave Annabella's green eyes an extra sparkle, and her complexion an extra glow, which led Miss Hurst to fume all the more.

The second day after the ball had dawned clear and sunny, and Mundell had announced casually at breakfast that he proposed to join the villagers in making up a cricket team to challenge the famous Gentlemen of Taunton to a match. Marcus Kilgaren and Will Weston readily agreed to participate, and Caroline, her blue eyes sparkling, proposed that the ladies should take a picnic along and support the contestants. Miss Hurst's expression mirrored shocked disapproval.

'Lud, a village cricket match!' She saw Mundell's quizzical gaze and added hastily, 'I am sure I do not dispute the privilege of gentlemen to mix with the common folk in such games, but I cannot believe my mama would approve of me attending!'

Caroline shrugged, doing little to conceal her irritation. 'As you wish, Ermina! Mrs St Auby and I shall get along very well if you and Charlotte do not care to join us!'

Surprisingly, Miss Mundell now spoke, blushing a little. 'For my part I should enjoy the fresh air,' she said, a little defiantly. 'Cricket is a very gentlemanly and sportsmanlike game, dearest Ermina. I am sure your mama could find no fault!'

'Upon my word!' Miss Hurst stared at her friend,

amazed Miss Mundell should speak out. Annabella also looked at her with renewed interest. She had dismissed Miss Mundell as a shy mouse in the shadow of her opinionated friend, but now she realised that some powerful feeling must be prompting the girl to speak thus. Charlotte Mundell's face was flushed and her eyes bright, and for once she looked almost pretty. She was very like her brother in appearance, but whilst the hawkish features and piercing grey eyes were handsome in a man, they were not very appealing in a woman. Yet now, Charlotte was animated, with a curious expression of excitement tinged with apprehension, almost as though, Annabella thought shrewdly, she were in love…

'Well!' Miss Hurst said crossly. 'If you *insist* upon going, Charlotte, I suppose I must join you! Though why you should wish to watch so tediously dull a game, I cannot imagine—'

Sir William Weston rustled the pages of *The Times* loudly and Annabella caught the tail-end of an ironic smile he exchanged with Marcus Kilgaren. Yes, clearly there was something going on here which might well become more plain during the course of the day.

The match was being held on the village green, and Caroline, Annabella and the other ladies arranged themselves comfortably under the spreading branches of a huge oak, in dappled sun and shade. It was a shame, Annabella thought, that Miss Hurst had insisted on accompanying them. She complained about everything. There were twigs and insects dropping off the tree and her flimsy parasol could do nothing to

ward them off, more insects had crept into her sand-
wiches, the seats were uncomfortable and the rules of
the game unintelligible.

Annabella secretly found the match rather entertaining. The Gentlemen players, in their white top hats
with black bands, were far more elegantly attired than
the motley selection of villagers who were, nevertheless, determined to win against their illustrious opponents. The village side were batting, Mundell and
the local blacksmith building up a creditable score of
runs. Across the pitch, Annabella could see money
exchanging hands as bets were taken on the outcome
of the match. There was also some heavy drinking,
but the day was hot and the thirst of the players in
particular was acute. As the beer was downed, the
support became more voluble and the language unbridled. Miss Hurst looked pained at being exposed
to such crass company.

Mundell eventually fell to a fast ball that hit his
middle stump so cleanly it knocked it out of the
ground. He walked off to a sympathetic round of applause and his place was taken by a tall young man,
loose-knit and ambling with a kind of gawkiness
which was rather attractive. Miss Hurst, who had been
in the middle of a peevish complaint about the slowness of the roads in the westcountry, broke off in the
middle of her sentence, staring hard.

'Good God, surely that cannot be John Dedicoat!
At a village cricket match?'

Annabella hid a smile. She was reminded of Lady
St Auby's astonishment that Mundell should have
chosen to patronise a country assembly. She had no
idea who the newcomer was, but now she observed

that Miss Mundell had sat up a little straighter and that her pale complexion was once again a becoming rose, her grey eyes brilliant. Miss Hurst, by comparison, was both unobservant and completely self-centred.

'Well!' She was preening herself with a satisfied smirk. 'Perhaps he is here because he knew I should attend! You must have seen, dear Lady Kilgaren, how Lord Dedicoat singled me out last night!'

Caroline's expression was hidden by the lid of the picnic hamper as she rummaged inside for something she had apparently mislaid. Her voice was muffled and Annabella wondered whether she had mistaken the note of amusement she thought she had detected.

'I am persuaded that Lord Dedicoat is here because he enjoys the game of cricket, Ermina, although…' Caroline shot Miss Mundell's rapt face a quick glance '…he *may* have another motive for attending!'

Miss Hurst smirked again. 'I knew it! Does he not cut a handsome figure! This is very pleasant entertainment!'

There at least, Annabella thought, Miss Mundell could be in full agreement with her friend, for the girl's eyes never left the tall figure at the crease. And Lord Dedicoat played with flair and grace until a wickedly spinning ball caught him off guard and he was out. He took his dismissal with the same good-natured ease that had characterised his innings and was succeeded by the village doctor.

'Lud, these vulgar people!' Miss Hurst said, with a sudden return to peevishness. 'Drinking and gambling on the village green! Why—' She stopped abruptly and blushed bright red. John Dedicoat, accompanied by Will Weston, had come upon them suddenly, both men looking rather dashing in their cricket whites. At close quarters, Lord Dedicoat was indeed a pleasing young man, but Annabella had eyes only for Sir William, whose athletic physique was peculiarly suited to the elegance of his attire.

Both men were carrying tankards of beer, Annabella noticed, and stifled a giggle as she caught Caroline's eye. Miss Hurst was unlikely to continue her diatribe now.

'I had a monkey wagered on John reaching fifty before he was out,' Sir William said cheerfully, sitting on the grass at Annabella's feet, and giving her a grin which suggested that he had also heard Miss Hurst's last utterance. He took a deep draught of ale.

'This local brew is very good, isn't it, John? I'm glad to see the villagers entering so wholeheartedly into the spirit of the occasion!'

Miss Hurst glared at him. Now that she had all but given up on the prospect of attaching Sir William, she felt quite comfortable in treating him with disapproval. Besides, there was metal more attractive in Lord Dedicoat who was equally handsome and had a title into the bargain.

'Do tell me a little about the game, my lord,' she gushed unbecomingly. 'Those men standing about over there—what is their purpose?'

John Dedicoat began to explain the fielders' positions to Miss Hurst whilst simultaneously watching Miss Mundell. Will Weston leant back on one elbow so that his head was on a level with Annabella's knee. She resisted the surprisingly strong impulse to touch his ruffled brown hair.

'Are you enjoying the game, Mrs St Auby?' Weston asked softly, looking up at her with those brilliant blue eyes.

'Yes, sir, I thank you.' Annabella smiled. 'I have absolutely no understanding of the rules, but that has not marred my enjoyment!'

'I could explain them if you like,' Weston offered, taking a bite out of a cucumber sandwich with his strong white teeth. He looked at Miss Hurst, who was insisting that Dedicoat give a running commentary of every ball bowled, and smiled.

'Pray do not put yourself to the trouble, sir!' Annabella said, following his gaze and scorning to behave in so foolish a fashion as Ermina Hurst. She spoke with gentle malice. 'I have no need of such guidance!'

Weston shook his head in mock sorrow. 'Spurning my offer, Mrs St Auby? You are very hard on a fellow's self-esteem! Can it be that you do not wish for my company?' There was a teasing light in his eyes, a challenge that Annabella rose to.

She was enjoying their sparring and he knew it too. There was an edge to the encounter that the presence of the others did nothing to diminish, an attraction that was instant and mutual. And dangerous.

'For shame, sir, that you need to fish for compliments from your friends!' Annabella spoke lightly, and caught her breath as he touched her hand fleetingly, almost accidentally.

'Is that then how you see yourself, Mrs St Auby?' Weston asked, dropping his voice even lower. 'As a friend of mine?'

Annabella tore her gaze away from his compelling one. 'Friendship is to be prized, sir…'

'Oh, as to that, I agree with you.' Weston selected another sandwich from the hamper. 'True friends are indeed to be valued. But from you, Mrs St Auby, I might ask for something more…'

'Just at the moment,' Annabella said tartly, 'your *friends*—' she emphasised the word '—are asking something of you, sir! I believe it is your turn with the bat! Pray try to concentrate on the game!' And, well pleased with herself for not succumbing to his flirtation, she watched Sir William lope away to take up his stance at the wicket.

Miss Hurst had exhausted the topic of field placings and Lord Dedicoat had, with some relief, moved away a little to converse in a low tone with Miss Mundell. And for the first time, Miss Hurst was watching her friend with a less than amicable expression, her brown eyes narrowed thoughtfully as she saw Dedicoat smile at Charlotte. A moment later, a shriek rent the air.

'A beetle! Oh, Good God, a beetle has just dropped from that tree on to my lap!' Miss Hurst leapt to her feet clutching Lord Dedicoat's arm and leaning heavily against him. Caroline shook her head in exasperation.

'Really, Ermina! It will do you no harm!'

'Oh! Oh!' Miss Hurst was drooping artistically. She allowed Lord Dedicoat to lead her gently towards his own seat with soothing words and much careful support. The beetle, Annabella observed, was nowhere to be seen. She watched, a small smile curving her lips, as Miss Hurst lowered herself slowly on to Lord Dedicoat's seat with small gasps of distress and shock.

Poor Charlotte Mundell was quite disregarded. Annabella leant forward. She had seen a bee, drunk with pollen, lurch onto the cushion beneath Miss Hurst's descending bottom. Annabella sighed and sat back again. She did not say a word.

## Chapter Four

It was later the same evening that they were sitting in the Blue Saloon after dinner, with Viscount Mundell and his sister engaging the Kilgarens at cards and Sir William and Annabella listening to Miss Hurst, who was exhibiting her proficiency at the piano.

Miss Hurst's recovery from the bee sting had been remarkable. Since the injury was to a part of her anatomy that precluded discussion, she had decided to bravely ignore the incident and soldier on with only the slightest wince whenever she sat down.

As Miss Hurst played, Annabella was covertly studying Sir William's profile. His blue eyes were distant, as though he were dwelling on matters far beyond the lamplit room and the music. The sweep of his lashes cast a shadow against the hard line of his cheek, and in repose that handsome mouth looked uncompromising, almost harsh. Though relaxed in his chair, there was something almost watchful in his stillness.

Annabella frowned slightly. What was it that caused this tension in him? She doubted that he was such a musical purist that Miss Hurst's rendition of Bach could offend him, although whilst technically brilliant the performance certainly lacked feeling… Suddenly, Annabella felt a hollow feeling in the pit of her stomach, a conviction that she scarcely knew Sir William, and understood him even less. The passage of time in his company had given her only a superficial knowledge of his interests and dislikes, for the conversations that one could hold in a group were inevitably very general, or hampered by the presence of its other members. Annabella frowned again. She had to admit to herself that she most ardently wished to have a better understanding of Sir William Weston.

The music rippled around her, and Annabella shifted slightly, trying to find a better position on the gilt sofa, which was no doubt most fashionable but made no concessions to comfort. Her wriggling disturbed Sir William from his reverie and he turned his head and looked directly into Annabella's eyes, and again she experienced that small tremor of shock which made it impossible for her to be indifferent to him. Worse, he then smiled, that slow, heart-shaking smile of his, and she was utterly lost.

'Mrs St Auby!' The music had stopped and Miss Hurst's voice was sharp. 'Did you not attend me? I asked if you would care to play now?' There was an equally sharp look in her dark eyes, for she had not forgotten Annabella's claim to play very ill. 'I am sure,' she added patronisingly, 'that we can find something suited to you!' She rifled through the sheets of music on top of the piano. 'Scarlatti? No, too difficult, perhaps…'

Annabella tore her gaze away from the compelling

blue heat of Sir William's, and took Miss Hurst's place at the pianoforte.

'Thank you,' she murmured, 'I shall sing, I think.'

'As you please.' Miss Hurst shrugged, moving across to Sir William's side with an ostentatious swing of the hips matched by the sway of the ostrich feathers in her hair. She seated herself and arranged her skirts, looking expectant. A minute later, she had started to chat to Sir William in an undertone, much to Annabella's annoyance.

After a few bars, Miss Hurst had fallen into chagrined silence, aware that her companion's attention had wandered. The card-players paused in their hand to listen. Annabella had not chosen a classical piece, but an old Scottish love song, 'The Wild White Swan', and sang with a depth and pathos that could not help but touch the listener. The melodic cadences fell gently, sorrowfully on the ear. And as the last notes died away there was a breathless hush before everyone broke into spontaneous applause and cries for more. This time Annabella picked a saucy little song calculated to shock a little, but the purity of her exceptionally fine voice somehow robbed it of anything but innocent naughtiness. The smiles were broad as she ended.

Finally, she was prevailed upon to sing a duet with Sir William, who turned out to have a fine tenor voice, rich and a little mocking in tone, and then she begged a rest and took her glass of lemonade out on to the terrace. Dusk was falling, casting its shadows across the sentinel cypresses and turning the formal gardens into a cool and mysterious place. Annabella leant her elbows on the parapet and looked across to the pleasure lake.

'You have been exceptionally reticent about your musical talent.' Sir William Weston, the same mocking tone evident in his voice as there had been in his singing, had followed her out and came to lean on the stone parapet beside her. 'I have seldom heard such a fine voice.'

Annabella smiled. 'Thank you, sir. I'll allow that on the occasion I was quizzed on the subject I saw no need to make my questioner free with the information! But,' she added seriously, 'you should not criticise in others a trait which serves you well!'

'You mean to imply that I give little of myself away?' It was becoming too dark to see his face, but Annabella thought that he was smiling slightly. 'Well, in the main I'll concede the truth of that! But I have no sinister motive, I assure you! It is simply that on board ship, living in each other's pockets, one becomes accustomed to keeping one's own counsel in order to avoid unnecessary disputes. It is a habit which has served me well on occasions such as this houseparty, which requires much the same approach!'

Annabella laughed despite herself. 'Surely you exaggerate, sir! I have been among you a few days only, but I see no sign of disputation!'

'You would be surprised, Mrs St Auby,' Sir William murmured. 'Why, only yesterday there was a heated debate between Miss Hurst and Miss Mundell over which had most recently used Miss Hurst's silver thimble, and Lord Kilgaren was called upon to arbitrate! I kept quite out of the matter, I assure you!'

'You are absurd, sir!' Annabella smiled. 'I suspect

that you really keep your silence just to appear more mysterious!'

'Acquit me!' Sir William said, humorously. 'Though,' he added with sincerity, 'I should be flattered to think that you would wish to learn more of me, Mrs St Auby. On what may I enlighten you?'

'Oh…' Annabella turned away to look out across the darkening garden. She essayed a light tone. 'Simple things only, sir! Of your family, your home…'

'Well…' Sir William spoke easily '…my father died a few years ago when I was away at sea, and my mother a year later. I have two elder sisters and I had a younger brother, who married the daughter of a Charleston plantation owner and lived abroad. He died last year.' He brushed aside her words of condolence as though it still hurt him to speak of it. 'And as for my home…' Sir William's voice changed, took on a deeper quality. 'There is a house on the Berkshire Downs, just north of the little village of Lambourn… In the winter the wind whistles down from the chalk hills and across the wide valley below with the snow on its edge, but in the summer the countryside drowses in a verdant, green peace. There is an ancient track which cuts its way across the hills, bone dry in the sun, and butterflies drift through the poppy fields.' His voice changed, became brisk. 'But it is a long time since I have been there. Are you cold, Mrs St Auby?'

Annabella had shivered suddenly as a stray breath of wind touched the back of her neck and trickled down her spine. She was aware of a vague feeling of disquiet, but she knew not why. She allowed Sir William to take her arm and steer her back into the lighted room, where the card-players had just concluded their game.

Caroline Kilgaren came across to sit by Annabella as Sir William moved away and was almost immediately pounced on by Miss Hurst, who demanded his opinion on a letter she had just received from her mother:

'For it says, dear Sir William, that Lady Frankland has inherited an estate of fifty thousand pounds from her uncle, Mr Cobbett, and yet I positively thought that she was cousin only to the Cobbetts, and surely the Drysdales are his closer relations…'

Caroline smiled ruefully as Miss Hurst bore Sir William away to a corner of the room to continue the discussion. 'Now my dear, there is a matter I wanted to broach with you. It is about the ball on Friday.' She hesitated. 'Tell me to mind my own business if you wish, but I could not help wondering… I have a dress, you see, a very pretty confection in silver and gold, which would be just the thing for you if you do not have something you prefer to wear.' She considered Annabella thoughtfully and smiled. 'We may have to add a flounce, for you are somewhat taller than I, but that should not be beyond the skill of Ellie, my maid. She is a most talented sempstress.'

Annabella could have hugged her for her tact and kindness. The ball had been on her mind, for although Miss Mundell had referred to it as a small gathering for friends, Annabella had the feeling that the small gathering could be both exclusive and very smart, a far cry from the Taunton assemblies. She had wanted desperately to go, but had almost cried off through a lack of appropriate clothing. But now, perhaps, that problem might be solved.

'You are very kind to me, ma'am,' she said, gratefully. 'I do not mind admitting that I was wondering how I might go on.'

'Come upstairs now,' Caroline urged her, 'and you may try it on. I'll call Ellie, my maid, and she can help us with any adjustments.'

Lord and Lady Kilgaren were occupying a well-appointed suite of rooms in the east wing of Mundell Hall, with charming views over the flower gardens and the deer park beyond. Caroline went across to the wardrobe, which seemed to Annabella's dazzled eye to be absolutely packed with dresses of all styles and materials. With a cry of triumph, she pulled out something from the back.

'Here it is! Now, what do you think?'

Annabella thought she was imagining things. The dreamy, ethereal creation draped over Caroline's arm could surely not be intended for her! When she tried it on, its softly flowing lines seemed to caress her body in the most seductive way, and she stood back in amazement to consider her reflection in the long mirror. The low bodice was cunningly cut to cross over in a V shape rather than the less sophisticated square or round necklines she was accustomed to, and she looked impossibly slender and elegant. Behind her in the glass, she could see both Caroline and the maid smiling.

'Perfect!' Caroline declared. 'It lacks length, of course, but with a ruffle of silver taffeta, Ellie...' the maid nodded in silent agreement '...if the dressmakers of Taunton can run to that...' She swooped on a bandbox at the back of the wardrobe, 'And here is the silver circlet which is intended to match.' She placed it on Annabella's honey-coloured curls and stood back to admire. 'Oh, my dear, you will look divine!' Then, as Annabella remained silent, she said anxiously, 'What is the matter? Do you not care for it?'

Annabella shook her head slowly, a lump in her throat. 'It is the most beautiful thing... I cannot believe that I am really going to wear it!'

Caroline smiled, reassured, and Ellie, her mouth full of pins, instructed Annabella to turn around slowly so that she could see the rest of the fit. A tweak here and a tuck there, and the maid nodded her satisfaction.

'You will be the belle of the ball, my dear,' Caroline predicted, 'and I'll warrant Sir William will think so too!'

Annabella smiled, still dazzled by the subtle, shifting patterns of silver and gold. Her eyes were like stars as she turned before the mirror. 'Oh, do you really think so, ma'am?' She sounded quite wistful and very young. To Caroline she looked suddenly so like her sister that she too felt a lump in her throat.

'If Sir William tells you of something—' she began, stopped then started again. 'You must never think that Sir William is interested in you other than for yourself, my dear.'

Annabella's wide, uncomprehending green eyes turned on her in puzzlement.

'I do so hope that you are right in thinking he likes me, ma'am.'

Caroline gave up. It was not her story to tell, anyway, and she had already told Will Weston in the

most forcible tones possible that the sooner he told
Annabella the truth, the better. Will had argued that
he had wanted the chance for them to get to know
each other properly first, before this matter interfered
to muddy the waters. Caroline thought he was a fool,
but knew she could not sway him. She sighed. There
was such a clear, innocent light in Annabella's eyes
as she stood, rapt in wonder at her own appearance,
that Caroline hoped she would never suffer disillu-
sionment. Like Will Weston before her, she contem-
plated the curious mix of characteristics that was Annabella St Auby. Sometimes so collected, so
sophisticated, and at others so young and lacking in
confidence. And she was, after all, only twenty-one,
with no one to show her how to go on or help her
form sound judgement. Caroline thought it was extraordinary that she had turned out as well as she had.

When Annabella came down the stair at Mundell
Hall on the night of the ball, she was delighted to see
that William Weston, who was waiting with Marcus
Kilgaren, actually stopped talking when he saw her.
There was uncomplicated admiration blazing in his
blue eyes and a more complex, and far more exciting,
emotion which set Annabella's pulse racing. As Weston moved forward to take her hand, Marcus Kilgaren
crossed to Caroline's side.

'You seem to have played the fairy godmother
rather successfully, my love,' he murmured to his
wife, with a grin. 'Little Mrs St Auby looks quite
ravishing tonight. Certainly, Will looks as though he
would like to ravish her!'

Caroline dug him reprovingly in the ribs. 'Marcus!

She's a sweet girl, and she deserves to enjoy herself. But—' a tiny frown marred her brow '—Will still hasn't told her about Larkswood! I worry that if she finds out some other way, it may all go wrong…'

Marcus's shrewd blue eyes scanned her face. 'You really have taken her under your wing, haven't you, Caro? But there's nothing we can do. Will must sort it out for himself.'

Caroline looked across to where the two heads were bent close together as Sir William scrawled his initials on Annabella's dance card. She sighed. 'I know… But Annabella is only twenty-one and I know she has been unfortunate before, even though she has not confided the whole to me. It would be most unlucky if something was to spoil her current happiness.'

Nothing was further from Annabella's mind. She felt truly beautiful in the gold and silver dress, and the admiring glances cast her way were a delicious contrast to the pitying looks usually reserved for her at such events when she was obliged to turn out in her old, outmoded gowns. Then there was the warmth of Sir William's hand beneath her elbow as he guided her into the first dance. Her dance card was already filling up, her company sought by plenty of eligible young men. It was promising to be a delightful evening.

'You look quite captivating tonight, Mrs St Auby,' Sir William observed, as he led her into the dance. 'I might wish not to have to share your company with all these other gentlemen!'

Annabella smiled, a little flirtatiously. It was an evening made for romance and the experience was most enjoyable. She cast him a look from under her lashes.

'Are you always so direct, sir?'

'No…' Sir William's smile broadened '…generally I am only so outspoken when I want something a great deal!'

The movement of the dance fortunately separated them at that moment and gave Annabella the opportunity to compose herself.

'I cannot believe that you speak to all young ladies like that, sir,' she said severely when they came together again. 'They would likely slap your face or faint dead away!'

'I never give them the chance,' Sir William said laconically.

'Oh, indeed?'

'No, for I have never addressed myself thus to a young lady. As a type they bore me!'

Annabella choked back a laugh. 'Upon my word, sir, you are very severe! To condemn all my contemporaries thus—leaving aside the doubt it cast upon my own status in your eyes! Which do you dispute? That I am young, or that I am a lady?'

Sir William's gaze considered her enchanting face. 'Ah, now you are trying to trap me, ma'am, and it is too bad of you! You must know that I consider you to be indisputably a lady!'

'Punish you, rather, for your dismissive view of my sex!' Annabella considered him thoughtfully. 'Do you really have such a low opinion of us, Sir William?'

'Why, not in the least! But I would never generalise.' Sir William turned her expertly. 'My interest usually lies in people as individuals and at the moment—' his smile was mocking '—one individual in particular!'

Annabella's euphoria lasted until just before supper, when she happened to find herself in the ladies' room at the same time as Miss Hurst, who was pinning up a torn flounce. Miss Hurst watched, her brown eyes bright, as Annabella tweaked a curl back inside the silver circlet.

'La, what a charming dress!' she said with gracious condescension. 'Lady Kilgaren is the kindest creature in the world, always taking care of waifs and strays! And Sir William…' here Miss Hurst paused, her brown eyes brimful of malicious laughter '…well, he is the kindest creature too, except when he wants something—when he has a *particular* reason for acting the gallant!' She gave a little trill of laughter. 'But I expect he has told you *all* about that by now, Mrs St Auby!' And she gathered up the skirts of her dress in one hand and, laughing still, went out of the door.

Annabella stood quite still before the mirror, her comb forgotten in one hand as Miss Hurst's words began to do their poisonous work. A particular reason, Miss Hurst had said. But what could be Sir William's reason for acting the gallant with her? She had no money, and he had no need to hunt a fortune anyway. Certainly he was a friend of Alicia and James Mullineaux, but then all of Viscount Mundell's set had been kind to her because of that connection. Her heart missed a beat. Surely Miss Hurst did not mean to imply that Sir William was interested in setting her up as his mistress? Though he had perhaps been more explicit in his attentions than a more conventional man, there had been nothing disrespectful in his attitude, no indication that he intended to offer her *carte blanche*.

There had been such a spiteful look on Miss Hurst's face…but then, Annabella reasoned, Ermina Hurst had never liked her… She gave up and tried to forget about it. She was certainly not going to please Miss Hurst by asking her to explain her meaning.

Some of the enjoyment seemed to have gone out of the evening. The light from the chandeliers was not so sparkling and bright now and the animated chatter of Mundell's guests seemed to wash over Annabella rather than involve her. Nor was her heart in the dancing any more, and when the next set of country dances ended she excused herself to her partner and slipped into a cool alcove behind a pillar and sat down in the shadows. Whatever had Miss Hurst meant…?

'Mrs St Auby…' When Sir William's voice spoke in her ear, she jumped a mile.

'Oh, Sir William! You startled me, sir! I was not attending…'

Those searching blue eyes scanned her face thoughtfully. 'No, indeed, I can see you were thinking of something else entirely, ma'am. A penny for your thoughts?'

Annabella shifted uncomfortably. 'They are not worth it, sir!'

Sir William raised one dark brow. 'No? Then perhaps you will tell me why you are hiding yourself away behind a pillar? I met a most disconsolate fellow on my way here. Apparently you were supposed to be his partner for the boulanger, but he could not find you. But…' Sir William shrugged and sat down beside her '…his loss is my gain,' after all!'

Annabella's answering smile felt stiff and insincere. Oh, why could she not put Miss Hurst's malicious remarks from her mind? And Sir William was not unaware of her discomfiture, for his gaze had not wavered and he was studying her face with relentless intensity.

'You look as though you need a pleasant diversion to take your mind away from these melancholy thoughts,' he observed after a moment. 'Would you care to come for a sail on the lake with me?'

'On the lake? In the dark?' Annabella's green eyes widened to their furthest extent at this audacious plan, distracted as he had intended her to be.

'In the moonlight,' Sir William amended. 'There is a full moon tonight. This is one of those moments, Mrs St Auby, when I find that I miss the soothing influence of the sea. A sail on Mundell's artificial lake is a poor substitute, I know, but it must suffice!'

Annabella smiled in spite of herself. 'That is definitely the sort of invitation I should refuse, sir!'

'Indeed it is…' Sir William also had a smile lurking in his eyes '…and it is the sort of invitation I should not be offering. However…'

'That would be delightful, sir,' Annabella said with a small, demure smile.

It was indeed a very clear night. The moon glittered on the water and cast their shadows across the lawn. The turf was springy and already wet with dew, but the air was warm. Sir William took Annabella's hand as they crossed the lawns to reach the jetty and the small rowing-boat that was tied up there.

'Not a sail, to be precise, but a row,' Sir William said. 'Well, Mrs St Auby? You should think carefully now, for you cannot change your mind once out in the middle of the lake!'

Annabella cast him a sideways look. 'No, sir? Can I not trust you to bring me safely back again?'

There was a split second of tension. 'Let us hope so,' Sir William said, cryptically, holding out his hand again to help her step into the boat.

The splash of the oars in the water seemed magnified in that still night, but the sounds of music and laughter floating from the windows of the terrace ballroom masked all other noises. Annabella glanced around, a little fearful of being seen, for she could still only half-believe that she had had the temerity to do this. But the shadowed gardens were empty of movement and in a few moments she sat back in the boat, relaxing. The cushioned seats were very comfortable, and she trailed her hand in the cool water, looking up at the stars shining in their cold, lonely splendour.

Neither of them spoke. Sir William had the habit of silence, and Annabella was too wrapped up in the enchanted beauty of the night. Somewhere at the back of her mind a quiet voice was counselling that this was no fairytale and that she should be very careful of what she did, but she did not wish to regard it. This seemed pure romance and she knew she was tumbling head over heels in love with Sir William Weston. It was so agreeable an experience that she had no inclination to put a stop to it with common sense.

Sir William rested on the oars and smiled at her in the darkness. 'We are almost at the island. Would you care to step ashore?'

This time Annabella hesitated for fully five seconds. 'I think perhaps...yes, that would be very pleasant.'

The island was tiny, with a small decorative summerhouse in the middle, surrounded by neatly trimmed lawns and flowering shrubs. On hot summer days it was the scene of picnics by the water, but now its shuttered windows had a secretive look. The boat grated on the shingle and Sir William leapt ashore, securing the rope to an overhanging branch. He turned back to help Annabella, taking her hand in a firm grip as she stepped from the swaying boat onto the shore.

'It's very beautiful, isn't it?' she said, a little wistfully, for there was something magical about the night which seemed quite unreal. The moonlight shimmered on the black lake as the slight breeze stirred the water. The cypress trees stood clear against the sky and the air was filled with the scent of flowers. And then, like the snake in paradise, Miss Hurst's words slid into Annabella's mind again, poisoning the night. She shivered.

'What is it?' Sir William spoke from close at hand. 'Something is troubling you, is it not, Annabella? You would do far better to tell me what is wrong.'

Annabella drew in her breath at his use of her name, but there was something about the intimate darkness that encouraged confidences. She took a deep breath.

'Sir William, I must ask you—' She stopped. Oh, how difficult this was! What could she say?

'Yes? Ask me what?' His voice was cool, dispassionate, giving no indication of his feelings. It chilled her, but she was suddenly determined to continue.

'For what reason have you sought me out, sir?' The

words had tumbled out and Annabella felt her whole body burn with mortification. How could she have asked so naïve a question? She wished she had never started this.

'I take it that you mean to ask what prompted me to seek your company when we first met,' Sir William said, still with the same detachment. Annabella could not see his expression, for his head was bent, his hands deep in his pockets.

'Yes.' Her voice had shrunk as her embarrassment had grown. 'I thought perhaps that it was for my sister's sake...'

Sir William shifted slightly. 'I cannot deny that it was my friendship with James and Alicia which first brought you to my attention, Annabella.'

'I see.' Annabella's voice was now a tiny thread of sound. So he had only tolerated her company for friendship's sake. And no doubt Caroline Kilgaren's kindness had sprung from the same source... Annabella's fragile confidence wavered. The cold charity of it made her feel like crying. 'It is as I had supposed, sir. No doubt you are all acting from the same obligation to my sister—'

Sir William moved surprisingly quickly, taking hold of her upper arms and turning her so that the moonlight fell full upon her face. He gave her a little shake. 'Just a moment, Annabella! You do us all a disservice by that assumption! Yes, Mundell and all our friends initially sought you out because of your connection with Alicia, but do you think we would have done any more than merely acknowledge your acquaintance if we had not liked you for yourself?' His hands slid down to her wrists, but he did not let her go. 'As for me,' he said, an undertone of amusement in his voice, 'I like you all too well, and it is damnably difficult for me! It was foolish in the extreme of me to bring you out here when I have been avoiding just such a situation for days! I gave in to a reckless impulse tonight, and should have known better!'

Annabella freed herself and moved away slightly, her silver dress gleaming in the light. Her heart was suddenly beating light and fast. His touch had awoken in her something which could not be dismissed easily, a hunger that invaded her senses. 'I do not understand you, sir,' she said coolly, knowing full well that she lied.

'I think that you do.' Sir William sounded exasperated, though whether with her or with himself, Annabella could not tell. 'It was most imprudent for us to court scandal by stepping apart alone. For all your widowed state you are still young and inexperienced, and I would not care to risk your reputation or damage that innocence—' He made a sudden, violent movement away from her. 'Devil take it, Annabella, you understand what I mean…'

Annabella hesitated. Half of her was begging her to retreat from this hazardous conversation whilst the other half, the dangerous half she scarcely understood, wanted her to push him as far as she could. She shivered a little in the cool air, but more from the peculiar excitement that gripped her than from the cold. Sir William was standing half-turned away from her and she put her hand tentatively on his arm.

'We had better go back now.' Sir William's tone was uncompromising, but Annabella could feel the tension in him, taut as a spring. And she had to know...

'You flatter me with your protestations that you have sought my company for pleasure, sir,' she said lightly. 'Do you not, then, wish to know my opinion of you, in return? Or are you so confident of your own attractions that you need no reassurance?'

Sir William smiled then, but it was not a comfortable smile. Annabella had the distinct impression that she had bitten off more than she could chew, but she was filled with a wilful determination to see if she was right. She looked across the lake, where the lights of the ballroom glittered amongst the dark trees, and she spoke very deliberately.

'I thought when I met you that you were an interesting man, a man who held some...small...appeal to me. And I wondered whether I would find you more or less interesting were you to kiss me?'

It was, after all, exactly what she had asked for, and it proved conclusively to Annabella that she was well out of her depth in provoking a man like Sir William Weston. The kiss was shocking and frightening in its explicit demand. His hands were mercilessly hard as they held her against the tense lines of his own body, his mouth hungry as it plundered the softness of hers. Annabella pushed hard against his chest to free herself. In some things she was indeed the innocent he had suggested. Francis had never shown her any tenderness in their brief marriage, being concerned only for his own selfish satisfaction, but here she sensed emotions and needs far more complex, in both herself and in Sir William, and she was suddenly afraid of them. And when he let her go straight away, she was also disappointed and confused.

'Is your curiosity satisfied now, Mrs St Auby?' Sir William asked with scrupulous politeness, 'or are there some points on which I can offer further clarification? You need only say the word!'

She could not see his expression in the darkness, but there was something so cold in his tone that Annabella shrank, transformed from the provocative sophisticate she had pretended to be into the inexperienced girl who realised the extent of her wilful mistake. How could she have behaved so? To have encouraged him, flirted with him so outrageously, so immodestly, then withdrawn in maidenly haste and disarray like a startled virgin when he had taken her in his arms. Impossible to explain to him that she had never felt any affection for her husband and never received any in return, that he had never held her with love and that her feelings were as unawakened as any new debutante... And now, no doubt, Sir William would think her just a cheap flirt, the sort who would encourage George Jeffries, or indeed any man, because she was bored, but was not prepared to deliver on those promises...a shallow tease...

'Forgive me, sir,' she said, in a voice so stifled with mortification that it was scarcely hers. 'I have behaved very foolishly...I am not always so flighty and superficial...' She swallowed a sob. So much for her pretty dreams of romance in the moonlight! Could it have been any more embarrassing?

She had to take his hand to allow him to help her back into the boat, and she held out her own so gingerly that she heard him catch his breath with irritation. Every moment that prolonged this interlude was impossibly humiliating. Then he took her hand in his, and, extraordinarily, everything changed. There was a moment when they both stood quite still, then she found she was in his arms again, held wordlessly against him. Once again, as on that first evening at the assembly, her head was resting against his chest and she could feel the strong beat of his heart against her cheek, the warmth of his body close to hers. But this time he did not let her go. It was the first time Annabella had ever been held with love and the same sense of recognition and peace flowed through her as on that first evening. How long they stood there she did not know. An eternity could have passed, but she would not have cared, for she was truly happy. Then she felt him brush the hair back from her face and kiss her gently.

'There is no need to be afraid,' he said a little huskily. 'It need not be like you knew before.'

Annabella raised her head to look up at him. The moonlight cast deep shadows. 'How did you know?' she said, a little uncertainly.

'It seemed the logical explanation.' Sir William loosened his grip a little so that he could look at her properly. 'You were married to a man you did not love or respect, a man I have heard described—in no doubt more complimentary terms than he deserves— as a boorish cad. I do not imagine he showed you any consideration, not least in the physical demands he made upon you. But it is not always that way...' he touched her cheek lightly, sliding his hand into her hair '...let me show you.'

This time he was extraordinarily patient and gentle.

His lips touched first one corner of her mouth then the other, before returning to it fully with the lightest of tantalising kisses. Annabella felt some of the tension within her begin to uncoil. His lips drifted along her jawbone to her throat, causing delicious shivers to touch her spine. Suddenly her skin felt incredibly sensitive, just waiting for his touch. Involuntarily, her lips parted, and his mouth returned to hers with the same teasing, frustrating lightness. Annabella's senses were beginning to burn. She forgot all about Francis and his selfish demands, forgot her fears and nervousness, her foolish provocation. She slid her arms around Will's neck and brought his head down to hers.

'Kiss me properly,' she whispered, and heard the amusement behind his soft words.

'Whatever you wish, Annabella…'

Then it was like her imaginings. Warm and tender, yet somehow indescribably exciting as he led her step by step towards some mysterious conclusion. Her blood was racing through her veins, the smell and taste of him filling her senses. The world receded as she became lost in the pleasure of his embrace. Dizzy, melting with longing, she pressed against him with total abandonment.

Then Will raised his mouth from hers and said, in a voice that was a mixture of amusement, regret and something else she could not identify, 'I still think I should take you back now, Annabella. In fact, I should say the need to do so has become even more pressing…' But she knew that he was smiling, and only smiled in return as she snuggled closer to him, turning her face against his chest, for she knew that somehow everything was all right.

\* \* \*

'Whatever have you been doing, Will?' Marcus Kilgaren's voice was full of resigned humour. 'You have been away the best part of an hour, and Annabella St Auby looks almost incandescent with happiness. You may tell me to go to the devil if you wish,' he added pleasantly, 'but I thought to point out that if I had noticed, so had others.' He nodded significantly in the direction of Miss Hurst, who was whispering urgently to Miss Mundell. The two of them were standing, somewhat inappropriately, in front of a statue of the Three Graces. 'But perhaps I am to wish you happy?'

Will grinned. 'Not yet, but soon, perhaps…'

'Then you have not told her about Larkswood?' Marcus persisted. 'I only ask, because, again, there are those kind friends who may do the telling for you.'

Will's grin faded. 'Surely you do not think—?'

'Miss Hurst has not taken her implied rejection well,' Marcus said obliquely. 'She may feel it necessary to impart the truth to Annabella as one good friend to another… Evidently Annabella knows nothing of her inheritance?' he added quizzically.

Will shook his head slowly. He took a glass from a passing flunkey and drank deep. 'She told me a little while ago that the lawyers were still trying to sort out Bertram Broseley's business affairs. I had hoped to be able to negotiate an agreement with them, without involving Annabella.'

Marcus was shaking his head. 'But she will find out, Will. Someone will tell her—'

'Very well.' Will put his glass down with a decisive click. 'I had wanted to get to know Annabella properly, to make sure she understood my reasons for wanting Larkswood, but I know you are right. I must go away in a couple of days,' he added, 'but after that I will tell her…' And he strolled back to Annabella's side as though drawn by a magnet.

Marcus watched him go, watched Annabella's face upturned to his, her eyes bright with happiness, and sighed. 'Let us hope,' he said under his breath, 'that you are not too late, my friend.'

# *Chapter Five*

Annabella woke the next day to bright sunshine and warm happiness that made her smile even before she was fully awake. Mundell Hall was very quiet, for most of the Viscount's guests would not be rising so unfashionably early, but Annabella felt full of energy despite the lateness of the ball the previous night. She slipped out of bed, dressed swiftly in another of the gowns which Caroline Kilgaren had pressed on her, and sped downstairs for some fresh air. An impassive footman informed her that Lord Mundell was out walking his dogs, but that the rest of the party was still abed. Annabella thanked him prettily and ran down the steps into the garden.

Her steps took her, by accident or unconscious design, towards the ornamental lake which was glittering in the early morning light. A number of waterfowl preened and swam on its glassy waters; on the island in the centre, the windows of the pretty little summerhouse reflected the rays of the rising sun. It was very quiet. Impossible to believe, Annabella thought dreamily, that the scene between herself and Sir William Weston had really happened. Perhaps she had imagined it all, a dream conjured by the romance of the night and her own wishful thinking… She was still staring at the view, remembering the night before, when a voice called her name from near at hand. Turning quickly, she saw with a rush of disappointment that it was Viscount Mundell and not Sir William Weston who had accosted her. Mundell, his pack of King Charles Spaniels pressing at his heels, came up to her with a broad smile.

'Good morning, Mrs St Auby! A beautiful day, is it not? You must have plenty of stamina to be up so early after the ball! I imagine most of my guests will not appear until mid-afternoon!'

Annabella smiled at him. 'The sunshine beckoned me out, my lord, and it is too fine to be abed! I was just admiring your lake. You have a fine selection of waterfowl!'

Mundell, who was in his way quite an ornithologist, started to point out to her the different breeds, including the rare Cinnamon Teal which he had had specially imported from South America. 'Of course, it is difficult to prevent the ornamentals interbreeding with the native ducks who are attracted to the water here,' Mundell was saying, then realised from Annabella's glassy expression that birds were perhaps not really a point of interest to her. He smiled slightly. 'But I am boring on about the estate as I often do! I spend comparatively little time here, you see, and each time I return I discover afresh what draws me to the country…' They started walking along the edge of the lake, discussing the rival merits of town and country life, until they reached the point where the ha-ha divided the formal garden from the deer park, and Mundell bade her farewell, saying that he would give the dogs a run in the park.

As Annabella turned back towards the house, an amused voice from near at hand said, 'At last! I was afraid that he would never go!' And Sir William Weston stepped out of the shelter of the beech hedge directly on to the path in front of her.

'Sir William!' Annabella was annoyed to discover that her voice came out rather squeakily, with a combination of shock at seeing him so suddenly, and residual embarrassment over remembering their encounter in the clear light of day. Last night had been an enchanted evening, but now the sun was bright and showing all too clearly the vexatious blush in her cheeks. She looked at him a little accusingly.

'Have you been skulking in the bushes for long, sir?'

'I have. I thought that Hugo would never leave you alone!' Will looked completely unrepentant. The early morning breeze had ruffled his brown hair, and he put up a hand to smooth its disorder. He was dressed very casually in an old hunting jacket and breeches, a cravat tied carelessly about his neck, but the ensemble still had a distinction which was hard to define but immediately obvious. Annabella, running a mental eye over her own toilette, was glad that she had made the effort to wear the pretty straw-coloured dress and matching cloak, but she had little idea how appealing she looked with the breeze tugging at the tendrils of honey-fair hair and accentuating the pink of her cheeks and brightness of those green eyes.

'Come into the rose arbour,' Will said abruptly. 'There is something I wish to say to you.'

A little apprehensively, Annabella followed him through the archway, out of the sight of prying eyes, and into the heady-scented shadows of the walled garden. The sun had not yet warmed the old walls, and she shivered a little within the cloak from a combination of anticipation and cold. What was it that he wished to say to her? She looked up into his face, and discovered that it appeared Will Weston did not wish to talk after all. His arm went around her waist and he drew her deeper into the shadows. Mindful of her reaction the previous night, he kissed her very gently, waiting until he felt some of the tension leave her and her body become pliant against his own. Encouraged, he deepened the kiss a little, leading her by skilful stages to the point where he could tell her innocent but heartfelt response to him was sliding over the edge into genuine desire. So far he had given little thought to his own pleasure, but suddenly his awareness changed. The seductive softness of her in his arms awoke a need in him that almost pushed him beyond all restraint. He teetered on the edge, within a hair's-breadth of abandoning caution and crushing her to him. Then there was the sound of steps on the gravel beyond the archway, and Miss Hurst's tones could be heard addressing a nameless companion.

'Of course, whatever they say, the family is bad *ton*. How could it be otherwise when the father was that disgusting nabob Broseley, the elder sister married some degenerate septuagenarian for his money, and the younger one set her cap at Francis St Auby in that shameless way? Why, do you know, I heard the most *delicious* piece of gossip from Lady Oakston last night. Apparently Annabella Broseley was in the habit of making illicit trysts with Francis in the woods. This was well before the wedding, and they say he was not the first…' Her voice faded away.

Will straightened and let Annabella go gently, watching with regret as the intrusion of reality caused the colour to leave her stricken face and the bright light fade from her eyes. He captured both her hands and held on to them.

'You have nothing to reproach yourself with, Annabella,' he said gently, 'neither now nor in the past. Miss Hurst has a vicious tongue, and at the moment her disappointment leads her to exercise it on you. I beg you not to regard it.'

'Who was she with?' Annabella whispered.

'I do not know. Miss Mundell, perhaps, for no one else would bear her ill-bred prating!' There was real violence in Will's tone. He saw how upset she was and added gently, 'As I say, do not regard her, Annabella. She is bitter with disappointment.'

Annabella nodded slowly. To have returned to reality with such an unpleasant shock had somehow spoilt the sweetness of what had happened before. Spoilt it, but not put it from her mind altogether. She had never felt like that before. It had been a little frightening, but at the same time entirely pleasurable and it had left her wanting more…

'Don't look at me like that, Annabella, or I will forget my good resolutions,' Will said a little roughly. 'There really was something that I wished to say to you. I have to go away for a few days.' He saw her face fall and added, 'I have business with my lawyer in London, or I would never go away at such a time. Will you stay at Mundell until I return, so that I know that you are safe here?'

Annabella shook her head again. The memory of Miss Hurst's spite was still in her mind and she would have been quite happy never to have to see her again. To spend several days in her company, without the protective presence of Will Weston, was not to be considered. Even Lady St Auby was a preferable option.

'No,' she said slowly, 'I will go back to Taunton, I think. I was intending to return today, and I find I do not wish to stay here in such company.'

Will tightened his grip on her hands. 'Very well, I shall not seek to dissuade you. But there is something most particular I wish to say to you, Annabella. I doubt we shall have the opportunity to speak privately again until I return from London, but when I do, do I have your permission to call in Fore Street to see you?'

Annabella caught her breath. She could not misunderstand him. He intended to make a proposal in form. Even as she smiled her acquiescence, and felt his lips brush her cheek in the tenderest of kisses, her heart cried out for him to speak here and now. But he was silent, and in a moment he pressed another kiss on her hand, tucking it through his arm.

'We must go back to the house now.' He scanned her face and his expression softened. 'Can you try to look as though our attention has been concentrated on nothing more exciting than the roses? At the moment there is a certain air of distraction about you which, whilst completely charming, will certainly put ideas into the heads of the more observant of Mundell's guests!'

Inevitably Annabella blushed all the more at this, and equally inevitably Will found himself obliged to kiss her again as a result. It was a long, delicious, passionate time later that they finally managed to disentangle themselves. Annabella's hair had completely escaped its pins and her cloak had become snagged on the thorns when Will had precipitately pushed it from her shoulders so that his mouth could trace the delicate line of her jaw and throat. Her lips felt swollen and beestung with kissing and her eyes were bright with unsatisfied desire. Nor did Will look any less shaken than she. He took several deliberate steps away from her.

'Enough of this! I'm not made of stone, sweetheart! We really must seek the safety of the house!'

He took her arm again, and this time they wended their way slowly through the maze of garden paths to the house. It was unfortunate that Miss Hurst was just crossing the marble hall as they came up the steps, for she paused and her sharp gaze took in every aspect of their appearance.

'Lud, Mrs St Auby, you look as though you have been pulled through the hedge backwards! Why, there are twigs in your hair!' Her gaze moved to Sir William's inscrutable face, and whatever she saw there made the words wither on her lips. 'Well,' she said, with playful lightness, turning back to the easier prey, 'you must be sharp set after such a morning's activity, Mrs St Auby, though from all I hear, it is not new to you! Breakfast is being served in the dining-room, I believe! You must have worked up quite an appetite!'

And with a trill of laughter at Annabella's furious, mortified face, she set off up the stairs.

'So, has the navy stolen your affections away from the militia, my dear?' Mrs Eddington-Buck asked, her bright brown shrew's eyes darting maliciously. Lady St Auby drew a sharp breath before Annabella even had time to think of an answer.

'It's a scandal, Millicent! First she has young Jeffries paying court and then she goes jaunting about the country with that ramshackle Sir William Weston! But—' she gave a thin smile '—it's all of a piece! Her mother was another such, by all accounts, forever throwing out lures to any man who would take her! Why, how do you suppose she ended up with that Cit, Broseley? Do you know, I heard—'

Annabella rose and quietly left the room. She had become reasonably inured to criticisms of her own conduct, but unjustified attacks on the mother she had never known had the power to hurt her more deeply. Lady Julia Broseley had been a gentle girl, shy and unsure of her own worth, momentarily dazzled by Bertram Broseley's golden good looks and supreme self-confidence. He had married her for her family connections, and when her parents had disowned her for the runaway match, had treated her with the crushing contempt he had for all commodities that no longer held any use for him. Poor, sad Julia had provided him with two daughters, and died as quietly as she had lived, when Annabella was only a few days old.

Annabella went up to her tiny bedroom, the only place where she could escape Lady St Auby's sharp tongue, and sat by the small window, trying to read. After the airy simplicity of the rooms at Mundell, the St Aubys' poky old house felt particularly claustrophobic, especially as her mother-in-law had picked up immediately on her happiness with the curious awareness that unhappy people have for the joy of others. She had chipped away at Annabella with the same bitter comments as before, and though she could not touch her daughter-in-law's inner contentment, she soon had Annabella wondering whether the veiled malice of Miss Hurst might have been easier to bear.

It was only two days since she had left Mundell Hall, and yet it seemed much longer. Annabella sighed. She found she could not concentrate, for her mother-in-law's mention of George Jeffries had brought back the extraordinary conversation she had had with him the previous day.

She had hardly been expecting to see Jeffries at all, for their quarrel several weeks previously had seemed final, and her head was full of Sir William Weston. They had been riding on the afternoon of the previous day, up on the Quantock Hills in the bright summer's day, and it was the last in a series of happy memories which remained with Annabella from the time they had spent together. She had been vaguely surprised when Jeffries was announced, but too secure and wrapped up in her new-found love to spare much thought for why he was there.

He had strolled into the drawing-room as though their disagreement had scarcely occurred. He had brought with him a bunch of gaudy red roses, well past their best bloom and with the petals about to drop, and had laid them carelessly on the table as he had come in.

'Annabella, my love!' He took her hand and pressed a damp kiss on it, looking at her languishingly. 'You are in excellent looks today! All this fraternisation with Mundell and his set must be good for you! It is the talk of the town!'

Annabella felt the irritation rising in her at this odious familiarity of his. Worse, the drawing-room door was ajar, and she could see her mother-in-law's flushed red face in the opening as she eavesdropped shamelessly, and the maid grinning in the hallway behind her.

'I scarce expected to see you again, sir!' she said coldly. 'The last time we met, your departure suggested that you would be taking your compliments elsewhere in future!' Too late, she realised that he had interpreted this as jealousy on her part, for he was grinning complacently. He had a round, impudent face with pale grey eyes that somehow always managed to appear over-familiar, and now he was admiring her figure in a way she found frankly insolent. She sat down hastily, and Jeffries took a chair opposite, continuing his ogling. Annabella itched to slap his face.

'You must forgive me,' he said, with an obvious assumption that she would. 'I was disappointed by your reticence on the occasion of the ball, but I understand that you feel you must observe the conventions of mourning a little longer.'

Annabella felt her temper rising. 'My reticence did not stem from hypocritical conventionality, sir,' she said, frigidly. 'I infinitely regret that you find it difficult to believe that I have no interest in your attentions!'

'Ah, the respectable widow!' Jeffries's tone was still easy, but Annabella saw a flash of anger in his eyes. 'Say no more, my love—we shall not quarrel again over this! But remember—' his lips tightened into a humourless smile '—your distinction by Mundell and his set may be short-lived. They may drop you as quickly as they have taken you up, and then my attentions may not be so unwelcome!'

Sighing, Annabella wondered how obtuse, or just plain conceited, a man could be, and also how rude she was going to have to be to get rid of him. She raised an eyebrow. 'Was that all you had to say to me, sir? If so—'

'No, there was another matter.' Jeffries was still smiling, and there was an unpleasant edge to it. 'I came to warn you.'

'To warn me?' Annabella was so surprised that she forgot to be angry. 'About what, pray?' She watched him sit back, very much at his ease, and her mystification grew.

'About Sir William Weston.' Jeffries's grey eyes slid away from hers. 'He is not…a man to be trusted.'

All Annabella's bad temper returned with a rush. 'And what can you know of the case, sir?' she asked scathingly. 'I was not aware that the gentleman was known to you!'

'I had not met him before that night at the ball,' Jeffries admitted, 'but he was known to me by reputation.' He shifted a little in his seat, still avoiding her gaze. 'And that reputation is not a sweet one, Annabella. I speak only out of concern for you.'

'Very fine of you, sir,' Annabella snapped. 'I scarce consider you to be the man to criticise another's apparently unsavoury reputation!'

Jeffries had the gall to look more sorrowful than angry. 'I did not mean to imply that he had a penchant for women,' he said apologetically, 'although there were tales—'

'I thank you, I do not wish to hear them!'

'No, indeed,' Jeffries murmured, with an unctuous smile, 'I should not sully your ears. But this is more serious, Annabella.' There was something in his tone which caught her attention. Her anger died a little. Could this really be as serious as he implied? She did not want to hear this, and yet…

'What do you mean?' she asked slowly.

'I mean treason,' Jeffries said, in the same ingratiating tones as before. There was a silence. On the mantelpiece the clock ticked loudly.

'I think that you must be quite mad, sir,' Annabella said faintly. 'Treason? Whoever could think such a thing?'

'I wish I was.' Jeffries was determined to finish. 'There was talk when I was serving under General Ross out in the United States. Weston was the captain of a frigate which was involved in the naval battle for Lake Champlain in '14. When he came under fire, they say he retreated and ran instead of coming to the aid of a fellow ship… There was talk of dereliction of duty, but no charges were ever brought, for as you know, Weston has friends in high places. I had already heard some tales of him falling in with privateers when he was in the Indies, for how do you think he made his fortune? But again, no charges were brought…I thought you should know…'

Annabella found that she was full of wild, unreasoning rage. Her thoughts were spinning in a kaleidoscope of colour and images. Chief amongst them was the memory of Sir William's face. How could this man, who had not one ounce of Will's integrity or courage, come here to make such outrageous accusations…? She stood up. 'I thank you for coming to spread your wicked, unfounded gossip, sir,' she said, her voice shaking with suppressed rage. 'You will oblige me by leaving the house immediately. I want to hear no more of this poisonous tale. If no charges were ever laid against Sir William, it ill behoves you to raise such slanderous defamation again! Upon my word, this rings with spite and malice, nothing more! Good day, sir!'

Jeffries stood up too. There was an ugly look on his face, blurring the good-natured features into a sneer of malevolence. 'Oh, it suits your purposes to disregard my words, madam, for I know you have high hopes of Weston! Well, he will never marry you, for what are you, after all? The destitute daughter of a disgraced merchant, whose own family want nothing to do with her! Weston is after bigger fish and don't give a toss for you!' He marched to the door and flung it open, sending Lady St Auby flying. Annabella felt sickened. She had temporarily forgotten her mother-in-law, with her habit of listening in to every conversation within the house. Now it could be guaranteed that the whole of Taunton society would hear the shocking tale, much embroidered, and before teatime. Lady St Auby's features were a compound of delight at the insults Jeffries had heaped upon Annabella, and unholy glee at being in possession of such a prime piece of gossip. As the front door slammed behind the Captain, Annabella caught her mother-in-law's arm in a grip that made the older woman wince.

'I had forgot your vulgar habit of eavesdropping, madam! If this story goes the rounds I shall have no hesitation in laying it at your door!' She gave Lady St Auby's arm a shake. 'Further, I shall advise Sir William to sue you for slander! He is a rich man and can well bear the expense—which you can not, can you, madam? Now, for once in your life, make a decision based on sense rather than gratification!'

Lady St Auby recoiled from the fury she saw in Annabella's eyes, but her daughter-in-law had already dropped her arm, privately shocked at the violence of her own emotions. She had known that she was falling in love with Sir William, had revelled in the romance and the pleasure of his attentions, had been looking forward to the declaration that she knew to expect when he returned. But first there had been Miss Hurst's spiteful insinuations, then Lady St Auby's sniping, and now Jeffries's vicious slander. Was everyone determined to spoil her happiness? And how intolerable for Sir William that men such as George Jeffries should go around repeating their poisonous tales simply to cause trouble, and that women such as Lady St Auby would batten on them! Jeffries should be careful, Annabella thought, that Sir William did not call him out. But then, what did one do about such unpleasant gossip? Should it be given consequence by acknowledging and responding to it?

Remembering the incident, Annabella threw her

book aside in vexation and looked out of the dusty window on to Fore Street. She would have to speak of the matter with Caroline Kilgaren, whom she had arranged to meet for a shopping trip the following day.

Caroline would reassure her that it was all a hum and not worth a moment's thought. And soon Will would be back, and it could all be forgotten. With a little sigh, Annabella picked up her book again and forced herself to concentrate on the page. At least it helped to pass the time.

A wet morning greeted her when she rose next day, with skies of an unrelieved grey to match her mood. It was still early when the knocker went and the maid brought in a bouquet of roses from the gardens at Mundell, the dew of morning still fresh upon the velvety petals. Unlike Jeffries's tribute, these roses were still tight buds with a heady scent that promised the richness that was to come, and the card that accompanied them was written in Sir William Weston's hand, telling her not to forget, and that he would see her soon. Annabella smiled a little dreamily as she put the roses into water, and hummed as she went about her tasks for the rest of the morning. The impact of Jeffries's cruel words was receding, and she knew it would not be long until Sir William returned. Lady St Auby's malice slid off her without touching, deflected by a love she was sure must be reciprocated.

The town was busy when she went out to the market. Since the incident with the pail of water, Lady St Auby had given her only the lightest of household tasks, and Annabella was quite amenable to doing the marketing. She had an eye for good produce and the stallholders liked her friendliness. Where the maids tended to return with old vegetables about to rot, either because they wished to buy cheap and keep the change, or because the vendors fleeced them, Annabella usually found a bargain. But this morning the experience was far from pleasant.

Small knots of women stood about, baskets over their arms, their eyes sharp as Annabella walked by. The whispering started behind her back: comments about Sir William Weston's sudden departure from Mundell Hall, allusions to the gossip Annabella had heard, speculation that he had dropped her. All of it was murmured in an undertone, the speakers looking hastily away when she turned to challenge them. She had seldom had so uncomfortable a trip out. So it seemed Lady St Auby had been unable to hold her tongue, or else Jeffries had been dropping his venom into other ears as well as hers... Annabella hurried back to confront her mother-in-law, only to be thwarted by finding her out on a visit to Mrs Eddington-Buck.

It was almost midday when the sharp rat-a-tat of the knocker startled her again. Annabella was so sunk in despondency that she scarcely wondered who it was. There was the sound of voices in the passage, and then the drawing-room door opened.

'My dear Mrs St Auby! How do you do, ma'am?' With a slight shock, Annabella recognised the stooping gentleman in the doorway as her father's lawyer, Mr Buckle. She had not seen him since the time, immediately after her father's death, when he had had the unfortunate task of telling her that Broseley's estate had nearly all been swallowed up by debt. He tipped the rain from his hat and handed it to the maid, gratefully accepting Annabella's offer of a cup of tea.

'An inclement day,' he observed, divesting himself of his coat and fussily laying it out to dry, 'but not a day of ill tidings, I am glad to say!' He beamed at Annabella over his half-moon spectacles. 'I have good news for you, young lady! Very good news indeed!'

Annabella got up and closed the door. There could be nothing untoward about an interview alone with her father's man of business, and she was damned if she was going to share the news of any good fortune with her mother-in-law's servants.

Mr Buckle was unpacking his case, shuffling papers self-importantly. 'We have finally wound up your father's business affairs,' he said a little pompously, 'and I am pleased to tell you that there is a residue from the estate—a very small residue given the significance of your father's fortune at one time—but, nevertheless, enough to give you a modest income.'

Annabella's gaze had wandered back to the tiny unfurling buds of the red roses, glowing softly on the corner table. She dragged her attention back. 'But that is excellent news, Mr Buckle! Is it…' she was almost afraid to ask the question '…is it enough to live on?'

Mr Buckle primmed his lips. 'A moderate sum only, but with proper investment…yes, I should think that, if you are careful, it could be enough.'

Enough to help me escape from this house at least, Annabella thought, and found her attention almost imperceptibly drifting back to Sir William Weston again. Perhaps she need not worry about continuing much longer in the St Aubys' household… But this could only make it easier for her, for she would feel that it was less of an unequal match if she had some money of her own… Scolding herself for letting her mind wander to Sir William yet again, she realised that the door had opened to allow the maid in with a steaming cup of tea, and that Lady St Auby was lurking expectantly in the corridor. The door closed quietly and Annabella realised that Mr Buckle was still speaking.

'…all the property has been sold to cover the debts,' the lawyer was saying, 'but there is one estate left. Well,' he corrected himself, 'perhaps estate is not the right word, for the property is small, but thirty acres, with a farm and a modest house…'

Modest was evidently one of Mr Buckle's favourite words, Annabella reflected. And it suited his own moderate and respectable demeanour. It had always been a surprise to her that Bertram Broseley had chosen such a demonstrably honest lawyer, but then perhaps that was precisely why he *had* chosen him.

'There is a problem, however,' Mr Buckle was saying, suddenly fixing Annabella with a severe look as though the obstacle was of her own making. 'The title to the property is in dispute.'

'In dispute?' Annabella was confused. 'Do you mean that the house is not really mine?'

Mr Buckle made a deprecating movement. 'No indeed, my dear Mrs St. Auby! The property is yours, inherited from your father who, in turn… erm…bought it from the late owner some five or six years ago. What is apparently in dispute is the manner in which—' he cleared his throat discreetly '—your father purchased the estate.'

'Extortion?' Annabella asked politely. 'Blackmail? The possibilities are endless...'

Mr Buckle looked scandalised, as he always did when someone suggested that Broseley's business methods had been less than scrupulous. 'Mrs St Auby! No, indeed, nothing of the kind! The house was offered as repayment for some gambling debt—a wager between your father and the owner, which he later regretted. But the deal was sound, if a little...' he cleared his throat '...a little unorthodox, shall we say? Your father,' Mr Buckle added, nodding sagely, 'always preferred property to money in these circumstances. It's value always increased handsomely and made him a splendid profit!'

Annabella sighed. Mr Buckle sighed too, but for a different reason.

'But now the owner's son is threatening to take the case to court, claiming that the arrangement was illegal. He evidently feels very strongly about the manner in which his father lost that particular piece of his heritage! He is not a poor man, but I believe he wants the property back for family and sentimental reasons.' Mr Buckle frowned. 'I have to say that he has been somewhat intemperate in his demand to settle the issue.'

The faintest scent of roses drifted across the room to Annabella, and at the same moment the faintest shadow touched her heart, the smallest of suspicions...

'Where is the house?' she asked, her throat suddenly dry.

Mr Buckle shuffled the papers again. 'In Berkshire, I believe...'

'…a house on the Berkshire Downs, just north of the little village of Lambourn…'

'…the late owner was a Sir Charles Weston…'

'…my father died a few years ago… But it is a long time since I have been there…'

Annabella could hear the echo of her own voice: 'For what reason have you sought me out, sir?'

The blinding tears came into her eyes, blurring the outline of the beautiful red roses. Through her numb despair, she remembered that she had suspected that Sir William Weston had had a reason for pursuing their acquaintance. He had soothed her doubts, made her fall in love with him, pretended that he cared for her too. How ironic that Miss Hurst had been correct all the time, that Sir William's charm was a means to an end, a means of regaining his patrimony one way or the other… Mr Buckle carried on speaking for some time, but Annabella had no idea what he said.

'I understand how you feel, my dear,' Caroline Kilgaren said, her piquant face creased with anxiety and distress, 'but will you not wait a little? This hasty departure surely cannot aid matters. And I am persuaded that Sir William would wish to explain the situation to you himself—'

She broke off. Long experience of Annabella's sister Alicia had taught her when she was wasting her breath, and in the past few weeks she had realised that Annabella was more like her sister than anyone had ever realised.

Annabella was very pale, sitting tense and upright in the chair opposite Caroline's. Her eyes burned with fury and her expression was set. 'I do not wish to hear any of Sir William's excuses, ma'am.'

The wind hurled another flurry of rain against the parlour window.

Caroline sighed, abandoning that particular tack. 'And I was so hoping that Alicia would send a letter soon, and invite you to stay with her! That would have solved all your problems! You did write to her, did you not?'

Annabella nodded slowly, regretting the impulse that had prompted her to set pen to paper and contact her sister. 'I did, but I do beg you, ma'am, not to tell her of this. Sir William's friends should not be embarrassed by a division of loyalties! I have no wish to cause trouble for my sister, nor indeed for you, ma'am.' Her hard tone softened a little. 'You have shown me nothing but kindness, and I do thank you for it! But my mind is made up. I travel on the morrow.'

Caroline gave a graceful shrug. 'I can see that there is no dissuading you! The house is fit for habitation, I take it?'

'Oh, yes!' Annabella lied brightly, trying to dismiss the memory of Mr Buckle's horrified face as he had begged her to allow him at least to have the house cleaned for her. He had been deeply disapproving when she had expressed her intention of travelling to Larkswood immediately. Realising that something had upset Annabella, but not understanding the cause, he had entreated her to be reasonable and had evidently thought her a half-wit to go to a place that had not been inhabited for three years. His protestations had fallen on deaf ears, however. In the space of a few minutes, Annabella had become so determined to claim her inheritance from under Will Weston's nose that she would stop at nothing.

Will Weston... First, he had made it impossible for her to continue living under the St Aubys' roof by showing her another, far more desirable existence. She had fallen into the very trap she had wanted to avoid, the trap of thinking that the life led by Will and his friends was for her, that she could become a part of it. Worse, she had allowed herself to fall in love with romance and with him equally, and now the romance had gone but her painful love for him remained, twisted out of all recognition. She could not bear it, but it seemed she must...

'And you have a companion to accompany you?' Caroline pursued, recalling Annabella to the present, to the musty room and the claustrophobic life she was trapped in. 'It would not be the done thing at all for you to live at Larkswood alone!'

'Have no fear on that score!' Annabella had already chosen the only maid in the St Auby household who was not slovenly and sullen. Whether she would pass muster as a companion was another matter entirely, but she would have to do, for there was no one else.

Caroline still looked dubious. She got to her feet and picked her reticule up from the table. 'Then I can only wish you good luck. But, Annabella—' she gave her an impulsive hug '—if you ever need anything at all, please let me know! I do not like matters to end this way!'

Annabella blinked back the tears. 'It is far better—'

'Will was only ever interested in you for yourself,' Caroline said abruptly, to cover her own emotion. She could not bear the heartbreaking, stricken face of the girl before her. It was so clear that Annabella St Auby was hopelessly in love with Will Weston, and that love made her feelings of anger and betrayal all the more intense. And Caroline was a loyal friend who could not bear to see two people she cared for make such a mull of so promising a situation. 'Will would never have married you just for Larkswood,' she said, trying again when Annabella's stony silence was her only reply.

'Oh, I am persuaded of that,' Annabella said, with bitter anguish. 'He would never wish to tie himself to an unloved wife for the sake of so small a property, not when he is so rich!'

'Then why cannot you believe that he cares for you?' Caroline asked, perplexed.

Annabella shrugged angrily. 'Because he did not tell me about Larkswood in the first place! Because he did not tell me the truth, did not trust me! Perhaps he thought to make me fall in love with him so that he could persuade me to sell Larkswood back to him at less than its value, hoping that I, poor fool, would be so besotted that I only wished to please him! Perhaps he was just trifling with me as a small revenge against the family which cheated his father out of a pretty property! I do not know, since he did not see fit to tell me the truth!' Her voice fell again. 'He did not trust me,' she repeated.

Caroline shook her head, aware that it was pointless to persist. Annabella's sense of betrayal was too raw, too new, for her to listen to reasoned argument. 'I shall not say goodbye, for I am sure we shall meet again,' Caroline said slowly, devoutly hoping it would be true. 'Farewell then, Annabella, and good luck!' And she went out, tripping over Lady St Auby in the doorway and giving her so searing a glare that the older woman positively shrank away.

The carriage took Caroline swiftly back to Mundell Hall, her shopping trip forgotten. She was greeted with the news that the men were out shooting, and she had no taste for the company of Miss Mundell and Miss Hurst. She hurried to the study, paused briefly as she remembered Annabella begging her not to tell anyone about the dispute with Will, then called for pen and ink and settled down at the escritoire to write a hasty note to her oldest and dearest friend, Alicia Mullineaux.

Annabella's sense of misery and disillusion had grown with the passage of time. Too inexperienced and too in love to be able to achieve even a degree of equanimity over Will Weston's behaviour, she had dwelt on his betrayal until she was quite sure that she hated him. It angered her that her mind seemed incapable of blocking him out, surprising her at the most inappropriate moments with the image of him, or a memory of some time they had spent together. When she dreamed one night that she was in the rose arbour at Mundell with him again, she awoke confused and tearful, feeling betrayed all over again.

To add to her woes, her impulsive decision to move in to Larkswood had proved to be nothing short of disaster. On the day after Mr Buckle's visit, she and the maid, Susan, had left Taunton at first light for the long and arduous journey into Oxfordshire. The coach had lurched and jolted its way along the roads until they both ached in every joint. Annabella had just enough money to pay their fare on the stage as far as Faringdon, and from there a kindly carter had taken them across the wide, flat valley towards Lambourn. The carter had dropped them by the gate of Larkswood just as the sun was sinking behind the hills, those sweeping chalk hills which Sir William Weston had described so memorably that time on the terrace at Mundell. They had been tired and dusty from the journey, the last part of it jarring over rough tracks behind the labouring horse. As the carter set off again up the steep track, a silence descended that seemed as old as time. The evening sky was bright blue, and the setting sun gilded the rosy sarsen stone of the house with a warm glow. A tabby cat was sitting in the deserted courtyard, its golden eyes watching them unblinkingly. And then a rat had dashed across the yard and into an outhouse, the cat had raced after it, and Susan had screamed and flung herself into the arms of a young man who had just come through the field gate to see what was going on.

It had turned out to be a useful introduction. The young man, Owen Linton, was the tenant farmer at Lark Farm, and Susan was a very pretty girl, and soon the besotted young man was at their beck and call for such matters as mending doors and hammering down loose floorboards. But despite that, they were fighting a losing battle.

Annabella sighed to herself, thinking of all that needed to be done. Larkswood was a neat and charming house, standing foursquare a little back from the track which linked Lambourn with the road east to Oxford. It had four bedrooms, a dining-room and a well-appointed drawing-room which looked out over the gardens and the orchard. Between the house and the farm was the cobbled courtyard, and at one end was all that remained of 'The Old House', as Owen Linton put it, a small medieval manor which had once stood on the spot and was now reduced to a couple of rooms and a pile of stones. Not, Annabella thought, that the old house was much less habitable than the new. Three years of neglect had left their mark in damp walls, rotten carpets and curtains, and mildewed furniture. There were mice in the kitchen, despite the presence of the tabby cat, and the only water had to be drawn each day from a well in the courtyard. Paint was peeling, tiles loose, floorboards squeaky. They were five miles from the nearest village, and had no transport…

Annabella sighed again. The spar that turned the well chain was rotten and the chain itself old and rusty from disuse. She could hear the bucket splashing about below but the handle stubbornly refused to turn. She could feel herself perspiring in the morning sun, feel her headscarf slipping back as her face grew redder with her exertions. It was just another of the small irritations which now made up their everyday life.

This is all Sir William Weston's fault, Annabella thought, turning her anger once more into the iron resolve that she would keep Larkswood as her own and never let it go. She would show him that she was not to be charmed and brushed aside when the fancy took him. Let him challenge her right to the house in a court of law if he wished! She would never yield.

The sound of hoofbeats on the track distracted her and she straightened up. Visitors were rare here, and except for the odd cart or hay wain, few vehicles used the track over the hills. Annabella pushed her head-scarf back from her honey-coloured hair and the cob-webs on it tickled her neck. It had proved unexpect-edly useful to have nothing but old clothes, for she had no need for finery here. It could not have been more different from the splendour of Mundell.

The horseman turned the bend in the track, cantered into the yard and slid out of the saddle, hitching his reins over the fence in a gesture which suggested that he had done the same thing a hundred times before.

'You!'

For a moment, Annabella stared in total disbelief. The ride across the valley had ruffled Will Weston's tawny hair, but it was the only sign of dishevellment to compare with her own disarray. Those compelling blue eyes were as vital as ever as they rested upon her and he moved towards her across the cobbled yard with the same contained grace that had always drawn her gaze. Annabella found that the passage of four weeks had done nothing to lessen the shock and pain of seeing him again. She could not be indifferent to him. She told herself that she hated him.

'Good afternoon, Annabella.' It was almost a phys-ical pain to hear her name spoken again in that well-remembered voice, the resonant tone, cool, consid-ered, authoritative… She had admired him so much, she realised suddenly, and felt all the more disillu-sioned as a result.

And now not even the courtesy of her formal name, now that he no longer had any reason to hoodwink her! For some reason, Annabella had never imagined that Will would seek her out again, let alone here at

Larkswood, which was the very cause of the dispute between them. But now that he was here, she wondered why on earth she had not thought to anticipate such a meeting, for she was indeed woefully unprepared to deal with him. Acutely aware of the cobwebs clinging to her skin, her flushed face and her stained and torn gown, she glared at him.

'You are not welcome here, Sir William! Leave my property immediately!'

Will showed no sign that he had even heard her, strolling imperturbably across the cobbles towards her. Annabella's fury locked in a tight pain in her chest.

'I want to talk to you.' Now he was standing in front of her.

'Well, I have no wish to talk to you!' Annabella raised her chin. 'Take yourself off, sir!'

Will seemed unmoved. He smiled slightly, as though she were a spoilt child. It made her blood boil even more. 'Must you be so melodramatic?' he enquired. 'I had hoped that we could go into the house and talk sensibly about this.'

Talk sensibly! It was the last thing Annabella wished to do! 'You are not listening to me, sir,' she responded furiously, her green eyes flashing. 'I do not want to speak to you. Now, go away!'

No gentleman that she had ever met, and certainly no one whose manners were as good as Sir William's, was likely to disregard her wishes in this and force his company on her. She had already turned away when Will picked her up and carried her, kicking and shrieking, into the house. Susan, who had come into the yard to find out what had happened to the pail of water, stood in open-mouthed amazement as Sir William strode past her.

'The devil you don't!' he said equably, as he put Annabella down on her feet in the drawing-room and prudently stood back out of range when she might have tried to slap him. He closed the door, then looked about him with what Annabella could only interpret as horrified surprise.

'Good God,' he said, quietly.

She could imagine what prompted his thoughts and it filled her with even greater anger. The once-delicate plaster of the ceiling was crumbling into dust and mould was growing on the walls. The floorboards had given way in one corner and the curtains were rotting where they hung. There was barely any furniture and a fusty smell filled the air.

'You cannot possibly stay here,' Sir William said, still in the same quiet tone.

'Yes, I understood that was what you came to tell me,' Annabella said nastily, suddenly afraid that she might cry. The temerity of the man in pretending to care about her was too much. 'So, do you intend to try to buy me off, sir? Or perhaps you have no wish to offer money for such a ruin of a house, and have simply come to tell me that you will take the case to court? You are too late, sir—my lawyer has told me as much already!'

Sir William sighed, driving his hands into his trouser pockets. 'I meant only that the place is not fit for you to live in and you will make yourself ill in the trying. Good God, the walls are running with damp— you will succumb to a chill within a week!'

'Your concern touches me, sir,' Annabella said,

filled with a perverse enjoyment that she appeared to be able to be as horrible to him as she wanted without him retaliating. 'You need pretend no longer, however! Had you had any genuine consideration for me, you would have told me of your interest in Larkswood from the start, instead of cozening me with soft and sweet words!'

'So now we come to it,' Will said softly. He opened the door again, letting in the fresh air and the sunlight. 'It is not as you imagine, Annabella. How could I have told you? I was caught— I knew that if I told you about Larkswood as soon as we met you would assume that the house was my only interest in you, or that I was trying to charm you into letting me have it back for a minimal price…I knew that you would not believe I was interested in you for yourself alone!'

'Whereas now, of course,' Annabella said sarcastically, 'I know just how true your sentiments really were!'

She saw a muscle tighten in Will's jaw and felt even happier to see that she could pierce his indifference and make him angry when he was trying so hard to be rational. She felt almost drunk with the pleasure of it.

'Have you now come to tell me that you have changed your mind and will not be claiming Larkswood back?' she demanded, and saw her answer at once as he turned away.

'If you would let me explain,' he said, with constraint. 'My father regretted the wager he made with Bertram Broseley by which he signed away this house. He tried to buy it back several times, I believe, but your father would have nothing to do with it. I am willing to try to prove that the wager was illegal because I need the house—'

'*You* need the house!' The hurt burst in Annabella in a huge, angry tide. 'No, sir, *I* need this house— really need it! You, who have so much, think of taking from me the only thing that really is mine! What am I to become—a pensioner of my sister and her husband, or worse, the continued object of Lady St Auby's charity?'

'I had once hoped,' Sir William said very quietly, 'that you would become my wife.'

'Oh!' The cruelty of his words touched Annabella to the quick. She felt all the breath go out of her as though she had been punched. She turned on him in blazing fury. 'There is no need to gild the lily, sir! All pretence between us is at an end! You never cared for me, and I never had any feelings for you!'

'Is that so?' Sir William had moved with surprising agility to catch hold of her and pull her into his arms, despite her struggles. Annabella could not free a hand to slap him, so she kicked his shins viciously.

'You little vixen!' Sir William still sounded amused and it infuriated her. If he had tried to kiss her, she would have bitten him. He did not do so, however, merely holding her so tightly that she could barely move. He spoke into the golden curls.

'Now, my love, I remember thinking once that honesty was one of your greatest virtues. Be honest now, and tell me that you are indifferent to me.'

'I see that you are amusing yourself at my expense as well—' Annabella said hotly, only to be interrupted.

'Amusement be damned!' There was angry vehemence in Weston's tone now behind the quietly spoken words. 'You are determined to think the worst of me, are you not, madam? What, then, if I live up to your opinion of me?'

It was unfair, Annabella thought desperately. Held close in his arms, all she could concentrate on was the treacherous persuasion of his body against hers, the feeling of attunement that was both familiar and yet intoxicatingly exciting at the same time. She looked up into his eyes, her own darkening with despair.

'You need not make your feelings any more plain, sir—'

'Oh, indeed!'

She could not fight him, nor, she found, did she have any inclination to do so. This time there were no concessions to her inexperience. He kissed her with a ruthless demand and she returned the kiss in full measure. They were so swept away that neither of them heard the carriage that rumbled up the track, or the voices in the yard and the footsteps in the hall. They did not break apart until an amused masculine voice behind them said,

'Well, William, I have found you in some extraordinary situations before now, but none so remarkable as this!'

It was a moment of some delicacy. James Mullineaux was lounging in the doorway, a whimsical smile on his face as he regarded the couple. Annabella, her heart sinking, saw that Alicia was at his shoulder, immaculately beautiful as ever in a dress of bright yellow that should have clashed horribly with her auburn hair, but of course did not. And worse, behind them, but still with an undoubtedly clear view of proceedings, stood her grandmother, the Dowager Countess of Stansfield, whom she had never previously met but whose identity was obvious. Lady Stansfield, in vivid emerald green that matched her bright green eyes, was watching Annabella with an incalculable expression.

'We had thought to invite you back to Oxenham with us, Annabella,' Alicia said to her sister, hurrying into the sudden silence, 'but perhaps, if you have settled your differences with Sir William…' Her thoughtful gaze travelled from Annabella's bright red face to Will's studiously blank one.

'I have not!' Annabella snapped. 'Sir William has made some arrogant and groundless assumptions that his suit would be welcome! Well, it is not, whatever appearances may say to the contrary!'

'It was a good try though, Will!' James Mullineaux observed with a broad smile, and Annabella glared at him, quite forgetting that she had always been in awe of her sister's devastatingly handsome husband.

'Well, then…' Alicia said, a little inadequately, as the silence again threatened to become embarrassingly long, 'would you care to stay at Oxenham for a little, Annabella, just until Larkswood is made more comfortable for you?'

Annabella caught Alicia's eye and was shaken out of her self-absorption. Preoccupied with her feelings for Will Weston, appalled that she had responded so fervently to his kiss, humiliated to have been discovered thus, she had not really thought how difficult such a meeting could be for Alicia. Now she came forward with a sudden, shy smile to kiss her.

'Oh Alicia, I am so sorry! I am really so very glad to see you again, and nothing would please me more than to spend some time with you, but only—' her gaze fell on Will and hardened again '—as long as it is understood that I do not give up my claim to Larkswood! I do not care if our father robbed, cheated or murdered his way into this property—I intend to keep it!'

Alicia hugged her, a little apprehensively. Seeing her own temper reflected in someone else was a rather nerve-racking experience. 'Of course! We can talk about it all later. For now, let us get you out of this place before the whole house comes tumbling about our ears—'

'Annabella!' The autocratic tones stopped them all in their tracks. Lady Stansfield had drawn herself up to her full—tiny— height. 'Come here, my gel.'

Annabella's heart was suddenly in her mouth. She knew of her grandmother only by repute, but had heard that the old lady was sharper than a needle and never minced her words. She dropped her a demure curtsy. Lady Stansfield's jewel-bright eyes scanned her face thoughtfully.

'Hmph! Don't seek to cozen me with your milk-and-water airs, miss! It's a bit late for that! I saw you just now, aye, and heard you too!' She took Annabella's chin in her hand. 'You have a great look of your mother about you, child,' she said surprisingly, 'and a Stansfield through and through, to judge by that temper!' She gave a dry cackle of laughter. 'You'll have to try harder, Sir William, to win this one's heart!'

'So it would seem, ma'am,' Sir William said expressionlessly.

The bright green eyes moved on to search his face for a moment, then Lady Stansfield laughed again. 'You'll do,' she said, with a malicious smile, 'and I shall enjoy the entertainment of watching you try to prevail!'

'Grandmama,' Alicia said severely, 'we are not all here simply as a diversion for you! James, I shall take Annabella off to pack now, if you wish for a word with Will! Annabella, I think that little maid had better come with you…' And she shepherded her sister and her grandmother out of the room.

As she packed her meagre belongings for the second time in a month and instructed Susan to do the same, comforting the lovelorn girl with the thought that they would soon be back, Annabella was prey to very mixed emotions. She had no intention of letting go of Larkswood now that she had found it, nor of falling victim to Will's convincing lies for a second time. And whilst she was glad to have the chance to get to know both her sister and her grandmother better, she was aware that it could distract her from the problem of the house, and that could be dangerous. Besides, whilst neither Alicia nor James had expressed any view on her relationship with Sir William, they were both great friends of his and could therefore not be impartial… Annabella sighed. Looking out of the window, she saw James and Will emerge from the house and part with a quick word and a handshake. No, it would not do to let her defences down.

# Chapter Six

Alicia Mullineaux was reading, but her mind was not on the written word, and when the door opened softly to admit her husband into the bedroom, she cast the book aside on the bedspread with little regret.

'James, I need to talk to you!'

James Mullineaux raised one black eyebrow and sat down beside her, taking her hand in his. His wife looked distractingly lovely in a diaphanous lace night-dress, but he doubted whether she would appreciate being told so at the moment, for her face was crumpled with worry in a way that made her look absurdly childlike.

'What is it, my love?' he asked gently. 'Surely you cannot be worrying about Annabella again? She is with your Grandmother in her room, chatting nineteen to the dozen, so that is one of your fears allayed, at least!'

The frown on Alicia's brow lightened for a moment. 'Yes, I must own that I had the gravest doubts that they would like each other, and yet they have taken to each other in such a way!'

'Your grandmother,' James said, toying with a curl that was lying seductively in the hollow of Alicia's collarbone, 'recognised instantly what the rest of us have only just started to realise, which is that Annabella, like you, is a Stansfield after her own heart! So, if that is not your concern, what—?'

Alicia's frown returned. 'It is just that I cannot believe Annabella is happy,' she said in a rush. 'She loves Will, but she refuses to see him, and will not listen to a word in his favour. Oh, I can see that she believes herself deceived and, indeed, it was unfortunate that he did not see fit to tell her about Larkswood before, but...'

James's lips had replaced his fingers in stroking the delicate skin of her neck, and Alicia stopped, trying to remember what she was trying to say. 'James...'

'Yes, my love?'

'About Annabella and Will...'

James raised his head slightly. 'Alicia, I love Will Weston like a brother, and I want your sister to be happy, but we must leave them to sort out their differences. And just now I could wish them in Hades...' His fingers had found the ribbons which tied the nightdress and were giving them short shrift. He slipped his hand inside the lacy bodice. Alicia gasped.

'Do you still wish to talk?' James asked teasingly, his lips brushing hers, 'or may it wait until later?'

Annabella St Auby and Will Weston were also awake, but for different reasons. Annabella had parted company with her grandmother a few minutes before, having spent an entertaining evening being regaled with stories of Lady Stansfield's experiences in *ton* society. She was feeling too restless to sleep, pacing about in the pretty yellow bedroom which Alicia had had furnished especially for her, picking up a book, casting it aside, turning to her needlework and sighing before she even attempted a stitch.

Once she was on her own these days, she found that her thoughts reverted to Will Weston in the tiresome but inescapable way that they had done for the past three weeks. When she had first come to Oxenham, he had called to see her several times and she had refused to speak to him, but in the past week he had neither written nor called. She supposed that she deserved this but, annoyingly, his absence had done nothing to keep him from her mind. Nor did Alicia or James ever mention Will to her, an omission which Annabella was beginning to consider as rather sinister.

She wondered whether they were all conspiring against her behind her back, then scolded herself for her obsession. Whatever the case, in a strange way his absence only seemed to reinforce his presence in her mind and prevent any possibility of her forgetting him.

Other young men had called at Oxenham and had been introduced to her by Alicia, who had seemed overly anxious that she should find at least one admirer in local society. Contrarily, Annabella found herself taking random dislikes to these unsuspecting fellows: they were too young, too old, too fat, too thin, too miserable, too *cheerful*… Even Richard Linley, a neighbour of her own from Lambourn, who had every grace and circumstance to recommend him, was found to be at fault simply for not being Will Weston. And through all her bad temper, Alicia would smile tol-

erantly and James would look amiable and Lady
Stansfield would tease her for being a fickle madam
until she wanted to scream with frustration that they
did not understand. But, of course, they did, which
was part of the trouble.

Had Annabella but known, she was in the thoughts
of the very man whom she found so difficult to dismiss. Will Weston was sitting alone in his study with
nothing but a glass of malt whisky and his thoughts
for company. He had been turning the wooden globe
on his desk, a faint, reminiscent smile on his lips as
he remembered his travels to Zanzibar and Antigua
and the Cocos Islands… He had never wished to settle
on land for any length of time until now, and until
now he had never met a woman he had wished to
marry… He took a sip of the whisky, enjoying its
aromatic flavour. From the first he had been drawn to
Annabella St Auby, finding both her person and her
individuality deeply attractive. It was an irony that the
same characteristics which had endeared her to him
in the first place were now the stumbling-block in
their relationship. Had she been more tractable he
would have risked another attempt at an explanation,
but he had no confidence that they would not end up
quarrelling. So perhaps he would simply have to try
to woo her once more… He smiled again. It did not
sound like a hardship.

'I am not certain whether the colours of that flower
border work well together,' Alicia sighed, eyeing the
drift of purple and blue with disfavour. 'What do you
think, Annabella? I must discuss the matter with

Fisher, I suppose, and plan a new planting scheme for next year!'

Annabella jumped guiltily. Her mind had not been on Oxenham's delightful gardens, nor indeed on much that her sister had said for the past five minutes, for she had been thinking of Will Weston yet again.

During the lazy late summer days, she had gradually grown to know Alicia better and had spent much time with her grandmother, who showed all signs of doting on her newly found grandchild. Little Thomas Mullineaux, her nephew, was also an adorable distraction. Meanwhile, James had sent a team of men to lick Larkswood into shape and soon it would be fit for habitation again. Larkswood, her inheritance. She blotted from her mind the memory of Will's strained face as he had tried to tell her that he needed the house. The mingled misery and anger rose in her once more, and she was glad when Alicia spoke again and distracted her.

'Caroline writes that Ermina Hurst has gone back to London,' Alicia said, reading from a letter that had just been delivered. 'Apparently Viscount Mundell is under siege from another young lady now, a Miss Hart, who has taken Taunton by storm! Poor Hugo! I wonder how he bears it! And Caro has also met an erstwhile admirer of yours, Annabella, one George Jeffries… Oh!' She pulled a face. 'I do not think she likes him a great deal!'

'Neither did I!' Annabella said, with feeling. She pushed the memory of Jeffries's insolent face from her mind, but the mention of his name raised other recollections, which she had forgotten until then. She had been intending to ask Caroline about the dreadful slander of Sir William Weston's name, she remembered, and whether such rumours had ever surfaced before. Their quarrel had put such thoughts from her mind, but even now, believing him false in his affection for her, she could not quite also believe that his integrity was also a lie. He had seemed too fine a man, too honourable... Stop it, Annabella, she chided herself furiously, as a warmth invaded her heart, threatening to banish her anger and undo her completely.

'Alicia...' she began, intending to ask her sister about the rumours, but at that moment, Thomas chose to crawl towards the flowerbed and put a handful of soil in his mouth. In the ensuing excitement, the nursemaid swooped on her charge with cries of alarm, and Alicia took him on her knee, wiping the dirt from his face.

'I have an errand to run in Challen village,' Alicia said, when things had calmed down, 'but I wondered whether you would mind going for me, dearest Annabella? I promised Mrs Coverdale, the vicar's wife, that I would pass her some of Thomas's old baby clothes...' Her gaze fell on her baby son again, gurgling blissfully on her lap. 'But James is due back soon, and I wanted to spend some time with him and Thomas alone. Would you mind, Annabella?'

In fact, Annabella was quite glad of the trip out. The even tenor of life at Oxenham bored her at times, but only, she told herself severely, because she was so unhappy in herself. And that brought her to the only point of Alicia's request that was inconvenient, for Will Weston's home was at Challen Court, and she knew that he was staying there despite his absence from Oxenham. She told herself that she did not want to see him—and knew that she was lying.

Alicia's landaulet was very pretty and the drive to the village was accomplished with ease, Annabella having no difficulties in controlling the matched pair that drew the carriage. She had met Mrs Coverdale the previous week, and spent a pleasant half-hour chatting and admiring her newborn baby. She drove back down Challen high street, suddenly noticing that there appeared to be babies and small children everywhere, squalling in their mothers' arms on cottage doorsteps, or playing by the side of the road. A strange feeling, part-longing, part-envy, stirred in Annabella and she blinked in surprise. That was a train of thought that was even less profitable than her hopeless dreams of Sir William Weston...

She did not see him, as she had half-hoped she would. But as she drew out of the village, past the first set of cross-roads which led to Challen Court, she saw that the stage was before her, setting down its passengers at the junction with the Oxford Road. She reined in and waited until it set off again in a cloud of dust, and was about to drive on when her eye was caught by the two passengers who had descended on to the grass verge.

The first was a young woman little more than Annabella's age, and she was heavily pregnant. A large, battered portmanteaux, surely too heavy for her to carry, lay in front of her, and a child of about three clutched her hand. More babies and children, Annabella thought exasperatedly. She pulled out to pass them. At the same moment the girl called out, 'Your pardon, ma'am! Can you direct me to Challen Court, if you please?'

Annabella paused, looking more closely. The young woman was very pale and there was a sheen of sweat on her face, no surprising thing in the heat of the afternoon, but suggestive of illness rather than mere warmth. Her thin dress was sticking to her, and a sudden grimace of pain crossed her features, causing her to grip the child's hand so tightly that she started to cry. Annabella got down carefully. She took the girl's arm as she swayed.

'Challen Court is up this road, but it is almost a mile, you know, and you cannot possible walk it! It is obvious that you are very unwell!'

'It will pass in a minute,' the girl whispered. 'The jolting of the coach…' She swayed again, catching the wheel of the landaulet to steady herself and closing her eyes for a moment.

Enlightenment burst on Annabella in a flash. 'But we must get you to the house at once! Are you able to endure the short distance in the carriage? I am afraid that it is the only way…'

The girl gave her a faint, reassuring smile. 'You are very kind, ma'am. It will be some little time yet…' Her voice trailed away and she closed her eyes again briefly. She had a sweet voice, Annabella thought, momentarily distracted, with an unusual accent… A servant girl from Cornwall, perhaps, for her tones were similar to Susan's rich West Country voice. But what did she want at Challen Court?

She helped the young woman up into the seat with some difficulty, and bent to pick up the little girl and pass her up to her mother. The child wriggled on to the seat and turned to survey Annabella with the serious contemplation of children. She was a pretty little thing, fair and sturdy, and she had the most vivid blue eyes that Annabella had seen. Unmistakable eyes... Weston eyes... At the same moment, the young woman said softly, 'I know that Will can help me...he wrote to tell me to come...' and she smiled very slightly.

A cold wave of shock broke over Annabella, and she stood back. The woman, who was slumped in her seat, had not noticed anything odd, but the little girl continued to watch her with Will Weston's bright blue gaze. Annabella gave herself a shake. Later, she told herself sharply, later you can think about this. For now, you must get her to the house. But she felt cold, and her body seemed slow to act, and her fingers felt clumsy on the reins.

A mere few minutes brought them in sight of Challen Court, which was fortunate, for the young woman had turned an even pastier shade of white and had her eyes closed as spasms of pain wrenched her body. Annabella drove straight into the stable yard. Several grooms, who had been working in the tackroom, came running at the sound of the wheels, and one, brighter than the rest, sped off into the house calling for help.

A number of servants now came hurrying forward, and Annabella's eyes fell with some relief on the unmistakable figure of a housekeeper. She jumped down from the carriage and went up to the woman, grasping her arm. There was no time for long explanations.

'Please help us, ma'am! I found the young lady at the crossroads, asking for Challen Court. I think she is about to be confined!'

The housekeeper swept one comprehensive look over the huddled figure in the carriage. 'Yes, you are right, ma'am! John, Harry, lift the young lady down. Beatrice, run inside and heat some water. Has someone gone for the master? What—'

In the confusion, no one had noticed the arrival of Sir William Weston until the girl, now standing in the yard supported by two burly footmen, looked up and a smile broke across her strained features.

'Will, oh, Will, I am so very glad to see you...' She started to cry. Annabella felt very much like following suit. This tender reunion, following on so swiftly from the shock of meeting the woman and the child, was a little too much for her. She watched as Will swept the girl up into his arms with negligent ease. Her arms went about his neck and she turned her face against his chest. The housekeeper was holding the little girl by the hand as they followed them indoors. A pang of pure jealousy wrenched at Annabella so fiercely that she almost cried aloud.

'Don't try to talk now, Amy. You are quite safe.' Annabella watched as the girl's head drooped against Will's shoulder and her eyes closed. She turned away, her throat choked with tears, determined to drive straight out of the yard without another word.

Sir William paused momentarily. 'Jem, stable Mrs St Auby's horses; Barringer, show her into the green drawing-room, if you please. I shall be with you directly, ma'am.'

Their eyes met. Annabella opened her mouth to say that she was leaving, but the words died unspoken. There was something so compulsive in Sir William's gaze, compounded of a bright anger and even stronger demand, that made her hold her tongue. In silence, she accompanied the little party into the house and watched as Will carried the girl upstairs, before the butler's gentle voice broke into her thoughts and she followed him meekly into the drawing-room.

'Well, Annabella, what new calumnies have you imagined against me by now?'

Annabella had not heard Will enter the room, for she had been rapt in her attention to the portrait on the wall, which was of a man, presumably the luckless Sir Charles Weston, who had the same distinctive blue eyes as all his family. The contemplation of his picture had helped her to pass the long minutes since she had been left alone and also helped her not to think too much. Now she jumped and spun round.

'The lady… Will she be all right?' she asked spontaneously, then, realising that he had already spoken, said, 'I beg your pardon, what did you say, sir?'

A shadow of what might have been surprise touched Will Weston's face.

'Amy—my sister-in-law—will be fine. Mrs Jenner is with her now, and has some experience in such matters. She assures me that we do not need to send for the midwife. It will be a little time before I am presented with a new niece or nephew.'

Annabella sat down rather suddenly. 'Your sister-in-law!'

A faint smile touched Will's mouth, but left his eyes cold. With a small shock, Annabella realised that he was angry. It was a cool, contained anger rather than a wild fury, but nevertheless it was frightening. Even when she had provoked him so at Larkswood that day, he had only appeared amused with her. But now there was no amusement in him, and no kindness.

'You are so easy to read, my dear Annabella! In that split second in the yard, I had ascertained that you had seen Charlotte's blue eyes, noted—obviously—Amy's condition, thought about her asking for me…and made some rather large assumptions!'

Annabella blushed bright red. 'I did not… I was not aware…' Her voice faded away as she realised that she had no suitable excuses to hand.

Will's sardonic smile deepened. Annabella got to her feet again rather quickly. 'I really should be going now—'

'Oh, no,' Will said softly. 'Not this time!' He was standing with his back to the door, leaning his broad shoulders against the panelling and giving every indication that he was unlikely to let her out of the room. 'This time,' he added pleasantly, 'you will do me the courtesy of giving me a proper hearing.'

'But…' Annabella cast about desperately for a reason to escape '…I am expected back directly! I am already late, for we have guests tonight and I was supposed to be collecting some vegetables from the farm on my way back…' Again her voice trailed off under his pitiless gaze.

'I have already sent a messenger to Oxenham to assure your sister that all is well,' Will said calmly. 'No doubt they will make shift to provide for their guests in some other way!'

Annabella sat down for a second time. 'Oh, but—'

'I wish to explain about Larkswood.' Will drove his hands hard into his pockets. He moved across to the fireplace beneath the picture of Sir Charles, and rested one booted foot on the fender. 'But first I should tell you about Amy—' those very blue eyes met hers expressionlessly '—in order that there is no misunderstanding.'

Annabella flushed bright scarlet again. So he thought her a gossip who might damage his sister-in-law's reputation, did he? The idea that he had so low an opinion of her was a hurtful one, but then she had done little to make him think well of her. Suddenly she deeply regretted the pride and disdain that had made her refuse to listen to him when he had tried to explain about Larkswood. Her arrogance did not reflect well on her. And now he had read her reaction to Amy Weston so accurately, and was angry, not indulgent.

'You may remember that I told you at Mundell that my brother had married an American girl and lived abroad until his death last year,' Will was saying. 'He took a fever—it was a terrible tragedy. Since the death of Amy's father, Peter had run the family plantations, but when he fell ill and died she could not continue there alone. She is not strong and, of course, there was the new baby on the way. She wrote to tell me that she would sell the estate and come to make her home in England.' He shook his head. 'I counselled her to wait until after the baby was born, fearing that such a journey would be too much for her, but I never heard from her in reply.' He sighed. 'Her letter telling me of her departure for England must have been lost in the post and is probably at the bottom of the sea by now. I had no notion of her coming here until today. Now, God willing, the baby will be delivered without difficulty…'

There was a knock at the door and Barringer entered with a tea tray. 'Mrs Jenner has asked me to tell you that all goes well, sir, but that it will still be some little time,' he said, primly. 'Shall I put the tray here, sir?'

Will did not look as though he cared in the slightest about the location of the tea tray, and it was Annabella who gestured to the butler to put it down in front of her.

'Only Barringer could serve tea at a time like this,' Will murmured in exasperation.

Annabella poured a cup. 'It is the done thing for expectant fathers, unless they are on the hunting field,' she said, commiseratingly. 'No doubt your butler felt the situation also applied to expectant uncles!'

That won her the faintest flicker of a smile. Will took the proffered cup and sat down.

'You must be desperately concerned, sir,' Annabella continued. 'Surely anything else you may wish to say to me can wait until later? Larkswood is of no importance in comparison...'

Once again, that unfathomable blue gaze rested on her and Annabella, feeling discomfited, made a business of stirring her own cup of tea.

'It surprises me to hear you say so, ma'am,' Will murmured. 'But I prefer all matters to be out in the open.'

Annabella's heart sank. 'As you wish, sir.'

Will stirred his tea vaguely, still looking at her in that reflective way, then he appeared to pull himself together for, when he spoke, his voice had regained its usual incisive tone.

'You should know that I have decided to give up all claim to Larkswood.'

Annabella almost dropped her cup. He did not appear to notice. 'My brother and I grew up there and it holds many of the happiest childhood memories for me. We moved here when my father inherited Challen, but I always preferred Larkswood, modest a property as it was.' His gaze rested for a moment on the benign, fair figure in the portrait. 'I was at sea when my father wagered the house. He wrote to me that he had been unable to find a tenant because of the isolated location, and that it had been easier simply to sell the place. I was surprised, but not suspicious.' He put his empty cup down. 'To his death, I never imagined that there was anything sinister in the sale. And then Peter told me what had happened.' His gaze came back to Annabella and she almost flinched.

'It seems my father had wagered foolishly in a game of Hazard against Bertram Broseley. The house was his stake. My father regretted it and later tried to buy the property back several times, but Broseley always refused…' He made a slight gesture. 'Father was too ashamed of what had happened to tell anyone, but when he was dying he let slip to Peter what had happened. His lawyer confirmed it.'

'And you wanted Larkswood back,' Annabella whispered.

'It seemed only fair,' Will said savagely. 'I was willing to pay the gambling debt, plus a generous rate of interest. I had been lucky with the prizes I had captured at sea, very lucky. And then a distant cousin of mine died and left me a tidy fortune. This estate, which could turn a good profit once it was properly managed, was no drain on my resources. My father had been ill for some time, and his revenues had been declining, but I had little difficulty in improving matters. So you see…' he shrugged '…if it had not been for my father's misjudgement or pride, the house need never have been lost.'

It was an untimely moment for Annabella to remember George Jeffries's words, but for some reason they rose in her mind and would not be dismissed. 'I had already heard some tales of him falling in with privateers when he was in the Indies…how do you think he made his fortune?'

So there had been nothing in that particular nasty piece of gossip, she thought thankfully. Sir William's money had come by the conventional routes of success as a navy captain and inheritance. And the other charge of cowardice—

'What is it, Annabella?' Will asked sharply. 'You look as though you have seen a ghost!'

Annabella shook herself. 'It is nothing… You do not surprise me, sir, with your account of my father's dealings. He was ever one to drive a hard, if not an illegal, bargain, and he always preferred property to money for it appreciated in value.'

Sir William shrugged. 'Naturally, the deal in itself was legal, if unethical. On my return from the war, Lovell, my man of business, told me that Broseley had recently died and had been found to have debts greater than anyone might have expected. It seemed a good opportunity to take Larkswood back. But Buckle—your lawyer, I suppose—refused to negotiate, and so I was reduced to making somewhat stark threats of legal action. And then there was Amy. I thought that Larkswood would be the ideal home for her and Charlotte. Then I met you and was obliged to reconsider my position on the house, but since I hoped that you and I—' He broke off, and began again with more constraint. 'Anyway, I want you to know that I no longer wish to reclaim Larkswood. You pointed out to me, quite rightly, that without it you have nothing. I would not wish to take that from you.'

'Why did you not tell me before…about Larkswood—?' Annabella started to say, then broke off in confusion as she realised how close she was to tears. Will was right, of course; through her own ill-considered reaction to his behaviour she had lost the chance of an alternative future. She put her cup down on the table with a rather abrupt thump and got to her feet. 'Your pardon, sir. That was foolish of me. I do not require an answer to that question. I really must go…'

'Wait…' Will had also got to his feet and the movement brought him closer to Annabella than was quite comfortable.

'No, really…I must get back…the others… dinner—' She knew that she was gabbling. 'I am so very glad to understand a little of why you wanted the house…' she swallowed hard '…and even more grateful that the rumours I had heard about your fortune were unfounded—'

There was a moment of complete stillness.

'And which particular rumours would those be?' Will asked, quite without expression.

Annabella was edging towards the door when he took her arm in a grip that was not painful, but which she certainly could not have broken without effort.

She knew that she had made a mistake but, preoccupied with escaping from the turbulent effects of his presence and the intensity of her own emotions, she had not been thinking about what she was saying.

'I suppose,' Will said, with the same hard, angry edge that had been in his voice earlier in the evening, 'that I should not be surprised that you had been listening to unfounded gossip about me! After all, you have interpreted all my other actions in the worst light possible!'

'That is unfair!' Stung by his words, Annabella wrenched her arm from his grip and glared up at him. 'I did not give any credence to what I heard! And I could not ask you—'

'Why not?'

'Because you had already gone—'

'Of course, I forgot.' Will's tone was savage. 'By then you assumed that I was trying to trick you over Larkswood! Was *that* the rumour you had heard, or were there other tales? Good God, what must your opinion of me have been, when all the time I was thinking—'

'You are despicable to twist my words so!' Annabella cried. 'Yes, I'll admit that Miss Hurst planted a doubt in my mind that you had some interest in me other than for myself! That was why I asked you, that night in the summerhouse...' Her voice broke. 'But you assured me that it was not so, and I believed you!'

'Then what else has been said? Good God, I had no idea that Taunton was such a hotbed of speculation!' But there was no humour in Will's voice and he waited in stony silence for his answer.

Annabella was twisting her hands together in dis-

tress. She knew she was getting into a terrible tangle.
'Oh, this is all so stupid! I never meant—'

'You will oblige me by telling me exactly what you
did mean.' There was steel in the smooth tones now.

'Very well!' Annabella's green eyes were suddenly
defiant. 'A good friend warned me about you, Sir William.
He said that you were not a man to be trusted!
He said,' Annabella added, with unforgivable exaggeration,
'that you had made your money conspiring
with pirates and that in the American Wars you forgot
your duty sufficiently to abandon a fellow ship to its
fate and save your own skin!'

She thought later that she had been fortunate Will
had not struck her. Out of her own hurt and misery
she had spoken more wildly than she had intended,
but it was no excuse. She saw the stark fury in his
face as he stared at her, then he turned away as though
he wished to turn his back on her forever. After a
moment of silence she took an impulsive step forward,
touching his arm tentatively, but he shook her
off as though she were contaminated.

'Stories such as those are so vile they do not warrant
any explanations,' he said at length, in a low
voice. 'And for you to believe them...' He shook his
head slowly.

'But I did not!' Annabella was really frightened
now. She had thought him so calm, so slow to anger.
Little had she known! But then, she had impugned his
honour and integrity with her words, and he would
not forgive her that...

'This is all so foolish,' she said helplessly. 'I told
you I never believed ill of you! The rumours were

idle malice, prompted by jealousy, nothing more! You must believe me!'

Will shrugged indifferently. 'If you say so. I suppose it does not matter now.' He swung round and his blue gaze chilled her to the bone. 'Well, I must keep you no longer, Mrs St Auby. Pray give my best wishes to your sister and to James Mullineaux.'

He was holding the door open for her, still with that detached, cold courtesy that was somehow more frightening than any anger. Annabella hesitated, uncertain how to reach him, wanting only to banish this hostile stranger, who looked on her with such formality and dislike.

'Will…' she said beseechingly, using his name for the first time in a desperate attempt to put matters right before it was too late.

'Good evening, Mrs St Auby.'

He was not going to relent. The unshed tears bright in her eyes, Annabella raised her chin and marched out of Challen Court, praying that she would not disgrace herself by crying until she was out of sight.

The journey back to Oxenham was a nightmare for Annabella, as she could not see where she was going. The tears came in floods, blurring her vision, dripping on to her cloak and pretty muslin dress. Fortunately the horses knew their own way home, for Annabella was utterly incapable of giving them direction. She abandoned them in the stableyard and ran into the house, oblivious of the wooden-faced footmen in the hall, and cried all over Alicia's silk evening gown when her sister emerged to see what on earth was going on.

'Oh, Alicia, it was so dreadful! I am sure that he has nothing but contempt for me… I thought his sister-in-law was his mistress, and the poor woman is but recently bereaved, and he had wanted to marry me and now he has told me that he will not press his claim to Larkswood, but I wish he would…' Annabella's voice dissolved into a wail of inconsolable despair.

Alicia bore all this with fortitude and steered her sister into the library away from their dinner guests. She asked no questions, simply sitting with her arm around Annabella until the sobs had abated a little.

Annabella raised a face blotchy with tears. 'There was the poor woman standing by the side of the road in the extremes of pain and misery, and all I felt was a vicious jealousy, and it was the most *lowering* thing imaginable! And then when he came out into the courtyard and smiled on her with *such* tenderness, I wanted to scratch her eyes out! Oh, Alicia, I know I should be ashamed of myself, but I can't because I love him, you see, and it is so painful…' And her tears started afresh.

Alicia, abandoning hope of the delicious fillet of beef which would be rapidly congealing on her plate in the dining-room, hugged her sister all the harder. 'Love can be a very difficult matter,' she allowed. 'If you have never felt like this before—'

'I haven't.' Annabella wept piteously. 'I cared nothing for Francis, and I was nothing but a stupid child to imagine him as a way of freeing myself from our father. It took me very little time to realise my mistake! And then, when I met Sir William, I thought

I had been given another chance, but I threw it all away…'

'Surely it cannot be so bad—'

Annabella raised drowned green eyes to meet her sister's gaze. 'There is worse!'

'Surely not!'

Annabella was determined to make a clean breast of matters. 'I called him a traitor!' she announced tragically.

Not surprisingly, Alicia was somewhat startled at this extraordinary statement. 'Go back to the beginning and tell me the whole story,' she besought Annabella. 'I cannot make head nor tail of this!' This was hardly surprising, since her sister had been crying so much as to be practically unintelligible. Annabella blew her nose, took a deep breath and related the whole of her meeting with Amy Weston once again, and the events which had followed.

'So, when Will explained about the money he had inherited, I realised that the scurrilous story I had heard about him consorting with privateers was false,' Annabella finished, 'and I said so. I was too upset to be thinking properly, Liss, or I would never have breathed a word! But then, of course, Sir William thought that I had believed the rumours about him and became unbearably stuffy! I was so angry with him for thinking the worst of me that I told him the whole tale! It was stupid and childish of me, but I was so furious!' Her voice caught on a sob. 'Oh, it was dreadful, dreadful! And now we will never be comfortable together again!'

A small frown marred Alicia's forehead. 'So there

were rumours that Will had made a fortune through piracy? I have never heard such tales!'

'Oh, worse than that.' Annabella grimaced. 'At least, I suppose it's worse... Which would you say was the greater dishonour, Liss—to be accused of piracy, or cowardice in battle?'

Alicia looked as though she would have liked to put her head in her hands. 'Oh, Annabella! You didn't—'

'I know it was foolish of me...' Annabella looked away from her sister's accusing gaze, on the verge of bursting into tears again. 'You need not reproach me—I shall never forgive myself!'

Alicia bit her lip. 'Cowardice in battle?' she repeated carefully. 'Were there specific facts mentioned, or was this just another wild tale?'

Annabella made a hopeless gesture. 'I don't know! It was something to do with Lake Champlain—a few years ago—in '14, I think he said...'

'Who said?'

'Captain Jeffries...' And Annabella dissolved once more into tears.

'That troublesome man! Well, I have never heard these charges!' her sister said stoutly, 'and we all know Will Weston is too fine a man for them to be even remotely true! But you know how dangerous gossip can be. Such talk is very damaging, Annabella—'

'Oh, do not!' Annabella wept. 'I know! I never believed it, but Will thinks I did, and now he will never speak to me again!'

Alicia thought that this was probably true and was too honest to try to comfort her sister with false promises. To impugn the reputation of a man like Will Weston was no light matter. She made a mental note to ask James if he had heard anything of such rumours, and shepherded her unresisting sister to the door.

'You had best go to bed, Annabella,' she said gently. 'Matters will seem better in the morning. Fordyce, a tray for Mrs St Auby in her room, if you please. I will rejoin my guests for dessert.'

But, in the event, all of Cook's delicacies were wasted on Annabella, for they turned to dust and ashes in her mouth.

Annabella felt no better the next day, nor the one after that. Her days at Oxenham had fallen into a pattern: riding early in the morning, visits with Alicia, visits from neighbours and friends, trips out, walks about the estate, talking to her grandmother, playing with Thomas, and helping her sister entertain the guests in the evening. There seemed to be any number of sports and entertainments devised purely for pleasure. It was not an onerous existence and was, in fact, rather a pleasant one. Alicia had summoned her own dressmaker to provide Annabella with a wardrobe of clothes, she had every material need satisfied and she had the affection of her family.

Compared to the drab routine of life with the St Aubys, it was well nigh blissful. And yet, Annabella felt that she did not have a place. James and Alicia would never have treated her as a poor relation and Lady Stansfield had even indicated her intention to alter her will to include Annabella, but she had no function to fulfil in the pattern of life at Oxenham.

And she was not sure how long this could continue. She began to long fervently for Larkswood to be finished so that she could go back to a place that was her own.

It was five weeks before Amy Weston made her appearance in local society. She had been delivered of a boy, called Peter after his late father, and both mother and baby were thriving. Alicia had called early to convey their welcome and best wishes but, not surprisingly, Annabella had felt herself unequal to another visit to Challen Court. Her misery over Sir William was never far from her thoughts and it was more than she could bear to see him again. She had thought herself unhappy before, but this second misunderstanding between them, based on so foolish an error, was almost too much to stand. Once or twice she thought of asking James to intercede for her with Will, but could not bear the thought of her apologies being rejected.

When Alicia announced a few days later that she was giving a dinner in Mrs Weston's honour, Annabella almost invented a sick headache out of pure terror, but she knew she had to face Will some time. She managed to work herself up into a fine anticipation of the evening, but in the event it proved to be a sad disappointment. Alicia had prudently placed Will at quite some distance from Annabella down the table and when she did dare to raise her gaze to meet his, it was to notice that he scarcely even glanced in her direction. To Annabella's besotted gaze he looked compellingly attractive but frighteningly forbidding.

Annabella's company was monopolised by an elderly neighbour of James and Alicia, Sir Dunstan Groat, who was much taken with her prettiness, called her a buxom little wench, and spent a large part of the evening ogling her.

Amy Weston made a special point of thanking Annabella for her help that day at Challen, but when the gentlemen rejoined the ladies after dinner, Will steered her away to more congenial company and poor Annabella was left feeling as though she had the plague. She was asked to sing, but the occasion reminded her too sharply of the time she had sung at Mundell, and her voice faltered sadly on the notes. The applause at the end was merely polite. All in all, it was a miserable evening, and Annabella retired early to bed, pleading a headache.

The second time they met, it was easier. Their mutual friends, the Linleys, hosted an evening party with impromptu dancing; although Will did not ask Annabella for a dance, he did at least manage to be civil to her and exchange a few pleasantries. Once again, Sir Dunstan Groat monopolised her company, which Annabella bore with as much equanimity as she could. She still felt very miserable. The dispute over Larkswood had been painful enough, but the misunderstanding about the gossip was so silly and could have been avoided if only she had thought. Now it only served to underline the permanent estrangement between herself and Will. Annabella could visualise a series of empty social occasions, stretching into infinite time, at which they met and smiled stiffly, exchanged a few words and separated once more. It could not be worse. But, of course, it could be worse, for he could marry... Once again, she went to bed with a headache and awoke feeling unrefreshed.

As the late summer days slid into autumn, Annabella and Will were often in each other's company. In some ways, matters grew easier; in other ways, they were more difficult. Though Will never asked her to dance at any of the events they attended, Annabella found that they could at least converse pleasantly enough on superficial topics. Once, she had started to try to apologise for their misunderstanding, only to be cut off by the cold look in his eyes and harsh words of rejection. She did not try again. Then there was the torment just of seeing him, particularly when he was in company with some lady of his acquaintance. Annabella was miserably aware that envy was becoming one of her besetting sins.

On the morning following one party, when Will had paid such particular attention to a certain Miss Watts that eyebrows were raised, Annabella rose early, determined to shake off her blue devils with a ride. The day was bright, with a soft wind off the downs and the promise of an Indian summer heat when the sun got up. The mist lay wreathing the fields as Annabella and her groom set out. She was surprised to feel her spirits lifting almost immediately. The cool air stung her cheeks to rose pink and ruffled her hair. She let her feelings dictate a speed that was perhaps a little unwise, galloped across the fields and left the toiling groom on his old bay horse far behind.

When she looked back it was to see that another figure had come upon the groom, paused for a few words, then set off towards her. It was impossible to distinguish the horseman from this distance, but Annabella had a sudden and unwelcome conviction that it was Sir William Weston. She watched for a moment as he galloped towards her, setting a killing pace on the black hunter. Then she deliberately turned her horse's head and set it at the high brushwood hedge which blocked her access to the next field. They scrambled over, but only just. The horse pecked on landing and almost threw Annabella, but she managed to stay in the saddle, urging the mare onwards with a speed that almost seemed borne of panic. There was the thunder of hooves behind her and her reins were caught in an iron grip.

'A moment, Mrs St Auby!' Sir William Weston said, very politely.

Annabella swung round defiantly. 'Yes, sir?'

'This is my land, and—'

'And you would rather I did not trespass?' Annabella said sweetly. 'I beg your pardon, sir! I shall be on my way directly!'

Sir William did not scruple to hide his exasperation. 'I was about to say that there is a treacherous bog up ahead. I was concerned that your headlong flight might lead you into it unawares.' He ran a hand through his disordered tawny hair. 'Damnation, why must you be so—?' He broke off, the lines of his mouth tightening in irritation.

The hot colour flooded into Annabella's face. 'I beg your pardon, sir,' she said with reserve. 'I thought you were about to ring a peal over me!'

'For your reckless riding?' Sir William laughed shortly. 'Well I might, Mrs St Auby! You gave the

impression of someone anxious to break her neck!'
He paused and looked at her consideringly. 'However,
you ride magnificently. Not one in ten riders would
have recovered the way you did after that jump.'

He pulled his horse alongside hers, and they continued at a more decorous pace. Annabella was surprised that he sought her company at all. Surely his
behaviour previously had only served to underline to
her the dislike in which he must hold her. She found
that she was nervous.

'From what were you trying to escape, Mrs St
Auby?' Sir William asked now, the searching blue
eyes scanning her face. 'Speed such as that is usually
indicative of a need to evade something unwelcome!'

Annabella jumped. Damn him, he was too astute!
She could hardly say that she wanted some time on
her own away from Oxenham, for that would appear
too ungracious after the welcome accorded her there.
As for admitting to a need to avoid her thoughts of
him—well, that was impossible. She hesitated, whilst
he watched her pensively.

'Such reticence, Mrs St Auby!' Sir William's smile
was mocking now. 'It is not what I have come to
expect from you!'

'No, sir, for you are forever trying to provoke me!'
Annabella snapped. 'Let us talk of other matters, or
we shall only argue! How did Mrs Weston enjoy herself last evening?'

'I believe she liked it very well,' Sir William said
carelessly. 'I have not seen her this morning, but on
the journey home she was forever talking of your sister's warmth and kindness, and what good company
we had. I think it would please her if you felt able to

call at Challen Court, Mrs St Auby. Though Amy has the children for company, I fear she must be lonely sometimes.'

'I imagine it must be horrid for her,' Annabella said sincerely, 'having lost her husband but recently, travelling alone to a foreign land and being amongst strangers! I shall be happy to visit her—if you should not mind, sir.'

'I?' Will still sounded careless. 'Not at all, Mrs St Auby!'

Annabella began to feel rather cast down. It was indubitably better to be thoroughly disliked by Sir William Weston rather than be the recipient of such indifference. At least it meant that she had some effect on him! Unseen by Annabella, Will smiled slightly.

'Of course,' he continued in the same offhand tone, 'if you are contemplating matrimony with Sir Dunstan, you may have little time to spare for Amy!'

'Marriage with Sir Dunstan!' Annabella had risen to this before she thought about it.

'Sir Dunstan Groat,' Will said, as though further clarification were required. 'He is very rich, you know, and though he has buried three wives already, you might be considering him as a potential way out of your difficulties!'

'Difficulties?' Annabella's green eyes were flashing with anger now. 'I do not understand you, sir!'

'Oh, surely...' Will sounded vague. 'You said yourself—you cannot be Alicia's pensioner forever!'

'And what business is it of yours, sir?' Annabella returned furiously. 'It may interest you to know that I have inherited a small competence from my father's estate, and have every intention of going into business!'

'The circulating library?' Will murmured. He looked so cool, so detached, so elegant in the severe style he favoured, that Annabella suddenly wanted to slap him. She forgot that she had resolved to behave with circumspection whenever she met him. He really was the most infuriating man!

'A confectioner's!' Annabella said wildly, making it up as she went along. 'Alicia has promised to invest in my enterprise!'

'Ah.' Sir William smiled pleasantly. 'Your knowledge of sugar cane will come in useful there, Mrs St Auby! How providential! And what an imagination you have, ma'am! I commend you!'

Annabella ground her teeth.

'Of course,' Will continued, as though struck by a sudden thought, 'I was forgetting that you are now rumoured to be your grandmother's heiress! That should alter your prospects considerably! But Sir Dunstan need not marry for money, though he has always wanted Larkswood land. It completes a corner of his own estate, you see! So perhaps he has an eye on your little legacy when he is paying you those lavish compliments!'

'I had not thought that you had noticed his attentions, sir!' Annabella said sweetly.

A rueful smile touched Sir William's mouth. 'Ah, you have me there, ma'am! I noticed it very well!'

There was a silence as blue eyes and green met and held for a long moment. Then Sir William raised his whip in a mocking salute, dug his heels into the hunter's sides, and galloped off across the fields without a backward glance.

Larkswood was at last ready for habitation again.

'Stuff and nonsense!' Lady Stansfield declared strongly, when she heard that Annabella intended to move there forthwith. 'You should be settled here until you marry, miss! In my day no young gel would set up home where and when she pleased! Quite unsuitable!' She settled in her armchair and fixed her younger grand-daughter with her piercing glare.

'You forget, Grandmama, that I am a widow, not some debutante,' Annabella said indulgently, for she had seen the twinkle her grandmother had been unable to banish and she refused to be bullied. 'If Alicia could do such a thing before she married James, I fail to see why it should be different for me!'

Lady Stansfield snorted. 'Oh, do you! Your sister, miss, was another such, always thinking she knew best! Aye, and a fine mess she made of matters too!'

'Now, Grandmama, that is too harsh!' Alicia caught Annabella's eye and tried not to laugh. 'Besides, Annabella will have a footman and a gardener to help her keep Larkswood in order, as well as several maids! And she will only be situated down the road. It is all most convenient!'

Lady Stansfield made a rude and dismissive noise. 'No good will come of it, you mark my words! Young gels! In my day...'

Both sisters sighed, knowing full well that they were about to be treated to another diatribe on the shortcomings of the current generation. Both also knew that Lady Stansfield had actually been accounted quite wild in her youth, in the days when eighteenth-century society had been a lot more rumbustious than at present.

'Grandmama, tell me again how you disguised yourself as a boy in order to go alone to the races,' Alicia said sweetly, to be rewarded by a scowl from Lady Stansfield.

'Pshaw! I can see your tricks, miss! To think that I should be so beset by disobedient grandchildren—'

'In your own image, Grandmama,' Annabella murmured, leaning across to tickle Thomas's tummy where he lay gurgling on the rug.

'Well, well,' Lady Stansfield said gruffly, 'if you have that henwit, Emmeline Frensham, with you, I suppose it will be accounted quite respectable! Though Emmeline is not the woman she was—not after that incident at Bathampton!'

'No,' Alicia agreed regretfully, 'Emmy's nerves have never been strong since she was abandoned at that inn the time I was abducted! But she should do very well for Annabella—she is quite excited at the prospect of a change of scene, you know, for she has lived quite retired since my marriage!'

'Should have taken Will Weston when he offered,' Lady Stansfield said suddenly, with her famed lack of tact. She ignored Annabella's blush and added astringently, 'There's a man for you! He'd have known how to keep you in order, miss!'

'Grandmama—' Alicia began, but Annabella cut in,

'In point of fact, Sir William has never asked me to marry him, ma'am!'

'Well, why not?' Lady Stansfield looked offended. 'If you'd played your cards aright, miss, you could have whistled him up! Young people today! Always fiddle-faddling around, never getting to the point! You would do better to take Will Weston as a lover—'

'Grandmama!' Annabella besought, at the same time as Alicia said,

'Not again, Grandmama! I seem to remember you offering me similar advice about James…'

'Well, then!' Lady Stansfield looked triumphant, as though Alicia had just proved her point. 'You mark my words, no good will come of this business of living alone, Annabella! No good at all!'

# *Chapter Seven*

James Mullineaux and Will Weston, having spent the afternoon sizing up a horse which James had eventually decided not to buy, were sitting in the library at Challen Court and were talking over a glass of excellent brandy. Amy had brought Charlotte and Peter in to say goodnight to their uncle, and James had watched with indulgent amusement as the little girl had clambered on to Will's knee and planted sticky kisses on his face.

'Thinking of setting up your own nursery soon, Will?' James asked slyly, taking a chair opposite the fireplace, where the portrait of Sir Charles looked benevolently down.

Will gave him a straight look. 'I may be. I'm sure you'll be amongst the first to know, James! You've put a lot of work into Larkswood,' he added, as a logical extension to his train of thought.

James grinned, immediately perceiving what was troubling his friend. 'You can pay me back one day,' he said coolly, 'when you take possession of the house again!'

Will laughed reluctantly. 'You'll be waiting a while for your money! Your little sister-in-law has given me to understand that she won't sell to me and I doubt she'll succumb to sweeter persuasion! She don't trust me!'

'Thought the boot was on the other foot,' James said lazily. 'Annabella certainly believes you don't like her much!'

Will shifted a little uncomfortably. 'You of all people should know, James, that you can dislike someone and still find them damnably attractive!'

'None better!' James agreed cheerfully. 'So that's why you keep avoiding Annabella! Thought you just couldn't stand to spend any time with her!'

Will smiled reluctantly. 'No, you didn't, James! You know I like her too well, not too little!'

James raised his eyebrows, not denying it. 'Then why put so much effort into avoiding her? I think you're being a little unfair to Annabella, Will.' Their eyes met for a moment and he added, 'She's very unhappy, you know. I'm sure you'd agree that there was fault on both sides in your original quarrel, and as for those ridiculous rumours—well, Annabella never truly believed them!'

Will shrugged. 'Maybe not. I don't know… Devil take it, I thought those stories had all died. That's the hell of it, James—gossip is as difficult to pin down as air, but as damaging as a stab in the back, and it's never possible to trace and destroy it. When Annabella repeated the tales to me, I was so furious to hear them from her I suppose I just overreacted. If it had been anyone else I wouldn't have cared so much. But she just stood there, looking so sweet and so desirable, and repeating such debasing tales…' Will looked away, his face strained. 'I had been hoping against hope that there was still a chance for me, but there was the complication of Amy's arrival and our quarrel, and her refusal to see me—damn it, she has the pride of the devil!'

'Alicia once told me hell would freeze over before she accepted my hand in marriage,' James said cheerfully. 'It's the Stansfield temper, I'm afraid! But you don't strike me as the faint-hearted type, Will! Why don't you put your fate to the touch—if you still *want* to?'

There was silence.

'Annabella certainly seems to have healed the breach with her sister and Lady Stansfield,' Will said, turning the conversation. 'You must be pleased for Alicia's sake.'

James nodded, willing to allow the subject to change. 'Oh, Alicia's thrilled, and the old lady dotes on Annabella!' He laughed. 'And I must admit I like my little sister-in-law! I didn't really expect to, but she's not like any of us anticipated. Proud to the point of obstinacy, perhaps, and I know how it feels to be on the receiving end of that!' He shrugged. 'Milk-and-water misses are more to some men's taste, I know, but…'

Will grinned, reaching across to refill the brandy glasses. 'But there are those of us who prefer beauty and wit! Well, you may wish me luck then, James! I think you have persuaded me to try…but she'll probably tell me to go to the devil!'

The new moon was sharp and clear in a sky of black as Annabella lay in bed at Larkswood that night.

She had soon discovered that living in the country on her own was a very different prospect from living as a member of the family in a large country house where there was constant company and entertainment. Although she still had visitors and, indeed, had the use of a pony and trap to convey her to civilisation, when the blue twilight of evening fell over the hills, she was, to all intents and purposes, alone. Miss Frensham, with her endless needlework, never seemed to lack occupation. Annabella, on the other hand, had already taken to reading with far greater fervour than she had previously shown, and was even contemplating gardening. She reflected ruefully that she had few friends with whom to maintain a correspondence, and she was going to need to find new resources for solitude if life at Larkswood was not to leave her lonely and dull. Still, there were always her ideas for going into business, which might bear further investigation were she to become too bored.

She found that she missed Alicia in particular over the days that had followed her move, and her grandmother to a scarcely lesser degree. As she had got to know Alicia at Oxenham, they had begun to exchange childhood memories and experiences in a way Annabella had been unable to do with anyone else. Both had been treated harshly by their father and both found solace in the other's company. From the start, Alicia had made it clear that she would not ask Annabella any difficult questions about her marriage, but Annabella needed to confide and feel that one person at least knew the entire story.

Then there was Lady Stansfield, ancient now, the

relic of a previous generation, but the most marvellous raconteur of society stories from the previous century, and fiercely protective of the family she had left. She made no secret of her delight in seeing Alicia settled so well, and her desire to see Annabella suitably married before she died. When Annabella had tried to explain haltingly about her estrangement from Alicia, Lady Stansfield had cut her off with a brief gesture.

'Bertram Broseley—out-and-out bounder!' she had declared roundly. 'As for the St Auby family, nothing for them to be proud of! No need to apologise for anything that's happened, my girl!' Her green eyes were bright. 'You're a Stansfield, remember, and you're a good girl for all your contrary ways!' And she had given Annabella a hug and a kiss that had made her feel much better.

Annabella sighed now, turning over in her bed. For some reason she felt particularly restless that evening. Normally she had no difficulty sleeping, but tonight she found that Will Weston was invading her thoughts with the same relentlessness that had dogged her when first she came to Larkswood from Taunton. It was tiresome and rather depressing that she could not dismiss him. He was not for her—fate and her own pride had seen to that. Unfortunately, her emotions could not relinquish him so easily.

She slipped out of bed and sat on the window seat for a while, listening to the sounds of the night, the wind in the trees and the scuttering of little creatures in the undergrowth. Everything sounded magnified by the quiet of the house and the stillness outside. The tiny sickle moon rode high in the cold sky, and Annabella shivered. There was something curiously compelling about the shadowy night. Without conscious thought she got dressed and slipped down the stairs.

The old house cast its silhouette over the cobbles of the courtyard as Annabella slipped past. She heard Owen's cows bumping gently against each other in the barn, and the rustle of the mice in the hay. The track to Lambourn lay bright and white in the moonlight, but Annabella turned aside from the road, slipping along the field path that edged Larkswood garden. She passed the still pond that was all that was left of the old millhouse, and paused in the shelter of the hedge to consider the empty landscape. The breeze off the hills was cool and she shivered deep within her cloak. Well, a breath of fresh air should at least help her to sleep…

Without warning, there was a rustle of leaves beside her and a man stepped out directly onto the path. Annabella drew breath on a scream, but before it reached her lips, strong arms seized her from behind and a hand came down over her mouth as she was dragged backwards against a hard, male body.

'Be still and keep quiet!'

Annabella went still with shock at the sound of Will's voice. When he realised she was not about to scream he took his hand away, but only to scoop her up into his arms. Annabella had the confused impression of someone stepping past them, then Will had strode off down the path, to put her back on her feet only when they had gained the shadow of the hawthorn hedge. They stared at each other in the fitful moonlight.

'What the *hell* are you doing here?'

This time, Annabella thought inconsequentially,

Will did not sound particularly angry with her, only exasperated. She smoothed her cloak with fingers that were still shaking a little. Her whole body was tingling from the contact with his, her blood racing with a mixture of fright and excitement.

'I might ask you the same, sir! Whatever are you about? Do you go creeping around in the night often?'

'I asked you first,' Will said pleasantly. He took her arm, guiding her deeper into the shadows. 'What are you up to, Annabella?'

'I couldn't sleep,' Annabella said sulkily. 'There is no mystery! I thought to take a breath of fresh air—'

'It is past two o'clock! Scarcely an hour for a young lady to be out for a stroll! Not one woman in a hundred would go out for a walk in the middle of the night if she could not sleep! A cup of warm milk, perhaps, a book to induce sleepiness—'

Annabella shook his hand off her arm, annoyed by his attitude. 'A dose of laudanum?' she said crossly. 'Perhaps you would approve of that instead? I am sorry if my behaviour offends you, but I did not expect to find the countryside so crowded! As I said, sir, I was unable to sleep and stepped outside for a little. I imagine my purpose is less sinister than yours!'

Will sighed. 'I am out after a poacher, that is all. The man you saw with me is my gamekeeper! We had been following the fellow for several miles and knew he had taken a hare or two, but suspected he was after bigger game. We were about to catch him snaring a deer when you appeared out of nowhere and he made a run for it. A night's work wasted!'

Annabella was not about to apologise for taking a

walk on her own land. 'I suppose it does not matter that you gave me a monstrous shock!' she complained. 'Was it really necessary to grab me like that?'

She saw Will smile. 'Probably not, but it was rather enjoyable! And I did deserve some recompense for you spoiling the evening!' He heard Annabella let her breath out on an angry sigh. 'Come, let us call a truce! If it is any compensation, you gave me a hell of a fright too!'

They were walking slowly up the path towards the house.

'Your language, sir,' Annabella said primly, 'is not that of a gentleman to a lady!'

Will sketched a mocking bow. 'Your pardon, ma'am! But if you choose to wander about at night, you have to deal with what you find! You should be more careful, perhaps.'

'Perhaps so!' Annabella looked at him. There was an undertone in his voice which suggested that she was not, perhaps, as safe as she might have imagined. It was a disturbing thought, and not in an entirely unpleasurable way. Will kicked aside a fallen branch to clear her path, and she struggled to keep a grip on her practicality. It would do no good to allow her susceptibility to him to distract her.

'Those are strange sentiments from a man who has been out on the dangerous enterprise of catching a poacher!' she said, with deliberate lightness. 'But I shall be more careful on my next moonlight stroll, and will carry a pistol with me!'

She saw Will grin in the moonlight. 'Can you shoot?' he enquired. 'It would be an advantage!'

'Strangely enough, I can,' Annabella said demurely. 'My father considered it a useful accomplishment, which no doubt says a great deal about him! I forgot to mention that when Miss Hurst quizzed me on my achievements! Lord, it would have been worth it to see her face!'

They had reached the door of Larkswood, and Will stood back to let Annabella go inside. 'You do not intend to invite me in?' he enquired, when she made to say goodbye. This time there was no innuendo in his voice, but somehow Annabella wondered at his meaning.

'Certainly not!' she said primly. 'That would be a most unorthodox thing for a young lady to do at two of the clock!'

And she shut the door firmly in his face.

Amy Weston called the following day, bringing little Charlotte with her, but not the baby, Peter, who was still a little too young to travel. Charlotte was full of excitement over the kite her uncle had taught her to fly on Weathercock Hill nearby, and Annabella was forced to endure both Amy and Charlotte praising Will Weston extravagantly. It was not that she grudged others their good opinion of him, but just to hear his name repeated and his virtues rehearsed was difficult for her when her emotions were so deeply engaged. She was constantly afraid that she would give her feelings away.

Amy was also warm in her admiration of Larkswood, which gave Annabella a pang as she remembered that Will had intended Amy to have the house. Then, fortunately, Mrs Weston put it all right.

'It is a lovely house and a beautiful situation,' Amy

said, as they sat down for tea on the lawn, 'but do you not find it rather isolated here, Mrs St Auby? I assure you, I could not live miles from anywhere, with only the farm for neighbours! Surely you must be lonely!' Her anxious brown eyes took in the empty expanse of cornfields and the sweep of the hills.

Annabella began to realise that Amy's life on the plantation must have been far more pampered and less hardy that she had imagined. She encouraged her to tell her more about it and for a while was regaled with breathless tales of Charleston society, and how happy Amy had been with Will's brother. Then Amy seemed to droop like a delicate flower and sighed.

'But, of course, that is all gone now. It is so very hard, is it not, Mrs St Auby, to lose a husband! There are times when I still feel his loss very strongly. No doubt you feel the same!'

Annabella was tempted to say that she had been very glad to lose Francis, but thought this might upset her visitor. 'I think I understand how you must feel,' she said diplomatically. 'And you have been very brave in leaving your home and coming all this way for the sake of your family! You must have been glad to receive such a welcome at Challen Court.'

'Oh, yes, Will has been all a brother could be,' Amy said enthusiastically, accepting one of the scones Miss Frensham passed her. 'He is looking for a house for us, Mrs St Auby, but I hope it will not be far distant from Challen, for I find the society hereabouts most congenial! Your sister has been all that is kind to me, and I hope…I am sure…I could make friends here…'

Annabella smiled at her reassuringly. It seemed odd

that Amy Weston had the brand of courage that could take her from one continent to another, and yet was uncertain of her welcome in country society.

'I am sure of it,' she said warmly, and saw the relief reflected in Amy's eyes.

'Of course,' her new friend continued, 'when Will marries it will be even more pleasant! I do so hope I shall like his wife!'

Annabella jumped and spilt her tea. Miss Frensham tutted and patted ineffectually at her skirt with a lavender-drenched handkerchief. Down the garden, Charlotte Weston was pursuing a brightly coloured butterfly with her little net. Annabella dragged her gaze away and fixed it on Amy's pretty, undisturbed face.

'Is that event imminent, Mrs Weston?'

'Oh!' For a moment, Amy looked confused. A little colour came into her cheeks. 'Well…that is to say, I am not really certain… But,' she said brightly, 'I heard Will talking to your brother-in-law the other day and making some mention of the changes he would make at Challen when he got married. Then Lord Mullineaux made some comment that I did not catch but I heard him say that half his female relatives had been in love with Will in their time! And,' Amy added, digressing to show her partiality, 'I cannot be surprised at it, for Will is a fine man, is he not, Mrs St Auby?'

'He is very well, I suppose,' Annabella said, a little coldly. 'He is not so handsome as James, of course, but…'

'Oh, no,' Amy agreed, with a little smile, as many women had done before her, 'but then Lord Mulli-

neaux is so prodigiously attractive, and so devoted to
your sister that it makes one quite envious! But Will
is a very agreeable man, and I think any girl would
be fortunate to call him husband!'

Annabella could not but agree. A chill touched her
at the thought of the lucky girl who would do so.
Some female relative of James Mullineaux…a highly
suitable alliance between two of the county's illustrious families… *Surely* Alicia would have told her
about this! But perhaps not, if she knew it would upset
her sister.

'Was the name of the lady mentioned?' she asked
Amy, as casually as she was able. Amy wrinkled up
her small nose.

'Not precisely, but I did hear Will remark later that
Lord Mullineaux had said that a cousin of his was
coming to stay at Oxenham, a Miss Shawcross, who
I believe currently lives with his sister in Worcester-
shire.'

Miss Shawcross. Annabella bit viciously into her
third scone and decided that she disliked the sound of
her intensely. Amy, quite unaware of the trouble she
had caused, regretfully refused Annabella's offer of a
second cup of tea.

'I should be going back to Challen before the light
fades,' she said anxiously. 'The autumn evenings
close in so fast here, and I fear there may be footpads
in these hills!'

Miss Frensham, who had been dozing in her chair
in the warm sunshine, now woke up with a start.

'Oh, no, my dear Mrs Weston, I have not heard of
any such thing! I am persuaded that Lord Mullineaux

would never have let us come here if there had been the slightest chance... Oh, dear!'

Annabella, finding herself out of sorts with both her visitor and her companion, was seized by a malicious impulse.

'I believe Serena Linley's coach was stopped by a highwayman on the Lambourn road only last week,' she said sweetly and entirely untruthfully. 'She said that it was most exciting!'

Miss Frensham looked up at the hills and shivered histrionically. 'Upon my word, we continue to live in very lawless times!'

'Did the villain take anything?' Amy enquired, looking round a little nervously.

Annabella shrugged. She was already regretting the whim that had prompted her to tell such a story, for no doubt Will Weston would hear of it now and put her down as a troublemaker. Still...

'Only a kiss, I believe,' she said lightly.

Miss Frensham gave an outraged gasp but there was a definite twinkle in Amy's eyes.

'Well, that could be quite fun!' she said brightly, and left Annabella with the impression that they might, after all, become friends.

Annabella spent the next couple of days helping Susan to make butter and cheese in the Larkswood dairy. They were fairly self-sufficient, for Lark Farm kept them supplied with the items they could not grow or make for themselves and Owen Linton frequently travelled to market and would undertake a commission for his neighbours in return for a melting look from Susan's brown eyes. Annabella had found her-

self being drawn more and more into the household
activities. She had never had the running of a household before, for her father had paid all the bills when
she and Francis were first married, and after that she
had always been a pensioner in someone else's home.
It was strangely enjoyable to make plans with Susan,
who was proving a capable manager and a staunch
ally.

Even more pleasant was the prospect of a change
of scene and some different company. Alicia had written to invite her sister to stay at Oxenham for a few
days, with a view to going to the Faringdon Goose
Fair. Annabella grasped the opportunity eagerly.
Whilst she did not regret staking her claim to Larkswood, she imagined she might turn into a mad recluse
if she never went into the outside world at all and had
no fresh entertainment. Perhaps, she thought, churning
the butter with unnecessary violence, the fortunate
Miss Shawcross would be of their party...

Both Susan and Owen Linton frowned when Annabella borrowed a horse and told them she was off
for a ride in the hills on her own that afternoon. Neither of them told her she should not ride alone, although Susan looked as though she would have liked
to have done so. Their expressions were so reminiscent of disapproving parents that Annabella almost
laughed. As she set off up the track to Lambourn she
remembered Will's comments a few nights ago and
reflected that most people found independent women
uncomfortable. She knew that most of her acquaintance thought it odd in the extreme that she had chosen to live on her own at Larkswood, and clearly believed her to be an eccentric. Neither Alicia nor James

had tried to dissuade her from living there, but Annabella sometimes wondered whether this was not because they approved but because they wanted her to realise for herself that it did not suit her. Shrugging, she encouraged the horse to a gallop across the rolling chalk down.

There were some ancient standing stones which stood close to the track on the top of the hill. Annabella stopped to consider the view, picking out Larkswood nestling in its hollow, and beyond it in the distance the villages of Challen, Oxenham and the others that dotted the flat valley floor. She dismounted, and hitched her horse's rein over a fence post whilst she looked at the ancient stones. They were not particularly impressive for many were leaning or tumbled into the field, covered with mosses and lichens, yet there was something peaceful about the spot that made Annabella sit down in the long grass with her back to one sun-warmed stone, and contemplate the scene. Before her, a field of late poppies bobbed and swayed in the light breeze like a shifting red scarf between the heads of corn. Annabella's eyes closed.

She was not sure how long she dozed for, or what had woken her, though she thought she had felt movement nearby. A skylark was twittering away up above her head and as she opened her eyes, a shadow fell across her and blotted out the sun. For a moment she was gripped by panic, but almost immediately she recognised the newcomer.

'Oh!' She struggled to sit upright. 'You startled me, sir! Whatever are you doing here?'

Will Weston straightened up from where he was leaning against a nearby stone, and viewed Annabella's prone figure with amusement mixed with appreciation. 'I would hope that I am protecting you from footpads and highwaymen,' he said dryly.

Annabella's face flamed. She scrambled to her feet. 'Oh, she told you! It was only in jest—'

'I am more concerned that you choose to go riding alone,' Will said, 'and that you then fall asleep in the middle of nowhere! You are not very wise, are you, Mrs St Auby, despite what I said to you the other night!'

Annabella raised her chin. She knew that he was right, but unfortunately it only brought out the worst in her. 'I was in no danger,' she said hotly.

'Really?' Will stepped closer. 'There may not be highwaymen in these hills any more, Mrs St Auby, but it is no sensible thing to go out alone. I wonder that you dare to live at Larkswood, to all intents and purposes remote from civilisation…'

'But you intended it as a home for Mrs Weston,' Annabella reminded him in honeyed tones, 'so you must have considered it suitable then.'

She saw a smile touch Will's mouth. 'Very true, and quite right of you to remind me! It would not have served for Amy at all. Well…' he stepped back to allow her to pass him and regain the path '…I am glad to see that you are thriving at Larkswood. I am for Lambourn, for I visit the Linleys this evening. I should be on my way.' But he did not move, and his thoughtful gaze travelled over Annabella slowly and unreadably, appearing to linger on her flushed face and bright, tumbled hair.

Annabella found herself suffering a constriction in her breathing. She tried to steady herself.

'How did you know I was here?' she asked, a little breathlessly.

'I saw you riding up the hill.' Will's voice had dropped. There was suddenly something oddly intimate about the stone circle, the heat pulsing off the ancient stones, the skylarks twittering in the bright arch of the blue sky. Annabella swallowed, her throat dry. An intense longing for the golden happiness of Mundell, before Larkswood and the rest had driven a wedge between them, took hold of her as though she was in a vice. Their eyes met and held as the tension spun out between them.

'Don't look at me like that!' Will said harshly, stepping back with such recoil that Annabella felt shocked. There was more violence in his tone than she at first understood, but then she remembered that he was an affianced man now—or as good as such. Crimson with mortification at the thought that her face had betrayed her longing for him, she turned away hastily, caught her foot in the hem of her riding habit and stumbled against one of the stones. She scored her hand painfully on its roughened surface as she tried to break her fall.

'Oh!' She stared at the red weal as it came up on her skin, the desire to cry so ridiculously out of proportion to the injury. She looked up into Will's face and from there it was suddenly an easy step into his arms, and he was kissing her with a violence that was both terrifying and tender as the tears dried on her hot cheeks, and he drew her down into the grass in the shelter of the stone circle.

Their passion rose to consume them with a force only intensified by its long denial. Will's lips were hard and bruising, but Annabella only pressed closer, revelling in their demand and the suppressed violence of his need for her, their need for each other. Her lips parted and opened beneath the pressure of his. The taste and the feel of him filled her senses. Neither of them said a word.

The urgency between them was inexpressibly exciting. Will's imperative fingers unfastened Annabella's riding habit to reveal the flimsy chemise beneath. Annabella's breasts were rising and falling rapidly with her fevered breathing, her nipples taut against the fine material. Will caught his breath, almost ripping the fabric aside so that his mouth could take one rosy tip in his mouth. Annabella gasped, her hands tracing an urgent path of their own over the hard muscles of his back, delving under his jacket and shirt to feel the delicious smoothness of his skin. All fear had gone, all thoughts of Francis and the undignified, painful act that he had inflicted on her. All she wanted now, at once, was the exquisite conclusion of such delicious pleasure.

Will's mouth had returned to hers, its explicit demand making clear that he wanted it too. Every yielding line of Annabella's body was pressed against his as he forced her back against the stone. The warmth of the sun, combined with the burning in her blood created a feeling of languorous abandonment. Then Will's grip eased abruptly and he moved away from her.

'Forgive me…I should not…'

'Oh!' Annabella was bewildered for a moment. Dazed by the intoxication of her senses, she was slow to understand that he had withdrawn from her. She

opened her eyes reluctantly. The sky above her head
was still bright, the sun still shone, the grass tickled
her skin… And Will was supposed to be marrying a
certain Miss Shawcross.

Will was propped on one elbow, watching her with
those very blue eyes. And suddenly Annabella forgot
about his prospective bride, for she saw that it was as
it had been at Mundell, only far, far better, for his
eyes were full of love and tenderness.

'Oh!' She was in his arms again, tumbled back
amid the grasses, laughing and crying at the same
time.

And when he said, very seriously, 'Will you marry
me, Annabella?' there was never any possibility that
she would answer other than yes.

Later, when they were sitting with their backs to
the warm stone, Will's arm holding her possessively
close to him, Annabella was able to say all the things
she had wanted about Larkswood and their quarrel
and how she had thought he was betrothed to someone
else. Will seemed astounded.

'Betrothed to Miss Shawcross! No such thing, I assure you! Why, I haven't even seen her since she was
about twelve years old! How on earth did you imagine
that?'

Annabella wrinkled up her nose. 'But Amy said…'
She blushed a little, and went on, 'She had heard you
talking to James, and him mentioning that Miss Shawcross was to come to Oxenham, and also James saying
that half his female relatives had been in love with
you at one time or another…'

She could feel Will's chest move as he laughed. 'I

rather think,' he said gently, 'that Amy must have confused two separate conversations. James was referring to you. I had just implied that I intended to ask you to marry me.'

Smilingly, he pulled her to her feet and helped her to remove most of the grass seeds that appeared to have attached themselves to her crumpled clothing. Annabella's hair was tumbled in profuse disarray, but she did not care. Will himself looked scarcely less dishevelled.

'I shall have to go all the way back to Challen to change my clothes now,' he said, with a rueful smile. 'But I will take you back to Larkswood first, my love.' He brushed the hair back from her face and smiled again. 'I wish I didn't have to leave you, but I promised Richard Linley that I would see him tonight, for he travels abroad on the morrow. But we shall spend the day together tomorrow, if you would like...' Seeing the luminous delight in Annabella's green eyes, he took her hand and led her back to where the horses were patiently tethered, eating their way through a large proportion of the hedge. Will hitched both pairs of reins over his arm and led the puzzled but docile creatures behind them as he and Annabella walked slowly, hand in hand, down the hill to Larkswood.

Susan was in the courtyard, hands on hips, watching them as they wandered dreamily homewards. Her eyebrows rose as she noted Annabella's disorder, the brightness of her eyes, the curve of her lips in a tender smile.

'Susan,' Annabella began vaguely, 'Sir William

and I...' She looked at Will, smiled, and forgot what she was saying.

'You may wish us happy,' Will said, a twinkle in his eyes. 'Mrs St Auby has consented to be my wife.'

Susan's smile broadened. 'Congratulations, sir, congratulations, ma'am! And about time too!' She took Annabella's unresisting arm. 'Come, ma'am! I need to do something with your appearance before you break the good news to Miss Frensham! She may appear to be henwitted, but she is neither blind nor stupid!'

After Will had kissed her goodbye, with a reminder about seeing her the next day, and ridden off down the hill towards Challen, Annabella submissively allowed Susan to take her up to her bedroom, help her change into fresh clothes, and tidy her hair. She then went to acquaint Miss Frensham with her good news, accepted her congratulations charmingly, and sat in the garden for the rest of the afternoon, doing nothing but thinking of Will. When the chill of dusk finally drove her inside, she sat in the little drawing-room and spent more time thinking about the future. Tomorrow, after Will had called, she would go to Oxenham to tell her grandmother and Alicia the news...

Finally, when the house was quiet, and there was nothing but the steady tick of the long-case clock at the bottom of the stairs, she got up to go to bed.

It was another bright moonlit night and there was no sound except the wind in the trees outside. Annabella crossed to the hall window, still too happy and full of ideas to rest, and pulled the heavy curtain aside. She peered out. The night was suddenly dark, the full moon hidden momentarily behind scurrying clouds. Annabella shivered. Although she was beginning to love this wide landscape with its sweeping hills, there were times when there was something elemental about it, something that she could not understand. She was not a superstitious girl, but when the sun went down over the flat fields of the valley, or the moon topped the ridge of the hills behind the house, she would find herself held by a spell as old as time. But soon she would not be alone at night any more. She shivered again, but this time with remembered pleasure, not cold. She drew her shawl closer around her shoulders and picked up her candle to light her way upstairs. She had reached the first step, had her hand on the newel post, when the quiet of the night was smashed by the sound of horses being ridden hell-for-leather into the courtyard, followed by a confusion of voices and a hammering on the front door. Annabella jumped violently.

'Open in the King's name!'

A door opened upstairs and Miss Frensham's voice quavered: 'Mrs St Auby! Mrs St Auby! Whatever is happening?'

Swallowing the retort that she had not the least idea in the world, Annabella moved across to the door and started to pull back the heavy bolts. By the time she was ready to swing it open, Frank, the footman, had appeared, pulling his coat on, obviously having dressed very hastily. Miss Frensham was hovering on the half-landing in a dressing-gown of formidable respectability and an even more terrifying bedcap. Behind her the pale faces of Susan and the other maids could be seen peering out of the shadows.

Frank opened the door and almost immediately the hallway was full of jostling men, one of whom was barking orders. Miss Frensham drew back with a terrified squeak.

'You two, search the house from the attics down. Benson, go around the back. And, Jenkins—'

Annabella raised herself to her full height. 'I am mistress here and you, sir, will not search my house without first giving good reason why!'

The effect of her words was remarkable. Everyone froze. Then the gentleman turned slowly to face her.

He looked young at first glance, until Annabella weighed up the lines of age and experience on his face and put him at closer to thirty than the one or two-and-twenty she had first thought. Like his men, he was dressed in a uniform she did not recognise, for it was a sober black, very different from the scarlet regimentals of Jeffries and his like. And he was fair, with a youthful complexion which was turning a little rosy at the arctic tone of Annabella's voice.

'I beg your pardon, ma'am.' He executed a stiff bow. 'Captain Harvard, of His Majesty's Royal Navy, at your service. I was not aware that Sir William Weston was married.'

Annabella blinked, beginning to wonder if she had been drawn unwittingly into a farce. 'He is not, as far as I am aware. At least not yet. But what is that to the purpose?'

The gentleman looked at her properly for the first time, taking in her old dress and the hair loose about her shoulders. A shade of familiarity came into his manner whilst behind him his men fidgeted, uncertain whether to follow their orders or wait for other directions. A gust of air blew in and Frank tried to shut the door, only to be restrained by one of the burly posse.

'We are looking for Sir William to arrest him,' the Captain stated, with ill-concealed impatience, 'and you would do best not to obstruct us in our duty, ma'am! I must ask you to stand aside!'

Annabella lost her temper. 'You there, unhand my servant! And you, Captain, are looking in the wrong place! I am Annabella St Auby, sister-in-law to the Marquis of Mullineaux, and this is *my* house, not Sir William's! Now, explain your business, if you please! Arrest Sir William! I never heard such arrant nonsense! Miss Frensham—' the companion quailed before the martial light in Annabella's eyes '—please accompany us to the drawing-room!'

Captain Harvard looked slightly abashed as he followed her meekly into the room she had so recently vacated, with Miss Frensham bringing up the rear, somewhat embarrassed in her night attire. Annabella closed the door behind them and fixed him with a quelling gaze.

'Well, sir?'

'It would seem that there has been some mistake,' Harvard began, reluctantly admitting to his error. 'I understood that this was Sir William Weston's house, which was why we were sure he would be making for here!'

Annabella raised an eyebrow. She remained standing and deliberately did not ask him to be seated, and it was only Miss Frensham who perched uneasily on the edge of one of the armchairs.

'I fear you are making little sense, sir,' Annabella

observed coldly. 'It lacks but five minutes to midnight. Is it likely that Sir William would be abroad at this hour, particularly out here in the middle of nowhere?'

'No,' Captain Harvard said slowly, his gaze resting on her, 'it is not likely, but it is…possible.' Clearly he had not totally relinquished the idea that Annabella was Sir William's mistress, housed discreetly away from civilisation, and with her lover visiting her at this odd hour of the night. Remembering the encounter in the stone circle, Annabella thought how easily this could be true and felt the first cold touch of a censorious world on her happiness.

'However,' Harvard continued after a moment, 'the Master of Arms from Sir William's own ship recognised him just now on the road and we imagined he would be seeking shelter here.'

Annabella raised her brows with sceptical exasperation. 'I still do not understand you, sir. What of this cock-and-bull story about an arrest? Upon whose authority do you act thus?'

'On the authority of the Lords of the Admiralty,' Harvard said with a quiet satisfaction. 'Sir William Weston is accused of treason, and I am here at the behest of Admiral Cranshaw to arrest him on that precise charge.'

There was a deep silence. Annabella reached blindly behind her to grip the hard edge of the escritoire, leaning back against it for support. Her lips formed the word to repeat it, but no sound came, and it was Miss Frensham who spoke for both of them.

'Treason…' Miss Frensham whispered, white to the lips. 'Sir William! Surely not!'

Once again, despite her misery and confusion, Annabella observed a barely definable hint of satisfaction in Captain Harvard's face. It was banished as he felt her scrutiny.

'Yes, ma'am,' he said with wooden countenance. 'Sir William is called to answer certain charges that he abandoned the sea battle at Lake Champlain in '14 when he had not been given the order to cease his fire. And,' Harvard could not resist adding, with an unattractive pleasure in the words that was far from professional, 'the fact that he sought to resist arrest suggests to me that he feels his guilt most keenly. It was not the action of an officer and a gentleman!'

It occurred to Annabella, through the anguish of hearing the cruel gossip repeated as a formal charge, that Captain Harvard did not like Sir William Weston. Her protestations that it was only gossip and Sir William was surely innocent, died a death as Harvard's cold grey eyes rested on her face, weighing her reaction to his deliberately callous words.

'You look shocked, ma'am,' Harvard observed gently. 'Pray sit down. May I offer you some restorative?'

'Of course I am shocked,' Annabella snapped, disliking him all the more for his presumption in offering her comfort when he had been the cause of her distress. 'Sir William is a particular friend of the family—'

'Most distressing, ma'am,' Harvard concurred smoothly, 'especially as Sir William was wounded—'

Miss Frensham let out a small shriek, which fortunately masked Annabella's quieter, but no less heartfelt, gasp of alarm. This midnight burlesque was becoming more bizarre, more shocking, by the moment.

'Wounded?' she repeated faintly, and saw a faint look of gratification cross the Captain's face as he noted her pallor.

'Yes, ma'am, shot as he tried to escape.'

Annabella took a deep breath, determined not to show her panic. Miss Frensham had given a slight moan at the word 'shot' and was clutching the lapels of her dressing-gown together, as though she expected Captain Harvard's men to burst into the room at any moment and shoot the lot of them.

'So,' Annabella said as coolly as she was able, meeting the Captain's eyes very straight, 'let me understand you correctly, Captain. You are seeking to arrest Sir William Weston. You thought that you identified him on the road hard by here, you presumably called out to him to stop and identify himself, he declined to do so, and you shot him.'

The stark words seemed to resound in the quiet drawing-room.

'I can only repeat, ma'am,' Captain Harvard said with stilted courtesy, 'that Sir William is a wanted man whose own actions condemn his criminal behaviour.'

Annabella felt sickened. The Will Weston she knew bore no resemblance to the Captain's harsh description. And yet, how could Will, who prized integrity so highly, seek to evade capture and bring such disgrace on himself? As for the charge of treason, Annabella had never believed it true and did not do so now. And she had no intention of revealing her feelings to this hard-faced stranger who had invaded her house with such a lack of consideration. With a supreme effort, she looked him in the eye.

'I fear I cannot help your enquiries, sir. You may have rather more success looking for Sir William at his own house, Challen Court, of course. Now it is late, and you will oblige me by leaving.'

A faint tinge of colour crept back into Captain Harvard's face at her tone. He was clearly annoyed at the cool way Annabella appeared to be taking the news and he chose to ignore her instruction.

'How well do you know Sir William, ma'am?' he challenged. 'When did you last see him?'

Annabella moved towards the door. 'As I have said, Sir, Sir William is an acquaintance of my family,' she said with chilly courtesy, 'and I last saw him earlier today when he passed on his way to dinner in Lambourn.'

'You are certain,' Harvard persisted, 'that he has not been here this evening?'

Annabella raised a haughty eyebrow. 'Captain Harvard, do you think that I do not know the comings and goings of my own household? To my certain knowledge, Sir William has not called by here this evening.'

Harvard's chill grey eyes rested on her face. It was clear that he disbelieved her, even suspected her of hiding his quarry. Annabella faced him out bravely.

'I suggest you concentrate your search elsewhere, sir. You are wasting your time here.' She opened the door and stood politely to one side to allow him egress.

'And, sir, if you have any further questions for me,

you may return in daylight to ask them. It is late and I am for my bed. I bid you goodnight!'

Annabella was unsure how she preserved her calm whilst the disgruntled Captain marshalled his men and took them off into the night. By this time, the entire house was in uproar. Frank was giving a greatly exaggerated account of his involvement to the wide-eyed kitchenmaid whilst Miss Frensham was wringing her hands and showing all signs of giving way to the vapours. After a worried glance at Annabella, Susan led the companion tenderly back to her bed with murmured promises of hot milk laced with a sleeping draught. Annabella sat down nervelessly on the bottom step and put her head in her hands. She wanted to run out into the night to find Will. She wanted to hurry to Oxenham to seek help. Neither course of action would be profitable. She needed to think...

The door was still ajar, for Frank had neglected his duties to seek consolation in the kitchen and could be heard exchanging sweet nothings with the maid as she put the milk on the hob. Wearily, Annabella got to her feet and reached for the door. It swung inwards before she could touch it.

'Will you help me then, Annabella, in spite of everything you have heard tonight?' Will Weston asked softly, stepping over the threshold.

Paradoxically, Annabella found that she was angry, rather than pleased to see him. Having sustained the shock of Harvard's words and successfully concealed her desperate concern, she found that the sight of Will alive and well was curiously irritating.

'Will!' Her words came out with rather more ferocity than she had intended. 'What on earth is the meaning of this?'

Will tried to smile at her fierceness but the effort was rather strained and it was only when Annabella had had a few more moments to consider the rather greyish pallor of his face and the tight lines of pain about his mouth that she realised that he was hurt after all. His boots were covered in mud, his jacket torn and stained and he held his left arm stiffly, cradled by his other hand.

'You're injured—' she began, anger melting swiftly into concern as she stepped forward instinctively to take a grip on his good arm.

'The veriest scratch to my shoulder, but it has bled overmuch.' Will sounded weary and strangely detached. He swayed a little, leaning briefly against her. Annabella tightened her grip.

'Bandages, perhaps...' there was a trace of rueful amusement in his voice '...and do I ask too much for some food and wine? I am sorry to trouble you this way—' the blue eyes, clouded with pain, searched Annabella's face '—particularly when I am a fugitive.'

'Don't be foolish,' Annabella said shortly. 'Of course we will help you! You must come upstairs—'

'No!' Will's gaze narrowed with the effort of concentration, of holding off the faintness that threatened him. 'The servants—'

'Can be trusted.' As Annabella spoke, she heard Susan's footsteps on the stair and looking up, saw the maid leaning over the banisters. 'Quickly, Susan, to me! I think he is like to swoon...'

Susan asked no questions. With her help, Annabella

managed to help the semi-conscious Will up the stairs, then paused on the landing.

'Best put him in your own room, ma'am,' Susan said practically. 'The other bed is not aired and Sir William looks in dire need of rest. Here—' she helped Annabella steer Will into the bedroom '—I will go and fetch some food—do you go to Miss Frensham's closet and bring bandages and some of that revolting ointment she keeps…' She saw Annabella's look of alarm and added, 'Never fear, ma'am, Miss Frensham is already asleep. Just the mention of a sleeping-draught was enough to do it! No need for her to trouble herself any more this night…'

Miss Frensham was a confirmed hypochondriac and had a whole collection of bandages, dusting powders and ointments in her closet. Annabella trod softly up to her door and scratched quietly on the panels. A muffled snore was the only response. Tiptoeing into the darkened room, Annabella paused only briefly to check her companion's unconscious figure, bundled up in severe gingham with the huge lace bedcap perched atop her head and her curling papers rustling beneath it. Miss Frensham wheezed again. Reassured, Annabella started to take a vast amount of pots and potions from the cupboard, Miss Frensham's regular snuffling her only accompaniment. She backed out of the room and bumped into Susan again on the landing. The maid had her arms full of blankets and a pitcher of water held precariously in one hand. She ran a careful eye over Annabella's haul of medicines and nodded with approval, holding out her own load.

'Take these to Sir William, ma'am,' she ordered. 'I'll go to the kitchens and get him some food.' And, giving no time for Annabella to wonder at her complicity, she hurried off downstairs.

## Chapter Eight

Annabella found that Will had managed to prop himself against the pillows, but his eyes were closed and his colour bad, giving the lie to his earlier claims that he was not much hurt. There was dried blood on his sleeve, and a fresh, bright stain on his chest. As Annabella touched his hand, he opened those very blue eyes and tried to smile.

'Annabella… Thank God…'

Annabella poured some water with hands that shook a little, and helped Will into a more upright position so that he could drink. His head rested against the curve of her shoulder and, as she watched him, she felt a great wave of fear and tenderness overcome her. She brushed the tumbled hair back from his forehead with gentle fingers.

'I have bandages and some blankets,' she said a little gruffly, to cover her emotion, 'and Susan is bringing some food for you. I think, perhaps, that it would be a good idea to bind up that wound first…'

Will looked down and seemed vaguely surprised that the wound was still bleeding.

'Damnation…' He moved uncomfortably. 'Will you help me off with this shirt? A strange request to a lady, I know—' despite his pain, his blue gaze mocked her '—but we shall do better without it.'

Annabella was annoyed to find herself colouring up fierily. She slipped his jacket off and started on the shirt buttons with fingers which slipped slightly. The wound was to his shoulder, a deep gash that looked clean but was still bleeding slowly. Further down his arm was another, a smaller laceration that was nevertheless an angry red. Annabella's breath caught on a small gasp. She had never seen such injuries before, let alone had to dress them. She had not the first idea where to start.

'Annabella,' Will said patiently, after several minutes had elapsed, 'I would as lief not lie here forever! If you wash the wound, dust it with that powder and bind it up, I shall do well enough. The other is a mere scratch that will heal on its own given time.'

His matter-of-fact tone steadied Annabella, as it had been intended to do. She reached a little uncertainly for the cloth and dipped it in the bowl of water, dabbing gently at the gash until it was clean. She heard Will catch his breath and bit her lip in wordless sympathy, but though his face had paled visibly, he said nothing and made no further sound. The pale yellow powder from Miss Frensham's collection of medicines looked horrible, but once Will had reassured her again that it was perfectly safe to use, she dusted the wound and started to try to bind it up. Here she got herself into a considerable tangle, and it was Will who, having tended to plenty of men injured in action, took the end of the bandage and showed her how to wind it around him securely. Halfway through, Annabella became inexplicably distracted by the smooth, bronze skin of his chest beneath her fingers. She could feel the warmth emanating from him, smell the scent of his skin. She dropped the bandage, reached clumsily to pick it up again, and found her hand caught and held by his.

There was a light in those blue eyes, at once tender and demanding, which held her captive. He raised her hand slowly to his lips and kissed her fingers.

'Thank you,' he said huskily. 'You have been very kind.'

Annabella freed herself reluctantly and managed to finish tying the bandage. She found she could not meet his eyes. This sudden shyness was extraordinary, after the passion of earlier in the day. But that seemed like another world now. She busied herself in tidying up, pouring him another mug of water and fussing with his blankets.

'We will have some food for you shortly. You must be hungry...'

'Thank you,' Will said again, softly. He was still watching her with that odd mixture of tenderness and speculation. Then his expression changed. 'Annabella, I owe you an explanation. I heard what Harvard said tonight—or the majority of it, at least. I was outside... But—' the bitterness crept in '—you had heard the rumours about Lake Champlain already, of course.'

'Yes, and I never believed them!' Annabella was vehement in her need to reassure Will that she had never doubted him. 'When I heard them in Somerset I counted them as spiteful malice and nothing more. And now I have no more reason to believe them than

I did before!' She hesitated. 'The only thing I do not understand, Will…' her voice wavered, but she was determined to continue '…is why you did not agree to go with Harvard to clear your name. Surely you have nothing to fear? Surely you could establish your innocence beyond all doubt!'

A faint, rueful smile touched Will's mouth. 'You are more generous to me than I deserve, my love! What you should be saying is that a man who resists arrest rightly forfeits the claim to be treated as a gentleman and may expect to be thrown into chains! My actions suggest I have something to hide…that I must indeed be guilty! No doubt that is what Harvard will say! And all my acquaintance would expect me to have surrendered to him tonight, to be dealt with justly and considerately, escorted to London to explain myself to the Admiralty, perhaps, but not hunted as a criminal!' He turned his head away and closed his eyes for a moment.

'Then…' Annabella began, uncertainly, 'why did you choose—?'

Will's eyes opened again. They looked shadowed and very tired. 'Oh, yes, Annabella, you are right in that I could have cleared my name had I been given a chance. But that choice was never mine. Harvard did not challenge me as he claims. He shot me without warning. Oh, I do not doubt that, now he has lost me, he will tell everyone I ran from arrest. But the truth is that he tried to kill me and now he wants me dead!'

Annabella put a hand to a head that was spinning. She wondered fleetingly whether Will was delirious, but though he was clearly in pain, there was no real fever—not yet. But even so…

'You think I have run mad,' Will observed, reading her thoughts all too accurately. 'I assure you that it is true. Harvard never identified himself to me, never challenged me to stop...' He sighed. 'I had been dining with the Linleys over in Lambourn, as you know, and it was later than I expected when I rode back. It was dark, but I saw two men riding towards me. As I say, there was no challenge—they shot at me without warning. The first shot grazed my arm and, naturally enough, I rode off, thinking they were footpads. I had a pistol with me and could have taken them on, but it was dark and I could see no point in taking the risk... Then the second shot took me in the shoulder.' He shook his head. 'I fell off my horse, which was terrified and took off down the road as though the hounds of hell were after it. But I managed to scramble into cover, and in the darkness they could not find me. It was then that I heard them talking.'

The lines of anger and bitterness set deeper in his face. 'Harvard was swearing violently because they had lost me. He said that they had to find me, that I could not be allowed to live and tell the tale. I recognised his voice, for they were standing a bare twenty yards from me. And he addressed Hawes by name, which gave me pause for thought. Hawes was the Master at Arms on my last ship, but before that—and after—he was Harvard's man.'

'Then you are saying that it was quite deliberate,' Annabella said slowly, and Will nodded.

'Oh, yes, there can be no mistake. They set out to take me—and not alive, either. The tale that I was running from arrest was made up afterwards, to discredit me in case I came forward to claim Harvard had tried to kill me.'

There was a silence. The candle flame guttered. 'But why should Harvard do such a thing?' Annabella asked slowly. 'It is not that I disbelieve you, Will, but—'

Will shrugged a little irritably as though his wound pained him. 'That's the devil of it! I do not know! His original orders must have been to take me in, they can hardly have been to shoot me! And Harvard and I were never close friends, but I had no notion he bore me such a grudge! Damnation, I cannot think straight! I have spent the best part of the night since it happened trying to understand why he would do this to me!'

Annabella put a soothing hand to his forehead, concerned that it was starting to burn with a feverish heat. 'Try to sleep a little,' she counselled. 'Doubtless much will fall into place when you have a clear head! Now is not the time to puzzle yourself with this!'

Will gave her another faint smile. 'You speak much sense, sweetheart!' A shadow touched his face and he plucked a little fretfully at the blankets. 'But I should not stay here, bringing you into danger—'

'I am your future wife,' Annabella said strongly. 'Who should have a better right to look after you? Now go to sleep. You are feverish...'

She heard him laugh softly. 'So I am, but not the sort that you mean! I have been burning for you, Annabella, for a long time!' He caught her hand again. 'For a long time I have been afraid of what I would do, for I wanted you so much, and now here I am in your bed, but not in the sense I would have envisaged!'

'You *are* feverish,' Annabella reproved, trying not to smile.

She wrapped him in the blanket and left the water within reach. It seemed that Susan's food would not be needed, for Will seemed to be falling asleep before her eyes, and no doubt it was for the best. She stood for a moment, looking down on him, filled with love and tenderness as she considered the curve of his cheek, the silky thickness of those dark eyelashes, the determined line of his jaw, somehow softened now that he was so vulnerable. A faint knock at the door broke her reverie, and Susan slipped into the room.

'Sorry I was so long, ma'am. One of them oafish sailors came back asking some questions, but I sent him off with a flea in his ear!' She saw Annabella's look of alarm. 'No cause to worry, ma'am! Now, I'll sit with Sir William, for you look done up and no mistake!' She was shepherding Annabella towards the door as she spoke. 'Owen will be setting off to market early tomorrow and will get a message to Oxenham— I was thinking you'd be wanting them to help... And don't worry, ma'am—we'll take good care of Sir William, seeing as you're sweet on him!'

Annabella slept late, completely exhausted, and only awoke when Susan pulled back the bed curtains and put her cup of morning chocolate carefully down on the bedside table.

'He's proper feverish today, ma'am, I'm afraid,' she said, in answer to Annabella's enquiry about Will's health. 'Frank sat with him through most of the night. I've changed the dressing on his wound and it's starting to heal, but he's very hot and he hasn't woken. If you're going in to see him, ma'am, try to give him some more of that draught. It looks nasty, but it works well.'

Annabella dressed hurriedly and slipped quietly out of the spare room and across the landing. Though the entire household appeared to know of Will's presence and accept it with silent connivance, Annabella had no wish for Miss Frensham to stumble on a wanted man in her bedroom. The consequences of that would be too difficult to deal with. She abandoned the challenge of thinking up ways to distract her companion for the day, and pushed open the door of her room a little apprehensively.

Will had thrown back his covers and was tossing and turning restlessly. His forehead was hot and damp with fever, and he was murmuring a little in his dreams. Annabella bathed his face gently, but he did not wake, and after a moment she sat down on the edge of the bed beside him, just holding his hand in hers.

He woke suddenly a few minutes later. The blue eyes, glittering now with pain and delirium, raked Annabella's face but she was not sure if he knew who she was. She gave him some water, then the noxious black draught, which he tried half-heartedly to push away, before swallowing a small mouthful.

'Where am I...?' Will's voice was a whisper, his gaze narrowed with the effort of concentration. 'Annabella? Then it is true...' He tried to sit up and fell back with a groan, closing his eyes.

'Keep still.' Annabella pressed a soothing hand to

his cheek. 'You are quite safe, and soon you will be well again.'

Will smiled a little, his eyes still closed. 'Safe… A ministering angel…' Suddenly his eyes opened wide again and fixed on her face. 'Do you love me, Annabella? Tell me!' His hand was gripping her arm with surprising strength for one so ill, and his tone demanded an answer. A small chill touched Annabella's heart. Surely he could not have forgotten their betrothal so quickly? But then, with a fever, one might forget many things…

'Yes,' Annabella whispered, 'I love you very much, Will. I have done for a long time.'

Will relaxed almost at once, his eyes closing like those of a sleepy child reassured by her words. His hand slid from her arm and his breathing deepened into what seemed to be normal sleep. Annabella watched him, feeling her love for him uncurl inside her and expand until it felt as though it filled her whole being. No consideration of the crime of which he was accused could alter her feelings for him. But how they were to untangle this knot was less clear.

The door opened softly and Susan stuck her head around it.

'You must take some breakfast, ma'am,' she chided gently. 'Miss Frensham has just woken and is in a very delicate state this morning. I have persuaded her to stay in her room for the time being.'

Annabella sighed. Miss Frensham's delicate state, no doubt induced by the shocks of the previous night, was another trying circumstance to contend with whilst she tried to see her way clear to helping Will.

She stood up and went downstairs, her footsteps slow, her mind dogged with anxiety.

The day dragged by. Annabella, torn between worrying over Will's condition and puzzling over his allegations towards Captain Harvard, moped about the house, spent half an hour desultorily cutting roses in the garden, and watched the hands of the clock drag themselves round towards the afternoon. A hasty council of war between herself, Frank and Susan had led to the decision to move Will across to Lark Farm, where they felt he would be safer from both the attentions of Captain Harvard and any unexpected forays Miss Frensham might make into Annabella's bedroom.

The next problem was how to move the invalid, for Will had not regained consciousness and Miss Frensham was up and prowling about the house in an irritable sort of a way. In desperation, Annabella brought out the piece of embroidery which she had been working on for at least six months and which Miss Frensham had frequently criticised for its poor workmanship. The half-hour she spent going over its defects with her companion was tiresome and boring, but had to be time well spent. Fortunately, the exercise put Miss Frensham into far happier a frame of mind and after lunch she graciously agreed to arrange the roses Annabella had cut that morning.

Annabella, meanwhile, was beset by further doubts. When Susan had told her the night before that Owen Linton would take a message to Oxenham, it had seemed the best solution. Now, however, she was not so sure. James Mullineaux was, after all, a Justice of the Peace and probably the first person Captain Harvard would turn to in his hunt for the fugitive. Will and James might be the best of friends, but how would that friendship be sustained when Will had been denounced as a traitor and a criminal? Still, it was too late now. Annabella picked up a magazine to while away the tedium of the afternoon and almost immediately heard the sound of a coach pulling into the yard followed by voices in the hall.

'Annabella!' Alicia, immaculately beautiful as ever in a gown of deep green, hurried in to greet her sister. 'We had the most extraordinary message from Owen Linton this morning! Are you all right? What on earth has happened?'

It was not just the Mullineauxs who had arrived, Annabella realised, but Caroline and Marcus Kilgaren as well. Suddenly overcome with a rush of emotion at seeing them all, Annabella threw herself into Alicia's arms with rather more fervour than might be expected after a separation of only five days. Her sister, however, took this all in good part and only hugged her back.

'Oh, Alicia,' Annabella said, muffled, 'I am so glad to see you!' She let her sister go reluctantly and tried to compose herself. Caroline and Alicia guided her to the chaise-longue and sat down on either side of her, their faces showing identical expressions of woe. It would have been amusing had Annabella not been too upset to appreciate it.

'Well, Annabella,' James said bracingly, with the directness for which he was well known, 'what the hell's going on? All we have heard is some cock-and-bull story from Linton, in which he claims Will Weston was accused of treason and shot whilst evading arrest!' He moved across to the window and propped himself against the sill. 'I'd have thought him barking mad,' he continued, 'were it not for a visit this morning from some chap—Harvard, I believe he was called—looking for Will on behalf of the Admiralty! So?'

To her surprise, Annabella discovered that this abrasive unsentimentality was just what she needed. Where Alicia's sympathy might have encouraged the tears, James's straight talking forced her to confront the problem. Nevertheless, the mention of Harvard's name caused her to shiver.

'What did Captain Harvard say?' she asked tonelessly.

James moved restlessly to look out of the window. 'Why, he told us that the Admiralty had sent him to bring Will up to London to answer the charge of treason which had been levied. He said that he and one of his men had been given the intelligence to expect Will to be returning from Lambourn last night, and they had intercepted him on the road. They challenged him, at which he shot at them and rode off. They returned fire and brought him down, but could not find him.' James's face was sombre. 'Harvard was not slow to point out that Will's actions damned him as a guilty man trying to escape. He even hinted that Will might be unbalanced. I fear I did not take to Captain Harvard,' James finished, a little grimly.

'Harvard was here last night, after it happened,' Annabella said, with another shudder. 'He said much the same to me. He was sure that Will would have made for here to seek shelter.'

James raised his eyebrows. 'Harvard seems very sincere in his wish to find Will,' he observed gently. 'He even said that he was afraid Will might be dying on a hillside and asked for my help in mounting a search party!' James smiled for the first time. 'But I thought I should save myself the trouble!'

Their eyes met. 'Will is not here,' Annabella said truthfully, looking at them all very straight, 'so you need have no fear on that score!'

Alicia stirred. 'But is he safe, Annabella? Oh, don't worry about James—' she had seen her sister's look of apprehension '—as long as he does not know where Will is, he can answer all questions put to him by Harvard quite openly! We are more concerned that Will is injured!'

Annabella capitulated. There was such genuine worry on all their faces that she could not believe they would ever betray Will. Especially when they knew the truth. 'He has a wound to the shoulder and is in a fever,' she said carefully, 'but I do not believe it to be life-threatening, unless Miss Frensham's powders and potions carry him off! He is quite safe, but unfit to move for now. But pray do not tell Captain Harvard any of that! The more time he spends out on the hills searching for Will, the better!'

Caroline leant forward, going straight to the heart of the matter. 'But what does Will have to say about this, Annabella?' She frowned unhappily. 'I do not need to tell you that none of us can believe either the charge of treason or the accusation that Will shot at Harvard and escaped. Can there have been some mistake?'

'There is no mistake,' Annabella said bluntly. 'Will

told me that Harvard tried to kill him. They shot at *him* without warning, then tried to hunt him down. I assure you—' she had seen the shocked, disbelieving horror on the faces of them all '—it is true.'

There was a stunned silence.

'The charge of treason in itself is sufficiently bizarre,' Marcus Kilgaren said quietly, after a pause, 'but this beats all else. Will is certain that there can be no misunderstanding?'

'None,' Annabella said, with another very straight look. 'But, of course, it is only his word against Harvard's, and Harvard has a witness who will back his own story. Worse, Will is currently too ill to put his side of the story and Harvard is taking advantage of his disappearance to suggest that Will is condemned by his own actions! Will cannot simply come out and accuse Harvard of attempted murder—not when the evidence looks so bad against him! And he has no notion as to why Harvard acted as he did!'

'Now we see why Harvard seemed so mighty put out to have lost Will,' Marcus said grimly. 'No doubt he would prefer to find him dead on a hillside somewhere—or captured and locked up, with no one taking seriously his counter-allegations!'

'But what is it all about?' Alicia asked plaintively, putting in to words the one thought that was troubling them all. 'The charge of treason is the start of all this, and to accuse Will of such a crime is the biggest piece of nonsense I ever heard! Why, a man of greater integrity it would be hard to find!'

'Someone has been planting poison in the ear of the Lords of the Admiralty,' James said quietly. 'You may remember that there was some foolish talk a cou-

ple of years ago about how Will had run out of a naval
engagement and left another captain to face the enemy
alone. It was complete nonsense, but unfortunately the
story never quite died. Though how it has blown up
again now, I cannot tell.'

'I heard that malicious tale myself when I was in
Taunton,' Annabella said hesitantly, glancing at her
sister. Marcus's words had hit precisely upon what
had been troubling her, for surely a man such as
George Jeffries had no influence to raise such a serious charge against Will Weston. There had to be
someone else involved...someone with power, or at
least greater influence.

'In Taunton? From whom?' Marcus leant forward.

'Why, from Captain Jeffries,' Annabella said, still
hesitant. 'He told me of that and of other unsavoury
rumours about Will making a fortune from being in
league with pirates. But Jeffries has no standing—he
would never be given credence!'

'Maybe not,' Marcus reflected, 'but someone else
might...' He caught James's gaze across the room. 'If
Jeffries had repeated the rumour to someone with both
influence and a grudge...'

'Ermina Hurst has a cousin, or some such, at the
Admiralty,' Caroline said slowly. 'I remember her
mentioning it in passing one evening, but I was not
really attending, for you know how that woman rattles
on!' She caught herself up, and looked appalled at
what she seemed to be suggesting. 'Oh, but surely...
No! Even Ermina would not—'

'Miss Hurst did not take her rejection by Sir William in good part,' Marcus pointed out coolly. 'Perhaps she saw this as a means of revenge...'

'But we do not even know if Ermina knew this Captain Jeffries,' Caroline burst out. 'Oh no, this is too far-fetched for words! I am sure we wrong her even by thinking of it!'

Judging by the looks on the faces of the two men, Annabella thought that they were not so sure. And nor was she, when she considered it. After all, she had been a witness to the frustrated spite of Miss Hurst as she realised that both Viscount Mundell and Sir William were slipping beyond her grasp.

'Miss Hurst danced with Jeffries at the subscription ball in Taunton,' she said quietly. 'I remember thinking it odd at the time, for a man like Jeffries was far beneath her touch! But all the same...'

'It will bear investigation,' James observed, 'along with a number of other matters.'

The others looked at him enquiringly. 'Well,' James enlarged, 'it seems singular to me that Harvard should choose to seek his man in the middle of the night when he might have called at Challen in the daylight! That in itself is suspicious and suggests he wanted no witness to the encounter! I would like to know Harvard's original orders!'

'Admiral Cranston could probably tell us that,' Marcus said speculatively. 'Harvard mentioned this morning that he was acting under Cranston's authority—although he appears to have exceeded it somewhat!'

'But why did Harvard try to shoot Will?' Caroline said crossly, in the tone of voice that suggested the attempted murder was a tiresome parlour game. 'If only we knew...'

'If we knew that, my love, we would have solved the whole case,' Marcus said with a twitch of his lips.

James stirred in his chair. 'There's plenty we *can* do, however, whilst we wait for Will to recover and state his case! We need to trace some of Will's colleagues—those who could give testimony and clear his name of the treason charge. Then we can try to discover the background to all this from Cranston. And I will try to find some witnesses—any witnesses—to last night's events. It's a long shot, I know, but it's possible… When we've turned up anything useful I'll send word,' he added to Annabella. There was an irrepressible twinkle suddenly in his dark eyes. 'You have to hand it to Will—he has certainly hit on a novel way to effect a reconciliation!'

Annabella looked flustered. She had forgotten that she had yet to impart what had previously been the most important piece of news of all. She turned to Alicia, her green eyes suddenly bright. Despite their situation, nothing could dampen her happiness in her engagement to Will.

'Oh, Liss, the most marvellous thing! Will and I became betrothed yesterday afternoon! I had almost forgot!'

Announcements of marriage were usually followed by a flurry of exclamation and congratulation, Annabella thought with irony. Twice she had declared her intention to marry, and on both occasions the news had sunk like a stone. The first time, her father had stormed and raged, refusing his consent until she had lied that she had already given herself to Francis in the most intimate of ways. This time was little better, for no one said anything at all until Alicia recollected herself and got up to kiss her.

'I am glad that you have settled your differences, Annabella,' she began carefully, 'but—'

'I know!' Annabella sighed. 'You do not think it wise to contemplate a betrothal to a man who is under suspicion of treason and attempted murder!'

'Well, not precisely—' Alicia caught her husband's eye and fell silent just as the door opened.

'Mrs St Auby,' Miss Frensham said peevishly, 'the mildew has taken those roses and they are quite unsuitable! I have done my best, but no one will dispute that they are not up to scratch! And,' she added as an afterthought, 'that tiresome Captain Harvard is here again, poking about in the kitchen and asking questions! It's enough to give me a megrim! I am retiring to my room!'

Harvard was already lurking in the corridor, even as Frank, wooden-faced, made the unnecessary announcement of his presence.

'Captain Harvard is here to see you, ma'am.'

Annabella saw the mingled speculation and concern on the faces of her companions, and felt them range themselves behind her in a wordless show of solidarity. She got up and faced the door, a martial light in her eyes.

'Please send the captain in, Frank,' she said sweetly. 'Does he have his band of merry men with him?'

It was evident that the Captain had heard this last, for his colour was high as he came into the room and there was an angry look in his eye. This turned to greater annoyance as his gaze took in Annabella's visitors, especially when James came forward cordially to shake his hand and remind him of his fruitless trip to Oxenham earlier in the day. It was clear that Harvard had neither expected nor sought such an audience, and he too could feel the unspoken unity of the group ranged against him. He bowed a little abruptly.

'If you will excuse me, ladies and gentlemen, I have private business with Mrs St Auby...'

This did not have quite the desired effect. There was just the right degree of hauteur in Alicia's raised eyebrows to make him feel uncomfortable, and Annabella was quick to capitalise on this.

'I have no secrets from my sister, sir,' she said in honeyed tones, 'nor indeed from any of my friends. You may speak freely.'

It was obvious that the Captain did not wish to speak freely before everyone. He ground his teeth. 'If you would grant me a private interview, ma'am—' he began, but this time it was Alicia who intervened.

'Come, come, sir, it would not be at all proper for me to permit my sister to speak with a gentleman alone,' she chided. She settled herself more comfortably in her chair as Annabella gestured the irate Captain to join them, turning wide, innocent eyes on the Captain she did so.

'Well, sir? You find me positively agog... Have you had any success in your hunt for Sir William Weston?'

Captain Harvard swallowed hard. 'No, ma'am, we have not. Which is why I am here once more. You did not disclose last night that you are betrothed to Sir William! We have reason to believe that he is hiding here and I have a warrant to search these premises!'

This assertion was met with veiled amusement by Caroline and Alicia, and James turned aside to hide a smile, as though they thought Harvard was playing a part in a bad melodrama. Captain Harvard looked put out.

'This is no matter for jest, madam—'

'No indeed!' Annabella tried to look suitably grave. 'I do apologise! Only you see, sir, we have so little excitement out here in the country that I fear you have quite overset us! Please search to your heart's content! You will find the attics sadly dusty, I fear, but you must not neglect them! And we have cellars, too... Oh!' Inspiration hit her. 'And make sure you include the farm outbuildings in your search! Mr Linton will not mind!'

Larkswood was a relatively small house, but Captain Harvard was determined to be thorough and the search took three hours, during which time he became progressively more bad-tempered as his men found nothing. Nor could he get Annabella on her own as her guests settled down to play a game of whist in her drawing-room.

From the house they progressed to the farmyard where a furious Owen Linton, protesting volubly, was ordered to give the sailors access to his outbuildings. Annabella's confidence in him was not misplaced as he deliberately forgot to warn them of the uncertain temperament of the horse tethered in the far barn. Having sustained bruised shins from kicking, and painful bites to arms and shoulders, the search party shot out of the building straight into the cow byre where the floor proved unpleasantly slippery. Liberally smeared with dung, they assembled in the yard under the frosty eye of the Captain, who certainly could not see the funny side of the situation.

'I did warn you last night that it was all a hum,' Annabella remarked helpfully after Captain Harvard had admitted defeat and was standing in the hall calling his men to order. She brushed some straw and a few cobwebs off his uniform, smiling sympathetically at him. 'You will not find Sir William Weston here, sir. You would do better concentrating your attentions elsewhere!'

'I will be over tomorrow morning to pay my respects to Admiral Cranshaw,' James said, appearing in the drawing-room doorway and giving Harvard a civil nod that made him feel even more uneasy. 'I shall be interested to hear of the progress of your enquiries!'

Harvard shifted uncomfortably from one foot to the other. To have his incompetence rehearsed before his senior officer was almost more than he could bear, but he could not afford to antagonise a man of James Mullineaux's position and influence. He swallowed hard.

'You will find the Admiral at The Old Crown in Faringdon, my lord,' he said, as politely as he was able. 'I shall hope to join you there with good news of the hunt as soon as I am able.'

James allowed the faintest flicker of a disbelieving smile to lighten his face. 'Good man! Then we must not keep you from your search, Harvard! Have you tried the caves on the far side of Weathercock Hill?

They used to be used by highwaymen preying on travellers from Lambourn and might be worth a look!'

The Captain nodded his thanks and marched off down the drive as James said softly, 'What a pity I forgot to warn him about the marshes over that way! My tiresomely bad memory…'

It was late when Annabella trod softly down the garden, across the yard and up to the farmhouse door. A full moon had risen, shedding its bright white light across the gardens and accentuating the black shadows. Susan was waiting for her.

'He's still feverish, ma'am, I'm afraid.' Somehow she still managed to sound reassuring. 'If you could sit with him for a few hours, ma'am, Owen will come along to be with him through the night.'

'Of course.' Annabella paused, her hand on the doorpost. 'What happened when the sailors came, Susan?'

In the candlelight she saw the maid smile. 'Oh, Owen showed them round the farm before they went out to the barns… He had secured the door somehow—he claimed it was bricked up and even kicked it to prove his point! He's a fly one, is Owen! I could hear them talking outside, but they didn't suspect nothing, and Sir William never stirred. All's well, ma'am!'

Annabella looked at her, wondering at the unquestioning loyalty the servants seemed to have towards Will Weston. They had slipped into connivance without a word, just as James and the others had done earlier. It was extraordinary, considering that Will

Weston was a wanted man, yet no one, it seemed, doubted Will's innocence…

'Sir William is a good man,' Susan said stolidly, in answer to Annabella's unspoken question. 'Owen says that he was always a fair and just man, and his father the same before him. And Frank says that any friend of Lord Mullineaux must be in the right of it, so that's good enough for all of us, ma'am.' She bundled up the soiled bandages and picked up the lantern. 'There's fresh candles over by the wall, ma'am, and some water in the pitcher. If he wakes, give him some more of that draught. And if he's too hot, try sponging him down!'

The attic room of Owen's farm was painted white with a makeshift bed against one wall, tucked under the sloping eves. Annabella knelt down beside Will, attempting to bring some order to his tumbled sheets as he tossed and turned uneasily. Each time she tucked him back in he would throw the covers back as though burning up with the fever and desperate for cooler air. His skin was scorching hot. Try sponging him down, Susan had said. Annabella picked up the sponge a little gingerly. She had never considered herself to be a missish girl, but bandaging Will's wound the previous night had shaken her, and now she was not sure she could help him.

Will threw his covers off again, intolerably hot, and Annabella stared transfixed at his powerfully muscled torso, tapering with perfect symmetry to the flat stomach and narrow waist. Just like the previous evening, his smooth, tanned skin fascinated her. She began to gently soothe it with the cool sponge, encouraged as his restless movements slowed and he seemed calmer.

The blankets lay low across his flat hips and a little colour came into Annabella's cheeks as she tried to continue her ministrations and preserve his modesty at the same time. For a widow she was very prudish, she told herself severely.

The change in Will happened abruptly. It was not cold in the little room, for the evening was mild though clear, but suddenly he started to shiver violently as though all the heat had drained from his body. Annabella hastily pulled all the blankets over him, wrapping him up as tightly as possible, but it did no good. He was racked with shaking, his teeth chattering. Try as she might, Annabella could not kindle any warmth in him.

'I'm so cold…' Will's eyes had not opened, it was not possible to tell if he were really conscious, but the pitiful whisper seemed all too true. Without thinking, Annabella lay down beside him, wrapping her arms about him in an attempt to put some warmth back into his body. She burrowed under the covers, pulling them back over both of them to cocoon them around. It was not long before she was very hot indeed, whilst Will appeared scarcely less cold. Her clothes, whilst keeping her warm, prevented the heat from reaching Will. Annabella sighed with irritation. There was only one solution to both problems.

She got up, blowing out the candle and taking off her dress with brisk, practical movements. Her shawl made an excellent additional blanket, and in her shift she was able to curl up closer to Will and transmit her body heat to him. It was cosy and relaxing in their retreat and Annabella felt herself drifting into sleep. At the back of her mind she was wondering what on earth Owen Linton would think when he came in to sit with Will, and what Miss Frensham would say if she found her missing. Neither thought seemed to trouble her sleepy mind much. She slid into dreams.

Annabella woke to find herself cradled in Will's good arm, her face turned into the curve between his shoulder and his neck. His skin felt cool and fresh, and he was not tossing with fever or shivering with cold. Bright daylight was creeping into the attic room and with horror Annabella guessed it must be at least seven in the morning.

Worn out with emotion and worry, she had slept the night through and never even stirred. But Will seemed better, and that was the important thing. Better still, he had not woken and she was likely to be spared any difficult explanations of her presence. Annabella slid carefully out of his warm embrace, wincing as her bare feet touched the cold boards of the floor, and bent a little stiffly to pick up her dress.

'What the *devil* is going on?'

She had not heard Will move, but now she saw that he had raised himself a little against his pillows and was regarding her with amazement and disbelief in the pale light. Annabella was acutely aware of her semi-naked state, the transparent lawn of the low-cut shift. She clutched her dress in front of her.

'Oh! I had no notion you were awake! Are you feeling better now?'

'I feel much recovered, thank you!' Will's tones were clipped, but with a hint of puzzlement as though he could not recall precisely what either of them were doing there. 'Annabella—'

'I am so glad the fever has broken,' Annabella gabbled desperately. 'You have been ill for a day and night and we feared you would remember nothing—'

'I remember nothing of the past day, but I am not so ill as to think I am imagining the sight of you standing there in your shift,' Will said sharply. 'What's going on, Annabella?'

'I...we...' Annabella made a hopeless gesture with the dress, saw Will's gaze follow the curve of her breasts as revealed by the flimsy shift, and gave a squeak of desperation.

'Please, Will! Could you look the other way whilst I put my clothes on?'

'It seems a little late for modesty,' Will said grimly, but he turned over heavily and waited whilst Annabella fumbled clumsily with the fastenings.

'Now—' he turned swiftly back and caught her wrist as she would have scuttled past him '—you will oblige me by explaining exactly what you are doing here!' He looked at her scarlet, defiant face, and added, 'It does not take much thought to realise that you have just spent the night in my bed!'

'You were cold,' Annabella said crossly, 'and I could think of no other way to help you!' She saw his raised eyebrows and added, 'I did not expect my ministrations to be met with such ingratitude!'

'You were fortunate not to be in receipt of any ministrations from me!' Will said dryly. 'I may be sick, but you are enough to tempt a saint!'

Annabella snatched her shawl up. 'I am glad to find you so restored to health and bad humour!' she said, still cross. 'I will send Owen in to help you wash. I have no wish to offend your sense of propriety still further!'

* * *

'Mrs St Auby!' Miss Frensham's thin figure was stiff with outrage. 'As your companion, I feel I must make a stand against these night-time walks you persist in taking! I sought you out last night only to find you gone—'

'And I explained to Miss Frensham that you had thought to take the air, ma'am!' Susan finished, her impishly pretty face for once expressionless.

Miss Frensham rustled her magazine irritably. 'I shall be glad to see you married and off my hands,' she said, as though Annabella was a troublesome sixteen-year-old. 'Your sister was just as difficult—I fear it is the Stansfield blood!'

'So I have been told, ma'am,' Annabella returned politely, slipping into her seat at the breakfast table and applying herself to her food with enthusiasm. The sight of Will recovering from his fever had lifted such a burden from her that she felt ravenous.

'Sir William fancies himself recovered, Susan,' she later told the solemn-faced maid. 'Please ensure that Owen keeps him indoors for at least another two days to give his wound time to heal. I shall stay here to allay Miss Frensham's concerns and in case Captain Harvard returns.'

The day dragged by as slowly as the previous one. Annabella, prudently keeping out of Will's way to give his temper time to cool, went riding in the afternoon and came across a small party of sailors toiling through the heather on the hill, gloomy and streaked with mud and slime. She greeted them cheerfully and watched in satisfaction as they headed away from Larkswood. That night she resisted the urge to go to see how Will progressed, and slept soundly alone and in her own bed.

'He's asking for you, ma'am,' Owen Linton said the next morning, and with a little apprehension Annabella thought it was perhaps time.

She found Will up and dressed in an old frieze coat and pair of breeches which were clearly Owen's cast-offs and had seen better days. There was three days' stubble darkening his jaw, which Annabella inexplicably found rather attractive and, though he was still rather pale and moved carefully, he looked so much better that she found tears of relief prickling the back of her throat. His tousled brown hair added to his air of general dishevellment, but his eyes were alert and unclouded by pain or fever. He took Annabella's hand and gave her the searching look she was coming to know well. He drew her across to sit beside him on the bed, his eyes never leaving her face.

'I did not have the chance yesterday to thank you properly for your care of me,' he said, with a hint of a smile. 'I understand that you have been nursing me and it can have been no work for a lady. I am sorry—'

'I am not made of spun sugar, sir!' Annabella said sharply, taken aback a little by his formality. This was not the Will Weston she had come to know; that man would have taken her to task, perhaps, for her unconventional behaviour, but would not have treated her with this painful correctness.

'No, but...' Will frowned. 'Forgive me, I cannot remember anything about that night...I hope that I did not take advantage, or behave improperly.'

He looked so concerned that Annabella burst out laughing despite herself.

'For shame, sir!' She wiped her eyes. 'What can you be thinking of? You were a sick man, and I did nothing but try to make you comfortable! Neither of us should feel concerned by the situation!'

Will did not smile, and Annabella began to wonder what was wrong. Something was clearly worrying him.

'I know I have compromised you, but I fear I cannot offer you marriage whilst my name is under a cloud,' Will said, in a rush.

Annabella was silent, looking at him. The concern and misery was clear in his blue gaze; he looked as though he was begging her to understand. And the hurt and anger his words had caused melted away as Annabella realised what he was trying to tell her. His code of honour simply did not permit him to marry her when he felt he had nothing but ignominy to offer her.

She moved closer to him, until she was brushing against his body and could reach across to graze her mouth against his. She heard his breath catch in his throat as her lips traced a warm line down the strong brown column of his neck. It filled her with excitement to think that she could do this to him. She could feel his tension, the control he was desperately trying to exercise. Her fingers untied the laces of his shirt so that she could spread her palms gently against his chest, careful of the wound to his shoulder, but questing, searching, nevertheless.

'Annabella…' The word came out as a groan as Will fell back against his makeshift pillows.

'It is not acceptable for you to spend the night with me and then change your mind and refuse to marry me,' Annabella said, her voice prim but her drifting hands demanding as they moved lower. 'It is not the action of a gentleman, sir… I insist,' she added softly, 'that you give me demonstrations of your good intentions.'

Will was evidently not as weak as she had at first supposed. He moved swiftly to tumble her beside him on the bed, his mouth claiming hers ruthlessly. Their lips met and clung tenderly, sweetly, until he let her go reluctantly and sat up with a rueful smile.

'Enough of this! I have to think, and you have to help me, and it simply cannot be done when you distract me so. That was a very wicked trick, Annabella!'

Annabella snuggled closer to him. She had heard the amusement in his tone and pressed a lazy kiss against his throat.

'You did not want to resist me,' she said perceptively. 'If you had chosen, you could have done so! You wanted me to persuade you to keep your word!'

Will looked at her with his searching blue eyes. 'You are right,' he agreed slowly, 'and how well you understand me already, my love! As a gentleman I should not press my suit with you for you deserve better than this. But I shall take what I want, nevertheless! I love you and I will marry you as soon as I can.'

'It does not matter,' Annabella said stoutly, 'for we shall soon clear your name.' She reached for the food basket. 'Let's eat,' she said, ever practical. 'Susan has prepared you the most marvellous breakfast!' She gave him a naughty smile and stretched luxuriously. 'I am so hungry…'

'Minx!' Will said, his mouth full of one of the

freshly baked rolls and honey which Susan had packed for him. He ate ravenously and drank a fair draught of the new milk from Owen's herd, before settling back against the wall with a contented sigh.

'Ah, that's better!' Will's tone changed, became intent. 'Now, Annabella, you must tell me what has been happening these three days past. I need to try to piece it all together.'

Annabella obediently related the visit from Captain Harvard and also the call made by James, Alicia and the Kilgarens.

'James has been working on your behalf and said that he would be in touch when he had some information to impart,' she finished. 'Oh, Will, you do not think that this whole matter could be some outrageous mistake? I have been thinking about it the whole time and can make no sense of the matter!'

She heard Will sigh. 'I wish I could say it was easy to explain,' he responded heavily. 'I truly wish I could claim it all as a misunderstanding. But I know what happened that night, Annabella.' The conviction rang in his voice. 'Harvard set out to kill me. When he knew that I had somehow got away, he was determined to find me and silence me. I do not know why, but I know it is true.'

'When they came here that night, Harvard had a whole troop with him,' Annabella observed suddenly. 'Yet you say that there were only the two on the road…'

Will was looking at her with sudden concentration. 'I had not thought of it before, but that is both true and also suspicious. Now I come to think of it, I heard the troop approaching up the road just after I had reached Larkswood land. It would be interesting to know just what orders he had given to them. I imagine he intended to present them with my corpse, telling them that he and Hawes had courageously tried to arrest me whilst they waited for reinforcements to arrive, and that I had been shot trying to evade capture!'

Annabella shivered, folding her arms for warmth. 'You mean to imply that Harvard would not have wanted an audience for what he planned,' she said quietly. 'But Will, this is monstrous! What can we do?'

'Get to Oxenham as soon as James sends word,' Will said, a little grimly. 'There's strength in numbers and this house is already under suspicion. Then, perhaps, we may untangle the threads and try to work out what to do. Is your carriage ready?'

'Yes—Frank has it all prepared, but it is only a surrey, Will, little more than a cart and with nowhere to hide you!' Annabella desperately tried to think of a solution. Suddenly a feeling of melancholy assailed her as her doubts of the previous day returned. If they could not clear Will's name...

Will caught her wrist, pulling her to him. 'Remember I love you,' he said softly. 'You are bright and brave and beautiful, and I love every little bit of you, Annabella, not just the beauty on the outside.' He kissed her hard and let her go. 'Now, this is what we will do...'

They spent the rest of the day playing chess to pass the time and in the evening Owen came to tell them that Captain Harvard had set a watch on the house.

'Good morning, Captain!' Annabella, a wide-brimmed straw hat crammed hastily on her head and a shawl about her shoulders, sallied forth from the house with the breezy greeting on her lips. It had been somehow inevitable that Harvard had materialised as the carriage was brought out into the yard and he was surveying them all with deepest suspicion. His cold grey gaze took in Annabella's appearance, then moved on to Susan, who was carrying a large case, and finally came to rest on Miss Frensham. The companion, trailing yards of scarves and jingling beads, was exhorting Frank to be careful with her baggage and had barely noticed the throng of men and horses coming into the yard. When she finally looked up and saw the Captain's inimical gaze, she drew back with a start of alarm.

'Oh, you startled me, sir! Whatever can be going on?'

Annabella took her arm in a firm grip. 'This is Captain Harvard, Emmy—you remember him, of course?'

Miss Frensham drew herself up. She had indeed remembered the Captain. 'I recall the gentleman bursting in twice and making rash accusations,' she said haughtily, 'on the first occasion at some ungoldly hour of the night! I hope, sir, that you are not about to repeat the exercise!'

Emmy could be surprisingly robust, Annabella reflected, with a slight smile, noting the Captain's discomfort at having to upset so proper and elderly a gentlewoman.

'I apologise for discommoding you, madam,' he said abruptly, making a stiff bow. 'I am only doing my duty.'

'Still chasing shadows, Captain?' Annabella enquired sweetly. 'You are wasting your time with us, I fear! Still, if you have nothing better to do...'

Harvard did not rise to this calculated provocation. 'You are going away, ma'am?'

'As you see.' Annabella watched as Frank stolidly continued to put the baggage into the cart. 'A visit to my family for a few days, that is all. It has been planned for some time. Nothing exciting, I fear...' And she turned her limpid green gaze on the Captain.

Harvard was also watching the bags being stowed. It was obvious that there was nothing—or no one—else hidden in the cart, for there was no room. His distrustful glance swept over them all again: Frank, poker-faced as he carried on with his work, Miss Frensham glaring at him with mistrust equal only to his own, Susan waiting respectfully for her mistress to ascend into the surrey, and Annabella, still smiling with carefree charm.

'Sir William Weston—' he began.

'Is not concealed about my person, sir,' Annabella said, smiling widely, 'as you can see. Nor is he disguised as my companion or my maid!'

Miss Frensham looked affronted. Susan giggled delightfully.

Harvard lost his temper. He seized Annabella's arm. 'I do not trust you, madam! It seems to me that you have something to hide—'

'Unhand me, sir!' Annabella said, green eyes flashing. 'I am not to be manhandled thus! Your commanding officer shall hear of this!'

There was a rumble of wheels on the cobbles as Owen Linton's haywain started its ponderous journey out of the farmyard, weighed down not with straw but with a load of root vegetables on their way to market. In the next field, his cowhand was guiding the herd out of their pasture and down the track towards Oxenham. In a flash, Harvard had dropped Annabella's arm and swung round on the cart.

'Stop that cart!' He ordered. 'You men, bayonet those vegetables! *That* will be where he is hiding!'

Susan started to giggle uncontrollably as the sailors began to stab randomly at the turnips. There was an outraged shout from Owen as the vegetables started to roll out of the back of the cart under this assault. Turnips and swedes tumbled to the ground and surged across the yard in a yellow tide. Owen was struggling in the grip of two burly sailors, swearing and shouting. And no one was hiding under the vegetables. As the cart emptied and the blank space stared back at him, the colour suffused Harvard's face in a rich tide. Annabella was watching him with the sort of detached interest that could only add to his embarrassment and his men were sniggering behind their hands.

'Well,' Annabella said brightly, into the pregnant silence, 'we will be on our way then, Captain. I trust that you will be compensating Mr Linton for the damage to his crop. If you are fortunate, he may permit you to take some of the less-damaged vegetables for your supper! Good day!'

Harvard watched the surrey down the road before ungraciously ordering his men to help a grumbling Owen pick up his load. A few fields away, the cowhand was driving the animals through the gate to a buttercup meadow. But no one was watching him, and no one saw the figure that crept away from the comfortable cover of the cows' heaving flanks, slipped along the hedgerow and disappeared in the direction of Oxenham.

# Chapter Nine

'Oh, it was priceless!' Annabella said, several hours later, wiping her eyes. 'There was Owen, his face as black as thunder, and Miss Frensham muttering that Captain Harvard was clearly deranged, and turnips rolling everywhere... And I have always wanted to say 'unhand me'! It's such a theatrical phrase!'

'Poor Harvard,' James said, with patently false sympathy. 'He must have known that there was something afoot! You clearly have a talent for pretence, Annabella!'

'Well,' Annabella said pertly, 'if I need to earn my living I could always go on the stage, I suppose!'

'Rather than open a confectioner's?' Will murmured, with a bright, enquiring look. 'Will you, perhaps, settle for a smaller enterprise? A husband and family?'

Annabella's lips twitched. 'A greater enterprise, you mean! But the whole idea was of your making, if the truth be told! How did you fare with those cows, Will?'

'They were very amiable creatures,' Will said. 'So what do we do now, James?'

They were all gathered in the library at Oxenham, James and Alicia, Caroline and Marcus and now Annabella and Will. Alicia had drawn the curtains against the fading light and prying eyes, and they were all sitting in a circle before the fire.

The first thing that Will had been at pains to explain was Harvard's unprovoked attack, and his determination to find Will and contrive his death. Despite Annabella's assertions that they all knew and understood, Will clearly felt he had to make his friends believe in his innocence. He had sat defiantly staring them down, almost daring them to contradict him. But no one had suggested that they disbelieved him, and gradually the tension had left him.

Then James had said feelingly: 'You'd damn well better be innocent, William, for I've spent the best part of two days buttering up that old duffer Cranshaw on your behalf, and Marcus has had to go to Portsmouth, a town he swears he hates more than any other in the country! We don't expect to be told now that it's all a mistake and you're about to turn yourself in!'

There was a pause, then they all burst out laughing.

'I pity you trying to pump Cranshaw for information, James,' Will said with feeling. 'The fellow's a tight as a clam when it comes to business!'

A grin lightened James's face. 'Oh, at first he was reticent, but after we had broached our second bottle he became more loquacious!'

'James!' Alicia was trying to look disapproving. 'I

hope you are not suggesting that you got poor Admiral Cranshaw drunk just to gain information!'

James gave her an unrepentant smile. 'All's fair in love and war, as they say, my sweet, and this is definitely war!'

'So…?' Alicia invited.

'Well…' James settled more comfortably and stretched his legs out before him '…Cranshaw said that someone at the Admiralty—unfortunately he was not quite drunk enough to name them!—had been stirring up trouble by raising the old rumours against Will. The Lords of the Admiralty, more with the intention of exonerating Will than anything else, decided to ask him to come in to answer the charge, all very gentlemanly and without any hint of arrest. Harvard was the man they chose for the commission.' James shifted slightly, his dark gaze resting on the intent faces of his audience. 'Now this is where the tale becomes particularly interesting. According to Cranshaw, Harvard was violently opposed to the plan. He said that the rumours were nothing but spite with no basis in fact, and that Will should not be called on to defend himself against such base allegations. He was most vehement on the subject, Cranshaw said.

'And yet,' Marcus continued softly, 'a few days later, Harvard tried to shoot Will dead—with only one witness to the deed, and a witness, moreover, he trusts to support him. They failed and then tried to hunt Will down to kill him… It is far removed from Harvard's impassioned pleas to his masters at the Admiralty that Will is innocent of all iniquity!'

'It doesn't make sense!' Caroline said despondently. 'How can the man argue in Will's favour one minute and try to murder him the next?'

'And then brand him a criminal and outlaw!' Annabella finished indignantly.

Everybody exchanged glances. There was silence.

'My head is spinning,' Alicia complained, voicing the feelings of all of them. 'I feel as though I am looking at a mirror which turns everything back to front—'

Marcus gave an exclamation. 'Back to front! Of course!' He looked around their intent faces, his eyes suddenly bright with suppressed excitement. 'There is one possible theory that makes sense!'

Everybody waited patiently.

'Suppose for a moment,' Marcus continued in the same thoughtful tone, 'that the rumours are true.' There was a quick, collective intake of breath. 'I do not mean that they are true in relation to Will,' he added quickly, seeing the militant light in Annabella's eyes and smiling a little, 'so there is no need to glare at me! But suppose that there is a grain of truth in them. It is often the way with gossip and scandal. It has its origins in fact, but the real details become obscured.'

'I collect that you mean to imply that the rumours relate not to Will but to someone else,' Annabella said carefully, feeling her way towards the solution Marcus was proposing.

Marcus leant forward. 'Precisely,' he said in the same quiet tones. 'I suggest that we have been looking at this the wrong way up—or back to front, as Alicia said. We have assumed that the rumours are untrue, because we know that Will never abandoned battle as he has been accused. But what if it was true that a Navy captain *had* turned tail in the heat of battle and left his colleagues to fight on alone? And how if that captain was not Will Weston, but Charles Harvard?'

'And Harvard,' James added, 'knows what he has done, knows that he was safe whilst the rumours blamed Will, and knows that any investigation might exonerate Will and point the finger of blame elsewhere!'

'So,' Marcus finished, 'he tries to remove Will first, and with him the possibility of the truth coming out!'

There was a silence.

'Oh Marcus, what a splendid idea!' Caroline burst out, her eyes shining.

Marcus smiled modestly. 'It is good, isn't it! The point is whether or not it could be true!'

'Would it be possible, Will?' Alicia asked, a little hesitantly. 'I mean, would it be possible for one ship to be mistaken for another in the heat of battle? After all, most of us have no idea of how a sea battle is conducted!'

Will had been sitting back in his chair whilst Marcus propounded his theory. His pose was relaxed but his gaze was watchful, although a blue light had started to blaze in his eyes at the suggestion of Harvard's culpability. Now, he put his empty glass down gently and sat up.

'Yes, it's possible,' he said slowly. Everyone caught their breath. 'But unlikely,' he finished. Everyone sighed. Seeing their blank, disappointed faces, Will tried to explain. 'Even in a naval battle where you're intent on your own ship's position and that of the enemy, even with all the smoke that's generated and the hideous noise and confusion, a good captain is aware of the tactical movement of the fleet around him. If a ship of the line were to slip away and abandon the action, it would surely have been noticed!'

He sat back and took Annabella's hand in his, aware of the way in which her face had lit up with hope at the possible explanation, and fallen with disappointment a moment later.

'But surely that's the point,' she said, after a moment's silence. 'Someone *did* see something suspicious and that is where the rumour came from! Maybe not something conclusive, such as a ship just sailing away, for no doubt that would have ended in court martial! But something odd, something questionable...'

'You are very hot in my defence, my love,' Will said with a slight smile. 'Believe me, if I could make the facts fit...! But what of Harvard's crew? They would have known if he had abandoned the fight!'

'Not necessarily!' Annabella urged. 'Why, I read in the papers only recently of a ship that had run aground on Lundy Island when its entire crew were convinced it was still off Cornwall! They did not even believe the lighthousekeeper who rescued them when he told them where they were! So you see, Harvard's crew might never have realised precisely where they were!'

'I had no idea that you had such an interest in naval matters, Annabella,' Alicia teased slyly, watching her younger sister colour up.

'But Annabella's right,' James interposed. 'It could happen!'

Will was still looking sceptical. 'I'd like to believe it,' he said slowly, 'but—' He broke off.

'What is it?' James asked sharply. 'You've remembered something, haven't you, Will?'

'It may be nothing,' Will said slowly, 'but Harvard and I were next to each other in the line. Towards the end, when it was clear that all was lost, I went to the aid of the *Bellepheron,* which was under heavy fire. Harvard broke line at almost the same time. I did not see where he went, for there was much smoke and a mist coming up, but I assumed he had gone to the rescue of another ship just as I had. That was what he *said* he had done.'

'But surely the captain of the *Bellepheron* could exonerate you—?' Annabella began, only to break off at the bleak look on Will's face.

'Dunphy died,' Will said, 'and the ship went down.'

There was a gloomy silence.

'Then surely we could find out which ship *Harvard* claimed to have helped,' Caroline said bracingly, after a moment, 'and prove that he did no such thing! I'll wager that he lost his nerve and chose to run, pretending later that he was answering a call for help from another ship.'

'And then he hears that there are rumours that one of the ships was seen breaking the line, and is afraid that he will be correctly identified as the defaulter. So he decides to blame you, Will,' Marcus continued. 'He simply reverses your roles. In fact, I'd guess he was one of the first to stir the scandal, subtly of course, suggesting by implication that you had deserted. Nothing could be proved either way, for the *Bellepheron*'s captain is not alive to defend you, and equally no one identified Harvard as the real deserter.

But the mud sticks, and Harvard knows that for as long as you are suspected, he is safe.'

'It's a good theory,' Will admitted, a little grudgingly. 'But we will never be able to prove it!'

'Could we get Harvard to implicate himself, perhaps?' Caroline suggested hopefully.

'A trap…' Marcus and James looked speculatively at each other. 'Perhaps if we were to tempt him by letting him know Will is here—'

'No!' Annabella spoke strongly, her fingers clutching at Will's sleeve. 'It's too dangerous! Harvard does not trust us, he will be suspicious, wary… It's too much of a risk!'

'I'm afraid you're correct, Annabella,' Will said reluctantly, covering her fingers reassuringly with his own. 'Harvard would sense the trap, I think, if we were to use me as bait. No, there must be another way, though I cannot for the life of me think of it for now!'

'Do you remember which ship Harvard claimed to have rescued?' Annabella asked tentatively, determined to exhaust every possible possibility. 'If we could find the captain—'

'It was Dowland in the *Détente*,' Will said thoughtfully, 'but he is away at sea and has been since '14—' He broke off, seeing the triumphant look which flashed between James and Marcus. 'What is it? What have I said?'

'That's where you are wrong, old chap,' Marcus said, with satisfaction. 'Dowland isn't at sea any more. He's in Portsmouth. I should know—I saw him yesterday!'

This riveting piece of news seemed to call for another drink, and James refilled their glasses. The atmosphere in the room had lightened considerably.

'Why did Dowland never say anything?' Caroline enquired. 'If our theory is correct, one would have expected him to have exposed Harvard's fabrication.'

Will was shaking his head. 'You must remember, Caro, that Dowland probably never even knew what Harvard was saying. Immediately after Champlain, Dowland was given another ship and sent to the Indies. The rest of us were stationed off Canada until the end of hostilities. Until now, no doubt no one has asked him the right questions!'

'And neither did I yesterday,' Marcus admitted. 'But the one thing I did ask him was to come up to Oxenham as soon as he was able. I thought he might be able to help us. He arrives tomorrow!'

'So, James, do you have any further surprises to spring?' Will asked. He had changed completely, his blue eyes sharp and alert, the pain in his shoulder forgotten in this new excitement.

James grinned, catching the atmosphere. 'Just one! I had been trying to find a witness to Harvard's actions on the night he shot you, Will. And against all the odds, I have got one!'

The news was electrifying. 'But who on earth would be out at that time of night?' Annabella marvelled.

'Not you, then, my love?' Will asked, with a teasing look which suggested that he remembered Annabella's peregrinations at two in the morning.

James laughed. 'As it happens, Will, I know you will appreciate the poetic justice of this! You may remember that you were after a certain poacher who had dealt heavy losses to both the Challen and Oxenham estates. Well, last night we caught him! And last week he was in the vicinity of Larkswood... So, it is fortunate you did not catch him on the night you met Annabella!'

'Annabella!'

Annabella was still asleep when the knock came at her door. The lights had burned late in the library the previous night and she had not seen Will again. She and Alicia and Caroline had sat with Amy Weston, Miss Frensham and Lady Stansfield, chatting in desultory fashion, each trying to preserve the illusion that all was as normal. Amy had not suspected anything, but Lady Stansfield, with her sharp perception, had scanned the faces of both her grand-daughters, noted some hint of tension and kept her own counsel.

'Annabella!' The scratching at the door was insistent, as was the whisper outside. Annabella slid out of bed and went across to the door. The light had begun to seep around the bedroom curtains but it was still very early.

'Who is it?' she whispered, suddenly nervous.

'It is I. Alicia.' Her sister slipped into the room, fully dressed. Behind her was Caroline Kilgaren. Both were smiling, almost radiant with bright excitement. It struck Annabella as most inappropriate given the somewhat grim circumstances.

'What on earth—?' she began crossly, only to be shushed by Alicia. Caroline shut the door with exaggerated care.

'We have come to help you get ready for your wedding,' Alicia said, her eyes sparkling. 'Will would have come to ask you himself, but James and Marcus would not let him out of his room lest he were seen! But he says that if you refuse he will come for you anyway! He gave me a message for you, Annabella.' She frowned slightly in an effort to remember the words precisely. 'He said that he had told you he would marry you as soon as he could, and the time is now. Will you come?'

She watched as Annabella's green eyes filled with tears. 'I think he loves you very much,' she said gently, adding as the tears started to overflow, 'Caroline and I have been discussing it and we really feel you should agree to marry him!'

That fortunately had the happy effect of making Annabella laugh, although the sight of Caroline bringing forward the silver and gold dress she had worn for the ball at Mundell almost made her cry again. The two girls worked silently, helping Annabella into the dress and arranging her hair in an elegant cascade of golden curls. At the end, Alicia stepped back and sighed.

'Oh, you look so beautiful!' She had a lump in her own throat now. 'And here—' she produced a battered jewel case '—are the Stansfield diamonds. A fitting occasion for them to be worn again!' She hugged her sister. 'Our grandmother gave them to me to give to you specially. She is to be there this morning, for she says that, having missed my marriage to James, there is no chance that she will miss yours as well!' She clasped the jewels around Annabella's neck where they glowed softly with pale fire.

The little chapel at Oxenham had not been used for many years and the old priest was in retirement on the estate, but he had answered a summons from James Mullineaux to come to officiate at his sister-in-law's wedding. There, with two candles burning on the altar, Will Weston took Annabella St Auby as his wife.

At the last minute, descending the faintly lit stair, Annabella had clutched at Alicia's arm. 'Oh, Liss, is it not rather dangerous?'

Alicia had paused. 'Not really. Marriage is difficult sometimes, perhaps, as you well know, but not dangerous precisely…'

'No…I meant this…now. It is morning and if anyone were to be about…'

'Oh, yes…' Alicia was preoccupied with keeping her footing in the dark. 'But if Will is prepared to do this for you, Annabella—'

'I know, but suppose Harvard were to guess and burst in!'

'This isn't the Middle Ages, you know! This is a private house, and I doubt that even Captain Harvard would be prepared to risk everything by attempting to raid the premises!'

There was a moment's silence, then Annabella stopped again. 'Liss…'

'Yes?' Alicia had started to sound quite irritated.

'How can Will and I be married when the banns have not been read?'

'Because Will has a special licence, Bella! I believe he procured one a while ago—'

'Oh, I see! Will *assumed* that I would agree to marry him—'

'Yes, he did! And he was right, wasn't he?'

And now they were indeed man and wife, and the

priest was saying the blessing, his benign face wrinkled in a smile. Behind them, Alicia and James were looking besottedly at each other, Caroline and Marcus were holding hands, and even Lady Stansfield had a misty look on her face. Annabella stood on tiptoe to kiss her new husband.

'Now you have Larkswood back again,' she whispered irrepressibly, and saw him smile, but he did not answer.

Lady Stansfield, trying not to yawn at the earliness of the hour, kissed her grand-daughter and her new grandson-in-law, and then Alicia and Caroline escorted Annabella back up the stair to her room and helped her out of the wedding dress.

'Well,' Annabella said, a little inadequately, 'what shall I do now? It can only be nine o'clock, but I suppose I should get dressed properly.'

'Why not go back to bed for a little?' Caroline suggested pragmatically, but with a twinkle in her eye. 'You had a very tiring day yesterday, and Will has been ordered to rest, but perhaps he would like to share a breakfast here with you first...'

She dismissed Annabella's high-necked cotton nightdress with a wave of one hand, bringing forward one of Alicia's delicious gauzy creations. To Annabella's mind this was rather filmy, revealing far more than it concealed, and she was suddenly overcome by an extraordinary wave of shyness.

'Oh, but surely—' she could feel herself colouring up '—is this not a little impractical for breakfast? Something more modest...'

Caroline raised an expressive eyebrow at Alicia.

'There will only be yourself and Will here,' Alicia

said, trying not to laugh, 'and there is a wrap to go with the nightdress…here…'

The wrap was no more concealing than the night-gown, Annabella thought, obediently putting it on. She was suddenly beset with nerves. It did not appear to help when she told herself that she was no innocent, and that she had already spent a night with Will, albeit in different circumstances. She had longed for this moment, but now she was afraid. Her experience of Francis's lovemaking had not been a pleasant one, after all, and despite the pleasure she had found in Will's kisses, there was no guarantee that matters would be any easier with him… She managed to frighten herself so much that when Will came into the room some fifteen minutes later, he found his bride huddled under the blankets and looking at him with distinct nervousness.

Will smiled a little, bringing a bottle of champagne and two glasses over to the bedside and sitting down on the edge of the bed as though it were the most natural thing in the world for Annabella to suddenly find him invading her bedroom. He poured for them both and raised the glass in a toast to her. The champagne bubbles tickled Annabella's nose as she looked at him warily over the rim of the glass, the sheet tucked tightly around her.

As well as the champagne, Will had brought soft bread rolls, still warm from the oven, with rich golden butter and honey. Annabella, surprised to find herself hungry, ate and drank her fill and finally set her glass down rather reluctantly. Will yawned suddenly.

'Lord, I'm still so tired! My shoulder aches…

Could I…would you mind if I were to rest for a while…?'

Annabella immediately felt guilty. 'Oh! Your shoulder! I almost forgot. Of course…' She turned away, deliberately averting her gaze in an agony of shyness as Will wearily stripped off his clothes, slid into bed beside her and blew out the candle. There was a moment of tense silence, then Will sighed again.

'Annabella, I'm so sorry, would you mind if I just hold you gently? I feel a little cold…' He did indeed sound very fatigued and Annabella reproached herself for her self-consciousness when Will was evidently too tired to care about anything other than his physical discomfort. The flimsy, transparent nightdress need not matter, she reassured herself. He would not see it, and at least it would provide a barrier between them…

Will moved closer to her and Annabella was suddenly acutely aware of his body curved against hers, even through the almost non-existent encumbrance of the nightdress. Contrary to what he had said, he actually felt very warm. She could feel his chest brushing against her back, his thigh just touching hers, the gentle caress of his lips against the sensitive skin of her neck. He slid his good arm around her, pulling her closer, and settled down with a relaxed sigh.

Annabella found herself unable to rest. She was acutely and intensely aware of both him and the inconvenient demands of her own body. Her mouth was dry and it was not nerves that quickened her breathing now. The more she tried to distract her thoughts, the more they obsessed her. She imagined Will lifting the swathe of honey-coloured hair from her shoulder and sliding the silky material away so that he could press his lips to her naked skin. Suddenly she wanted him desperately. She gave an involuntary moan. Will shifted irritably.

'Whatever is the matter, Annabella?'

Annabella wriggled frantically to try to get away from him but he held her still. A delicious ache of anticipation in the pit of her stomach now threatened to overwhelm her. Her nerves had fled but she was frantic that Will should not guess her state, not when he was tired and hurt, and needed only to rest. She wriggled again.

Will rolled away from her, pulling her over on to her back in the process. Annabella opened her eyes to see him leaning on one elbow looking down at her. It was very dark in the room and she could not discern his expression. His fingers were absentmindedly entwining themselves in the curls of hair that nestled at her throat, just grazing her skin with the lightest of caresses. Annabella tried to ignore the tiny tremors of sensation which his touch was awakening.

'I'm so sorry,' she said in a rush. 'I know you are tired, but I find I cannot sleep. Perhaps I should read for a while, or get up and dressed—'

Will's mouth coming down on hers cut off any other inanities that she might have chosen to utter. Annabella's gasp of mingled surprise and pent-up relief was lost, as were any coherent thoughts that had previously been in her mind. She was helpless with desire, weak with the taste and feel of him. And he lingered over the kiss, prolonging their pleasure until Annabella was almost begging him to move on, digging her fingers into his back, pressing against him with abandonment.

It was then that Annabella discovered just how wickedly erotic her borrowed nightdress proved to be, for it fastened with a series of small buttons down the front which Will was now proceeding to undo with thorough and tormenting slowness. His lips brushed the hollow of her throat, pressing a trail of tiny kisses downwards. The material parted slightly, tantalisingly, and he traced its progress to the cleft between her breasts, sliding the silky fabric away slowly so that he could bend his head to her sensitised nipples. Annabella writhed beneath him, pulling him hard against her, but he resisted her blandishments.

'Oh, no, sweetheart… I've waited a long time for this and I don't intend to hurry…'

Annabella twined her fingers in his hair as his hands and lips continued their wicked provocation. The nightdress finally slid away from her shoulders and arms, leaving her naked to the waist. And Will had finally lifted his head from her breasts and was moving downwards again, hesitating once more over each button, his mouth still following the path of his fingers to stroke and caress and tease. His fingers skimmed the soft skin of her stomach, and the fluttery, demanding ache within Annabella intensified. She arched against him, desperate with need. With a gentle movement, Will turned her on her side so that she had her back to him and they were lying as they had been at the start. But this time Annabella was shockingly aware of his arousal, the hardness of him pressed against the curve of her bottom. She gave a little gasp.

Will's fingers moved to cup her breast and she

gasped again, willing him to end this torment. The nightdress was unfastened as far as her hips, but its slippery folds were entwined about them in a manner which suddenly seemed excessively stimulating. Then she felt Will's hands move to undo the last buttons and the material fell away.

His leg slid between hers, his fingers straying across the softness of her inner thighs. Annabella's eyes were open wide as she drifted with the unimaginable pleasure of Will's touch. She slid onto her back again, her lips parting as Will raised himself above her to reclaim her mouth in a kiss as deep as it was protracted. His hands were on her hips as he moved her beneath him. And when he finally put an end to all waiting, taking her with a fiercely gentle demand, Annabella thought nothing of the past and was enveloped in the exquisite fulfilment of the present.

Later, lying amidst their tangled sheets, with the candle relit and the champagne consumed, she looked somewhat accusingly at her husband.

'I thought that you were tired, Will! I was at great pains not to disturb you—'

With one swift gesture, Will pulled back the tumbled bedclothes and considered her naked body, holding the sheet out of her reach when she would have snatched it back.

'I defy anyone not to be disturbed by the feel and the touch of you,' he said softly. 'And if I was a little less weary than you imagined, well... No—' as she made another determined grasp at the sheet '—you denied me the sight of you before, Annabella—I insist that now I make up that deficit.'

Annabella shivered a little before the concentrated

desire in his face. She put out a hand and tentatively touched his shoulder. 'But your arm… Should you not be resting?' Unconsciously, her fingers brushed across the bronzed skin of his chest, revelling in the feel of him.

'The doctor tells me that I should spend some time in bed,' Will said with the shadow of a smile, 'and we have an entire day before we can put our plans into practice tomorrow night, so I intend to take his advice…'

Charles Harvard was ill at ease in the elegant dining-room of the Marquis of Mullineaux's house at Oxenham. It was not the grandeur of the company or the estate that overawed him, but the uncomfortable feeling of walking into the lion's den. At first, when he and Admiral Cranshaw had received their invitation to dine, Harvard had begged his superior officer to excuse him, arguing that his duty conflicted with the occasion. Cranshaw had called him a damn fool and looked at him as though he really believed Harvard to be mad.

'Can't afford to offend an influential man like James Mullineaux,' he grunted, shovelling his breakfast kedgeree down his throat as he spoke. 'Besides, Mullineaux's sound—may be a friend of Will Weston, but wouldn't do anything to prejudice the course of our investigation! Damn it, the man's a justice of the peace and a damned fine shot besides! Would have thought an ambitious young officer like yourself would be glad of an opportunity to further your acquaintance!'

Faced with his Admiral's monumental displeasure

and utterly unable to explain himself, Harvard had been persuaded to attend for dinner, and had almost immediately felt vastly uneasy. He found himself next to Lady Stansfield at dinner, an unkindness on the part of his hostess which could scarcely be matched.

The old Countess had eyed him up and down with disfavour and said, 'Harvard? Of the Yorkshire Harvards?'

It was impossible to tell from her tone whether it would be a good or bad thing to claim kinship with the unknown Yorkshire cousins, so the Captain had explained that his was the Sussex branch of the family. Lady Stansfield had sniffed her disapproval but offered no comment. As a fine turbot stuffed with spinach and ham followed the soup, Harvard began to relax infinitesimally. Lady Stansfield spoke again.

'Making any progress on your wild-goose chase?' she enquired affably.

Before the Captain could think of a tactful response, Alicia had interrupted from further down the table.

'Grandmama, it is not really appropriate to ask poor Captain Harvard about business whilst we're at dinner!'

'I should say not,' James agreed with deliberate tactlessness. 'I'm the sure the Captain don't want reminding of his lack of success!'

Harvard flushed.

'Have you seen the Regent's Pavilion at Brighton?' Lady Stansfield enquired, with suspicious affability.

'Yes, ma'am,' Harvard decided to risk it. 'I thought it most attractive.'

'Monstrosity! Carbuncle!' Lady Stansfield spoke

through a mouth of spinach. Harvard thought he also heard her say 'Stuffed shirt!' but he could not be sure.

Further down the table, as far away from Captain Harvard as possible, Annabella sat watching her grandmother bait him. Seeing Harvard, knowing what he had tried to do to Will—to her husband—made just sitting in the same room with him a trial for Annabella. But she understood the necessity for a cool head. Just as she had helped Will by hiding him through the time at Larkswood, now she would help them trap his would-be murderer.

Marcus was talking to Admiral Cranshaw, who was in high good humour as his glass was filled and re-filled and a loin of beef succeeded the turbot.

'I hear that John Dowland is back in port,' he was saying casually.

'Ah,' Cranshaw nodded sagely. 'Dowland's back, is he? Sound man, sound man. Bruising rider to hounds, too!' He took a swill of his wine. 'D'y hear that, Harvard? Dowland's back! Must be all of two years since you saw him, eh?'

Harvard dropped his fork on the floor and snapped at the footman who bent to retrieve it. He appeared to have gone very pale.

'Bad *ton* to blame the servants,' Lady Stansfield observed malevolently. 'Very bad *ton,* young man!'

Harvard ignored her. 'Are you sure, my lord?' He was addressing Marcus Kilgaren, who looked rather surprised.

'Why, yes, I heard it from Will Weston before he disappeared! I remembered it particularly, for Will said he planned to go to Portsmouth to see Dow-land…'

Harvard was already half out of his chair when he realised that all eyes were upon him and he sank back, reddening.

'Extraordinary behaviour!' Lady Stansfield said, looking down her nose.

Cranshaw, his face as red as the wine, seemed to have noticed nothing amiss. 'Aye, a good captain, Dowland was,' he reminisced. 'It would have been at Lake Champlain that you last saw him, eh, Charles? His was the only other ship the Americans couldn't take, apart from yours and Weston's...'

'Yes, sir,' Harvard said woodenly.

'I expect Dowland remembers Champlain well,' James said pleasantly. 'I'm sure he'd be an interesting man to talk to...'

'Oh, fine fellow!' Cranshaw agreed enthusiastically. 'Of course, he's been out of touch a long time; after the battle at Champlain he was sent to the West Indies... Portsmouth, you said, Kilgaren? Well, well, he'll be glad of some shore leave, no doubt... What's the matter, Harvard?' Cranshaw had flushed even more red with annoyance as his junior officer had stood up. 'Meal's not over yet, y'know!'

'Perhaps the Captain has been at sea too long,' Annabella murmured *sotto voce*. 'Here on land it is the *ladies* who retire first!'

There was general laughter. Cranshaw waved aside Harvard's impassioned 'Sir!'

'Later, man, later!' He was not to be denied his pudding. 'I declare, you're behaving damned oddly tonight!'

Harvard subsided again. But they had not finished with him yet.

'Heard an extraordinary story from my gamekeeper today,' James said, his eyes meeting Alicia's briefly with a wicked twinkle. 'Apparently he apprehended a poacher last night, a man from Challen, whose enterprises have taken him as far afield as the borders of Sir Dunstan Groat's land. Anyway, the man told a story that might interest you, Cranshaw.'

The Admiral grunted through a mouth of pudding. Harvard had gone a pasty white.

'Seems he was out the night Will Weston disappeared,' James continued, with blithe disregard for Harvard's sickly countenance, 'and says that he has some information that might be of interest. I promised to go to hear his tale tomorrow...'

Harvard raised his wineglass with a hand that shook slightly. Some wine splashed on to the white cloth.

'If he has information germane to our enquiry—' his voice sounded strained even to himself '—then he should be turned over to our authority...'

There was a sudden silence. James, who had been helping Annabella to some more dessert, turned and raised his black brows.

'My dear Harvard,' he spoke quite gently, 'the man was caught armed and resisting arrest, and with some of my deer! He is on a capital charge! But I am happy for the Admiral to accompany me if he wishes to hear the fellow's tale—'

'No!' Harvard caught himself. 'That is, a criminal such as that cannot be a reliable witness—'

'Nonsense, Harvard!' Cranshaw wiped his mouth on his napkin and laid it down with a sigh of satisfaction. 'If the fellow's got some information about Weston, I should be pleased to hear it!' He was feeling more generous now, more expansive. 'Tell you what, Harvard, you're always set on work, that's your trouble!' He waved an arm in effusive appreciation.

'Fine food, excellent cellar, pretty women...' he approximated a courtly bow at Annabella, who smiled back '...and all you can think about is questioning prisoners! Dashed dull, what!'

The door opened. Fordyce trod softly into the room and whispered urgently in James's ear. James threw down his napkin and stood up.

'Seems you will have a chance to speak to Dowland sooner than you might have expected, sir,' he said pleasantly to Cranshaw. 'He is here now, in fact, and asking to see you urgently. And I understand that he has Sir William Weston with him! Why, Harvard—' James's voice was suddenly as cold as ice '—wherever can you be going in such a hurry? Fordyce, Liddell, please detain the Captain for a moment. There is something I am sure he must be interested to hear...'

'Here we are like three grass widows,' Caroline complained disconsolately, two days after the gentlemen had left for London. She cast aside her magazine with a grimace. 'Why must we sit here tamely waiting for them to come back to us? Can we not entertain ourselves?'

Annabella sighed. It was raining, which seemed peculiarly appropriate. To have had Will snatched from her arms so soon after their marriage was particularly hard to bear, but she knew he had to go to clear his name and sort out all the unpleasantness occasioned by Harvard's own arrest for both treason and attempted murder.

When the Master-at-Arms, Hawes, had become aware of his captain's arrest he had hastened to vindicate himself and blame all on Harvard. His testimony, taken with that of James's poacher, was sufficient to clarify the matter of the attempted murder. Captain Dowland's assertion that he had seen Will Weston go to the aid of the stricken *Bellepheron* and that he had neither needed nor gained Harvard's aid at Champlain, was even more damning. It became apparent that Marcus's theory had been correct and that Harvard had lost his nerve in the dying stages of the sea battle, fearing capture so much that he had abandoned the conflict and fled. In the heat of the action no one had clearly seen or even guessed his deed, except for Hawes who was as guilty of treason as his master. And when Harvard had heard the first rumours swirl that a captain had abandoned the fight, he had been quick to pin the blame on Will Weston.

That left only the small matter of identifying the person who had stirred up the rumours again two years later and Will had been confident that he could find that out when he went to the Admiralty. It was ironic, Annabella thought, that Harvard had had more reason than anybody to prevent the Admiralty taking the rumours seriously, and that when they had done so he had been forced to revert to his murderous plan to try to save his own skin...

'So what do you suggest, Caro?' Alicia asked, cutting across Annabella's thoughts.

'Why, that we too should go up to London!' Caroline jumped to her feet. 'The Little Season will have started and anything is better than moping around here! Mrs Weston may not care to accompany us, but

I'll wager Lady Stansfield would be game! Come, what do you say?'

Annabella felt a sudden rush of excitement. She had never been to London and it would have the added advantage of bringing her nearer to Will.

'Well...' Alicia said cautiously, trying not to smile as she saw her sister's bright eyes fixed on her pleadingly, 'perhaps...'

'Capital!' Caroline clapped her hands. 'I will make arrangements at once! And,' she added, with a very naughty smile, 'we shall not send word to the gentlemen, I think! They will hear soon enough!'

The ballroom at Stansfield House had seen many a spectacular social occasion but none so impressive as the ball given by Lady Stansfield a week later. The *haut ton* had been stunned to discover her ladyship back in Town, accompanied by not one but both of her beautiful granddaughters. That those granddaughters appeared to be unaccompanied by their husbands was an even greater bonus.

In the days preceding the ball, Annabella had had to be almost forcibly restrained from going out to see the sights of the city and in particular to acquaint herself with the delights of the Bond Street shops. The impact of their arrival would be all the greater for having kept themselves hidden away, Alicia and Caroline argued, and Annabella acquiesced reluctantly, having extracted a promise from her sister that they would go on a shopping expedition as soon as possible. But on the night of the ball Annabella was forced to admit that her sister's strategy had been sound. The ballroom itself, decorated with tiny coloured glass lanterns and stained glass panels which cast ethereal coloured shadows, was the perfect foil for herself and Alicia. In a rich strawberry silk and lace dress Annabella felt more elegant than she had ever been, and the distinction of the company made the event a far cry from the provincial assemblies she was accustomed to.

Hugo Mundell, accompanied by his sister and her fiancé John Dedicoat, were amongst the first arrivals. Mundell seemed in high good humour to see Annabella again, pressing a leisurely kiss on her hand and complimenting her on her appearance.

'I understand that it is customary to congratulate a lady on her marriage,' he added with a smile. 'Alas, Lady Weston, I find I can only be sorry to hear of yours! Will has snatched you away before the rest of us had a fair chance!'

Annabella, diverted by the novelty of being addressed by her married name, thanked him prettily for the compliment and agreed to grant him two dances later in the evening.

'But where is Will this evening?' Mundell pursued, looking round. 'Surely he cannot have been foolish enough to leave you alone so soon after the wedding?'

Annabella smiled. 'Alicia, Caroline and I are all without our husbands this evening,' she confirmed. 'They have far weightier matters to contend with! Will has been at the Admiralty these ten days past over this business of Harvard and the treason trial!'

'Yes, I heard of that.' Mundell frowned. 'Extraordinary business, but I am very glad Will has finally been able to settle matters. Do you have any idea how the rumours started up again?'

Annabella had just seen Miss Hurst enter the ball-room on the arm of a very distinguished-looking elderly gentleman. 'I have a suspicion...' she murmured.

Mundell followed her gaze and raised his eyebrows. All he said was, 'I see Miss Hurst has her latest quarry in tow! She has great hopes of bringing him up to scratch! That, Lady Weston, is the Duke of Belston, and if he is not in the first flush of youth and does not have any land or fortune left, he is at least sufficiently important to engage her interest!'

It was much later in the evening that Annabella found herself in the ladies' withdrawing room at the same time as Ermina Hurst. Miss Hurst's bright brown eyes appraised her with dislike, taking in the beautifully cut pink dress and the elegant tumble of Annabella's honey-coloured curls.

'Lud, Mrs St Auby—or, Lady Weston, as I suppose I must call you now—who would have thought that you could have been transformed from country mouse to society matron so easily!' she gushed. 'To become your grandmother's heiress, and to catch Will Weston into the bargain! But...' her eyes sparkled with the malicious pleasure Annabella remembered all too well '...I hear Will has forsaken you already!'

'Only to pursue an important matter of business, Miss Hurst,' Annabella said sweetly. She swung round suddenly. 'A matter which you, perhaps, have some knowledge of? Gossip always was one of your accomplishments, was it not, albeit one you did not mention when we first met?'

Miss Hurst had started to flush brick red. 'I have no notion—' she began.

'No?' Annabella was still smiling pleasantly. 'No notion of a conversation at a ball in Taunton with a certain Captain Jeffries? No notion of some poisonous slander he passed on to you and you in turn saw fit to tell your cousin at the Admiralty? No notion of the misery and trouble your spite has caused? I envy you your ignorance!'

Ermina Hurst pushed past her to leave the room, her face a mask of twisted malice. 'You upstart little Cit!' she flashed. 'I wish I had spoiled sport for you! Will Weston deserves no better, and as for you, you will find that it takes more than a pretty face and a rich grandmother to be accepted in Society!'

She turned back to the door only to find it open and Alicia, Caroline Kilgaren and Lady Stansfield standing in the aperture. Behind them were the outraged faces of half a dozen of society's most influential hostesses.

'Appalling behaviour!' Lady Jersey said to Lady Sefton. 'One only hopes that Antony Belston will see fit to take her on a *very* long wedding trip!'

After the best part of ten days, Will, Marcus and James finally walked out of the Admiralty in Whitehall into the crisp wintry evening air. London appeared to be awakening for the night; lanterns flared, carriages trundled by and couples in evening dress strolled towards the first fashionable crush of the night. None of the gentlemen paid much attention. Their minds were still full of the events of the past week, the testimonies taken from Captain Dowland

and others, the statement made by Lynch the poacher, the impending court martial and trial of Harvard for treason and attempted murder.

They turned the corner into Horseguards and bumped into two slightly inebriated young men who hailed them with delight.

'Kilgaren! Mullineaux! Weston! I'll be damned!' The slighter of the two gentlemen clapped Will on the shoulder. 'Had no idea you were in Town! Thought the lovely ladies were all alone...'

The second young man blinked owlishly. 'Saw them at Lady Stansfield's ball last night,' he confirmed enthusiastically. 'What an entrance! What style! Had no idea Lady Mullineaux had a little sister! Would've made it my business to meet her sooner if I had!' He shook his head regretfully.

'Patrick O'Neill seemed damned pleased to see Lady Mullineaux again,' the first said slyly. 'Never forgave you for stealing her from under his nose, Mullineaux! Still,' he shrugged, 'no doubt we'll see you later? We're for Lady Cassilis's masquerade—should be a crush—word is Lady Kilgaren intends to go as Diana the Huntress!'

And so saying, they wove their way off towards Pall Mall.

James Mullineaux, Marcus Kilgaren and Will Weston stood stock still, staring at each other.

'What the devil—?' Marcus began, breaking off as he saw Will's rueful smile.

'I believe we have made a tactical error,' Will said slowly, 'in leaving our wives languishing alone and unattended—'

'It doesn't sound to me as though they have been

unattended for long,' James finished grimly. He set off purposefully. 'Damnation! Why can Alicia always do this to me?'

'Always could, always will!' Marcus said laconically, half his mind already preoccupied with the thought of Caroline attired as the Goddess Diana. 'As for Will, seems he must claim his bride before half of London tries to be before him!'

Annabella had just begun a waltz with the Earl of Manleigh when Lady Cassilis's butler announced the Marquis of Mullineaux, the Earl of Kilgaren and Sir William Weston. She had been having the most marvellous few days... From behind the disguise of domino and mask, she smiled a little and watched the proceedings with no little interest. There was no denying that the three men looked magnificent. They were in evening dress, which immediately singled them out amongst the coloured dominoes and fancy dress of her ladyship's other guests. Then there was about them a certain air of purpose, almost of sternness, as the set about tracking down their errant wives. Annabella's heart skipped a beat. Despite the concealing domino Will had been making a straight line for her when, fortuitously, he was delayed by an old acquaintance who had insisted in engaging him in conversation.

Marcus Kilgaren had come upon his wife chatting to a very old flame of hers, Lord Cavendish. Marcus was surprised to feel a real possessive jealousy stir within himself at the sight of Caroline, so exquisitely pretty, draped in a dress so diaphanous it should not have been allowed out of the shop. And Cavendish was certainly enjoying their reunion, leaning towards her, his eyes bright with admiration and something else which set Marcus's teeth on edge. He gave the unfortunate peer a nod that was barely civil and addressed his wife.

'I believe this is my dance, madam.'

Caroline's eyes widened in the flirtatious way he remembered from their courtship. He could not believe she was about to do this to him. 'I think you mistake, sir,' she said sweetly. 'I am not engaged for this dance—'

'You are now,' Marcus said grimly, grasping her wrist and almost pulling her to her feet. 'And, dear Caro,' he added in an undertone for her ears only, 'my preference at this moment would be to make love to you rather than dance with you! I am only conforming to propriety for the sake of Lady Cassilis's guests!'

For James Mullineaux, approaching Alicia was very reminiscent of the days before their marriage when his beloved had been besieged by a sea of admirers and it had been difficult even to get near to her. He cut a path ruthlessly through the crowd, not even pausing to respond to the greetings of his friends, and found Alicia at the centre, sensational in an emerald-green domino and black velvet mask, Captain O'Neill lounging by her side. The dazzling Lady Mullineaux, very sure of her power... *His* Lady Mullineaux...

He took her hand and, with the wicked smile that had always made Alicia's heart turn over, pressed a kiss on the palm. He did not even speak, simply drawing her out of the group and guiding her expertly towards a secluded alcove. Several ladies in their vicinity exchanged rueful looks. No point in wondering whether the Marquis of Mullineaux would be interested in a flirtation. The Marquis and his wife were giving off so much white-hot intense heat that to get close would be to risk burning! So much for the dictum which said that a husband and wife paying each other attention in public was unfashionable!

Annabella was scarcely aware of the moment that Will cut out Frederick Manleigh, so dextrous was his manoeuvre. One moment, the besotted Earl had been smiling down into her eyes, the next he appeared to have vanished completely. Will's arm slid about her waist, his thigh brushed against hers, hard muscle against sliding silk, and she almost lost her step through sheer sensual awareness.

'Well, madam?' Will was unsmiling, but Annabella was up to the challenge.

'I am very well, I thank you, sir.' She gave him a melting smile. 'I have been having such a delightful time!'

She saw Will's blue eyes narrow. 'So I see. I have heard that Lady Mullineaux's little sister is the toast of the Town!'

Annabella smiled again, lowering her eyes so that their expression should not betray her.

'No doubt,' Will pursued, 'it slipped your mind to inform these gallant gentlemen that you are, in fact, my wife of only ten days!'

Annabella almost laughed. She was nearly certain that his stern tone was assumed, just as her flirtatiousness was. How could it be otherwise, when his body against hers was giving a very different message?

'Alas,' she said with every appearance of regret, 'it

has often slipped my mind, given my neglect by my husband!'

She saw the expression flare in Will's eyes, the mixture of desire and challenge that set her blood racing, heady as a draught of wine.

'Do I understand you properly?' he asked musingly. 'You fear that your attention may wander, given the delightful distractions of town and the lack of attention paid to you by your lawful husband?'

Annabella lowered her gaze again, managing a modest smile. 'It is all so new and exciting,' she said, by way of excuse. 'I am sure I could be forgiven for thinking I might be missing something, were I to settle into dull married life…'

She gasped aloud as Will turned them so that Annabella's back was suddenly against one of the ballroom pillars.

'I am minded to demonstrate to these poor, lovesick fools that they are wasting their time,' he said, his mouth an inch away from hers. 'Which would be the greater scandal, do you think, my love, to kiss you here and now, or to carry you out of the ballroom to make love to you?'

'Why don't you find out?' Annabella asked provocatively, as she raised her mouth to meet his.

\*     \*     \*     \*     \*

# The Neglectful Guardian
*by*
*Anne Ashley*

**Anne Ashley** was born and educated in Leicester. She lived for a time in Scotland, but now makes her home in the West Country with two cats, her two sons and a husband, who has a wonderful and very necessary sense of humour. When not pounding away at the keys of her word processor, she likes to relax in her garden, which she has opened to the public on more than one occasion in aid of the village church funds.

# Chapter One

The perfectly matched greys, admired by many of those august members of Society known as Corinthians, turned under one of the finest examples of an Elizabethan archway to be found anywhere in the County of Wiltshire, and came to a halt in the stableyard.

Marcus Ravenhurst, the much envied owner of the coveted pair, waited only until his trusted head groom had jumped down from the smart racing curricle, and had taken a hold of the spirited pair's heads, before alighting himself with the agility of a healthy, finely tuned athlete.

As Marcus stalked towards the house, the cold February wind caught at his many-caped driving-cloak, sending it billowing about his tall, powerful frame, and dead leaves swirled about the path in front of him before adding to the ever-increasing decaying piles dotted about the grounds.

His dark brows drawing together in one of his famed, heavy scowls, he cast the tall trees shrouding the fine building in a depressingly gloomy blanket a look of staunch disapproval before entering the relative protection of the stone porch.

Reaching out one gloved hand, he raised the highly polished brass door-knocker, and administered several short, sharp raps. It was a minute or two before his summons was answered, and the solid oak door was opened by an ageing, grey-haired retainer.

"Why, Master Marcus!" he exclaimed with genuine warmth, and a familiarity granted to loyal servants of longstanding. He moved to one side, allowing the unexpected visitor to pass into the hall.

"Her ladyship never said she was expecting you, sir."

"She isn't, Clegg. I'm on my way to Somerset, and on the spur of the moment took it into my head to pay a call. The visit is a very brief one. I shall be staying only one night."

After placing his curly-brimmed beaver hat and his gloves on the hall table, Marcus removed his cloak to reveal a blue superfine coat of impeccable cut, a snowy-white neckcloth and a pair of tight-fitting buff-coloured pantaloons, which encased his muscular legs without so much as a single crease. His plain double-breasted waistcoat was free from fobs and seals; the only embellishment he ever wore, in fact, was a plain gold signet ring, which emphasised his strong, shapely hands.

As always the elderly retainer was impressed by the sober, yet elegant, attire, and thought there couldn't possibly be a dozen gentlemen in the length and breadth of the land who could carry their clothes so well as his mistress's eldest grandson.

"Her ladyship is in her private sitting-room, sir," he informed him, relieving him of the cloak and placing it almost reverently over his arm. "I'll go up and inform her you're here."

"Save yourself the trouble, Clegg. I'll announce myself." Marcus's harsh-featured face was transformed by a rare smile. "Having no desire whatsoever to see a member of my own sex put out of countenance, I shall spare you the embarrassment of having to stand by while she rings a peal over my head for not having taken the trouble to visit her for some months."

"As you wish, sir," the butler responded gravely, but with a betraying twitch to his lips. "I'll arrange a bed-chamber made ready for you."

"Thank you, Clegg. And see to it my groom has everything he needs."

At the head of the stairs Marcus turned to his right, and went along the narrow passageway leading to his grandmother's private apartments. After a perfunctory knock, he entered the room to find the Dowager Countess seated in a chair by the fire, a rug over her legs and a book lying open on her lap.

"Was that a caller I heard, Clegg?" she enquired without bothering to turn her head to see who had entered.

"I cannot tell you how relieved I am to discover there's still naught amiss with your hearing, Grandmama."

"Ha! Ravenhurst!" She frowned dourly up at her favourite grandchild as he came striding in his usual purposeful way towards her. "Haven't set eyes on you in a twelvemonth. Was beginning to think you were dead!" she remarked with morbid humour.

"Three months, to be exact, ma'am." There was a suspicion of a devilish glint in his dark eyes as he placed a chaste salute on one pink cheek. "And, as you are no doubt overjoyed to discover, I'm still sound in wind and limb."

A wicked cackle answered this. "Nothing wrong with your limbs, Ravenhurst. You're the finest specimen of manhood in this family by a long chalk. You've no looks to speak of,'' she went on with brutal frankness, thereby eroding her former compliment somewhat, ''but, then, not all women are beguiled by a handsome face.''

He positioned himself before the fire, warming his coat tails, and looked down at her with lazy affection. Apart from the fact that she walked with the aid of an ebony stick, and that the hair beneath the fetching lace cap was completely white, there was little to betray that she had five-and-seventy years in her dish.

Her skin retained a satiny smoothness, her grey eyes were still brightly alert, and she had, much to her eldest son's discomfiture, and his wife's acute embarrassment, a mind as sharp as a meat cleaver and a tongue as corrosive as acid. Many had quailed beneath her blunt manner and astringent comments, but not so Ravenhurst. His grandmother numbered amongst that small handful of people he admired.

''I have never aspired to be an Adonis, ma'am.''

''Just as well,'' was the forthright rejoinder. ''But, then, when a man's as rich as Golden Ball, looks are a minor consideration to any discerning female of marriageable age.''

''Not quite that rich,'' he countered.

''Don't try to pull the wool over my eyes! You're one of the richest men in the land.'' She scowled up at him for several moments before enquiring irascibly, ''And how much longer do you intend standing there, warming the seat of those tight-fitting breeches of yours at my fire, boy? Go get yourself a glass of Madeira! It's from Henry's cellar. The only evidence of intelligence I've ever found in my eldest son is in his ability to pick a wine. And you can pour me one whilst you're about it.''

One dark brow rising sharply, he obediently went

across to the table on which the decanters stood. "I understood Dr Pringle to say, the last time I was here, that you were to drink only one small glass of wine with your evening meal."

"A pox on all physicians!" the Dowager responded crudely. "What does that fool know! And if you think I'm mutilating my insides by drinking a dish of tea at this time of the day, you're far-and-away out."

Knowing from long experience that to remonstrate further would be futile, Marcus dutifully filled two glasses, handing one to his irascible grandparent before seating himself in the chair placed on the opposite side of the hearth. After sampling the excellent Madeira and settling himself more comfortably in the chair, he enquired politely whether the Earl of Styne was in residence.

"No," the Dowager responded, not without satisfaction. "He's taken that whey-faced wife of his to Kent to visit her mother. Don't expect them back for a sennight or, with any luck, two. Why, did you wish to see him?"

"I cannot recall ever having evinced a desire to see my estimable Uncle Henry," he returned blandly, much to his grandmother's intense amusement. "But I really think he ought to do something about the trees surrounding this place. They make the interior dratted gloomy, ma'am. And the grounds are a disgrace. Nothing short of an eyesore!"

"I'll thank you not to interfere, Marcus!" she snapped. "Not one of those trees is being felled whilst I reside in the Dower House. They grant me privacy from all those prying eyes up at the mansion. And Wilkins will soon have the garden in order once he's recovered from his rheumatism."

As the ancestral home of the Earl of Styne was situated in the centre of the vast park, a quarter of a mile or more away from the Dower House, someone wishing to spy on the Dowager Countess from there would need to possess quite miraculous eyesight. Yet, here again he knew that to argue further would be a complete waste of breath, and so changed the subject by enquiring politely, if with precious little interest, into the health of the other members of the family.

As the Dowager Countess of Styne had seen fit to bless the late Earl with six pledges of her affection, it was some little time before she had finished casting aspersions on her five remaining children and their numerous offspring.

"Agnes was my first chick, and my favourite, Ravenhurst. I've never made any secret of that. Your mother was the best out of the lot of 'em by far."

"Perhaps I'm prejudiced, but I certainly thought so, too," he responded, a rare note of tenderness creeping into his voice.

"Never thought I'd outlive any of mine." She shook her head sadly. "And it had to be my little Agnes taken from me. I don't think she ever truly recovered from your father's death, Marcus. They were a rare couple, your parents. A real love match."

He did not respond to this, and after a few moments of dwelling on the deep sadness of loss, which for her had not lessened in six years, she gave herself a mental shake, and looked frowningly back at her favourite child's sole offspring to enquire what had prompted him to pay this unexpected call.

"I'd never hear the end of it if you discovered I'd almost passed your door and didn't pay a visit. I'm on my way to Somerset."

"Oh?" She cast him an enquiring glance. "Are you calling on that ward of yours in Bath, by any chance? Strangely, I was only thinking about her the other day. Agnes and her mother were great friends."

The shapely hand raising the glass to his lips checked for a moment. "No. I hadn't intended doing so."

The slight inflection in his deeply resonant voice was not lost on her, and she stared at him for several thoughtful moments before asking, rather censoriously,

"Do you never visit that child, Ravenhurst?"

Placing his glass down on the table conveniently situated by the side of his chair, he rose abruptly to his feet, and took up his former stance before the fire. "She has been well cared for," he said in a tone bordering on the brusque. "I placed her in that seminary in Bath, and then settled Cousin Harriet in Mama's old house in Upper Camden Place to look after the chit. I make her a quarterly allowance. She has everything she needs—my secretary sees to all that."

The reproachful look remained in his grandmother's eyes, and he found his ready temper coming to the fore. "Confound it, madam! What more could I have done? I know nothing of schoolgirls."

"Schoolgirl?" she echoed blankly. "Where have your wits gone begging, Marcus? Sarah Pennington may have been a schoolgirl, once, but her mother was knocked down by that runaway carriage not four months after your dear mama was taken from us. She must be nineteen, now, at least."

"Well? And what of it?"

She stared up at him in exasperation. "She was Agnes's godchild, Marcus. I don't think it would be expecting too much of you to pay some attention to your ward's future well-being. Why not fund a London Sea-

son for the girl? Bath is all very well, and I know dear
Agnes preferred it to London, but Sarah is far more
likely to find a suitable husband if she goes to the capital.
And if she favours her mother, I expect she's a very
pretty girl. Was she well provided for?''

"She's no heiress, if that's what you mean, but her
portion isn't contemptible.''

"There you are, then! I shall speak to your aunt Henrietta when she returns from Kent. She's bringing your
cousin Sophia out in the spring, so it wouldn't hurt her
to chaperon Sarah as well. Or, I might even do so myself.''

"No need to put yourself out, ma'am,'' was his almost indifferent response. "If I do decide to fund a Season for Sarah Pennington, and I have decided nothing
yet, then Harriet can chaperon her. That's what I pay
her for.''

"Pshaw! That pea-goose!'' the Dowager scoffed. "If
you're not careful, Ravenhurst, you'll have that woman
your pensioner for life. She came perilously close to ruining that husband of hers with her gambling, you
know.'' She looked thoughtfully beyond him to stare
down into the fire. "I suppose, though, at the time you
had little choice but to enlist your cousin's aid. I wish I
had done more, but it was so soon after Agnes's death.
I would have been poor company for the child.''

A tender look erased the annoyance from his eyes.
"Believe me, ma'am, there's no need to suffer pangs of
conscience. Sarah is well enough. I've received ample
very long and exceedingly boring letters over the years
from Cousin Harriet to leave me in little doubt of that.
And as far as a Season is concerned…?'' He paused for
a moment, looking thoughtful. "Of course, I'm not
against the idea, but a lot depends on circumstances.''

"Oh?" The Dowager looked questioningly at him again. "What circumstances?"

"There is every possibility, as you'll no doubt be pleased to hear, that I might be getting myself leg-shackled in the not too distant future," he confided somewhat crudely.

"And high time you were setting up your nursery, Ravenhurst!" Only a sudden glint in her grey eyes betrayed her delight at the news. "And who is the lucky gel? Do I know her?"

"You may do. It's Bamford's eldest daughter. She was engaged to be married to my friend Charles Templeton. You may recall he died several years ago in a riding accident, not many weeks before the wedding was due to take place. Broke his neck."

"Yes, I do remember that. But I cannot say I recall the girl. Is she pretty?"

"Pretty?" he echoed, frowning at an imaginary spot on the far wall, as though having difficulty in bringing a clear image to mind. "No, I wouldn't call her so. She's handsome enough, and has a deal of self-assurance and reserve. Some think her aloof, but I don't consider that a fault.

"She's six-and-twenty. Not in the first flush of youth, you understand, but then a chit out of the schoolroom who expected me to dance attendance on her all the time wouldn't suit me. We've been acquainted long enough to be sure we'd deal comfortably together. Yes," he went on as though trying to convince himself, "Celia Bamford will make an ideal wife. She knows what is expected of her. Once she's provided me with a son or two, there's no reason why we should see very much of each other."

He sounded so coldly dispassionate that it seemed almost as if he had chosen his future bride with the same impassive discernment as he would have used when selecting a brood mare. The Dowager stared up at her favourite grandchild in silent dismay, her delight, now, ashes at her feet.

"But do you love her, Marcus?" she enquired with unwonted gentleness.

"Love?" His thin-lipped mouth twisted into a cynical smile. "I don't look for that overblown emotion. I have learned over the years, ma'am, that most members of your sex become extremely loving especially when I am about to loosen the strings of my purse…no, mutual respect will suffice."

Unlike the Dowager, who passed a very troubled night, Marcus was up early the following morning and, after writing a brief note of farewell to his grandmother, set off on his journey to Somerset.

The wind had dropped considerably during the past twelve hours, and the day was bright, though very cold. Like their owner, the powerful greys were strong and healthy, and they reached the turn off to Trowbridge in good time. Ravenhurst, however, did not take this turning, much to his groom's intense surprise, but continued along the road to Bath.

It was most unlike his master to take a wrong road; those sharp, dark eyes, ever alert, seemed never to miss a thing. The groom debated for a moment, knowing that their eventual destination was a few miles east of Wells, then said,

"Did you not notice the signpost back along, sir? Trowbridge were off to the left."

"Yes, I saw it, Sutton, but I've decided to make a slight detour," was the only explanation forthcoming, but the groom, quite accustomed to his master's abrupt manner, was satisfied with that.

Mr Ravenhurst was renowned in polite circles for his sharp tongue and blunt language: traits undoubtedly inherited from the Dowager Countess. But those who knew him well knew him to be a just and honourable man: the sort of solid, dependable individual whom one naturally turned to in a crisis.

All his servants were devoted to him, and with good reason. Since his father's death he had proved himself to be a considerate and caring master who, in return for diligence and loyalty, paid every attention to his employees' well-being. So, naturally, it had irked him immeasurably when the Dowager had been censorious over what she saw as neglect of duty, but later he had had to own, if only to himself, that there had been some justification for the criticism.

He had just turned six-and-twenty when he had found himself in the unenviable position of guardian to a young girl still in the schoolroom. In the swift and decisive manner that characterised him, he had dealt with the situation promptly. Enlisting the aid of a recently widowed distant cousin, Harriet Fairchild, he had installed her in his late mother's Bath residence in order to take care of the orphaned Sarah Pennington, and then had conveniently forgotten the child's very existence, except on those rare occasions when he had taken the trouble to cast his eyes over one of his cousin's exceedingly boring letters.

With very few exceptions he held the entire female species in contempt. He was never vulgar, nor would it ever enter his head deliberately to embarrass any member of the fair sex, but he was a plain-spoken man with little patience for false gallantry.

His astringent comments and heavy scowls had sent many a hopeful young debutante scurrying back to the protection of her fond mama's side. He was impatient of vapours and megrims, and feminine tears rarely moved him. So what good would he have been in the rearing of a young girl?

None whatsoever, he told himself. It had been in Sarah Pennington's best possible interests for him to have kept his distance and not to have interfered. His heavy frown descended. But he could, he knew, at least have taken the trouble to write to the child from time to time, and it would not have hurt him at all to have visited her once in a while.

His conscience smote him. It was a rare experience, and one, furthermore, which he did not care for in the least. Consequently, by the time he had drawn his greys to a halt before a certain house in Upper Camden Place, he was not in the best of humours.

After giving orders to his groom to walk the greys until his return, he mounted the stone steps and rapped sharply on the front door. The young servant girl who answered the summons took one look at the forbidding countenance glowering down at her, and stuttered nervously that her mistress was not receiving any more callers that day.

"Oh, is she not?" he ground out, his tone as alarming as his expression, as he stepped, uninvited, into the hall. "Well, she shall most certainly receive me. You may tell her Ravenhurst is here."

After closing the door, the girl disappeared into a room on the right. Marcus, impatiently tapping one highly polished boot on the floor, heard a low murmur of voices before a high-pitched shriek rent the air.

Waiting no longer, he stalked into the room that the

young maid had entered to discover his cousin, prostrate, on the *chaise-longue,* the young maid wafting burnt feathers under her mistress's nose and a middle-aged woman, dressed in a very becoming dark blue walking dress and matching fur-trimmed pelisse, kneeling on the floor beside the couch, murmuring soothingly to his highly distraught cousin, who had taken one glance at him and then had promptly dissolved into tears.

"Good heavens, Harriet! What the deuce ails you?"

"You...? Here...? Today of all days!" came the muffled response from behind the lacy edging of a fine lawn handkerchief. "Gone, Ravenhurst. Eloped! Oh, the wicked, ungrateful child! How could she do this to me? And after all I have done for her, too!"

"I have already told you, ma'am, that Sarah has not eloped." The assurance came from the lady kneeling on the floor. She then cast her intelligent grey eyes up at the tall stranger and, easily recognising the signs of a gentleman containing his temper with an effort, hurriedly rose to her feet.

"Sir, you must be Sarah's guardian. May I introduce myself? My name is Emily Stanton." She held out her hand and found it taken for a moment in a warm, firm clasp. "Perhaps it might be best if we repair to another room."

Casting a final impatient glance at his, still, hysterically sobbing cousin, Marcus followed the lady across the hall and into a small parlour overlooking the street.

"Do I understand correctly from my sorely afflicted relative's somewhat garbled utterance that my ward has eloped?"

Mrs Stanton looked at him consideringly. "Would it disturb you if she had, sir?"

"Most assuredly it would! She was my mother's godchild. I would be failing in my duties if I permitted her to fall into the hands of some fortune-hunter.''

''Fortune?'' she echoed, failing completely to conceal her astonishment. ''Are you seriously trying to tell me that Sarah is a young woman of some means?''

His dark brows rose sharply, betraying the fact that he found the question an impertinence. ''You seem surprised, ma'am? Why should you doubt it?''

''Why, indeed!'' she muttered.

He could easily discern the frown of puzzlement before asking her politely to sit down. ''Perhaps you would be good enough to tell me what has been going on here this day? And, if you are able, enlighten me as to the whereabouts of my ward?''

''Be assured, Mr Ravenhurst, that it is not Sarah who has eloped, but my own daughter.''

Again his brows rose, but in surprise this time. ''You will forgive me for saying so, ma'am, but you do not appear unduly concerned.''

She smiled faintly at the dry tone. ''No, sir. I am not,'' she frankly admitted. ''My daughter Clarissa and Captain James Fenshaw have known each other since childhood. His family owns the property adjacent to our own in Devonshire. We enjoyed extremely cordial relations with our neighbours until my husband and Mr Fenshaw quarrelled over an unimportant strip of land.

''Since that unfortunate episode, my husband has strictly forbidden Clarissa to have any further contact with James, even going so far as to stop the poor child writing to him.'' She paused for a moment, absently twisting the strings of her reticule round her fingers. ''Several weeks ago James returned home from the Peninsular, injured. As soon as he had recovered sufficiently, he travelled with his mother to Bath to benefit from the health-giving waters, you understand.''

He saw the betraying twitch of her lips.

''But I was not fooled for a moment. He struck up an immediate friendship with your ward, and was a frequent visitor to this house, as was my own daughter.''

''Are you trying to tell me, ma'am, that my ward actively encouraged these clandestine meetings between your daughter and this man?''

Mrs Stanton raised her eyes to stare unblinkingly into angry dark ones. ''Yes, she did. Sarah and my daughter have been close friends since they attended the seminary together. Why, they are more like sisters! Your ward has stayed with us in Devonshire on several occasions. I am extremely fond of her. She's a very intelligent and sweet-natured girl.''

''After her involvement in this affair, it shows a generosity of spirit that you still think so, ma'am.'' He cast his eyes briefly in the direction of the clock on the mantelshelf. ''Do you wish me to go after the runaways?''

A slight frown creased her forehead as she rose to her feet and stared up at him, almost assessingly. ''Would you do that if I asked?''

''I am at your service. You have only to say the word,'' he assured her, and her frown deepened.

''No, sir. I do not wish to stop this elopement,'' she surprised him by responding. Moving over to the window, she stared down at the street to see a groom walking a pair of fine horses harnessed to a curricle.

''You must think me a most unnatural parent, but I hope with all my heart that they are successful and reach the border. It was cruel and unjust of my husband to try to keep them apart. They are well suited, and I know James will take good care of Clarissa. I was, unfortunately, duty-bound to adhere to my husband's wishes. Now, thankfully, all that has changed.

"First, I must pay a call on Mrs Fenshaw, and see what can be done to smooth things over here. Unlike our husbands, we have remained on friendly terms. I know she will be of a similar mind. I must, of course, write to my husband and inform him of what has occurred, and if he is foolish enough to go chasing after the pair... Well, so be it!''

She turned round to look at him again. "But all this is of precious little interest to you, Mr Ravenhurst. Your concerns are for Sarah, only.''

"You may take a light view of her involvement in this affair, ma'am, but I most certainly do not! I shall have a word or two to say to that young woman when she returns here," he remarked ominously.

"But, sir!" Her expression betrayed her complete astonishment. "Sarah won't be returning here. She, too, has left Bath.''

"What!" Disbelief was clearly writ across his face. "Do you mean to tell me that she is accompanying the star-crossed pair on this bolt to the border?" and much to his intense annoyance Mrs Stanton dissolved into laughter.

"Do forgive me," she apologised when she was able. "You do not know your ward at all well. That much is certain. Of course she hasn't gone with them.''

"Then where the devil has she gone, ma'am?" he demanded, not mincing words.

As her husband, too, had something of a peppery temperament, she did not bridle at the strong language, and once again regarded him rather consideringly. "Before I answer that, I should like to ask you a question. Why, after six years, have you suddenly taken it into your head to visit your ward?''

She smiled at the lofty glance he cast her. ''Yes, naturally, you find it a gross impertinence, and wonder what on earth it has to do with me. Well, sir, as I've already mentioned, I'm very fond of Sarah, and tell you plainly that I shall not help you to discover her whereabouts if your only reason for doing so is to berate the child for her involvement in my daughter's tiresome affair.''

A noise, something akin to a low growl, emanated from his direction. ''Let me assure you, ma'am, that I came here for the sole purpose of ascertaining whether or not my ward would care for a London Season.''

''I see.'' Once again Mrs Stanton subjected him to a long, penetrating stare. ''I think there is much that warrants investigation,'' she remarked at length, and somewhat cryptically. ''And I think I shall help you.''

''Do you know where my ward has gone, ma'am? And why, if it were not through fear of the repercussions of her involvement in your daughter's elopement, she found it necessary to leave this house?''

''I believe I understand fully your ward's reasons for leaving this place. With my daughter gone there would be precious little joy for her here if she remained. But I am no tale-bearer. You must discover the truth from Sarah yourself. As to where she has gone…? I'm afraid she did not see fit to confide in me. I wish I had been in a position to do more for the child, but…''

A deep sigh of regret escaped her. ''Sarah left letters for both your cousin and myself, but in neither did she explain where she intended going. In mine she merely begged forgiveness for her involvement in the elopement. Silly, silly child!'' she went on, an unmistakable catch in her voice. ''As though I blamed her!''

She paused for a moment, as though striving to regain her composure. "I have learned already that two ladies and a gentleman left the city early this morning in a hired post-chaise. One of the ladies was my daughter, and the other, by the description given to me, was undoubtedly Sarah. It's my belief she has asked my daughter to take her as far as the Bristol to London road, from where, I sincerely believe, she intends to travel into Hertfordshire."

His expression betrayed his incredulity. "What the dev—deuce does she want to go there for?"

Her smile was a trifle crooked. "You perhaps do not remember, sir, but before you became Sarah's guardian, she was in the charge of a certain Miss Martha Trent, who was employed, so I have been led to believe, as a sort of companion-governess. They were very close.

"After you dispensed with Miss Trent's services, she found employment in Hertfordshire as governess to two motherless little girls. Subsequently, she married her employer. Mrs Alcott, as she is now, visited Bath last year. I have never seen Sarah so happy! I overheard Mrs Alcott say on numerous occasions during her stay that she wished her former charge would make her home with her. And it is my belief that that is precisely what Sarah has decided to do."

"Do you know Mr Alcott's precise direction, ma'am?"

"I am sorry to say I do not. But what I can tell you is that he lives in a village not far from St Albans. He owns a sizeable property, and is a well-known figure in those parts. You should have little difficulty locating him."

"Thank you for your help, Mrs Stanton. You will forgive me if I leave you now, but the need is pressing. I must not delay in searching for my ward.''

"Please do not give me another thought. I shall remain here with your cousin a while longer.'' She arrested his progress to the door by the simple expedient of placing her fingers on his arm, and looked up into a face betraying deep concern. "For some years I have considered you a most neglectful guardian. I am beginning to think my judgement was at fault. Your ward is a capable young woman, but I shall not rest easy until you've found her.''

"Be assured, ma'am, I will!''

"Having now met you, Mr Ravenhurst, I do not doubt that for a moment. But—but, I beg of you do not return her to this house. If you have nowhere suitable to take her, then bring her to me.''

He refused to commit himself on this, but said, "Be assured I shall not neglect my duties again. Something has induced my ward to leave this house. Why the devil she didn't write to me if she was so unhappy, I don't know. But I mean to find out!''

Mrs Stanton, watching him collect his hat and gloves from the hall table, felt untold relief knowing that dear Sarah was being sought by such a very capable and obviously very concerned gentleman.

Her relief would have been short-lived, however, had she been standing in a certain inn yard not fifteen minutes later to witness the same gentleman stalking into the hostelry with a face like thunder.

The establishment's owner, a conscientious, hardworking man, had, through his own efforts, turned the hostelry into one of the city's finest. Before his marriage to the late innkeeper's daughter, six years before, he had worked since boyhood on the Ravenhurst estate. He had been devoted to the family, but after his beloved mistress's unexpected demise, he had decided to turn his hand to something new, and had never looked back.

He was manfully struggling with a large barrel of ale when he heard a loud voice raised in the tap. Unruly behaviour in his inn was something that he would not tolerate, and had not infrequently been called upon to evict disorderly customers by rough-and-ready means. Breaking off from his task, he strode purposefully into the tap-room, only to stop dead in his tracks, his belligerent look vanishing instantly.

"Why, Master Marcus, sir!" He came forward to clasp Mr Ravenhurst's hand warmly. "Haven't set eyes on you since...well, not since that sad time. How goes it with you, young sir?"

"Well enough, Jeb. But I need your help."

"Anything, sir. You know that."

"I had intended travelling to Wells, but have been forced to change my plans. Could you loan me a fresh team and look after my greys until I can arrange for their collection?"

"Course I can, sir! I'll let you have my bays. Wouldn't trust 'em to just anyone, you understand, but I know with you they'll be in safe hands."

They walked out to the yard and, whilst a young stable lad was harnessing the bays to his curricle, Marcus looked down the long row of stalls. Although the inn was not a posting house, several of Bath's residents stabled their horses here, knowing they would be well cared for.

"Which is my ward's mount, Jeb?" Marcus asked suddenly, his eyes resting on a particularly fine dapple mare. When he had received that letter from his cousin, requesting a horse for his ward, he had not left the matter in the hands of his efficient secretary, but had dealt with it himself.

In his reply he had requested her to seek Jeb's aid in finding a suitable mount. He had thought the price she had paid rather steep, and the cost of a riding habit exorbitant, but had not quibbled, and had increased Sarah's quarterly allowance to cover the costs of stabling. "Is it that mare?"

"No, sir. Miss Pennington don't stable her horse here. Fact is—" he scratched the side of his head "—don't ever recall seeing her ride. But I 'appen to know that the owner of the mare is wishful to sell her, if you're interested?"

Marcus did not respond to this, but looked at the ex-groom thoughtfully. "Are you acquainted with my ward, Jeb?"

"Well, I know of her, sir. Naturally, she don't come 'ere, but I've seen her about the city. My wife knows her right enough. Says she's a sweet-natured lass. Not too proud to stop and chat when they bump into each other whilst out doing a bit of marketing."

"Marketing?" he echoed, not hiding his astonishment. "But surely my cousin has servants enough to—" He broke off abruptly, his heavy frown descending, as he accompanied the innkeeper outside into the yard once again.

"Don't like the look of that sky, sir," Jeb remarked, glancing over to the west where dark clouds were gathering ominously. "Looks as though we're in for a spell o' bad weather. I hope your journey don't prove to be a long un."

"And so do I!" Marcus responded with feeling as he sat himself beside his groom in the curricle. "I'll return

your bays as soon as I can. Thanks again,'' and with
that he gave the horses the office to start.

The borrowed team were certainly not in the greys'
class, but were, none the less, sturdy animals, and Marcus soon reached the London to Bristol road. Although
he had tactfully refrained from divulging the nature of
his errand to the innkeeper, Bath being a positive hotbed
for gossip, he had explained to his groom the reason
behind the change in plans.

Sutton cast a concerned glance at his silent master as
the first flakes of snow fell to earth. ''I do hope we find
the young person, sir. I reckon we're in for a heavy
fall.''

''I'm determined to find her,'' Ravenhurst responded
grimly. ''Not even a snowstorm, Sutton, will deprive me
of the exquisite pleasure of wringing my sweet ward's
confounded neck!''

## Chapter Two

❧❧❧

Sarah Pennington entered the inn's infrequently used private parlour, and sat herself down on the wooden settle conveniently placed near the inglenook fireplace. The homely innkeeper's wife would not hear of a gently bred young woman remaining in the coffee-room where she might be forced to associate with the locals.

"Good enough people in their own way, ma'am," she had said, "but a little too rough-and-ready at times."

She had been all kind consideration for the poor young "widow's" plight. Sarah's lips curled into a wry little smile. How different her reception had been, here, at this small wayside inn!

When she had entered that busy posting house earlier in the day, she had been subjected to a display of hostile disapproval from the landlady who, after informing her in no uncertain terms that the common stage did not stop at that superior establishment, had begrudgingly furnished her with a cup of coffee before sending her on her way.

Odious woman! Sarah thought angrily, still nettled by the icy treatment meted out to her. How was she supposed to know where the London to Bristol Accommodation Coaches stopped to change horses and pick up passengers? She had never travelled by that means of transport in her life. But she ought, she knew, to have known that a young unmarried lady, travelling without so much as a maid to give her consequence, would certainly be viewed by many with staunch disapproval.

Fortunately, however, Mother Nature in her wisdom had seen fit not only to bless Sarah Pennington with a very pleasing countenance and a perfectly proportioned figure, but to bestow upon her a sunny disposition, a lively sense of humour and a good deal of no-nonsense common sense. She had, therefore, swiftly rectified the little oversight on her part.

As soon as she had been out of sight of any prying eyes watching her from the windows of that posting house, she had rummaged through her reticule, and had slipped her mother's wedding ring on to her finger. It was, of course, quite respectable for a married lady to be travelling about the country alone. More so a widow! she had decided, quickly placing the handsome husband of her fertile imagination six feet beneath the earth without suffering the least pangs of conscience.

Soon afterwards Fortune had chosen to look favourably on the young "widow". Sarah had not walked above a mile or two when she had been taken up by a kindly carrier who had generously offered to convey her to Chippenham to await the arrival of the Accommodation Coach from Bristol or, if she preferred, as far as Marlborough, where he was to have delivered his load of furniture.

As her purse was woefully slim, Sarah had not hesitated in accepting the generous offer of a free ride. Then, of course, cursed ill-luck had seen fit to demand its turn!

They had travelled no more than a few miles past Calne when snow had begun to fall.

The carrier, a seasoned user of the roads, knew the vagaries of the weather, and had predicted a heavy fall. Marlborough, now, was out of the question. He had fully intended to seek immediate shelter with friends, and had advised Sarah to take refuge at the wayside inn clearly visible from the main road.

He had assured her that the landlady kept a good, clean house, so she need not fear damp sheets, nor poor fare; and she was, now, very glad that she had taken his sensible advice, for the snow was falling harder than ever, rapidly adding to the three inches already covering the landscape.

Her reverie was interrupted by the landlord who entered the parlour, his arms laden with several substantial logs.

"Getting mortal bad out there, Mrs Armstrong," he remarked, piling the logs on the huge hearth. "You mark my words—there'll be more than one unwary traveller stranded afore this day is over."

"I dare say you're right. When I arrived at Calne, where my brother was to have met me," she remarked, her fertile imagination coming to her aid, and not for the first time that day, "the clouds were, even then, looking rather threatening. It was rather foolish of me not to have remained there, but it's such a busy posting house, and all the noise was giving me the headache, so I thought some fresh air would do me good. I expected, of course, to see my brother's chaise coming towards me at any moment."

By the sympathetic look on the landlord's craggy, weatherbeaten face, the explanation she had offered for her present predicament, accompanied by a forlorn little sigh, had sounded very convincing.

"I'm so very glad I noticed the smoke billowing from your chimneys from the main road, and had the sense to come here, instead of trying to return to that posting house at Calne."

"Would that be The White Hart, ma'am?"

"Er—yes, that's right."

"Did you leave the rest of your baggage there?" he enquired, recalling clearly that the young lady had arrived carrying only a smallish wooden case and a rather old and battered cloak-bag.

"No, my trunk was sent on ahead," she improvised quickly. "I've been staying with friends, just a few miles from here. I thought the few clothes I had brought with me would be adequate for my journey home. But I'm afraid I made no allowances for a deterioration in the weather and any possible delays on the road."

"Don't you worry your head on that score, ma'am. My good lady will provide you with any—er—little necessities you might need. And don't worry about your brother, neither. Stands to reason he won't be travelling far this day. As soon as the weather improves, I'll take you back to Calne in my old gig. No doubt we'll find him awaiting you at the posting house."

Sarah thanked him, and then watched, a flicker of regret in the depths of her lovely aquamarine-coloured eyes, as he left the room. How she hated lying to these kindly folk! But what choice had she?

She could not bear to be stranded here and be treated with contempt, her presence nothing more than a hindrance, a tiresome burden. She had endured more than enough years of feeling nothing more than a troublesome millstone about someone's neck. No, that wasn't strictly true, she amended silently. She hadn't been made to feel unwanted, at least, not by Mrs Fairchild. And her wretched guardian simply hadn't concerned himself about her at all!

She turned her head to stare down at the logs hissing and crackling noisily on the hearth, and began to recall the events in her life that had led to her present very sorry predicament.

Her father had been a courageous man, a captain in His Majesty's Navy, who had given his life for King and Country during the Battle of the Nile. Sad to say she could hardly remember him at all. She had been just a child when he had died; but she had almost reached the age of fifteen when her dear mother had been so cruelly and unexpectedly taken from her.

Keeping her tears firmly in check, she began to dwell on those idyllic childhood years when she had resided in her father's charming house near Plymouth, and those happy times when she had visited her dear godmother at Ravenhurst, that beautiful stone-built mansion situated in its many acres of Oxfordshire parkland. She retained many fond memories of her kind godmother, but her godmother's son she could not bring to mind at all.

In those early years, whenever she had visited Ravenhurst with her mother, he had been away at Eton, and then, later, at Oxford. The only vague memory she retained of him was on that day he had visited Plymouth shortly after her mother had died.

A hazy vision of a hard-featured face swam before her mind's eye. At the tender age of fourteen, she had been too afraid to look at the tall stranger in whose hands her future well-being had been placed, let alone disagree with any arrangements he may have undertaken on her behalf, and had kept her eyes glued to his highly polished top-boots, and her lips firmly compressed.

Honesty promoted her to admit that she had not disliked the idea of attending a seminary in Bath; she had not even objected to being placed in the care of his cousin, who had turned out to be quite a kindly soul, though slightly scatty and prone to fits of the vapours when things had not gone her way; but she had bitterly resented being separated from her beloved governess.

"No, my dear. It will not answer," Martha Trent had responded gently, yet firmly, to Sarah's pleas for them to remain together. "Your guardian is right. It will be much better for you to go to school and have the companionship of girls your own age. And with you attending a seminary, I would have no role to play in your new home. Mr Ravenhurst's cousin will, I'm sure, take very good care of you.

"I cannot live off your guardian's charity, Sarah. I must look about for a new position. And Mr Ravenhurst has very kindly insisted that on no account am I to take the first one offered, but am to look for a situation where I think I would be happy."

Sarah frowned slightly as Martha's words came back so clearly. Yes, to be fair, she had to own that her guardian had displayed some consideration for her beloved governess. Which was more than he had ever done for her! He was, by common report, a very rich man, and yet he had never seen fit to send her a little money of her own with which to buy a few little luxuries. What dresses she possessed, good quality garments, but sadly unfashionable, had been chosen for her by Mrs Fairchild.

Unlike other girls her age, she had never attended the balls held at the Assembly Rooms, and had rarely been invited to any private parties. The only times she had ever been truly happy were during those few short months each year when Mrs Stanton brought her daughter Clarissa to Bath, and those wonderful summer visits she had made to their home in Devonshire.

The weekday ventures to the Pump Room, where Mrs Fairchild sampled the waters and gossiped with her middle-aged cronies, and the twice-monthly card parties held in the large salon at Upper Camden Place, where Sarah had donned her best pearl-grey gown and had served Mrs Fairchild's guests with wine and tiny sweet biscuits, had proved to be the only slight relief from the tedium of living all year round in that, once, very fashionable watering place.

But it wasn't until Martha had paid that unexpected visit to Bath the year before that Sarah had become totally discontented with her lot. Her ex-governess had assured her that she would be most welcome to visit her in Hertfordshire, and to stay for as long as she wished, and had gone so far as to furnish her with enough money to hire a post-chaise for the journey.

Martha, also, had not attempted to hide her shock and dismay at her ex-pupil's drab, unfashionable attire, giving Sarah reason to hope that, perhaps, she wasn't so poorly circumstanced as she had been led to believe.

"As to that, my dear, I'm not perfectly sure," had been Mrs Fairchild's vague response to her charge's blunt enquiry. "Mr Ravenhurst has never seen fit to discuss your financial situation with me."

"But surely, ma'am, I was left some money?" Sarah had persisted. "We lived in a charming house near Plymouth. What has become of that? And my mother's family was certainly not poor. My grandfather was, after all, a baronet."

"Very true, Sarah. But what you, perhaps, do not realise, is that your mother became estranged from your grandfather when she chose to go against his expressed wishes and marry Captain Pennington. Worthy man though your father undoubtedly was, he hardly belonged to your mother's social class. And as far as your old home is concerned…? Well, I really couldn't say. Perhaps your mother left debts and Mr Ravenhurst was forced to sell it.

"And I cannot understand just why you have suddenly taken it into your head to concern yourself over such matters," she had gone on to say. "You reside in a charming house, have good food to eat and are expected to undertake only the lightest of tasks for your keep.

"I'm sure Mr Ravenhurst has your best interests at heart, my dear. And it most certainly wouldn't do for you to go parading round Bath in a lot of finery and giving the totally wrong impression to any eligible young gentlemen, now would it? But I'm sure that your guardian would not object to purchasing anything for you if it were really needful?"

"In that case, ma'am," Sarah had retorted, bitterly resentful at what she had deemed an unnecessary slight on her father, "perhaps you would be good enough to enquire, when next you write to my excessively wealthy guardian, whether he would be willing to furnish me with a suitable mount, so that I am able to accompany my friend Clarissa on her rides whilst she is in Bath. I do not think that that would be too much to ask!"

Of course, Sarah had not left matters there, and had written to Mr Ravenhurst requesting information regarding her circumstances, but had never received a reply, nor had the horse she had craved ever been forthcoming; not that she had been particularly surprised about that.

After all, a man who could not even bring himself to respond to the few letters she had written over the years was hardly likely to put himself to the trouble of purchasing a suitable mount for his tiresome ward.

Sighing, Sarah rose from the settle, and went across the room to stare out of the window. The snow was continuing to fall heavily in the rapidly fading late afternoon light. It was impossible, now, to discern the road from the grass verges.

She released her breath in a tiny sigh. Perhaps it had been rather foolish of her to leave Bath at this time of year, but she was not sorry she had. After all, with her friend Clarissa gone, and dear Mrs Stanton no doubt feeling quite out of charity with her daughter's conspiring friend, there was nothing left for her there.

Added to which, in June, when she attained her majority, her indifferent guardian would no doubt be only too eager to wash his hands of her completely. His obligations would then be at an end, and she would be forced to make her own way in the world. So, why wait until the inevitable was forced upon her?

It was as well to be prepared, she told herself, and look for a position as governess, or companion in some genteel household, and she felt certain that her dear Martha would aid her in finding a comfortable situation.

A smart racing curricle, making very slow progress along the road, caught her attention. The driver, his hat and cloak covered in white, put her in mind of a rather large and misshapen snowman; and she might have derived a deal of amusement from the spectacle had it not recalled to mind certain other travellers abroad that day, and she prayed with all her heart that dear Clarissa and James were not stranded on the road but, like herself, had found shelter at some inn.

The door opening broke into her disturbing thoughts, and she turned her head to see the innkeeper's kindly wife enter the room.

"Mrs Armstrong, we've another traveller just arrived wishful to shelter from the weather. Would you object if the gentleman joined you in the parlour for dinner? It's more fitting dining in here, him being a gentleman an' all."

"Of course I don't object," Sarah assured her. "Is he, perhaps, the person I saw just now tooling a curricle?"

"Aye, ma'am. Though what possessed him to go careering round the country in an open carriage in the month of February beats me. Mind, I thought it wisest not to ask. Didn't look in the best of humours when he walked in. But I dare say he'll cheer up and feel a deal better once he's got a decent meal inside him."

Sarah, her mind still dwelling on the long journey to the border her eloping friends had ahead of them, gave not another thought to the stranded gentleman traveller until, some fifteen minutes later, the parlour door opened yet again.

She watched a tall, broad-shouldered man, immaculately attired in a coat of blue superfine, tight-fitting pantaloons and shining top-boots—whose brilliance, no doubt, was attained from using a secret mixture containing champagne—enter the room. He came purposefully, yet gracefully, towards her, and she found herself staring up at a far-from-handsome and unsmiling countenance.

"I understand from the lady of the house that you have been gracious enough to permit me to share your private parlour, ma'am," he remarked in the most attractive deep masculine voice she had ever heard. "My name is Ravenhurst."

Her lovely smile of greeting fading, Sarah sat rigid on

the wooden settle, as though turned to stone. Ravenhurst…? The name echoed between her temples like some thunderous peal of bells. It couldn't be! Surely Fate could not be so wickedly capricious as to bring them face to face this day, of all days!

"Are you all right, ma'am?" The modicum of concern in his deep voice was lost on her. "You are very pale. I'll summon the landlady."

Sarah could not have responded even had she wanted to, and could only watch in a kind of trancelike state as he hurriedly left the room.

Placing a suddenly trembling hand to her throbbing temple, she tried to make some sense out of her frantically disordered thoughts. Was it, in truth, "the" Mr Ravenhurst? She hadn't recognised him, but that was in no way remarkable, considering she had set eyes on him only once in her life before, and then had taken precious little interest in his outward appearance.

Her finely arched brows drew together in a deep, thoughtful frown. Even supposing, by some cursed ill-luck, that the stranger did turn out to be her guardian, then what in the world was he doing in this part of the country? Although, she reminded herself, didn't Mr Ravenhurst have relatives residing in Wiltshire? A grandmother, or uncle, or some such? She felt certain that Harriet Fairchild had said as much.

If he had not been visiting his relations, then it must be pure coincidence that had brought him here, surely? He couldn't possibly have received word so soon of her leaving Bath. And even if by some mischance he had discovered her flight, he certainly wouldn't put himself to the trouble of coming after her… Or would he?

No, she thought, quickly thrusting this foolish notion aside, and focusing her mind on what course of action to take. Firstly, she must discover if the stranger was, indeed, her guardian; then, if the worst came to the worst, and it turned out to be so, she must try to discover what he was doing in this part of the world. She felt certain he had not recognised her and, given the circumstances, it might be wisest if she allowed him to remain in blissful ignorance.

By the time the object of her thoughts returned, with the very concerned landlady in tow, Sarah had regained full control of herself and was determined not to lose it so foolishly again. After hurriedly assuring the good woman that she was perfectly well, and that her "queer turn" had no doubt stemmed from a singular lack of nourishment since breakfast, she, once again reverting to her widowed status, introduced herself to the severe-looking man who then drew up a chair, and seated himself.

"Have you far to travel?" she enquired when the landlady had left them alone together.

His deep-set dark eyes held hers from the opposite side of the hearth. "As to that, ma'am, I couldn't say with any degree of certainty."

"You are not from around these parts, sir?"

"No," was the clipped response, but far from being annoyed by his abruptness, Sarah was amused.

He was, undoubtedly, a man prone to frequent bouts of ill-humour, the permanent crease between those almost black brows being adequate confirmation of this; and she recalled being told, on more than one occasion, that her guardian was a brusque, testy individual, much the same as her friend Clarissa's father.

Unlike Harriet Fairchild, however, who certainly entertained a lively dread of her untitled aristocratic cousin's unpleasant temperament, Sarah, strangely, experienced no such trepidation when in the company of such irascible gentlemen, and could not resist the temptation to goad him a little.

"No doubt you are feeling slightly peevish at having your journey interrupted, sir. Some gentlemen, I know, cannot brook the least deviation from their original plans, and fly into the boughs at the slightest hitch," and it took every ounce of self-control she possessed to stop herself from bursting out laughing as he regarded her much as he might have done a rare specimen in some fairground freak-show.

"But as there is nothing either of us can do to improve the weather," she continued, her voice not quite steady, "I suggest we try to make the best of our enforced stay here."

A sound, somewhere between the noise a gentleman makes when clearing his throat and that of a predatory beast's suppressed growl, reached her ears before he said, still with an unmistakable trace of annoyance in his voice, "Forgive me, ma'am, if I seemed—er—peevish, but the day has not turned out at all as I had expected. There hasn't been so much a small hitch in my original plans as a total abandonment, instigated by the completely unwarranted and feather-brained actions of my—"

He stopped abruptly, his lips for a moment compressed into a thin, angry line, though when he spoke again it was in a distinctly milder tone. "But as you correctly surmised, I do not reside in this part of the country, although I do have relatives living not far from here. My home is in Oxfordshire."

Oh, God, no! Sarah could have screamed in vexation. There wasn't a doubt about it. The wretch was her guardian!

It was perhaps fortunate that the landlady and her buxom rosy-cheeked daughter chose this auspicious moment to enter the room: one laying covers on the table; the other going about the room lighting the various candles and closing the curtains, offering Sarah time to calm herself down and rethink her strategy.

From what he had let fall, it was abundantly obvious that he was searching for her. But how on earth had he discovered, so quickly, her departure from Bath? There was only one possible explanation: against all the odds, he must have visited Upper Camden Place that morning. Wretched man! Why, today of all days, had he suddenly taken it into his head to visit Bath?

Not that that was of any relevance, she told herself, turning her head to stare down into the fire once more, blissfully unaware that he was studying the play of different emotions flit across her face. It was unlikely that Harriet Fairchild would have realised where her charge had intended going and, to be fair, Sarah knew she had given little away in the note she had left her. But Clarissa's mother might well have guessed Sarah's destination.

If Mrs Stanton had happened to be present when Ravenhurst arrived, how much information had he gleaned from her? Certainly enough to bring him thus far. Therefore, it stood to reason that he had learned of Martha Alcott's home in Hertfordshire. What beastly ill-luck!

"Something appears to be troubling you, Mrs Armstrong."

"W-what?" Sarah drew her head round with a start. "No, not really, sir," she managed in a moderately convincing voice, while silently cursing his astuteness. She forced herself to stare into those intelligent dark brown eyes. No, her guardian was certainly no fool.

Ought she to tell him who she really was? She dismissed the notion in an instant. His sole purpose in trying to locate her must be to return her to Bath. And she would not go back there! she thought determinedly. But she would need to be so very careful from now on, giving away no clue as to her true identity.

Had she mentioned that her destination was Hertfordshire to either the innkeeper or his wife? No, she felt certain she had not. Therefore, her destination now, if anyone should enquire, would be... Surrey. Yes, Surrey would serve very well, but she must ensure that she stuck to her original story, for if she made one slight slip, and he learned something different from either the innkeeper or his wife, she felt certain he would be on to her like a cat after a hapless mouse.

"I was just thinking about my brother. My friends left me at The White Hart in Calne where I was to have awaited his arrival."

"Then why didn't you?"

It was on the tip of her tongue to tell him to mind his own business, but she refrained, and said, instead, "I grew tired of waiting. I expected to see him at any moment coming along the road towards me in the chaise, but in the end was forced to seek shelter here. It was foolish of me not to have remained in Calne, I suppose."

"Exceedingly so, ma'am," he returned bluntly, the forlorn little voice that had gained the sympathy of the innkeeper earlier having no such effect on him. "Quite feather-brained, in fact!"

The green in her eyes became more prominent. "Yes, as totty-headed as driving about the country in an open carriage at this time of year, I dare say," she parried, and was astounded by the appreciative smile that curled his lips and completely erased the hard lines of his face, turning him into a most attractive man.

"*Touché,* madam." He rose to his feet. "I believe we are served."

Sarah accompanied him over to the table, not quite knowing what to make of him. He was certainly abrupt, and exceedingly rude, but he was not totally ill-mannered, for he did pull a chair out for her, and then proceeded to carve several slices of chicken on to her plate.

"I'm relieved to see that you have a healthy appetite, ma'am," he remarked after watching her help herself to the various contents of several dishes. "I cannot abide females who insist upon chasing morsels of food around their plates for the duration of a meal, and then have the crass stupidity to wonder, after eating so little, why they are prone to fainting all over the place."

She could not forbear a smile at his scathing tone. "Then you must be relieved to see that you are not in the company of such a one. I enjoy my food, and can assure you that I have never fainted in my life."

"You came perilously close to doing so earlier," he countered, and she cast him a wary look, but gained her composure almost at once.

"And that is precisely why I am rectifying that near-transgression on my part. I really could not bear the humiliation of having you step over me whilst on your way about the inn."

Once again she was privileged to see that rather wonderful smile. "I would never do anything so ungentle-manlike, I assure you."

He surveyed her for a moment over the rim of his glass, noting the strands of gold in her rich brown, plainly though neatly arranged hair, and the finely arched

black brows and long black curling lashes that framed
her lovely and unusually coloured blue-green eyes.

There was nothing classical in the lines of her small
straight nose, but her lips were pleasantly formed and
curled up slightly at the corners, and there was certainly
more than a hint of determination in that softly rounded
chin. All in all she was an exceedingly pretty young
woman who, he suspected, possessed a great deal of
lively wit and charm.

"Your husband must be concerned about you, ma'am.
Were you expected home this day?"

"I'm a widow, sir," she responded evenly, and just
for an instant thought she could detect a flicker of sympathy in his eyes as they rested for a moment on her
plain grey gown. "Are you married, Mr Ravenhurst?"

For some reason his dark straight brows snapped together, and his tone once again was clipped as he said,
"No, ma'am, I am not!"

"No, I didn't think so."

"Oh? And what gave rise to that assumption?"

"Because you had not long entered this room before
I became fairly confident that I was in the company of
a confirmed misogynist."

His deep rumble of laughter filled the air. "My word,
but you're forthright, ma'am! If that were, indeed, true,
I think I can safely say that I'm rapidly losing my ha-
tred."

For one dreadful moment she suspected him of flirting
with her, but then he changed the subject, and she felt
certain she must have been mistaken.

Unlike his cousin Harriet Fairchild, who rarely cast
her eyes over a printed word, and then only those set
between the hard covers of a Gothic romance, Sarah was
an avid reader who scanned the daily newspapers from

cover to cover, and so kept abreast of happenings in the world. She was, therefore, able to converse with Mr Ravenhurst on a wide variety of topics, from the progress of the war with France to the Prince of Wales's inauguration as Regent the previous year.

It transpired that her guardian had been amongst the two thousand guests who had attended the celebration party held at Carlton House; but from his scathing condemnation of the traffic blocking many of the capital's busy streets that day, and his caustic remarks on the oppressive warmth and the cluttered and vulgar opulence of the Regent's town dwelling, it was quite apparent that he had not enjoyed the experience very much.

They had no sooner eaten their fill of the excellent dinner than the landlady's daughter returned, carrying a bottle and a glass on a tray.

"Ma said as how you being a gentleman, sir, you'd be wanting this after your meal," she offered nervously, setting the tray down on to the table.

"What's your name, girl?" Marcus asked, reaching for the port and pouring himself a glass.

"Daisy, sir... Daisy Fletcher, sir."

"Be good enough to convey my thanks to your mother, Miss Fletcher. That was an excellent dinner."

"Oh, thank 'ee, sir! Ma do know how to look after gentlemen, right enough. She were in service when she were a girl. She do keep a good, well-stocked larder, so you needn't afear to go 'ungry whilst you're 'ere. And if the weather do stay bad for a few days to come, Pa be willing to slaughter the goose, and his favourite suckling pig, which'll do for several meals if you make use of the innards an' all. No, you won't be going 'ungry, sir."

Marcus, a look of comical dismay on his face,

watched her leave the room, and then turned once again to his dinner-companion to see her shoulders shaking with suppressed laughter.

"Has no one ever told you, ma'am," he said in a voice of mock censure, "that it shows a decided lack of breeding to laugh at rustics?"

"I was not laughing at her!" Sarah refuted hotly, but not quite steadily. "It was you who very nearly sent me into whoops. If you could have seen the look on your face when she mentioned slaughtering the pig."

"Dear me, yes. She spoke as though it were a pet. And do people consume the insides of a pig?"

"Some parts of it, certainly. The liver, and the chitterlings, I believe."

"Oh, God spare us! Let us hope it doesn't come to that. Though I'm sure if you're willing to tackle such fare, I can steel myself to do so. Where are you going?"

Sarah, who had risen, placed her chair neatly beneath the small table. "I was up very early this morning, sir, and am rather tired. So, I'll bid you good-night, and leave you to your port."

Picking up a candle, Mr Ravenhurst surprised Sarah by escorting her to the door, and then across the deserted coffee-room to the foot of the narrow staircase where he handed her the candle.

"Good-night, Mrs Armstrong," he said, his features once again softened by that warm smile. "I look forward to the pleasure of your company at breakfast."

Feeling not just a little confused, Sarah made her way up the narrow staircase and along the passageway to the spotlessly clean, low-ceilinged bedchamber that she had been shown into soon after her arrival at the inn.

At some point, while she had been in the parlour, someone had entered the room to fold down the bedcovers and to pull the floral-patterned drapes across the window. The candle on the small table in the corner had been lit and the fire had been made up, making the room pleasantly warm and cosy.

After going about the room lighting the other candles, she set the light Mr Ravenhurst had given her down on the chest of drawers by the bedside, and then went across to the table in the corner on which she had placed her wooden writing-case. She had been able to bring so few possessions with her—not that she had that many to bring—but she had refused to leave this, the last present her mother had ever given to her, behind in Bath.

She ran one finger lovingly over the delicate gold leaf of her initials, exquisitely carved into the fine wood, before flicking the catch and opening the lid. It was so beautifully made, having sections for ink bottles and pens.

There were two small drawers, one set in each of the back corners: the right quite inocuous; the left hiding a cunningly made secret compartment for billets-doux. There was also ample room in the centre of the box for several sheets of paper, the top one of which already contained several lines in Sarah's neatly flowing hand.

Lifting the sheet from off the pile, Sarah ran her eyes over the letter to her guardian that she had begun to write, ironically enough, shortly after her arrival at the inn, and groaned inwardly. The cool formality had seemed just the correct tone to adopt, but now, having met Mr Ravenhurst again after so many years, it seemed totally inappropriate, rude almost.

She raised her eyes to stare blindly across the comfortable room. And what an enigma the man had turned out to be! She had been given every reason to suppose, from remarks Mrs Fairchild had made over the years, and from snippets of information gleaned from visitors to Bath who were acquainted with her guardian, that Mr Ravenhurst was nothing more than an abrupt, unfeeling individual who had no consideration for his fellow man.

A wry smile curled her lips. He was most certainly abrupt, but his caustic remarks, far from giving offence, had amused her. She had enjoyed his company very much during dinner; and the simple thanks he had offered to the landlady's daughter had afforded a glimpse of his true character. He was far from the care-for-nobody she had thought him. Which made his seeming indifference towards her over the years even more puzzling.

She shook her head, genuinely perplexed. Something just didn't ring true. Added to which, he had come searching for her. Was that the action of an indifferent guardian? No, of course it was not! And, now, having come to know him a little, she felt she ought to tell him who she really was. After all, sooner or later he was going to discover the truth; and she felt certain that, once he understood her reasons for leaving, he would not force her to return to Bath.

Yes, first thing in the morning, she decided firmly, she would confess all. And who could tell, he might even be kind enough to escort her the rest of the way to Hertfordshire!

A sudden commotion below reached her ears. She could clearly hear the sound of several raised voices, and wondered what on earth was going on.

Curiosity got the better of her and, quickly thrusting the letter back into the writing-case and closing the lid, she picked up a candle and made her way back down the stairs to discover that a strange assortment of dishevelled travellers had invaded the coffee-room: some arguing amongst themselves; others calmly watching proceedings; and the very distraught landlord trying desperately to make himself heard above the din.

"What the devil is going on out here?"

The authoritative voice had an immediate effect. The hubbub ceased instantly as all eyes turned to stare at the imposing figure framed in the parlour doorway.

"Sir!" The landlord hurried towards Mr Ravenhurst, realising at once that here was a man born to command and, unless he was very much mistaken, accustomed to having those commands obeyed.

"These be the passengers from the London to Bristol Accommodation Coach. From what I can make out their vehicle be in a ditch, sir, a mile or so back along the main road. The driver and guard are walking the horses to Calne. And I been trying to tell 'em that that's what they should o' done, instead o' coming 'ere. We ain't a posting house, sir. We can't cater for such a large number."

"Now, Frederick—" his wife came forward "—you can't send these poor folk back out on a night like this. Why, it's blowing a blizzard out there. It would be positively unchristian!"

"And I for one won't walk another step!" declared a very fat woman who, much to Sarah's amusement, substantiated the statement by plumping herself down in the middle of the coffee-room floor.

Marcus, not so easily diverted by the action, shot the woman an impatient glance before casting his eyes over her fellow-travellers, his gaze coming to rest on a sandy-haired young man who was gaping back at him in astonishment.

"Ravenhurst! What the deuce are you doing in this out-of-the-way place?"

''I should have thought that that would have been patently obvious to anyone of the meanest intelligence, Nutley,'' he responded dampingly before addressing himself to the innkeeper's wife. ''How many of these persons are you able to accommodate?''

''Well, sir, if some wouldn't mind sharing, I dare say we can fix them all up.''

''One of the ladies could, perhaps, come in with me,'' Sarah offered kindly.

''No, there's no need for you to put yourself out,'' Marcus intervened before the landlady could accept the generous offer. Unlike Sarah, he had taken stock of the passengers.

Apart from the fat lady, who was still stubbornly seated on the floor, and who looked to be travelling with the thin man hovering nearby, there were only two other females amongst the passengers: a spinsterish-looking woman who bore all the appearance of a governess, and whose face was hidden by a large and rather ugly bonnet; and a twinkling-eyed female in a dashing red confection, whose saucy smile gave him a fair notion of what her particular calling might be.

''If you would be willing to change rooms with me, ma'am, I shall be happy to share with one of these gentlemen,'' he continued, raising a questioning brow at the tall young man whose broad shoulders were propped against the wall, and who had been silently viewing proceedings with an amused glint in his tawny-coloured eyes.

''Very decent of you, sir,'' he said coming forward. ''My name is Carter—Captain Brin Carter.''

Marcus acknowledged him with a nod before turning to the innkeeper again. ''I leave the rest of the arrangements to you and your good lady.''

Although having been granted little say in the matter, Sarah did not object to the new arrangements, and accompanied Mr Ravenhurst back up the stairs.

It took but a few moments to repack her meagre belongings into the cloak-bag and carry it across the narrow passageway into her newly allotted and much smaller bedchamber. She was genuinely fatigued after the events of the day, and long before the harassed innkeeper and his wife had the remainder of their unexpected guests accommodated, she had fallen sound asleep.

Marcus did return downstairs for a short while. He joined Captain Carter and one of his fellow travelling-companions in the tap to sample a tankard of the innkeeper's excellent home-brewed. The Captain, it transpired, was on his way to Bristol to board the next vessel leaving for Spain, and Mr Stubbs was merely paying a visit to the city to stay with his daughter.

Mr Stubbs's explanation for travelling at such a time of year sounded plausible enough, and Marcus might have accepted the reason at face value had the middle-aged, stockily built individual not betrayed an inordinate interest in the other customers: locals who had braved the elements for their evening tipple.

"An odd character, Stubbs," the Captain remarked later, when they entered their bedchamber. "Friendly enough, but a mite inquisitive, wouldn't you say?"

Marcus's lips twisted into a crooked smile. "Yes. Our friends at Bow Street do travel far and wide these days."

"A Runner?" The Captain's brows rose. "That would account for it, then! He was very chatty during the journey, asking a great many seemingly innocent questions. In fact, that weasel-faced fellow in the black coat, who started all the commotion earlier, was quite put out when Stubbs asked him what he did for a living. Can't imagine why. Turns out he's only some damned clerk in a lawyer's office.''

Marcus did not respond to this, for his attention was focused on the gold letters carved into the lid of the very handsomely made wooden box resting on the small table in the corner of the room. Without experiencing the least qualms he calmly opened the lid, ran his eyes over the unfinished letter lying on top and, much to the Captain's unholy amusement, suddenly uttered a string of decidedly colourful and unrepeatable oaths.

# Chapter Three

Sarah awoke with a violent start the following morning when the daughter of the house, entering the bedchamber, thumped a pitcher of warm water down none too gently on the top of the wash-stand.

"Sorry, Mrs Armstrong, did I wake you?"

"Oh, that's all right." Rubbing the sleep from her eyes, Sarah watched the flat-footed Daisy stomp across the room to draw back the curtains. The morning looked remarkably bright, and for a few elated moments she retained the hope that she might be able to continue her journey, until assured that nothing had passed along the road that morning.

"I overheard one of the locals saying last night that there be drifts ten foot deep in parts, blocking the main road," Daisy voiced dampingly. "Although the sun be shining, there be precious little warmth in it, and Pa reckons there'll be more snow afore long. You won't be leaving 'ere today, Mrs Armstrong. Nor tomorrow, I don't reckon."

"Never mind. It cannot be helped," Sarah responded, resigning herself quickly to remaining at least one more day at the inn. Fully awake, now, she sat up and pushed her tousled brown hair away from her face. "Did you manage to accommodate all those passengers off the stagecoach?"

"Aye, we did that, ma'am, but it were a bit of a squeeze. I had to give up my bed to that farmer and his wife. The young sprig and another man had Ma and Pa's room, and Mr Ravenhurst's groom kindly agreed to share with our Joe, so the lady in the pretty red bonnet could 'ave 'is old room. And the spinster lady and that man who be forever carping on 'ad to make do with the smallest rooms down the far end of the passageway."

Having always taken an interest in the welfare of others, Sarah looked up in some concern. "But where on earth did you and your parents sleep?"

"We bedded down in our parlour next to the kitchen. But from tonight I'm to sleep at me aunt's 'ouse, just down the road. And we're to 'ave me cousin Rose 'elping out." She pulled a face. "She be a right flighty little wench. And as sly as bedamned. I'd never trust 'er. She'll come to a bad end one o' these days, ma'am. You see if she don't."

So, Daisy evidently didn't care for her cousin very much, and most certainly wasn't looking forward to her presence at the inn. Sarah regarded her with an understanding smile. "I expect you could do with the extra pair of hands, though."

"Aye, we could that. Ma's been up since daybreak, baking and the like. Which reminds me. She wants to know if you'd like your breakfast brought up on a tray, or are you wishful to eat in the parlour again?"

"Definitely in the parlour, Daisy. You will have enough to do without running up and down the stairs with breakfast trays all morning."

After washing in the contents of the pitcher, Sarah

donned her detested grey gown, and stood before the wash-stand mirror to tidy her hair, twisting it in a long plait before securely pinning it to the back of her head. Vanity, thankfully, had never been one of her failings.

Yet she was feminine enough, as she stood there staring at her reflection in the mottled glass, to crave pretty dresses to wear and to long for the ministrations of an abigail, whose skilled fingers could arrange those silky brown tresses in a more becoming style.

A sigh escaped her. Elaborate hairstyles and elegant gowns were not the hallmarks of a governess, she reminded herself and, desperately trying to resign herself to her possible future station in life, left the bedchamber, blissfully unaware that her unfashionable attire and plainly arranged hair did not diminish her prettiness one iota.

Young Captain Carter was most certainly favourably impressed with what he saw, and cast an appreciative eye over both face and figure as Sarah entered the parlour a minute or two later. Unlike Mr Ravenhurst, who remained seated and merely acknowledged her with a curt nod, the Captain politely rose to his feet and, after introducing himself, thanked her for so generously giving up her bedchamber the night before.

"Not at all, sir. It was no inconvenience, I assure you." She sat beside Mr Ravenhurst at the table but, after a quick glance at his forbidding profile, decided to address herself to the far more amiable Captain. "I trust you both slept well?"

Captain Carter shot a wicked glance in his bedfellow's direction. "I'm quite used to sharing, ma'am. In Spain one is forced to adapt to many things, but I don't think our friend, here, is similarly accustomed.

"And it certainly didn't improve matters by being

awakened this morning by a young lass who threw open the door so violently that it crashed against the wardrobe, and then added insult to injury by tripping up over the mat at the bottom of the bed and very nearly drowning us both with the contents of the water jug she was carrying.''

"Clumsy wench!" Ravenhurst muttered, his eyes narrowing fractionally as he detected the slight movement of slender shoulders shaking in suppressed laughter. "By the by, Mrs—er—Armstrong, I believe you left that box in our room last night." He gestured to the small table by the window on which he had set the writing-case a little earlier. "At least I assume it's yours. It has the initials S.P. carved in the lid."

"Oh, yes. It is mine," Sarah confirmed after casting the briefest of glances at her most treasured possession, and cursing herself silently for leaving it behind in the room for him to find. "My maiden name was Postlethwaite," she managed after only the briefest of pauses. "Serafina Postlethwaite."

Marcus very nearly choked on his coffee, and hurriedly got to his feet. "If you will both excuse me, I think I shall take a wander outside and see for myself just how bad conditions are."

The Captain, frowning slightly, watched him leave. "He's an odd fellow. Don't quite know what to make of him. One minute he's as considerate as can be, and the next—" He broke off abruptly, and cast Sarah an almost apologetic smile. "I'm sorry, ma'am. Are you well acquainted with the gentleman?"

"No, sir, I am not," she responded truthfully. "He arrived here late yesterday afternoon, and we dined together. He is certainly a puzzling creature, though. I cannot make up my mind whether I like him or not."

She considered the point as she bit into a deliciously warm buttered roll. "Last night he was a charming companion, and yet, this morning…"

"Temperamental, I should say."

"Oh, he's most certainly that, Captain. I suspect he was thoroughly spoiled as a child," she went on, experiencing no qualms whatsoever at discussing her guardian with a complete stranger. "Needless to say he belongs to the aristocracy and is incredibly wealthy. So, I suppose, he's accustomed to having his way in all things."

"Ah, yes. Our privileged aristocracy. Where would we be without them?" he responded bitterly, but then seemed to collect himself and hurriedly rose to his feet. "I hope you'll not think me rude if I leave you to finish your breakfast in peace, ma'am. I think I, too, shall take a wander out of doors to indulge in a reprehensible habit I picked up in Spain."

"Not at all, sir." Sarah watched him leave, wondering why he should bear such an ardent grudge against a certain social class. There had certainly been more than a touch of acrimony in the attractive Captain's pleasant voice.

Shrugging, she quickly dismissed it as her own immediate problems came to the forefront of her mind and, rising from the table, went over to her writing-case, once again silently cursing for leaving it behind in that room.

Could her guardian possibly suspect? she wondered, staring down at those beautifully carved initials. After all, S.P. could stand for—well—almost anything. More importantly, though, why hadn't she been honest with him when the opportunity had arisen? She shook her head. No, she couldn't have confessed, then, not with the Captain present. Added to which, Mr Ravenhurst had not been in the best of moods, most unlike the convivial companion he had been the evening before.

She was still determined to tell him the truth, but she must choose just the right moment, catch him in a more agreeable frame of mind. In the meantime, though, it wouldn't do to add to any suspicions he might already be harbouring by hiding the case away. No, it made sense to leave it in full view for the time being, but she must certainly remove that damning evidence.

Quickly opening the box, she screwed the half-written letter into a tight ball and threw it into the fire.

The once intended recipient of that, now, burning missive was at that precise moment standing just inside the stable block, with his faithful groom beside him, gazing frowningly at the depth of snow in the yard. Captain Carter, who had emerged from the inn a few moments before, was standing by the door leading to the kitchen, enjoying a cheroot, and the innkeeper's massive son was busy with a shovel, trying to clear a path round the hencoop.

"Not a hope in hell of us getting away this day, sir," Sutton remarked, gazing up at the sky. "Nor tomorrow, neither, by the looks o' them clouds yonder."

"No, there's certainly more to come. We must resign ourselves to remaining here for two days, possibly more." Marcus glanced down at his trusted, middle-aged henchman. "How did you manage last night?"

"What a carry on, eh, sir? Never seen the likes before! You'd think folks'd be thankful to find shelter anywhere rather than be out on a night like that." He looked across at the innkeeper's son. "Joe be a big beef-witted lad, but there's no 'arm in 'im. And how did you cope, sir?"

he asked casting his eyes in the young Captain's direction.

"Well enough. But I don't doubt we'll all be sick and tired of one another's company before too long, and be more than ready to leave here when the time comes. Which reminds me..." Ravenhurst stared down in silence at the stable's earth floor for several thoughtful moments, then went on, "I've changed my plans, Sutton. When the roads do become passable, I want you to go to Sir Henry Bamford's place with a letter of apology from me. I most certainly shan't be staying with him now.

"You'll no doubt be able to get a seat on the stagecoach with this lot. Take it as far as Chippenham, from where you should have no difficulty hiring a horse to take you the rest of the way. Bring Quilp and my carriage to my grandmother's house."

The groom's brawny shoulders shook with wicked amusement. He had scant regard for his master's pernickety valet. "I reckon old Quilp must be miffed 'cause we ain't turned up, sir."

"I do not pay Quilp to question any change of plan I may choose to make," was the curt response. "I employ him to take care of my gear."

Sutton cast his master a surreptitious glance. "Will you be going after the girl again, sir?"

A not-unpleasant smile erased Marcus's heavy frown. "Be assured, Sutton, my darling ward isn't so very far away."

"Aye, sir. But where?" He shook his head, genuinely perturbed. "I don't like to think of the young lady about on 'er own. Why, anything might 'appen to 'er!"

"Come on, man! Use your head! How far away can she be? You know full well that that farm labourer saw a young female getting out of a post-chaise at the junction. The coach turned north on the road to Stroud, and she, on foot, went east.

"The landlady at that posting house gave us an accurate description, and we know a female answering that description was seen in a carrier's cart by that toll-gate keeper at Chippenham. We traced her as far as Calne. The carrier couldn't possibly have gone much farther."

"Aye, sir, but supposing it weren't your ward, but some other little lady riding in that cart."

"It was extremely remiss of me, before leaving Bath, not to have attained an accurate description of my ward and what she might possibly be wearing. But I harbour no doubts whatsoever, Sutton, that the young woman in the grey cloak and bonnet and my ward are one and the same person. Believe me, I shall have Miss Sarah Pennington safely installed in my grandmother's house long before you arrive there with the carriage," and with that positive assurance Marcus went back into the inn.

He was halfway across the tap when he was accosted by the innkeeper, who kindly enquired whether he would care to browse through a copy of the *Morning Post*. Marcus accepted politely and, with the briefest of nods to acknowledge the stagecoach passengers consuming a hearty breakfast in the coffee-room, carried the journal into the private parlour to discover Sarah still there, seated at the small table near the window, busily writing a letter.

She didn't look round to see who had entered, and for a few moments he studied her, his expression a strange mixture of exasperation and gentle appreciation.

"It's good to see you are able to keep yourself occupied, Mrs Armstrong," he remarked, seating himself at the dining-table.

"I think boredom will prove to be the malady of us all." She looked out of the window. The snow was so deep that it almost came up as far as the window-sill. The only tracks were those of tiny birds, braving the elements to search for scraps of food. Nothing, not even a farm cart, had risked travelling along the road. "How long do you think we shall be stranded here, sir?"

"By the look of the sky, I should say we're in for a further fall." No sooner had he spoken than the first flakes began to flutter to earth. "Certainly not tomorrow. Perhaps the day after, if we're lucky."

"Ah! May we join you?" The stylishly attired young gentleman who, Sarah noticed, had addressed Mr Ravenhurst by name the evening before entered the room, accompanied by a stockily built middle-aged man with penetrating grey eyes set in a kindly face. "Or do we intrude?"

"Not at all, sir." Sarah's warm, friendly smile encompassed them both. "I did not hire this parlour for my private use. You are welcome to use it whenever you wish."

"That is most gracious of you, ma'am," the younger man responded. "Ravenhurst, be kind enough to introduce me to this charming young lady."

His dark eyes appeared above the printed page. "Mrs Armstrong, the Honourable Mr Cedric Nutley and Mr—er—Stubbs. Mrs Armstrong, I should mention," he went on after the gentlemen had made their bows, "ought not to be here at all. But as she chose to go jaunting about in a snowstorm, found herself, like the rest of us, stranded here."

Sarah, wisely, ignored the gibe, and merely satisfied herself with casting him a darkling look before resuming her seat at the small table. After exchanging a few pleasantries with Ravenhurst, Mr Nutley came over to her.

"What a charming writing-case, Mrs Armstrong!"

"Yes, it is, isn't it." Sarah surreptitiously covered the letter that she had just begun writing with a plain sheet of paper. It was destined for an elderly lady, whom she had been in the habit of visiting regularly, and she did not wish him to catch sight of its contents, which might give rise to mention of a certain city.

"It's beautifully made, and has a secret compartment, here," she explained, pressing one of the tiny carved squares that decorated the sides of the drawers, and a small flap sprang open, revealing the hidden section. "Needless to say, it is empty. I never use it. In fact, the spring is a little stiff, I notice."

Mr Nutley looked at it keenly for several moments. "Why, unless one knew its secret, one would never suspect it was there! Which little square did you press?"

"This one—third from the end." Closing the flap, Sarah obligingly repeated the procedure before putting away her letter and closing the case.

"Heavens above!" Marcus ejaculated suddenly, drawing everyone's attention. He turned to the front cover of the journal. "This newspaper's over a week old. I thought the articles seemed familiar. Wait a moment, though… I've not read this before."

His eyes scanned the few lines at the bottom of one of the columns. "The Felchett diamonds have gone missing. There's a reward being offered for information leading to their return." He raised his head, fixing his eyes on Mr Nutley. "Did you know about this, Cedric?"

"I thought everyone knew," the young man responded casually, before joining Mr Stubbs on the settle. "Their disappearance was discovered on the morning after the betrothal party. You were there, Ravenhurst. Surely you cannot have forgotten?''

''I attended the party, yes,'' he concurred, ''but I left early for London the following morning, and haven't been back to Oxfordshire since.''

''Oh, well, in that case—'' Mr Nutley shrugged one slim shoulder ''—you probably wouldn't have heard. Deuce of a to-do about it the following day when the maid discovered the necklace wasn't in her mistress's jewellery-case. Been left open all night, apparently, on the dressing-table.

''My beloved sire had gone off with Lord Felchett and a few of the other gentleman guests for a spot of shooting. By the time they returned to the house, Lady Felchett had already sent poor Harry hot-foot to London to call in the Runners. Old Felchett was furious when he discovered what his good lady had done. Well expected him to burst a blood vessel the way he went ranting on. Didn't want any fuss, you see.''

''That seems rather odd, Mr Nutley, don't you think?'' Sarah remarked, frowning in puzzlement. ''You would have thought Lord Felchett would have applauded such swift action on his wife's part.''

''Perhaps. But half the gentry in the county had been invited to their son Harry's betrothal party. Some of them were staying on for the weekend, my family included. Wouldn't do to have the Runners sniffing round, asking a lot of fool questions. Might give offence. One cannot go about accusing one's neighbours, ma'am.''

''No, I suppose not,'' she agreed. ''Is the necklace very valuable?''

''Lord, yes! Worth a small fortune, wouldn't you say, Ravenhurst?''

''It is certainly reputed to be very valuable, yes,'' he

responded, gazing fixedly at an imaginary spot on the floor. "I wonder if there's a connection?"

He looked up to find three pairs of eyes regarding him questioningly. "Several valuable and well-known items of jewellery were stolen in London during the Season last year. And the famous Pelstone pearls were taken when the family was in Brighton during the summer. I was just wondering if the same person or persons were involved in the robberies."

Sarah frowned. "But how do they dispose of the items, sir? If they are all well-known pieces, surely they would be easily recognisable?"

Marcus looked directly into the grey eyes of Mr Stubbs, who had been listening intently to the conversation. "Now, there's an interesting point, sir, do you not think?"

Mr Stubbs's gaze did not waver. "No honest merchant would touch 'em, of course, so I would very much think that the items must find their way into the hands of some unscrupulous dealer who would, then, either sell them abroad, or separate the stones, melt down the gold, or whatever, and have them made up in some other form."

"I, for one, think that is monstrous!" Sarah exclaimed, appalled by the mere thought of such callous actions. "Those jewels have probably been in the respective families for years. They must be of great sentimental value, too."

"But not to the thieves, my dear lady," Marcus countered, getting to his feet. "It's turned out to be only a small flurry this time. Looks as though the sun is trying to come out again. I think I'll lend a hand at clearing the yard."

"What an odd fellow he is!" Mr Nutley remarked

when the door had closed behind Mr Ravenhurst. "Helping servants to clear away snow? Whatever next! Do you know, Mrs Armstrong, I've known that man all my life, and yet I still don't understand him at all."

"You live near him in Oxfordshire, Mr Nutley?" she enquired.

"Yes. My father's Sir Giles Nutley. Our home is some four miles from Ravenhurst." Slightly effeminate arched brows drew together above insipid blue eyes. "Deuced odd his being here, though."

"I don't see why, sir," Sarah responded in what she hoped was an indifferent tone. The last thing in the world she wanted was for Mr Nutley to start asking awkward questions. "I'm sure Mr Ravenhurst mentioned that he has relatives living not too far away from here."

"That's right, he has! I'd forgotten that." He giggled suddenly like a schoolgirl. "Lord! He must be smarting, having to put up at a place like this. Ravenhurst's accustomed to the very best. Well, he can afford it, not like some of us," he went on, his tone decidedly resentful. "Lucky dog! He's independent. He isn't forced to travel on the common stage because of the miserly allowance his father gives him." A glinting sparkle brightened his eyes. "But it won't be like that for much longer."

Evidently Mr Nutley was expecting to come into money. Sarah cast a brief glance over his fashionable, yet slightly dandified attire. He was certainly able to clothe himself in the first style of elegance on his miserly allowance, if nothing else. She decided she didn't care for this sulky young man very much, but masterfully disguised her feelings as she made an excuse to leave the gentlemen to their own devices, and went out into the coffee-room to find Daisy busily clearing away the breakfast dishes.

"Here, let me help," she offered.

"Oh, no, ma'am. There's no need for that. We've plenty of 'elp, now. Me cousin's 'ere. And that farmer and 'is wife offered their services if Pa could see 'is way to knocking a bit off their bill. They expected to be back in their own 'ome by now, and are a bit short of the readies. They've turned out to be good workers. Which is more than can be said for 'er," she added, gesturing to the archway by which one gained access to the stairs.

Sarah caught a glimpse of a golden-haired girl in a blue dress and white apron. From what she could see of her, the slender girl appeared to be rather pretty, and Sarah could quite understand, as she looked back at Daisy's plump figure and homely face, from where poor Daisy's dislike of her cousin stemmed.

Jealousy seemed a common affliction amongst certain inhabitants of this inn, she mused as she mounted the narrow flight of stairs. Mr Nutley was definitely envious of Mr Ravenhurst's wealth, and Daisy, Sarah suspected, her cousin's good looks. Captain Carter, too, had certainly betrayed a deal of resentment, earlier, to a certain class of persons.

As she reached the top of the staircase, she saw the spinsterish-looking female who had been among the passengers off the stagecoach hurrying purposefully down the passageway towards her.

"Good morning. I am Mrs Armstrong." Sarah stood at the head of the stairs, effectively preventing the woman's further progress. "I, too, have been forced to seek shelter here."

"Grimshaw. Miss Tabatha Grimshaw. Pleased to meet

you,'' she responded in clipped tones. Which betrayed the fact that she was anything but!

"I find all this most vexing, Mrs Armstrong,'' she went on in a most agitated manner. "As I particularly asked for peace and quiet, I did not object to being placed at the very end of the passageway in what is, I suspect, the smallest room in the house, but when I requested that no one should enter my room on any pretext, and find upon my return from breakfast that my belongings have been tampered with... Well, it is just too much!''

"Oh, dear. Have you discovered something missing?''

"Missing? On, no, no! Everything is there.'' The icy-blue eyes behind the pince-nez shot Sarah a furtive glance. "It is just that I have not been well of late. An irritation of the nerves, you understand. The slightest little thing seems to overset me. I am better on my own. I shall insist upon all my meals being brought up to me on a tray from now on. I must have my solitude. And I won't have my belongings touched!''

Sarah had come across many highly strung people during her years in Bath, and Miss Grimshaw gave every sign of belonging to their number. She was a tall, thin woman, whose greying hair was confined in a tight bun at the back of her head, and whose pallid complexion was evidence of poor health, as were the dark circles round the eyes.

Moving aside, Sarah cast her a sympathetic smile. "I'm sure when you explain that you have been unwell, Miss Grimshaw, the landlady will be only too pleased to send your meals up to your room.''

"Dried-up old stick!'' a voice behind her snapped, and Sarah, after having watched Miss Grimshaw scamper down the stairs with quite remarkable agility for a middle-aged woman who professed to be unwell, swung round to find the female who had been wearing the bright red bonnet the evening before regarding her from one of the bedchamber doorways.

Sarah's eyes began to twinkle. "Who...? Me?"

The woman gurgled with laughter, a light tinkling sound which instantly brightened the atmosphere. "No, Miss Grimstone, or whatever 'er name is. She never spoke a word to anyone from the moment she entered the stage at Marlborough. And when I asked, friendly like, if we'd met before, she deliberately snubbed me. Miserable old fossil!"

"Well, perhaps there's some excuse for her behaviour. She hasn't been well." A sudden frown creased Sarah's forehead. "And I don't think she's as old as she appears."

"She's certainly a lot older than you or me. My name is de Vine, by the way. Dorothea de Vine."

Sarah went smilingly towards her. "Mrs Serafina Armstrong."

"Is that your real name?"

"W-what?" Sarah was rather taken aback. "Of course it is! Why do you ask?"

The young woman entwined her arm round Sarah's and drew her into the bedchamber. "My name ain't really de Vine," she confessed in a conspiratorial whisper. "That's me stage name. Me real name's Dottie Hogg."

"Oh, you're an actress. How exciting!"

"It ain't all it's cracked up to be," Dottie confessed with a plaintive sigh. "I'm between jobs at the moment, as you might say. Tried me 'and in London, but it didn't work out, so I'm going back to Bristol. Me old mother still lives there, so I'll move back in with 'er until I can gets m'self fixed up, like."

"How I envy you! You must meet some interesting people," Sarah remarked, accepting the invitation to sit down beside Dottie on the bed.

"You come across all sorts, that's for sure. Like that lot off the stage. Mr *Stubble* is a good sort. Nice and friendly, not like old Grimlock and that weasel-faced clerk."

"I haven't met him yet."

"You ain't missed much, Mrs *Armitage*. What a fuss he were creating last night! The young sprig's not so bad. Kept giving me the eye, though, but I'm used to that. And I ain't just anyone's for the asking," she confided, much to Sarah's puzzlement. "But that 'andsome Captain, now. Cor! I bet he could show a girl a good time. Like that gentleman friend of yourn. He's a bit stern-looking. But I like a man to be a man, if you knows what I mean. I bet he knows 'ow to treat a girl, eh?"

"Gentleman friend?" Sarah echoed, still somewhat confused by Dottie's perplexing utterances. "Oh, you mean Mr Ravenhurst! He isn't a friend of mine. He arrived late yesterday afternoon, and we dined together."

Dottie looked slightly nonplussed. "Well, if that's so, you watch out, Mrs *Armshaw*. He's right taken with you. Believe me, I know the signs. The way he looked at you just before you went off to bed last—"

"You're mistaken, Dottie," Sarah cut in. She found herself, unaccountably, blushing and hurriedly rose from the bed. "Mr Ravenhurst isn't interested in me in the least."

"No offence intended, I'm sure." Dottie, too, got to her feet. "Anyone can tell you're a lady. It was just… Oh, well, never mind." She began to rummage through the contents of her cloak bag, which she had scattered across the bed. "Here, would you like to read this? A friend give it me. Trouble is, me eyes ain't what they were, and I can't make out the print too well.''

Sarah accepted the well-thumbed volume with genuine gratitude. ''Thank you, yes. It will certainly help to pass the time.''

''And I've a letter, somewhere,'' Dottie announced, arresting Sarah's progress to the door. ''Drat the thing! Where the devil did I put it?'' She delved into the pockets of a rather garishly coloured red-and-green striped gown. ''I know I brung it with me. Oh, well, when I do come across it, will you be kind enough to read it to me? It's me dratted peepers, you see.''

''Of course I shall. And thank you again for the book.''

Sarah wandered along the passageway to her own room, which had been tidied in her absence. The fire had been made up, and she was about to draw the chair nearer to its comforting warmth when the sound of voices caught her attention. As her bedchamber was at the front and very end of the house, she thought at first the voices were filtering up from the private parlour situated directly below, but then she realised that they were coming from outside.

Curious, she went over to the window to discover Mr Ravenhurst, Captain Carter and two other men she did not recognise busily clearing a path along the front wall of the inn. By the deep rumbles of masculine laughter that from time to time reached her ears, the four were enjoying their task hugely. She gazed at each man in turn before her eyes became fixed on one head of dark, slightly waving hair.

Discourteous and surprisingly thoughtful by turn, Mr Ravenhurst was, as his young neighbour had remarked, a very perplexing man. Unlike Mr Nutley, however, who evidently thought it beneath his social standing, Mr Ravenhurst did not hesitate to lend a helping hand at clearing away snow or, she reminded herself, to say a simple "thank you" to an innkeeper's daughter for a meal enjoyed.

She experienced a sudden feeling of deep regret that they had not become better acquainted during those years of his guardianship. It was unlikely now, given the overcrowded confines of the inn, that this omission would be rectified. But somehow she must contrive to attain a few precious minutes alone with him in order to declare her true identity.

The opportunity was destined not to be granted that day, however. Mr Ravenhurst was not among those who partook of a light luncheon, and Sarah did not see him again until the evening, when she entered the coffee-room to join her stranded fellow-travellers just before dinner.

She had spent most of the afternoon in the company of Dottie who, after skilfully arranging her own blonde tresses in a riot of bouncy curls, had contrived to arrange Sarah's hair in a more becoming style.

Donning her best pearl-grey gown, which she had worn on the occasions of Mrs Fairchild's exclusive little card parties, Sarah thought she looked quite presentable until Mr Ravenhurst, breaking off his conversation with Captain Carter and Mr Stubbs, came over and greeted her with,

"Oh, God! Not half-mourning again!"

She flashed him a look from beneath her long curling lashes. "You forget, sir, I am a widow, after all."

"You err, child. I forget nothing." His dark, intelligent eyes looked her over from head to foot. "The hair is a definite improvement, though."

"Why, thank you!" Sarah felt inordinately pleased by this mild compliment. "Miss de Vine arranged it for me. She's very clever with—"

"Miss who?" he cut in sharply.

"Miss Dorothea de Vine. Haven't you been introduced yet, sir?"

He clapped one shapely hand over his eyes. "No, I haven't. And you can spare yourself the trouble of introducing me to the 'Divine' Dorothea. Pure fabrication if ever I heard it! Still," he tutted, "there's plenty of that going on here." He removed his hand and cast a brief glance at the lively and not unattractive damsel who had positioned herself at the Captain's side. "What's her real name, by the way?" he asked, not giving Sarah the opportunity to assimilate his former remark.

"Dottie Hogg."

"Oh, dear me, yes. I suppose there's some justification for it, then. Only slightly worse than Serafina Postlethwaite, I should say."

This time Sarah couldn't mistake the underlying implication, and looked at him sharply, but his expression gave nothing away. In fact, he stared down at her with such a depth of warmth in his dark eyes that for some obscure reason her pulse became quite erratic, and she swiftly forgot her suspicions.

Whether or not by his contrivance, Mr Ravenhurst was seated beside her at dinner. She had suggested to the landlady earlier in the day that it would be more convenient, and involve less work, if everyone ate together in the coffee-room, after which they could all repair to the parlour, enabling the staff to clear away in peace.

The landlady had welcomed the idea, and had placed

two tables together to accommodate everyone. Only the farmer and his wife, whom Sarah assumed were eating in the kitchen, and Miss Grimshaw did not join the group.

Mr Ravenhurst, as had happened the night before, proved to be an ideal dinner companion, and only twice came close to oversetting her. The first occasion was when he asked Mr Nutley, who seemed for some reason in a very subdued frame of mind, to move the branch of candles further along the table as the light was catching his young neighbour's brightly coloured waistcoat and dazzling him.

The second occurred when the middle-aged clerk, Mr Winthrope, whom Sarah had met for the first time at luncheon, began to bemoan the fare, declaring the beef overcooked and the chicken tough. Mr Ravenhurst turned his head and spoke just one soft and very idiomatic sentence. Sarah did not quite catch what he had said, but knew it must have been extremely rude, for Mr Winthrope coloured to the roots of his sparse, greying hair, and said not another word throughout the remainder of the meal.

Apart from the chastened clerk, who sought immediate refuge in his bedchamber, everyone else repaired to the parlour once the enjoyable meal was over. The innkeeper had managed to provide them with a pack of decidedly sticky and dog-eared playing cards, and Sarah found herself making up a foursome at whist.

Mr Ravenhurst elected himself her partner, leaving Mr Nutley to join forces with Captain Carter as their opponents. Sarah and her partner won the first rubber, and then went on to win the second very comprehensively, which won her a modicum of praise from Mr Ravenhurst.

"However," he went on to say, his tone decidedly censorious, "it does lead one to suppose that your upbringing was not all that it might have been, Mrs Armstrong, if you were permitted to while away your formative years in the pursuit of gaming."

"Oh, yes. Such wanton dissipation! You cannot imagine to what extent I indulged myself. I became thoroughly depraved, in fact," she responded airily, much to the Captain's amusement and Mr Nutley's astonishment.

"The lady is but jesting, Cedric," Ravenhurst assured him. "Your deal, I believe."

"I'll sit this one out." Mr Nutley rose from the table, offering his place to Mr Stubbs. "I think I'll track down that rascally landlord. I have a fancy for a glass of rum punch."

When he returned to the room, after what seemed a very long absence, he was bearing a tray upon which stood several glasses and a large bowl. Pushing Sarah's writing-case a little to one side, he set the tray down on the small table by the window, and began to ladle out the warm liquor. "Who'll join me?"

Only Sarah and Mr Ravenhurst declined, but the others were happy to imbibe in the warming drink, though the Captain, Sarah noticed, grimaced at his first mouthful. She offered her place to Mr Nutley, who seemed far more convivial than he had earlier in the evening, and for a while she sat talking with Dottie before being the first to retire for the night.

She could hear, quite clearly, the murmur of voices from the room below as she curled up in the comfortable bed. She found the sounds reassuring, and was soon fast asleep.

\* \* \*

She awoke with an almost violent start sometime later. What on earth was that? A table being overturned…? A chair, maybe? For a few moments she lay there, not daring to move, her frightened eyes darting about the room, expecting at any moment to see a shadowy movement, but all remained still, all was quiet; not even the murmur of voices, now, from the parlour below.

Then, as the grandfather clock near the foot of the stairs struck two, she understood why. She had been asleep for several hours, not the few minutes she had first thought.

Cautiously, she eased herself into a sitting position, and felt for the tinder box. It took a moment before she had the candle on the bedside table lit; then she cast her eyes about the small bedchamber once more, just to reassure herself that there was truly no one there. All was as it should be, and yet she felt certain she had heard something…but what?

Wide awake now, she abandoned the notion of trying to get back to sleep for the time being, and decided to finish the letter she had begun writing the previous morning, but recalled that she had left her case downstairs in the parlour. She hesitated only for a moment then, throwing the bedcovers aside, she slipped her woollen shawl round her shoulders, and picked up the candle.

Her bare feet made hardly a sound as she tiptoed lightly along the passageway, but she was powerless to prevent the eerie creaking of the narrow stairs during her descent to the coffee-room. She had never been afraid of the dark, not even as a small child, and yet, without quite knowing why, something in the atmosphere of the place unnerved her.

It did not help matters when she bumped into one of

the chairs, sending it scraping across the wooden floor, but when she began to imagine every shadow had a life of its own, and a dozen pairs of villainous eyes were watching her every move, she took herself roundly to task for such childish fancies.

Consequently, when she opened the parlour door to discover a darkly cloaked figure standing by the window, she was disinclined to believe the evidence of her own eyes, and it was only when a sudden blast of cold air blew out her candle, and the shadowy figure perched itself on the sill and swung its legs out of the open window to disappear into the night, that she realised her imagination had not been playing tricks on her after all.

Her first impulse was to turn tail and run, but she checked it, and with the self-possession that characterised her she flew across to the windows and securely fastened them, lest the intruder return.

The terrifying possibility that she still might not be alone, that the intruder might have had an accomplice, now waiting in the shadows, ready to pounce on her at any moment, crossed her mind, and she stood perfectly still, not daring to move, hardly daring even to breathe; but the only sounds she heard were the heavy pounding of her own heart, and the solemn ticking of the grandfather clock in the other room.

Slightly reassured, she very slowly turned her head, darting quick glances about the room, trying desperately to pierce the gloom. The only faint light came from the dying embers of the fire and, after taking several deep breaths in a desperate attempt to steady her fraught nerves, she made her way cautiously towards it, very nearly tripping over something lying on the floor.

With trembling hands, she felt along the high shelf until her fingers came into contact with a taper. It was her duty to rouse the landlord, but she flatly refused to venture one more step without the aid of a light to guide her way.

Quickly thrusting the taper into the embers, she relit her candle and only just managed to stifle the hysterical cry that rose in her throat. It was not a chair leg that she had almost tripped over, but a man's leg, a thin leg encased in fashionable primrose knee-breeches, and she instinctively knew, even before she had edged her way round the end of the settle, and had forced herself to look down into those strangely staring insipid blue eyes, that Mr Nutley was dead.

## Chapter Four

For a few moments it was as much as Sarah could do to stop her knees from buckling and to remain standing, then without conscious thought she made all haste back up the stairs and along the passageway to the room situated directly opposite her own. Pausing only a second or two to catch her breath, she scratched lightly upon the door.

"Mr Ravenhurst…? Mr Ravenhurst, are you awake?" she called softly, her heart pounding against her ribcage, but only silence answered her. She raised her hand, about to knock again, when she detected the distinct sound of a bed creaking. The next instant the door opened a fraction, and that heavily scowling countenance, blessedly, appeared in the crack.

"What is it? What's wrong?"

How comforting, how reassuring that curt voice sounded! "It's Mr Nutley, sir. He's downstairs in the parlour. He's dead…I'm certain he's dead"

His heavy frown, if possible, grew more pronounced. "Wait there! I'll be but a moment."

The door closed, but opened again almost at once, and Mr Ravenhurst, looking surprisingly younger with his dark hair tousled by sleep, emerged from the room, dressed in a strikingly patterned brocade robe; and it was only by exercising the firmest self-control that Sarah suppressed the almost overwhelming urge to throw herself on that broad expanse of chest.

"Hold the dratted thing steady, girl!" he scolded, after trying unsuccessfully to light his candle from hers.

She had not realised she was trembling. She suddenly felt so very cold, and so very vulnerable standing there in just her nightdress and shawl, and with her hair tumbling down her back, but managed to gain control of herself sufficiently for him to achieve his objective at the second attempt. Then, without another word, he stalked along the landing, and Sarah almost had to run to keep up with his massive strides.

She followed him down the stairs and across the coffee-room, but flatly refused to re-enter the parlour and remained by the door, watching anxiously as he knelt down by Mr Nutley's body.

"He's dead right enough," he confirmed, after a brief examination. "His neck is broken." He turned his head, saw Sarah still hovering by the door, her face as white as her nightgown, and went slowly towards her, shielding her gaze from Nutley's body.

"What happened, child?" he asked in the gentlest tone she had ever heard a member of his sex use.

"I—I came in here to collect my writing-case." She remembered everything in minute detail, and yet it seemed so unreal, like a terrible dream. "There was someone standing over there by the window. Before I knew what was happening, he'd disappeared."

"Where? Through the windows?"

"Yes. I closed them. The draught blew out my candle,

you see. That's why I went across to the fire. And it was then—it was then that I saw…''

As her voice trailed away, Marcus went over to the windows, checked that they were securely fastened and then drew the curtains. He came back towards her, his expression thoughtful. Then he suddenly became aware of her state of dress.

"Where the devil is your dressing-gown? And you've nothing on your feet!" he admonished.

"W-what?" The scolding tone did manage to penetrate that veil of unreality which seemed to be shrouding her, but she still felt somewhat dazed by it all. "Oh, no, I know. There wasn't room in my cloak-bag for things like that."

He muttered something under his breath as he placed his candle down on one of the tables, and before Sarah could utter more than a stifled protest, he had lifted her into his arms.

"What on earth do you think you are doing, sir?" she demanded, indignation bringing colour back to her cheeks and restoring her self-possession with a vengeance.

"I'm putting you back to bed where you belong," he ground out, striding purposefully back across the coffee-room, and sublimely ignoring her continued demands to be put down at once. "And that is precisely where you are going to stay, my girl! And, for heaven's sake, hold that candle steady! I don't want covering in hot wax."

He carried her effortlessly up the stairs and along the passageway, just as though she had weighed no more than a child, and he was not even breathing heavily, she noticed, as he lay her gently down on her bed.

"You're absolutely frozen, girl!" he continued scolding, after briefly clasping one slender foot in his warm fingers, which had the effect of sending her pulse rate soaring. Casting her a far from approving look, he straightened the bedcovers, relieved her of the candle, and then went over to light the one on the wash-stand.

"Now, I'm going to leave you for a while, but I'll be back. And don't concern yourself if you hear people moving about."

"What are you doing?" she asked in some agitation as he removed the key from the door.

"I'm going to lock you in." Both expression and voice were much softer now. "But don't be alarmed, child. I shan't forget you." He made to leave, but turned back to ask, "You don't happen to know which room Stubbs is in, do you?"

"It's down the far end. First door on the right after the stairs, I think."

She heard the rasping of the key being turned in the lock, the reassuring sound of his firm tread moving along the passageway, and then nothing more for what seemed an interminable length of time, but was perhaps no more than a few minutes.

Then all was action: doors opening and closing; heavy feet descending and mounting the stairs; and a continual muttering of voices. The sounds of people talking below in the parlour eventually reached her ears, but she could not discern just what was being said. She felt certain, though, that one of the voices belonged to Mr Ravenhurst, and smiled to herself as she lay her head back against the pillows.

She felt, oddly, very comforted knowing that he was there. He was so capable, so dependable. It was strange, too, the way she had instinctively gone to him in those moments of panic and confusion after she had discovered poor Mr Nutley, as though to do so were the most natural act in the world. She closed her eyes, trying in-effectually to blot out the memory of Mr Nutley's twisted body and wildly staring eyes.

Her hand trembled as she gripped the bed covers. Re-action, at last, was beginning to set in. She wished des-perately that Mr Ravenhurst would return, but the grand-father clock in the coffee-room had chimed three before she heard the blessed sound of the key being fitted back into the lock, and turned her head on the pillow to see him, a cup in one hand and her writing-case in the other, enter the room.

"Ah, good! You're still awake," he remarked in an almost conversational way, just as though nothing un-toward had occurred. "Here, sit up and drink this."

Sarah automatically obeyed. Taking the cup of warm milk he held out, she took a large swallow, and then grimaced at its taste. "What on earth have you put in it? It's vile!"

"Only a little brandy, my dear." He placed the writ-ing-case down on the floor and then sat himself on the edge of the bed. "Now drink it up. You've had a nasty shock, and it will do you good."

He could not prevent a smile at the suspicious glance she cast the cup's contents as she tentatively raised it to her lips. "Why, anyone would think it was drugged!" His smile faded. "Drugged..." he murmured. "I won-der?"

"What do you wonder?"

"Nothing, child. I was merely thinking aloud. Come, down with that milk."

Feeling fairly sure that he would not let her get away with leaving any, and that he wouldn't balk at forcing the issue by pinching her nose and tossing the contents down her throat himself, Sarah gulped down the rest, and shuddered as she placed the empty cup on the bedside table.

"What has been going on?" She lay her head back down on the pillow once again, perfectly composed, as though it were quite the norm for her to be alone with a man in her bedchamber. "I heard a lot of moving about downstairs."

"Nutley's body has been removed and placed in one of the outhouses," he explained. "The parlour has been tidied, and a thorough search has been made of the downstairs rooms, and those bedchambers we were able to enter."

She frowned up at him. "Why? Surely the intruder wouldn't be foolish enough to return?"

"I should think that highly unlikely, child." His voice was very reassuring, as was his smile. "So rest easy. What we were endeavouring to discover was just how he managed to get in here in the first place. Although we found no sign of a break-in, the landlord freely admits that several of the window catches do not fit properly and could quite easily be forced."

"Then, if he did not break in," she said after a moment's thought, "he must have been in the inn already, or…"

"Or someone let him in," he finished for her. "Yes, child. They seem the only logical alternatives. In the ordinary course of events, a magistrate would have been summoned without delay. Unfortunately, the nearest lives some three miles from here. Getting a message to him is out of the question for a day or two, so we are obliged to deal with the investigation ourselves."

"Oh, dear." A wickedly mischievous twinkle brightened her eyes. "How tiresome for you, sir! You didn't expect to have anything like this thrust upon you when you sought shelter here, did you?''

"No, I most certainly did not! Nor have I any intention of taking responsibility for the unfortunate affair,'' he said determinedly. "And that, my child, is precisely why I did not hesitate to rouse Mr Stubbs.''

"Mr Stubbs?'' she echoed, perplexed.

A wry smile curled his lips. "Our friend Mr Stubbs is none other than a Bow Street Runner.''

"Good heavens!'' Sarah was astounded. "Well, it just goes to show one should never take people at face value.''

"It does indeed,'' he concurred, his twisted smile returning. "He wanted to question you tonight, but I wouldn't hear of it. But if you're not too tired, perhaps you could explain to me exactly what happened, precisely what you saw?''

Sarah was silent for several moments, her brow furrowed in deep thought.

"Something woke me,'' she began. "At first I thought there was someone in my room, but now, of course, I realise the sound must have come from the parlour directly below. I heard the grandfather clock chime the hour, and lit my candle. I knew I wouldn't go back to sleep, so I decided to finish a letter I had begun yesterday morning. Then I remembered I had left my writing-case in the parlour and went down to collect it.''

"Go on,'' he prompted when she fell silent.

"It might have been my imagination, but there was something in the atmosphere of the place…something eerie.'' She shuddered at the memory. "I kept imagining there were people lurking in every shadow. So, by the time I did enter the parlour, and saw someone by the window, I was fully convinced I was seeing things.''

"Were the windows open at this point?"

She frowned in an effort to remember. "Yes. Yes, they must have been, because the draught blew my candle out."

"I imagine, then, our intruder must have heard your approach."

"Well, I'm not surprised," she responded frankly. "I bumped into one of the coffee-room chairs, sending it skidding across the floor."

"That must have been what I heard. Go on," he urged again.

Sarah shrugged. "You know the rest, sir. He escaped through the window, I relit my candle, and then...and then discovered Mr Nutley."

"You said 'he', child. Are you sure it was a man?"

"Oh!" Sarah fixed her eyes on the strong column of his neck. Some detached part of her brain registered that there were dark hairs clearly showing between the lapels of his dressing-gown, but so hard was she concentrating on trying to conjure up a clear vision of the intruder that she paid little heed to this rather startling discovery. "I assumed it was a man. Whoever it was was certainly not as tall as you, sir, more Mr Nutley's height, or maybe an inch or two taller. I cannot be sure because he was wearing a dark cloak with the hood drawn over his head, which might have made him appear taller. He was certainly wearing boots and breeches—which, of course, would suggest a man—and yet...and yet something struck me as rather odd at the time, but for the life of me I cannot think what it could have been."

"All right, my child, that's enough for tonight." Marcus rose to his feet. "You'll need to repeat what you've told me to Stubbs in the morning, but do not worry—I fully intend to be present when he questions you."

The fact that he should insist upon being with her during the interview did not occur to her; she was just grateful that he was offering his support. She watched him move across to the window to check that it was securely fastened. "What's Mr Stubbs doing here, sir? Is he on the trail of some villain?"

"In a manner of speaking, yes." He picked up the candle on the wash-stand before moving back over to the bed, and looked down at her with his attractive smile. "But, unless you are a jewel thief, my dear, you've nothing to fear."

"Oh, I see." Her eyes glinted like those of a child who was about to indulge in some new and exciting game. "The diamond necklace you were discussing yesterday, I should warrant."

"Amongst others, yes. He's learnt of a certain gentleman in Bristol who doesn't bother asking too many questions about items brought to his establishment. Now, that really is enough for tonight!" he said authoritatively, like a strict uncle dealing with a recalcitrant child. "Try to get some sleep. I shall lock your door again, but don't worry. I shall sleep with mine open, and shall hear you if you should call."

It never entered her head to protest. The brandy was beginning to take effect, and she had no troubling in dropping off to sleep.

When she opened her eyes again it was to discover that it was morning and to find Daisy standing beside the bed.

"Ooh, ma'am, what dreadful goings on, eh? That poor young gentleman. Me and Rose learned all about it when we arrived. Ma and Pa's right upset. Never 'ad anything like this 'appen 'ere afore."

"Yes. It will be a shock to everyone."

"Aye. And you most of all, I'll warrant. It must of been terrible finding 'im that way. How are you feeling, Mrs Armstrong?"

"Dreadful!" Sarah placed her hand to her throbbing temple. "Mr Ravenhurst laced my milk with brandy. And now I have the headache!"

"You ain't the only one, ma'am," Daisy informed her, her plump face breaking into what Sarah considered an extremely callous smile. "Apart from Mr Ravenhurst, everyone seems to 'ave a sore 'ead this morning."

Sarah watched Daisy draw back the curtains, and then screwed up her eyes against the painfully bright light. "What time is it?"

"Getting on for ten, ma'am. Mr Ravenhurst said as how you weren't to be disturbed any earlier."

The dratted man seemed to be taking an awful lot upon himself! Sarah felt quite out of charity with him as she eased herself into a sitting position so that Daisy could place the tray on her lap. She found she had little appetite, but managed to force down a buttered roll and to drink a cup of coffee before placing the tray back on the bedside table.

When she went down to the coffee-room, half an hour later, it was to find Mr Ravenhurst and Captain Carter seated at a table. Mr Ravenhurst had his face buried between the printed sheets of a newspaper, but raised his head at her approach, and rose to his feet, his dark eyes scrutinising her face.

"How are you feeling this morning?" he enquired gently, and could not mistake the flash of annoyance in her eyes before she seated herself at the table.

"But for you, sir, I think I would have been perfectly

well. He took it upon himself to force brandy down my throat," Sarah explained in response to the young Captain's puzzled look.

"If it's any consolation, child," Marcus drawled, sounding sublimely unconcerned, "there are others similarly afflicted."

"So I have been reliably informed. But it is scant consolation."

He smiled at the pettish tone as he turned his attention once again to the journal. "How riveting!" he remarked in an attempt to change the subject. "It would seem the Fair Langley is rivalling Sarah Siddons in popularity."

"I have never been to the theatre, so have never been privileged to see either of them," Sarah admitted, placing her elbows on the table and resting her chin on her hands. "But I believe Mrs Langley is considered a very handsome woman."

"Like yourself, ma'am, I have never seen the lady perform," the Captain responded, "so cannot comment on her degree of beauty, but can safely say that although men may appreciate handsome women, we much prefer pretty ones. Eh, Ravenhurst?"

"Infinitely," he answered, his eyes resting on Sarah's delicately featured profile.

It wasn't necessary to look at him; she instinctively knew those dark eyes were turned in her direction, and could feel the heat glowing in her cheeks. There had been an unmistakable teasing quality in the Captain's voice, but not in Mr Ravenhurst's, and she felt untold relief when there was the sound of a door opening, and Dottie emerged from the parlour, holding a highly perfumed handkerchief to her temple.

"Oh, Mrs *Armitage!* What a to-do, eh?" she wailed. "It were bad enough waking up with the worst 'ead I've 'ad in years, but then to be questioned as though I was a common criminal. And 'ere I thought Mr *Stebbs* were such a nice man, too!''

"He is only doing his duty, madam," Marcus responded, displaying not a ha'p'orth of sympathy.

"I know that, Mr *Ravenleigh*, but the whole business 'as sent me quite unnecessary, and I think I'll lie down for a bit." She cast an appealing glance at the more sympathetic younger man. "Would you assist me up to my room, Captain? Me legs feel all queer."

Rolling his eyes in Mr Ravenhurst's direction, the Captain rose from the table. "It will be my pleasure, Miss de Vine."

Sarah frowned in puzzlement as her eyes followed their progress towards the stairs. "Do you know, sir, I do not think Dottie can be a very good actress. She cannot even remember people's names. So how on earth does she memorise her lines?"

His lips twitched as he rose from the table. "I think the theatre plays only a small part in our 'Divine' Dorothea's life, my little innocent. Her talents, unless I'm very much mistaken, lie in quite another direction. Now, do not let us keep Mr Stubbs waiting."

Only for an instant, as Sarah entered the room, and stared briefly at that portion of floor where Mr Nutley's body had lain, did she experience any slight trepidation. Mr Stubbs, looking very efficient, sat at the table with several sheets of his hand-written notes in front of him. She answered all the questions he put to her clearly and without hesitation, but she was unable to tell him any more than she had told Mr Ravenhurst the night before.

"And nothing else has occurred to you?"

The question came from her guardian, and she turned her head to look directly into his eyes. "Yes, sir, it has.

Why do so many people appear to be suffering from the headache this morning? Mr Stubbs, here, appears similarly afflicted.''

The Runner had, indeed, been massaging his forehead on several occasions, but his perceptive grey eyes had remained fixed on Sarah throughout the interview. He turned his gaze on to Mr Ravenhurst, one greying brow rising. ''I think we can tell her that, sir, don't you?''

''I don't think there's any need,'' Sarah put in before Mr Stubbs could explain. ''With the exception of Mr Ravenhurst, everyone was drugged.''

''Clever girl!'' Marcus's lips curled into an appreciative smile. ''Stubbs and I had come to that conclusion.''

''Normally, ma'am, I am a very light sleeper. It is essential in my line of work. But last night I slept heavily. I heard nothing. In fact, it took Mr Ravenhurst, here, a full five minutes to rouse me.''

''The drug could not have been in the wine,'' Sarah voiced after a moment's intense thought, ''because I had a glass with my dinner. Therefore, it must have been…''

''In the punch,'' Marcus finished for her. ''I did notice yesterday evening that although Nutley poured himself a glass, it remained on the table by his elbow, untouched. It's a pity, in this instance, that the lady of the house is such a diligent person. She cleaned both bowl and glasses before retiring for the night, so we are unable to confirm our theory.''

''I see.'' Again Sarah became thoughtful. ''Wait a moment, though. What about Miss Grimshaw and Mr Winthrope? They did not join us yesterday evening. Have you had the opportunity to question them?''

''Yes, I have, ma'am.'' Mr Stubbs referred to his notes. ''Miss Grimshaw is in the habit of taking a few drops of laudanum in water last thing to help her sleep, and so heard nothing. And Mr Winthrope came down to request more candles, as he'd been reading throughout the evening, and was accosted by Mr Nutley who, having just finished preparing the punch in the coffee-room, persuaded the gentleman to sample a glass.

"Mr Winthrope assures me that ordinarily he doesn't imbibe in strong liquor, but isn't averse to the occasional glass of rum punch. And as for the others…" Again he referred to his notes. "Not one of them heard a thing until roused by Mr Ravenhurst and myself. Although Mr Ravenhurst's groom mentioned that Nutley did try to persuade him and the innkeeper's son to sample a glass of the punch whilst they were keeping each other company in the tap, but they both declined."

Sarah's frown returned. "But why should Mr Nutley have attempted to drug everyone? Unless, of course, he had arranged to meet the man in the cloak and didn't want anyone to witness that encounter."

"A distinct possibility, child," Marcus agreed. "Or his intent was quite otherwise, and he was disturbed by our mysterious cloaked figure. But whether or not his death was accidental, we can only speculate at this juncture."

Sarah shuddered convulsively as she rose from the table. "Unless you've any further questions, Mr Stubbs, I think I shall return to my room."

She closed the door behind her, leaving the two men in private. Although Mr Ravenhurst had flatly refused to take any responsibility for the enquiry into the sad affair until a magistrate could be summoned, it was evident that, perhaps because he was acquainted with Mr Nutley's family, he felt obliged to take some interest in the proceedings.

And as Mr Ravenhurst had proved, beyond a shadow

of a doubt now, he was not a man to shirk any obligation. So why, then, a tiny voice reminded her, had he behaved so out of character during his guardianship of her? It just didn't make sense.

Sarah pondered anew over this rather puzzling circumstance as she made her way back to her room. At the head of the stairs she heard one of the bechamber doors close, followed by the sound of humming, and turned to see Daisy's pretty golden-haired cousin tripping lightly along the passageway towards her.

The girl cast her a rather furtive glance as she brushed past and Sarah's eyes narrowed suspiciously as she watched her progress down the stairs. Perhaps Daisy's dislike of her cousin was well founded, after all: there was something decidedly sly about that girl.

Dismissing the thought from her mind, she went along the passageway and into her own room. Although there were no signs, yet, of a thaw, there had been, thankfully, no further falls of snow during the night, and the day was dry and bright.

Sarah decided that she had had more than enough of being cooped up in the inn, and collected her cloak from the wardrobe. As she swirled it about her shoulders, the folds caught Dottie's book, which had been placed on the bedside table, sending it tumbling to the floor.

Bending to retrieve the volume, Sarah noticed a folded sheet of paper lying beside it and, believing it to be her own, cast her eyes over the few lines written in a rounded childish scrawl: *I am glad you did that to the little worm, Dottie. He had it coming to him. Hope everything turns out well for you. Eliza.*

Why, this must be the letter that Dottie had been searching for the previous day! She must have slipped it inside the back cover of her book for safekeeping, and then forgotten where she had put it, Sarah decided, and so took it along to Dottie's room.

After scratching lightly upon the firmly closed door, and waiting in vain for her summons to be answered, Sarah pondered on what she should do, for she could clearly detect soft moaning sounds and the creaking of bedsprings, so knew there was someone within.

Fearing Dottie might be unwell, she very gently turned the doorknob, opening the door sufficiently for her to poke her head into the room, and then promptly coloured to the roots of her hair at the sight that met her naïve, incredulous gaze.

She had often pondered with her friend Clarissa on the mysteries of the marriage bed, those untold, secret dealings between men and women that married ladies carefully avoided discussing with their younger and less experienced counterparts. Sarah realised in those few brief moments of acute embarrassment and stupefaction that she was witnessing, first-hand, those veiled relations between the sexes.

Then, before either Dottie or Captain Carter could detect her presence, she quietly closed the door, thrust Dottie's letter beneath, and flew down the passageway, only to collide moments later with a solid, immovable object at the head of the stairs. Strong fingers grasped her arms, steadying her, and she found herself staring up into laughing dark brown eyes.

"Anyone would imagine the devil himself were after you. Steady, child!" Marcus then noted the heightened colour and slightly erratic breathing, and his smile faded. "What is it? What's occurred to distress you?"

"Why, nothing! Nothing at all," she managed, but not very convincingly. "I'm just going out for some air," and before he could detain her further, she broke free from his gently steadying hold and rushed headlong down the stairs.

The cold air on her burning cheeks was refreshing, and it was such a relief to be out of doors after the previous day's confinement. The day looked set to remain dry and bright, giving one reason to hope that the thaw would not be long in commencing. No vehicle, though, had braved a journey along the road; the snow remained a furrowless thick blanket of white, sparkling brightly like some glinting bed of crystals.

A sudden gust of the biting northerly wind sent the brightly coloured inn sign swinging to and fro on its rusty hinges, drawing her attention, and she looked up to see the painting of an old man making his weary way towards a building whose windows were ablaze with welcoming light.

"The Traveller's Rest," she murmured with a wry little smile. There had been precious little rest for the weary travellers who had sought shelter beneath this roof, and she certainly didn't envisage that state of affairs changing after the tragic events of the previous night.

"Ah! So there you are."

Sarah swung round to see Mr Ravenhurst, seemingly oblivious to the icy conditions underfoot, striding towards her. Evidently, he had doubted her assurances that she was perfectly all right, and had come out in search of her. How very thoughtful! She felt strangely touched by this obvious concern for her welfare.

"Not that we can walk very far, but permit me to show you round the outside of our temporary dwelling place," and without giving her the opportunity to acquiesce or not he reached for her hand.

In those moments when those long shapely fingers,

strong yet gentle, curled about hers to entwine her arm through his, a vision of yet another long-fingered, shapely hand fondling a large white breast flashed before her mind's eye. What must it feel like to be caressed like that? she wondered, as Dottie's image was replaced suddenly by one of herself lying on a bed, a lean, muscular frame stretched out alongside her.

She was aware of a strangely powerful craving developing deep within. Only it wasn't the image of the tall Captain's well-muscled frame pressed against her soft white nakedness that aroused this frighteningly powerful yearning, but that of the man beside her.

A further gust of icy-cold wind brought her out of her reverie with a start. What on earth had come over her to imagine such things? she wondered, appalled at having had such abandoned thoughts. Surely she couldn't possibly be attracted to this man? No, unthinkable! Ravenhurst was her guardian, for heaven's sake! He stood in place of a…a father.

She cast a tentative glance up at that hard-featured profile. The trouble was, though, she just couldn't bring herself to see him in that light; and only hoped, as they set off on their stroll round the rambling old building, that if he should happen to notice the renewed scarlet flush mounting her cheeks he would put it down to nothing more than the frosty nip of the cold north wind.

The men had stuck to their task the previous day, and had managed to clear a path all round the inn, but Sarah's stout boots slipped occasionally on the exposed stones, and she was glad of that supporting arm. They inspected the exterior of the many outhouses, but Sarah carefully avoided enquiring into which Mr Nutley's body had been placed, and they ended their tour in the long stone-built barn, which contained only three horses and one cow.

They sat themselves down on the wooden stools placed near the open doorway, and after a few minutes Sarah realised that Mr Ravenhurst, who had been conversing quite amicably during their short tour, had grown very quiet as his dark eyes scanned the rear aspect of the inn.

''What are you studying so thoughtfully, sir?''

''That lean-to roof.''

Sarah turned her attention to the single-storey construction, which had obviously been added to the original building at some later date, and which ran along the whole length of the inn's back wall. Its sloping roof was tiled, and at its highest point was only a matter of a foot below the four bedroom windows.

''Are you thinking the intruder might have entered the inn that way?''

''It's a possibility, certainly. Climb on that water butt at the end there, and you can get on the roof without any trouble. Why, even a child could do it! If there is a loose catch on any one of those windows, it would be a simple matter to insert a knife or some other thin implement and flick open the catch.

''It's a great pity the landlord and his son cleared the snow off that roof yesterday. We would have seen footprints and known for sure, then. But as some of the timbers are not too sound, it's quite understandable why they did so.''

''Supposing our intruder did enter by one of those windows, he was taking an awful risk. After all, he wasn't to know that most of the occupants of those rooms had been drugged,''

''Very true.''

"And if that were, indeed, the case, surely the motive for doing so must have been robbery, and not to meet Mr Nutley."

"It certainly looks that way."

"More importantly, though, where did he go after climbing out of the parlour window? Travel is nigh impossible, even on a horse. Nothing has passed along that road for a day and a half. I know one can manage to walk into the village because Daisy and Rose have done so, but—" She gave a sudden start. "Oh, Lord! You don't think it was one of the local inhabitants, do you?"

"That, too, is a distinct possibility."

She looked searchingly at him. "But you don't think so, do you?"

"I'm not sure what I think, child. But Nutley drugged the rum for some purpose. And if we could uncover why he did that, it might give us the answers to a great many questions." He stood up and assisted Sarah to her feet. "Come, let us return indoors. It will soon be time for luncheon."

Leaving Mr Ravenhurst to quench his thirst with a tankard of the landlord's excellent home-brewed, Sarah made her way up the stairs, blushing slightly as she hurried past Dottie's room. She had only just hung her cloak back in the wardrobe when there was a knock on the door, and she turned, surprised, to see Miss Grimshaw quietly enter the bedchamber.

"Mrs Armstrong, I thought it my duty to come and see you. How are you feeling? What a terrible thing to have happened!" She slumped down, uninvited, on to the only chair. "Why, we might all have been murdered in our beds!"

"I'm fine, ma'am," Sarah assured her. "It was kind of you to take the trouble to enquire."

"You saw who killed poor Mr Nutley, so I've been told."

"I certainly saw the intruder, ma'am. But whether or not he was responsible for Mr Nutley's death…"

"Yes, yes. I suppose it might have been an accident, but… Oh, dear! My poor nerves won't stand much more of this. I can hardly wait to be away from this wretched place!"

"I think we all feel the same."

Miss Grimshaw cast her a rather penetrating glance before staring fixedly down into her lap. "Yes, yes. I dare say. But I expect you will need to stay to see the magistrate or—or someone. After all, you're the only one who saw the intruder."

"I saw a figure, yes, but I didn't see his face. I could pass him in the street and wouldn't recognise him."

"Oh, I see! Well, in that case, there would be little point in your remaining." Miss Grimshaw placed a hand to her temple. "I long to be with my sister in Bristol, Mrs Armstrong. Even though I didn't really know the young gentleman, I'm afraid this dreadful business has quite overset me. Did you know Mr Nutley at all well? Did you become acquainted yesterday?"

Sarah thought this rather an odd question to ask, but didn't hesitate to respond. "Naturally we had some conversation. It is rather difficult to avoid one another in this inn. But we had never met before. Mr Ravenhurst knew him, however. I believe he lives not too far away from Mr Nutley's parents. I suppose that is why he has taken an interest in proceedings."

"A very proper attitude!" Miss Grimshaw remarked, rising to her feet. "Well, I shan't detain you further, Mrs Armstrong. It will soon be time for luncheon, and you are no doubt eager to join the others downstairs."

"Why not eat with us yourself, ma'am?" Sarah suggested. "It might help to keep your mind off things."

"That is kind of you, but I'm not very good in mixed company. I think gentleman find me a little trying. No, I'm better on my own."

Sarah, watching the woman leave the room, experienced the most peculiar feeling of unease. Had that visit really been made out of the purest motives? She could not help thinking that it was quite otherwise.

## Chapter Five

Sarah was rudely awoken not by Daisy this time, bringing in the morning pitcher of warm water, but by a bedroom door being slammed, quickly followed by the sound of heavy footsteps hurrying along the passageway. It was in all probability only the farmer and his wife rising early as usual in order to help in the kitchen. In which case, it would be quite some time before the pitcher arrived, she thought and, turning on to her side, promptly went back to sleep.

When she awoke again, it was to see a bright ray of sunlight filtering though the chink between the patterned drapes. Swinging her feet to the floor, she padded across to the window, and could have wept for joy at the sight that met her eyes as she drew back the curtains.

Some time during the night the wind had changed direction from a biting-cold northerly to a much friendlier westerly. Although the landscape was still covered in its blanket of white, droplets of water were running down the window panes. The thaw had begun!

Deciding not to wait for Daisy, Sarah washed in the contents of the previous day's pitcher. It was unpleasantly cold, but she didn't care. The only thing that mattered was that she would soon be able to leave this place; perhaps not that day, but certainly the next, providing, of course, the wind continued to blow from its present direction and, perish the thought, there were no fresh falls of snow.

She refused, however, to be pessimistic and, hurriedly finishing her toilet, went downstairs, expecting to join the other no doubt equally jubilant stranded travellers, only to discover the coffee-room, surprisingly, deserted.

She frowned as she went over to the table at which they usually ate their meals. Not even the covers had been laid. How very odd! Although her stay at the inn had been far from pleasant, she had no fault to find with the landlady, who always had meals prepared on time. A quick glance at the grandfather clock, solemnly ticking away in the corner, confirmed that she was far from late in coming down to breakfast. So where was everyone?

It was then that she detected the sound of voices in the parlour. Surmising that breakfast for some reason was once again being served in there, she was about to enter when a noise behind her caught her attention and she turned to see Daisy, carrying a large tray, enter the coffee-room. One swift glance at those red-rimmed eyes was sufficient to warn Sarah that all was not as it should be.

"Why, Daisy! Whatever's the matter?"

"Oh, ma'am!" Depositing the tray on the table and herself down on a chair, Daisy sniffed loudly. "It—it's our Rose. She—she were found behind the hen-coop this morning by our Joe. She's been done for… Her throat's been cut!"

Sarah, joining her at the table, could hardly believe it, didn't want to believe it. "When did it happen?"

"During the night, they reckon." Daisy drew out her handkerchief and blew her snub nose vigorously. "I overheard Mr Stubbs say as 'ow she'd been dead for several hours."

Sarah frowned. "But I understood that you and Rose walked back to the village together, directly after serving dinner here in the evening."

"Aye, Mrs Armstrong, that be right. And we walked back to me aunt's house together last night. I been sharing Rose's room. We ate our supper, and then went to bed at the usual time, but when I wakes this morning she weren't there. I thought it odd, but didn't pay it much mind. I thought she'd just got up early and come 'ere by 'erself. Our Joe found 'er when he went out to collect the eggs for breakfast."

"So, at some point during the night," Sarah remarked after a moment's intense thought, "Rose got out of bed, dressed and came here. She must have arranged to meet someone, surely?"

"Aye, ma'am, that's what we all thinks. I know its wrong to speak ill of the dead, but she were a right flighty piece. There be no getting away from it. Our Joe were right fond of 'er, but she weren't interested in 'im. Kept calling 'im a slow-top and the like. You can bet your life she came 'ere to meet some man. She were forever teasing the village lads, setting one against the other. I reckons one of 'em 'ad 'ad enough, and did for 'er."

It was certainly a possibility, especially if Rose's disposition was flirtatious. But why arrange to meet someone here? Sarah wondered. It just didn't make sense. Surely if Rose had wanted the meeting with this man kept secret, she would hardly select directly outside her aunt's house as a trysting place?

Reaching for the coffee-pot, Sarah was about to pour herself a cup when the sound of hysterical sobbing reached her ears, and she turned her head in the direction of the parlour's closed door.

"Who on earth is in there?"

"Mr Stubbs carted Miss de Vine in there quite some time ago, ma'am," Daisy disclosed in a conspiratorial whisper. "Summat to do with a letter found on our Rose. Though what Rose were doing with it, I can't imagine. Couldn't read a word, she couldn't!" The pathetic sobs continued. "Sounds right upset, don't she? Wonder what they're doing to 'er in there?"

"I don't know, but I mean to find out!" Without a moment's hesitation Sarah stormed into the parlour to discover not only Mr Stubbs, but Mr Ravenhurst too, and poor Dottie, her elbows resting on the table, and her face buried in her hands. "What on earth is going on?" she demanded, the light of battle in her eyes.

"You should not be here, child." Marcus's tone betrayed his annoyance at the interruption, but Sarah stood her ground.

"I have as much right to be in here as you have," she countered and, ignoring that, now, all-too-familiar low growl, calmly closed the door and moved towards them.

Dottie grasped Sarah's hand in pathetically trembling fingers. "Oh, Mrs Armstrong!" she wailed, for perhaps the first time in her life remembering someone's name correctly. "They say I done it, but I didn't. I swear I didn't!"

"We're saying nothing of the sort, you foolish creature!" Marcus snapped as he continued to stare in a far-from-friendly fashion at Sarah. "We are merely trying to discover why a letter written to you was in that servant girl's possession.''

''And I keep telling you it ain't mine!'' Dottie cast her blue eyes up to Sarah in wide appeal. ''They won't believe me, but I ain't never seen it before in my life.''

Sarah turned to Mr Stubbs. ''May I see this letter?'' and without the least hesitation he handed it across to her. The ink was smudged, but the writing was still legible, and she had no difficulty in recognising it as the letter that had fallen from the book, and which, subsequently, she had slipped beneath Dottie's door. As the note had her name clearly written on it, it was extremely foolish of Dottie to deny ownership, unless...

Sarah gave a sudden start as a suspicion crossed her mind. Raising her eyes, she held Mr Ravenhurst's angry gaze above Dottie's head, and then quite deliberately turned the letter the other way up before handing it to Dottie. ''Just have one more look to make sure. I know your eyes aren't too good, and the ink is rather smudged. But, just to be certain.''

Sarah saw enlightenment dawn on the men's faces as Dottie, without turning the letter the right way up, cast her eyes over its contents, just as though she were reading every word.

''No, I ain't never seen it before,'' she confirmed.

''No, but I most certainly have,'' Sarah astonished them all by admitting. She calmly took the letter from Dottie and handed it back to Mr Stubbs, who was regarding her with intense interest now. ''Dottie loaned me a book the day after we all arrived here. Yesterday morning I accidentally knocked the book on to the floor, and that letter fell out. It wasn't until after I had apprised myself of its contents that I realised it wasn't mine, and so took it along to Dottie's room.''

"But you never gave it to me!" Dottie stated flatly.

"No, I know I didn't. You—er—were not alone at the time. I believe Captain Carter was with you, so I pushed it under your door." Sarah could feel the heat rising in her cheeks, and carefully avoided looking in Mr Ravenhurst's direction.

"There are one or two other rather important facts you ought to be aware of, Mr Stubbs…I have it on the best authority that the poor dead girl was illiterate. Furthermore, how did that letter come to be in her possession? More interestingly, though, the letter, I noticed, has been deliberately altered. It was signed by someone calling herself Eliza, not A Well-wisher."

"Eliza Cooper!" Dottie exclaimed. "She were working at that theatre with me."

Sarah cast a look of comical dismay at Mr Ravenhurst. "You're certain her name is Cooper?" she asked tentatively, knowing all too well the lively damsel's propensity for getting names wrong.

"Course I am!…or it might be Hooper," Dottie amended after a moment's thought. "Something like that, anyhow."

Sarah could not prevent a twitching smile. "And the—er—little worm your friend Eliza refers to is…?"

"Oh, 'im! He were the boss o' that rubbishing place. Dirty old demon! He were always after us girls. Wouldn't leave us alone."

Tears forgotten, Dottie gurgled with laughter. "I got 'im a bit tipsy one afternoon, took off all his clothes and got one o' the lads to 'elp me carry 'im on to the stage. Brought the house down, it did, when he stood up stark naked in the middle of the first act." She raised her shoulders in an indifferent shrug. "Course, he gave me the push afterwards, but it were worth it."

"I dare say all this can be confirmed, Mr Stubbs," Sarah remarked airily. She felt rather pleased with herself for coming so successfully to Dottie's aid and, although Mr Ravenhurst's brows remained fixed in a disapproving scowl, Mr Stubbs, before she went out, looked far from displeased with her interruption.

Her appetite having deserted her completely, Sarah went directly up to her room to collect her cloak. As she stepped outside the inn, the rapidly melting snow squelched beneath her boots. There were large puddles everywhere, and several wheel tracks, now, along the road. Life, it seemed, was getting back to normal.

But would life ever be the same at The Traveller's Rest? she wondered, walking across the yard. Certainly not for some considerable time. She shook her head in disbelief. It seemed incredible that such grisly events had taken place in this idyllic rural setting. Two deaths in as many days! A frisson of fear feathered its way down the length of her spine as the gruesome thought of who might be next crossed her mind.

"Oh!" She gave a sudden start as she walked into the stable. "I didn't see you standing there, Captain."

"Sorry if I startled you, ma'am." He stepped out of the shadows. "Came out to blow a cloud, as there were no signs of breakfast being served."

"It is ready now," she informed him, sitting herself down on one of the low stools. "What do you make of this sad business, Captain? I must confess it has me puzzled."

Flicking the cigar butt into the yard, he sat beside her on the other stool. "I don't know, ma'am. Nutley's death might well have been an accident. He might have fallen awkwardly, and hit his head on the edge of the settle, and it was that which broke his neck. But the young girl...?'' He shook his head. "That was murder...cold-blooded murder.''

"But why on earth should anyone want to murder a—a servant girl?''

"She might well have discovered something about Nutley's death. When Stubbs examined the body, he found a fragment of a five-pound note clutched in the dead girl's fingers.''

"Blackmail?'' Sarah's eyes widened for an instant, then she became thoughtful. "Yes. Yes, I should say Rose would have been capable of that. After all, where else would she have come by such a large sum of money? I wonder just what she had discovered...and, more importantly, about whom? Surely not someone staying at the inn?''

"It certainly looks that way, Mrs Armstrong. The weapon used in the attack was lying in the snow beside the body. The landlady recognised it as one of her own kitchen knives.''

"Oh, my God!'' Sarah's stomach lurched violently at the mere thought of someone at the inn being the culprit. "I know Dottie's letter was found in the dead girl's possession, but... No, I cannot believe Dottie would ever do such a thing!''

"Oh?'' His russet-coloured brows rose. "And why not? Women are as capable as men of committing dastardly, underhanded deeds.''

Sarah stared at him sharply. His tone had been flat, indifferent almost, as though it would not have mattered a jot to him if the murderer did turn out to be none other than Dottie. Yet, how could he remain so impassive after what had taken place between them only yesterday? Surely he must care something for the woman? Or could a man share those experiences with a female and remain totally unemotional…? Apparently, yes.

She felt, unaccountably, annoyed, and found herself saying, a touch of censure creeping into her voice, "But I thought you liked Dottie, Captain Carter?"

"I neither like, nor dislike her, ma'am," he responded with brutal frankness. "I have learnt the hard way that people are not always what they seem. And have been given little reason to trust your sex."

Sarah's annoyance faded and she regarded him thoughtfully. His voice had remained level enough, but she had easily detected the bitterness and underlying hurt. She gazed at his strong, attractive profile.

She had liked Captain Carter from the first and, had circumstances been different, had she not been forced to play the part of a recently widowed young woman, friendly but slightly aloof, wary of every word lest she give her true identity away, she would not have objected to getting to know him a little better. He was still a young man: twenty-four; twenty-five at most. Yet, already, life had begun to etch unmistakable lines of cynicism in his young face.

"So, you have been let down by a lady, Captain. And rather badly, I suspect. And now you have scant regard for the rest of my sex." She saw his strong hands clench, the knuckles growing white. She had no intention of prying, and was tolerably certain that he would not satisfy her curiosity if she did, but could not prevent herself from adding, "There is a great deal of bitterness in you, sir. And, I suspect, it does not all stem from unhappy dealings with women."

He looked at her then, his tawny eyes questioning. "What do you mean?"

"You made it abundantly clear, the very first morning

we met, that you bore a grudge against our privileged class."

His well-shaped mouth twisted into a begrudging smile. "And with good reason, ma'am. Although, I suppose, you might say I number amongst them."

"Oh?"

"My father was a younger son of a Viscount. But my mother, God bless her, came from rather different stock."

"Really? Then we have something in common, sir," Sarah responded, completely forgetting to put a guard on her tongue. "My mother was a baronet's daughter, and my father a naval captain."

"Well, well!" There was not a trace of bitterness, now, in his pleasant voice. "Tell me, ma'am, do you ever feel that you belong in neither one class nor the other?"

She shrugged. "To be honest, I've never given it much thought. I am what I am, sir, and there is nothing that can be done to change that. But it does anger me sometimes when people suggest that my mother married beneath her. My father was a courageous man. And I'll not hear a word said against him!"

"Good for you, ma'am!" His smile was full of appreciative warmth, and there was more than just a hint of respect in his tawny-coloured eyes, too. "And you are wrong, by the way...I do not hold all members of your sex in contempt."

"Do I intrude?" Mr Ravenhurst suddenly appeared in the doorway, his expression anything but warm. "Stubbs is looking for you, Carter," he informed him curtly. "Wants to ask you some questions."

"Lord! It's worse than the Spanish Inquisition in this place! In fact, I'll be glad to return to that country. It's a dashed sight more restful." The Captain reluctantly rose to his feet. "May I escort you back inside, Mrs Armstrong?"

"I am more than capable of performing that courtesy!" Marcus snapped out. "Therefore, do not let us detain you."

Sarah saw the Captain's smile fade and his eyes narrow, and hurriedly intervened. "You go on ahead, sir. I shall be along presently." For a few moments Sarah watched his progress across the yard, and then turned a reproachful look up at the man glowering above her. "Are you always in such a disagreeable mood before noon?"

"Only when I'm put into one by damnably foolish actions!" he retorted. "What do you mean by remaining out here alone with that man?"

How dared he adopt such a high-handed tone with her! Sarah rose from the stool, her bosom heaving. "And what, pray, has that to do with you, sirrah?"

"God give me strength!" he rasped through clenched teeth and, before she knew what he was about, he took a firm hold of her upper arms and shook her none too gently. "You brainless creature! A young female has been brutally murdered here within the last twelve hours, possibly by someone residing at this inn, and you wander about aimlessly, just as though nothing untoward had occurred."

"Oh, how dare you!" Sarah gasped, breathless from the shaking. She had never been so ill-used; nor could she ever recall feeling so angry with anyone in her life before. "Kindly remove your hands from my person. I dislike it excessively!"

Her lofty tone drew a ghost of a smile to his lips. "You might need to accustom yourself, my girl."

"Now you are being ridiculous! As ridiculous as suggesting Captain Carter is the murderer."

"I was suggesting nothing of the sort!" He released her then, his smile vanishing as he ran an impatient hand through his dark hair. "But, unlike you, I possess some discernment, and do not accept people at face value."

"And neither do I. But unlike you," she mimicked him with wicked sarcasm, "I try to look for the best in people."

"In the circumstances, my girl, that is singularly foolish. You would do better to cultivate the opposite standpoint. What do you know about Captain Carter? What do you know about any of them?"

"Not very much, I'll admit. But I know I am as safe with Captain Carter as I am with…with you."

"Oh, is that so?" he purred silkily. The sudden glint in his dark eyes should have warned her, but she took little heed. "So, you think you are safe with me," and before she knew it, she was in his arms and his lips had fastened securely on to hers.

Only for an instant did she struggle against the pressure of his mouth and the firm clasp of those muscular arms, then quite suddenly, unexpectedly, she found herself responding. Of their own volition her lips parted beneath his, and his kiss deepened, demanding and receiving a response.

Her imaginings of the day before were becoming a reality. That powerfully exhilarating sensation deep within began to stir once again, and her body seemed suddenly to have acquired a will of its own.

Her young breasts, pressed against that broad expanse of chest, grew hard, and she experienced an almost overwhelming desire to raise her arms, to entwine them round his neck, to run her fingers through that dark waving hair and to keep those tantalisingly disturbing lips securely fastened to her own, but his arms continued to encircle hers, restraining, keeping her his firm, but far from unwilling, captive.

When at last he released her, she was achingly aware that her traitorous body yearned to be pressed against that hard muscular frame once again, and could only stare up at him in wonder, in disbelief, almost.

"Now, let that be a lesson to you," he said in strangely hoarse tones, his breathing as ragged as hers. "It is unwise to be alone with any man. No matter how honourable he may be, given enough provocation, he might not always behave as he ought."

Sarah did not wait to hear more. Reality had returned with a vengeance, and she felt the red-hot heat of shame rising rapidly to the roots of her hair. Swirling round, she hurried back inside the inn, not stopping to catch her breath until she had attained the relative sanctuary of her bedchamber.

Slumping down on to the bed, she placed her hands to her burning cheeks. What must he think of her? She had behaved no better than a wanton! And yet she seemed, even now, powerless to quell that strange yearning in her newly awakened young body. If she were to grant the opportunity, could any man have such a devastating effect on her? She quickly thrust this disturbing thought aside, for she knew it couldn't possibly be true.

On one occasion when she had been staying at her friend Clarissa's home, she had been caught in the shrubbery by a neighbour's son. She had found his advances repugnant, and had boxed the spotty youth's ears soundly when he had tried to kiss her.

Yet Mr Ravenhurst's kiss had aroused no desire for such retaliatory actions, a taunting little voice reminded her. He, of course, was a man of experience. He had probably kissed scores of females, and had no doubt enjoyed the charms of many a beautiful mistress over the years, she thought bitterly, experiencing for the first time in her life that gnawing pain of jealousy.

She released her breath in a heartfelt sigh. It was a lowering realisation, but one much better faced—he had kissed her merely to teach her a lesson. It had meant less than nothing to him. And yet, her brows drew together in a deeply puzzled frown, if that was, indeed, the case, why then had he seemed just for one unguarded moment as disturbed by the experience as she had herself?

As no logical explanation came readily to mind, Sarah tried not to dwell on the disconcerting interlude, but this proved no easy task. In the end she decided she could not possibly come face to face with Marcus Ravenhurst again until she had herself, mind and body, well in hand. She remained incarcerated in her room for the remainder of the morning, and for the first time since her arrival at the inn requested a meal brought up on a tray.

Having not partaken of breakfast, she consumed every last morsel on her plate, and had only just set the tray back down on the bedside table when there was a knock on the door, and her tormentor, himself, walked boldly into the room, just as though he had every right to do so and, what was worse, as though he hadn't a care in the world.

"Over your sulks yet?" he enquired with a wickedly provoking smile, and that was all it needed to restore Sarah's equilibrium.

She glowered across the small room at him. "I have not been sulking!" she retorted. "And kindly close the door again on your way out," she added pointedly.

"Now, that is most impolite, my girl. Especially as I came here to see if you would care to leave."

"Leave?" she echoed, forgetting to be angry with him. "Do you mean the roads are passable?"

"Certainly. The Mail was spotted travelling along the main road quite early this morning. The local magistrate is here now, and I've cleared it with him for us to be on our way."

"How wonderful!" She was on her feet in an instant. "The landlord very kindly offered to return me to—"

"I know all about that," he cut in. "I've already told him I'll escort you. Do you think you can be ready in half an hour? I'll meet you downstairs."

Without giving her the opportunity to disagree with the arrangements he had undertaken on her behalf, he left the room. Not that Sarah had any intention of wrangling over who took her back to Calne. She was too excited at the prospect of continuing her journey to worry her head over such an insignificant detail, nor did it cross her mind to wonder why the magistrate had not insisted upon seeing her before she left.

It took no time at all to pack her meagre belongings, and after returning Dottie's book and bidding her farewell, she went down to the coffee-room where she discovered Captain Carter sitting quite alone.

"It would seem, sir, that I have been given permission to leave, and Mr Ravenhurst has kindly offered to escort me back to Calne. So, I must bid you farewell."

He rose to his feet and took her outstretched hand in both his own. "Godspeed, ma'am. I hope the remainder of your journey may pass without incident."

"I sincerely hope so, too." She looked earnestly into his attractive tawny-coloured eyes. "But do you know,

Captain, I should dearly love to discover just what has been going on here.''

''Probably no one ever will. But if by some chance the truth is ever unearthed, Ravenhurst has promised to write and let me know. Apparently he is acquainted with my commanding officer, Colonel Pitbury. So a letter should reach me.''

Sarah's smile was full of gentle warmth. ''Well, good-bye, Captain Brin Carter. Don't get yourself killed, will you?''

''I shall do my utmost not to.'' His smile was a carbon copy of her own. ''And let us say, rather, farewell. Who knows, my dear lady, our paths may cross again... I, at least, sincerely hope so.''

He made to pick up her cloak-bag, but she forestalled him by grasping the handle first, and as she walked away, she had the oddest feeling that they would meet again, and perhaps more than once, in the not too dim and distant future.

The landlord, awaiting her in the tap, informed her that Mr Ravenhurst had paid her shot, and then insisted upon carrying her belongings out to the curricle. Sarah thanked him for his hospitality, said all that was proper in respect of the death of his niece and then, after requesting him to pass on her farewells to the other members of his family, scrambled up beside her escort while the landlord placed her belongings beneath the seat.

''Is it not wonderful to be on our away again, sir?'' Sarah remarked, as Mr Ravenhurst gave the bays the office to start. ''But where is your groom? Surely you're not leaving him behind?''

''Sutton is taking a seat on the stage as far as Chippenham, and then hiring a horse. I've sent him on an errand.''

''Oh, I see!'' Sarah, then, bethought herself of something else, and began to rummage through her reticule. "You paid my bill, sir. How much do I owe you?"

He cast her an impatient glance. "Nothing."

"But, sir, I cannot possibly permit you to—"

"If you think I'm stopping this carriage," he cut in sharply, "so that you can grease my palm with a few paltry coins, you can think again. Put that confounded purse away, child!"

For some reason, best known to himself, he had fallen into one of his more disagreeable moods. Sarah cast him a furtive sidelong glance. Ought she now, at this the eleventh hour, to divulge her true identity? It wasn't that she had deliberately avoided doing so; it was simply that just the right opportunity had never presented itself. Which was hardly surprising, considering the tragic events that had taken place in the past days.

A tiny sigh of indecision escaped her. He was hardly in a particularly approachable mood, and yet...

She was still debating with herself when they arrived at the main highway. Instead of turning right, which would have taken them to Calne, Mr Ravenhurst confounded her by turning in the opposite direction.

"Sir, you have gone the wrong way!" she pointed out in some urgency."

"No, I haven't."

"But, sir, Calne is the other way," she reiterated, slewing round in the seat to look back at the signpost.

"I'm fully aware of that, child. I know this part of the country very well."

"Then why have you come this way?" she asked, not unreasonably, and watched a wickedly slow and infuriatingly smug smile curl his lips.

"Because, Mrs Serafina Armstrong, *née* Postlethwaite...alias Miss Sarah Pennington, my troublesome ward, I am taking you to a place where I can keep my eye on you!"

# *Chapter Six*

For several moments it was as much as Sarah could do to gape at him, hoping against hope that she had misheard, but his smugly satisfied smile was proof enough that she had not. The wretch had deliberately tricked her into going with him! And she, idiot that she was, had climbed willy-nilly into his carriage like a trusting fool!

"How long have you known?" she asked at length, striving to remain calm.

"Since that first night," he answered truthfully. "And I cannot tell you how relieved I am that you are not foolishly trying to deny it."

A little late for that, now, she thought wretchedly before cursing herself silently for a fool. What a complete and utter ninny-hammer not to have realised long before! Almost from the moment of his arrival at the inn he had shown such marked consideration for her welfare, and she had foolishly put it down to nothing more than a gentleman's concern for a young widow.

She raised puzzled eyes to stare blindly at the road ahead. But how on earth had he discovered her true identity? Had she foolishly given herself away? She cast her mind back, trying to recall in detail all of their many conversations, but could think of nothing she had said that might possibly have betrayed her. Curiosity got the better of her and she found herself asking outright how he had found out.

"The instant I saw those initials on your writing-case I became suspicious," he did not hesitate to admit. "And, of course, that damned impertinent letter confirmed it."

"What? You mean you read…?" Sarah regarded him in silent dismay for a moment, remembering all too clearly the pompous, not to say condescending, tone she had adopted when composing that half-finished missive, but then the sheer effrontery of his actions brought her temper to the fore. "How dared you rifle through my belongings, sir! How dared you! Stop this carriage at once!"

"No," he responded with infuriating calm. "And do not attempt to jump out," he continued while expertly overtaking a lumbering coach. "You might achieve your objective without suffering a sprained ankle, but you'll certainly end up with a sore rear. I'll see to that!"

He caught the tiny gasp of outrage, but missed the calculating look she cast him.

"That you would stoop so low as to lay violent hands on a defenceless female does not surprise me in the least," she informed him loftily. "But don't you think you've left it rather late to play the heavy-handed guardian? Or to take on the role at all, come to that?" she finished bitterly.

"So that rankles, does it?" He did turn to look at her then, and noted the stubborn set of the softly rounded chin. "Believe it or not, child, I refrained from interfering in your upbringing because I believed you would go on much better without it. But I see, now, I was wrong."

He cast a scowling glance over her dull grey garb. "Confound it, girl! Have you no dress sense at all? That dratted colour don't suit you in the least!"

"Dress sense?" she echoed, anger stirring once again at the unjustified criticism. "How was I supposed to dress anywhere near decently on the paltry allowance you gave me?"

"Paltry...?" His brows snapping together, he drew the curricle to a halt at the side of the road, and then turned in the seat to face her squarely. "Right, it's high time you and I sorted a few things out, young woman. Why did you suddenly take it into your head to run away?"

"I didn't run away!" she refuted staunchly. "I left...well, I left because I saw little point in remaining. I shall attain my majority in June, in case you have forgotten," she reminded him, a hint of sarcasm edging her voice. "Your guardianship will then be at an end, and I shall need to make my own way in the world. I thought to seek some genteel occupation—a companion, or governess."

"Governess?" he echoed, not hiding his consternation. "What foolishness is this?"

"It might seem foolish to you, sir," she retorted, flashing him an angry look from beneath her long, curling lashes, "but not everyone is blessed with a vast fortune. Most of us need to work in order to live."

"And what makes you suppose that you number amongst them?"

"I should have thought that was obvious!" she snapped. "I have no money."

"Who told you that?"

Sarah opened her mouth, closed it again, and regarded

him questioningly. "Are you trying to tell me that I do have money of my own?"

"Of course you have, you silly chit! Surely you cannot have forgotten your home near Plymouth? Which I have rented out, incidentally, on your behalf. And I suppose you have in the region of twenty-five thousand pounds on top of that, or perhaps a little more."

"Twenty-five…?" Sarah's jaw dropped perceptively. It was a fortune! And all these years she had assumed she was little more than a pauper. "Why didn't you tell me?" she queried, a touch of censure creeping into her voice now. "Surely I had the right to know my financial situation, sir?"

"You had only to ask." he responded airily.

"Ask? I did ask! Well, I wrote to you," she amended. "But you never once bothered to take the trouble to reply to any of my letters."

He did not respond to this, and after a few moments Sarah turned her head to look at him. There was a strange intensity in his gaze. He was looking directly at her, but she sensed that he was seeing something else. Then suddenly she saw it too. Everything became crystal clear. He had never received her letters, not one, simply because Mrs Fairchild had never sent them.

She realised, too, in those moments of astonishing enlightenment, that the allowance he had made her over the years must have been a generous one, but most of it had gone into Harriet Fairchild's pocket or, rather, had been squandered on her ruling passion—gambling.

The woman had been so very cunning, keeping her charge away from the assemblies, and denying her the pleasure of attending many parties where she might just possibly meet some eligible young man, because her comfortable existence would then have come to an end.

As long as Sarah had remained in Bath, Mrs Fairchild could continue to indulge in her vice at her wealthy cousin's expense.

"The lady I met in Upper Camden Place told me there was much that warranted investigation," he said ominously. "And she wasn't far wrong!"

"So, you did meet Mrs Stanton," Sarah remarked, instinctively knowing to whom he referred. "I thought you must have done. Your cousin wouldn't have realised where I intended going."

"Yes, I met your friend's mother." His expression was one of staunch disapproval as he gave the bays the office to start again. "And I shall have a word or two to say to you in the not-too-distant future, young woman, regarding your involvement in that elopement."

You carry on, then. See if I care, Sarah thought blithely before a thought struck her. "Why did you suddenly take it into your head to visit Bath? Did you go there especially to see me?"

"Of course I did, silly chit! Why else should I go to that confounded place?"

"Well, there's no need to snap my nose off! How was I supposed to know?" she retorted, having come to the conclusion long since that there was little point in trying to hold a polite conversation with him. "You've never bothered to pay me a visit before. Did you have a specific reason for doing so?"

"I intended asking whether you would care for a Season in London."

"Truly?" Sarah was startled by the admission.

"Yes. But, given your recent conduct, I'm not so sure the offer is still open."

For a few elated moments Sarah allowed her mind to dwell on the heady delights of a London Season, but then realised that it might be best if she didn't accept his offer. She had been confined for so many years, and the thought of being encumbered with yet another chaperon did not appeal in the least. During the past few days she had experienced the sweet taste of freedom, and had no desire to relinquish her new-found liberty.

No, she told herself, it would be better to stick to her original plan and stay with the Alcotts in Hertfordshire. Thankfully, having money of her own, she would not now need to seek a position, and once she had attained her majority, she could return to her home near Plymouth.

"It's kind of you to offer, sir, but I don't think I shall go to London."

"I-beg-your-pardon!" he ground out, turning the curricle off the main road and down a narrow twisting country lane. "What makes you suppose that you'll be given any say in the matter? If I say you'll go to London, you'll go, my girl! And that will be an end to it!"

"I have decided on exactly what I am going to do," she returned, completely unruffled by the autocratic tone. "And why have you turned down here?"

"Because I'm taking you to my grandmother's house until I can make more suitable arrangements."

"No, I won't go there!" Determination was very evident in her voice. "I am going to Hertfordshire."

"Sarah," he said with careful restraint, "you will do exactly as I tell you."

"Oh, do you really think so?" she parried sweetly. "I wouldn't be too sure of that if I were you."

He gave vent to one of his low growls, but managed to bite back the threatening retort that rose in his throat.

They continued the journey in chilling silence, but from time to time Marcus cast a suspicious glance in her direction. She kept her gaze firmly fixed on the road ahead, and her hands in her lap, looking for all the world quite innocently angelic, but he was not fooled. They had not spent those three days in close proximity without his gaining a fair knowledge of her character.

His eyes narrowed. The little minx was definitely plotting something: how to give him the slip, no doubt. He would need to watch her like a hawk for the next few days, he decided grimly.

Entering his uncle's vast Wiltshire estate by the north gate, Marcus turned the curricle on to the driveway leading to the Dower House. As soon as he had brought the team to a halt in the stableyard, and an aged groom had taken a hold of the horses' heads, he leapt out the curricle and, before she had time to alight herself, grasped Sarah's slim waist and swung her to the ground.

Ignoring the indignant look she cast him, he took a firm grasp of her wrist and almost hauled her behind him along the path to the front entrance; and only when Clegg had opened the solid oak door in answer to the summons, and they had stepped into the hall, did he release his hold.

"I take it my grandmother is in her sitting room, Clegg? Good," he went on in response to the nod. "This is my ward, Miss Sarah Pennington. And I should be grateful if you would keep an eye on her while I have a brief word with her ladyship."

While he was speaking he removed his hat and coat, and promptly handed them to the bemused butler, who was regarding the very pretty, but indignant young lady with considerable interest. Then, without so much as a glance in Sarah's direction, Marcus mounted the stairs, and went directly to his grandmother's private apartments. He entered the room without knocking to find her seated in her favourite chair near the hearth.

"Ah, good! You're awake."

The Dowager gave a start. "Heavens above! Must you creep up on a body like that!" she greeted him crossly, but with unmistakable warmth in her grey eyes, as he came towards her chair. "Well, and am I to congratulate you? Am I looking at a betrothed man?"

"What?" He looked nonplussed for a moment. "Oh, no. Never got as far as Bamford's place. Been careering about the country after that ward of mine. Little baggage had the temerity to run away from Bath! Caught up with her, though. She's here now. And that's what I've come to speak to you about."

"And so, too, have I."

They both turned to see Sarah framed in the doorway: the Dowager's expression one of surprised interest; her grandson's one of scowling disapproval.

"I thought you knew to await me below!"

Sublimely ignoring the reproof, Sarah turned and calmly closed the door before taking several paces into the room. She had removed her grey bonnet and cloak, and was embarrassingly conscious of the Dowager's shrewd eyes scrutinising the plain grey gown, but did not betray her discomfiture, and even lifted her chin slightly.

"Your grandson, ma'am, has brought me here for some perverse reasons of his own and, I might add, against my will. Unless I am very much mistaken, he was about to persuade you to house me under your roof—an arrangement, I'm sure, which would please you as little as it would please me."

The Dowager tapped her ebony cane on the floor. "Hoity-toity, miss! I shall say what pleases me and what does not." She looked up at her grandson. He was still staring fixedly across at his ward. There was more than a touch of annoyance in that gaze, but something else, too.

She looked back at Sarah. "Come here, child. Let me look at you." Sarah meekly obeyed, and stood before the Dowager, gazing solemnly down at her. "Why, you do look like your mother! Except prettier, I think. And you certainly did not get those lovely eyes from her, nor those dark brows. What unusual colouring!"

"No, ma'am. From my father, so I understand." Her lips curled into a shy smile. "Did you know my mother well?"

"Yes, child. Your mother and my Agnes were great friends since the days they both attended the seminary together. Your mother frequently stayed with us when she was a girl, but I saw little of her after she married your father." She turned to her grandson. "I cannot imagine why you are still standing there, Marcus. Go away and leave me to talk to Sarah in peace. You'll find brandy in the library."

"I could certainly do with one after what I've had to contend with during these past days!" he responded with feeling. He went over to the door, but turned back to add, "And don't you dare try to slip away, my girl! The library is downstairs. And I fully intend to keep the door open."

"Infuriating man!" Sarah muttered, much to the Dowager's intense amusement, as the door closed behind him.

"Has my obnoxious grandson been giving you a hard time? Do sit down, child, and tell me all about it. What induced you to run away from Bath?"

Sarah raised her eyes heavenwards as she settled herself in the comfortable chair opposite. "As I told your grandson, though he seems determined not to believe me, I did not run away, ma'am. I simply chose to leave."

She then went on to explain the reasons for her actions. The Dowager leaned back against the chair, listening quietly for the most part, but occasionally interrupting to ask a question. Her shrewd grey eyes never wavered from the lovely, expressive face as she learned a little of those years Sarah had endured in Bath.

Her grandson's arrival at the inn, and the subsequent events, brought more than one wickedly amused chuckle to rise in her throat, and Sarah's astringent comments on her guardian's perfidy at tricking her into accepting a ride in his curricle afforded the Dowager unholy amusement.

"The cunning wretch!" she exclaimed when she had learned all. "Little wonder you feel quite out of charity with him, my dear. But he is right, you know," she went on seriously. "You cannot go wandering about the country on your own. Look at what has befallen you already!"

There was a clearly discernible glint in Sarah's eyes. "Naturally, I was saddened by the tragic deaths, but I could not help being excited by it all," she freely admitted. "Nothing like that has ever happened to me before!"

"You poor child. You did have a very dreary time of it all in Bath, didn't you?"

Sarah could feel the colour rising in her cheeks, and was unable to hold that shrewd gaze. "Well, I—I..."

"There is no need to explain," her ladyship said gently. "That is all in the past. Now, we must look to the future. But first, you may go across to the decanters over there, and pour me a glass of Madeira. And pour yourself one whilst you're about it," she added as Sarah rose gracefully from the chair "It won't do you a mite of harm."

The Dowager watched her intently, scrutinising every fluid movement of the slender young body, and was more than satisfied with what she saw.

"My dear child, I'm beginning to like you already," she remarked, taking the glass held out to her. "You have a steady hand and you can fill a glass. Which is more than can be said for some people." She sampled the wine, then continued, "Now, we must decide what is best to be done with you. I can fully understand your being piqued at my grandson's high-handed attitude. Sadly, it is his way, and you must grow accustomed.

"For my part I see no reason why you shouldn't stay with your old governess. It is evident that you have a great fondness for each other. I shall certainly have a word with Marcus about it. But it is out of the question for you to travel to Hertfordshire alone, and on the common stage. So, until some arrangements can be made, would you object very much to remaining here with me?"

Sarah had the grace to blush. "I'm sorry if I appeared rude when I came in here, ma'am, but I thought Mr Ravenhurst might try to, well, bully you into housing me here."

A wicked cackle answered this. "Oh, my dear child! When you come to know me better, you will realise that even my dictatorial grandson is incapable of that feat."

She became serious again, and looked across at Sarah intently. "We are very alike, Ravenhurst and I. There are those who might disagree, but I believe I have mellowed over the years, and my grandson might well do so, given the incentive. But we're both plain-spoken, and spoilt enough to want our own way in all things. You might not find it easy staying here with me, and I shall not force it upon you, but I should very much like to have you as my guest, Sarah Pennington.''

Sarah did not doubt the sincerity, and felt touched by the invitation. ''Well, I—''

''Decide nothing yet, child,'' the Dowager interrupted. ''Take a little time to think it over. Now, be good enough to go over to the bell-pull.''

Sarah obeyed and, at the Dowager's request, gave it several sharp tugs. A few minutes later a gaunt middle-aged woman, with the most frighteningly piercing and almost black eyes, entered the room. She cast Sarah the briefest of glances before turning to her mistress and enquiring, quite disrespectfully, Sarah thought, what she required.

''Sarah, my child, this obnoxious creature you see before you is my personal maid, Buddle,'' the Dowager informed her with wicked amusement. ''Don't be alarmed. She might not appear so, but she is quite human, I assure you. She has been with me for more years than I care to remember.''

A loud snort answered this, and her ladyship turned to her maid without any visible signs of having taken offence. ''Has a bed chamber been prepared for Miss Pennington, Buddle?''

''Naturally.''

''Which one?''

''Master Marcus always has the largest guest chamber, as you very well know,'' the maid answered impatiently. ''Miss Pennington's belongings have been placed in the other guest room.''

The Dowager was silent for a moment, then said decisively, "Then remove them! Put Miss Sarah in the room next to mine. See that she has everything she needs, then come back here to me."

Only for one unguarded moment did the maid betray surprise. "Very good, my lady." She turned to Sarah. "If you would care to come with me, Miss Pennington, I'll show you the way."

Sarah wasn't so very sure that she did care to go with the forbidding-looking woman but, after hurriedly finishing the contents of her glass, rose to her feet, and followed Buddle down the narrow passageway and into a room where the drapes had been pulled halfway across the window. She was immediately aware of the delicate fragrance of lavender and rose petals sweetening the air, and turned her head to see a good fire burning welcomingly in the grate.

Buddle went over to the windows, and opened wide the drapes, allowing the fading afternoon light to filter fully into the room, and then turned to see an unmistakable look of delight on Sarah's face as her eyes wandered over the room's decor, picked out in delicate shades of blue.

"It is a pretty room, isn't it, Miss Pennington?" she remarked, with a modicum of warmth in her voice.

"Yes, it is," Sarah answered, running her fingers lightly down the pale blue velvet bed hangings.

"I'll just go along and collect your things from the other room. Now, is there anything else you'll be wanting?"

"If it isn't too much trouble," Sarah replied, casting the abigail an apologetic smile, "I'd dearly love a bath. I've not had one since leaving Somerset."

As soon as the door had closed behind Buddle, Sarah examined her surroundings more closely. The drapes at the windows matched the bed hangings exactly, and the pale blue wallpaper was patterned with delicate bunches of flowers in shades of pink, and white. A beautifully made lace cover with scalloped edging adorned the dressing-table, on which stood several dainty scent bottles, a comb and a silver-backed hair brush.

It was undoubtedly the boudoir of a lady of fashion. And she was anything but! She grimaced at her reflection in the dressing-table mirror, disliking more than ever the dull grey gown and her plainly arranged hair. Her appearance seemed even dowdier in these lovely surroundings. But why, suddenly, did it matter so much to her how she looked? Her appearance had never worried her unduly before.

She was still pondering over this when Buddle re-entered, carrying the battered old cloak-bag and writing-case. As a result of the hasty packing back at the inn, her best pearl-grey gown was badly creased, and she looked at it in dismay. Everything, but everything seemed to be going wrong for her that day!

"Don't you worry your head over that, Miss Pennington," Buddle said, noting the forlorn expression. "I'll soon have it pressed. The bath is on its way. Ring when you've finished, and I'll come back to you."

Later, when Sarah emerged from the rose-scented water, clean and refreshed, and having washed her hair, she felt slightly less disgruntled. Wrapping herself in the robe a young maidservant had brought with the towels, she rang for Buddle, and then sat at the dressing-table and studied her reflection in the glass.

The Dowager Countess had said that she had unusual colouring. Sarah turned her head on one side, considering this, as she dragged a comb through her long wet tresses. She had never given it much thought before, but she supposed she had. The finely arched dark brows and long dusky lashes made a striking contrast with hair that looked more golden than brown when touched by sunlight or a candle's glow.

Her features were regular and, looking at them dispassionately, she supposed her blue-green almond-shaped eyes were her most striking feature. She did not consider her small straight nose anything out of the common way, nor did she realise that many men found her sweetly curving lips very provocative and extremely kissable. But she had been given reason to suppose that Mr Ravenhurst considered her a pretty young woman.

She found herself, unaccountably, blushing, and was angry with herself for the unalloyed pleasure his appreciation gave her, especially as she still felt completely out of charity with him for his duplicity and high-handed treatment earlier in the day.

Buddle entering the room, accompanied by the young maid carrying several dresses over her arm, gave Sarah's thoughts a new direction, and she gazed across at the vibrantly coloured garments in wonder as the maid laid them very carefully down on the bed.

"Her ladyship said you were to make use of these, miss, until you have more suitable garments of your own to wear," Buddle informed her, picking up the blue velvet gown and casting an expert eye over Sarah's slim, shapely figure. "Yes, I think this will do nicely for this evening. Her ladyship has decided to eat downstairs in the dining-room, miss. So we'll need to look lively. The mistress has always kept early hours when in the country."

"But—but who do they belong to, Buddle?" Sarah asked, gazing longingly at the dark blue velvet gown with its high neck and long tight-fitting sleeves, and wishing fervently that it was hers.

''They belong to Miss Caroline, one of her ladyship's granddaughters. She visits every year, and left a trunk full of her belongings here after her last visit. More hair than whit, that one, Miss Pennington, but she does know what suits her. Now, while Betsy's bringing the rest of the things in, I'll see to you.''

Sarah had grown accustomed to doing most everything for herself during the past six years, and found it more than a little embarrassing to have someone else in the room while she scrambled into freshly laundered underthings. Buddle, however, seemed not to take the least notice, and set about drying the long hair on a fluffy towel.

''You have very pretty hair, miss, but it's rather heavy and is in desperate need of cutting,'' the abigail remarked in her usual forthright manner and, without giving Sarah the opportunity to acquiesce, or otherwise, whipped out a pair of sharp scissors from the pocket of her starched white apron and made several judicious snips.

Sarah glanced down apprehensively at the growing pile of prettily waving long strands of hair about her feet, and earned herself a severe reprimand, much as her old governess had given her on more than one occasion when she had been a child; but she could not prevent a reluctant smile as she sat obediently rigid on the chair.

For the next few days, at least, she would find it difficult not to be in the company of at least one of three very domineering people; and unless she was prepared to make a stand right from the start, she would no doubt find herself scolded and bullied and far from gently per-

suaded into doing precisely what she had no earthly desire to do.

So, it would be far more comfortable in the long run
if she made it abundantly clear, right from the start, that
she was a young woman with a mind of her own, and
had no intention whatsoever of becoming submissively
docile and kowtowing to the unreasonable demands of
the members of what could only be described as a des-
potic household.

Raising her eyes from the contemplation of the dressing-table's lacy covering, she promptly forgot her resolve to be assertive as she gazed in astonishment at her
reflection in the mirror.

Buddle had gathered her hair high on her head,
twisted and pinned a large portion of it into a tight circlet, and then had pulled the remaining hair through, so
that it hung over one white shoulder like a silken pony's
tale. She had also cut several strands very short at the
front, and tiny curls now feathered across her forehead
and on to her cheeks.

"Oh, Buddle, what clever fingers you have!" she en-
thused, still somewhat in awe over the result. "I could
never achieve anything half so elegant."

The compliment had been spontaneous, and had
sounded so sincerely meant that a suspicion of a smile
hovered about the abigail's thin-lipped mouth. "It's
quite a simple style, Miss Sarah, but effective. And it's
as much as I can do for you this evening. Now, let us
get you into that dress. They will be awaiting you downstairs."

Quickly hooking up the velvet gown, Buddle barely
gave Sarah time to cast her eyes over the finished result
in the full-length mirror before she whipped a blue-and-
white silk shawl about her shoulders, and then showed

her the way downstairs to the drawing-room where the Dowager and her grandson sat talking.

As the door opened, Marcus broke off what he was saying to turn his head, and for one unguarded moment could only stare in rapt admiration of his ward's transformed appearance as she moved gracefully towards them.

He rose to his feet. "Certainly an improvement," was the only mild praise he offered, however, before turning to his grandmother. "Where did the dress come from?"

"It belongs to your cousin Caroline. She left one of her trunks behind the last time she paid me a visit. I doubt the silly chit has missed it." She smiled up at Sarah. "My dear, you look charming. Don't feel uncomfortable about making use of the other things, but we must not delay too long in purchasing some new garments of your own. There's quite a respectable little establishment in Devizes that might be worthwhile visiting."

"I should dearly love to, my lady. Unfortunately, I have only sufficient funds to cover the rest of my travelling expenses to Hertfordshire." She bestowed a rather sweet, but slightly provocative smile on her, now, frowning guardian. "Unless, of course, I may have a little of the money my mother left me."

"No, you may not!" was the unequivocal response. "You secure your inheritance upon marriage, or attaining the age of five-and-twenty. Whichever comes first."

"But—but that is monstrous!" Sarah was hard pressed not to scream at the injustice of it all. What had her mother been thinking of? Under the terms of the will she had been effectively prevented from becoming an independent young woman. And, what was worse, she would be virtually tied by the caprice of another for a further four years. It really didn't bear thinking about!

The Dowager could easily discern the resentment in Sarah's eyes, and cast her a sympathetic smile. "It is in no way unusual, my dear, for matters to be settled thus. But it need not prevent us from acquiring a new wardrobe for you."

Scant compensation! Sarah thought bitterly, but it was not in her nature to agonise over what could not be altered, and resigned herself very quickly to making the best of it.

During dinner the Dowager and her grandson kept up a lively conversation. It soon became abundantly clear to Sarah that they were very fond of each other, and their pithy remarks and bantering exchanges caused more than one chuckle to rise in her throat.

As soon as the meal was over the ladies returned to the drawing-room. The Dowager wasted no time in extracting a promise from Sarah that she would be willing to remain at the Dower House for the time being, and then her ladyship made plans to go on the shopping expedition the following day.

"Of course, you cannot expect a provincial dressmaker to rival a London modiste, Sarah, but I do not think you will be disappointed."

"Oh, I shan't, ma'am. I assure you. Anything has to be better than what I have at present."

"That much is certain," Marcus concurred, earning himself one of his ward's darkling looks as he came back into the room. "In fact, I think I shall accompany you when you go on this trip to Devizes, just to ensure that you do not continue to tog yourself out in half-mourning."

"If I thought that by doing so I could annoy you, I would be almost tempted," Sarah retaliated.

"Now, now, Marcus," the Dowager intervened quickly. "You are not to tease the child. Sarah has agreed to stay with me for a while. But what plans have you for her future?" She saw a ghost of a smile hovering about his mouth. "Do you intend that she should go to London for the Season?"

"Perhaps," was his non-committal response.

"Well, you had better hurry and make a decision, my boy. It will soon be March. Precious little time to organise everything."

At this he turned to his ward. "Would you care for a Season, Sarah?"

His polite enquiry surprised her: she wasn't accustomed to such courtesy from him. Then her eyes began to twinkle rather wickedly. "The object of a Season being to find a suitable spouse, I rather think I would, sir. If I am successful in my endeavours, I shall then be free of your pernicious influence."

"Hornet!"

Sarah rose to her feet, and merely curtsied in response before turning to the Dowager. "If you will excuse me, ma'am, I think I shall retire early. What with one thing and another, it has been a rather trying day."

"Oh, Sarah," Marcus said in suspicious tones, arresting her progress to the door, "do I need to lock you in your room tonight to prevent a furtive midnight departure?"

She turned her head on one side as though giving the question due consideration. "No, I do not think there is any necessity for that. I rather have a fancy to lull you into a false sense of security, and then abscond when you're least expecting it. That would be far more re-warding.''

''Little baggage!'' he muttered after the door had closed behind her.

''Do you know, Marcus,'' the Dowager remarked, highly amused, ''that gel ain't in the least afraid of you.''

''Of course she isn't! Why the devil should she be?''

''Well, you're not exactly renowned for your polite drawing-room conversation, you know.''

He dismissed this with an impatient wave of his hand. ''Sarah's not such a wigeon as to boggle at a bit of plain speaking.''

''Just as well,'' responded the Dowager, eyeing her grandson for a moment with a mocking glint in her eyes, but then she became serious. ''What has been going on, Marcus? From the snippets Sarah let fall earlier, the child has had a pretty poor time of it all in Bath. And those dreadful clothes she brought with her…they are positively dowdy! Why, even my servants are better clad!''

''You may well ask,'' he responded grimly.

She looked at him with interest, but when he offered nothing further, she changed the subject by remarking, ''I'm glad Sarah has agreed to a Season. I don't think you'll have the least trouble in getting her off your hands, Marcus. She's a lovely, prettily behaved young woman.''

''Prettily behaved?'' he echoed, incredulous. ''It's quite evident that you do not know her very well, ma'am. You've no notion of the worry she's caused me. She's the most outrageous little minx! She's friendly to a fault, she'll mix with any raff and scaff and she's as trusting as bedamned! And when I think I shall need to keep an eye on her every minute throughout the Season, just to make sure she doesn't fall into any more scrapes, I'm almost tempted to retract the offer!''

The Dowager considered his remarks a trifle inflated, but refrained from further comment. In fact, during the rest of the time she remained downstairs with him, she did not mention Sarah's name again, but that night as she lay in her bed, sipping her customary cup of warm milk, she had a very thoughtful expression on her face.

Buddle, who was in the process of hanging her mistress's gown back in the wardrobe, looked suspiciously across at her. ''I know that look of old,'' she remarked, coming across to the bed to relieve the Dowager of the cup. ''You're up to something.''

The Dowager did not so much as blink; her eyes remained glued to an imaginary spot on the far wall. ''What do you think to Sarah Pennington, Buddle?''

''Ah! So that's it, is it! I knew as soon as you wanted her put in Miss Agnes's old room you were up to no good. If you want my advice, you'll leave well alone, and not interfere in Master Marcus's concerns.''

''But he likes her, Buddle,'' the Dowager murmured, almost to herself. ''There is that in his eyes when they rest upon her… There is such—such tenderness there. It is unmistakable. I've never seen him look at anyone that way before.''

Her lips curled into a satisfied smile. ''And he hasn't offered for that Bamford chit,'' she went on to divulge to the woman who was not only her personal maid but also a friend and confidante. ''And I cannot say I'm sorry. Sounds a cold, heartless chit to me. Wouldn't suit him at all!''

''Be that as it may, Master Marcus still wouldn't

thank you none for meddling in his private concerns. And you know it!''

The Dowager's brows snapped together as she fixed her gaze on her maid. ''Do you know, Buddle, you are becoming quite testy in your old age. Cannot imagine why. Now, go away, and leave me in peace! I need to think.''

# *Chapter Seven*

Sarah, too, had much to ponder over before she eventually fell to sleep that night. Her main concern was not her immediate future. The Dowager Countess seemed genuinely eager to have her as a guest, and Sarah was not unhappy at the prospect of remaining in a place where she knew her presence would be welcome. But her stay here could not be an indefinite one.

Once she had attained her majority, of course, she could seek shelter with the Alcotts, and her guardian would be powerless to remove her from their sphere, but he still retained control of her fortune for a further four years. Curse him! That still rankled, but she forced herself to swallow her chagrin and concentrate her thoughts on the options open to her.

She was still determined to go to Hertfordshire and remain with dear Martha and her family for a few weeks, but, here again, to impose upon the Alcotts' hospitality for any great length of time was unthinkable. Independence had effectively been denied her until she had attained the age of five-and-twenty.

So, unless she stuck to her original plan and tried to seek employment as a governess, or was prepared to bind herself to Mr Ravenhurst's will, which would no doubt involve living quietly somewhere with yet another female of his choosing acting as chaperon, the only other course open to her was marriage.

Sarah frowned as she stared up at the velvet canopy above her head. Strangely enough, she had never considered marrying. She didn't quite know why this should be, because all the young females of her acquaintance thought of nothing else. Perhaps, she mused, it was because she had had precious little experience of men.

Her father had died when she was very young and, with the exception of James Fenshaw, whom she had liked very much, but who had never figured in her thoughts as a prospective husband, the only other men with whom she had ever had any real dealings were the middle-aged husbands of Harriet Fairchild's friends.

Naturally, she had come into contact with many young men during her years in Bath. The Pump Room was a favourite meeting place for ladies of all ages, many of whom were dutifully escorted by some young male relative; but with very few exceptions, Sarah had considered those budding sprigs of fashion empty-headed nincompoops, who had little thought for aught else other than the latest vogue in tying a cravat, or the way to achieve a looking-glass shine on a pair of boots.

Her frown grew more pronounced. Perhaps the only man she had ever been attracted to on sight was Captain Brin Carter, and yet her feelings for him had been—well—more sisterly, really, like her feelings towards her friend Clarissa's beau... And the only other man, of course, with whom she had ever had more than a passing contact was...

Sarah's frown grew so heavy her brows almost met above the bridge of her nose. No woman in her right mind would ever consider Marcus Ravenhurst as a prospective husband! He was rich, certainly, but all the wealth in the land could never compensate for being joined in wedlock to such an arrogant, dictatorial creature! He was without doubt the rudest man she had ever met in her life. It would be impossible to find another ruder! And yet...

A soft, reminiscent little smile erased the scowl as her mind returned to those days spent at that inn. Her guardian could be quite kind at times, touchingly so in his little acts of thoughtfulness. Beneath that hardened exterior lay a benevolent, generous spirit. The right sort of woman, one who would not be cowed by his sharp-tongued brusqueness, could, she felt certain, mellow him in time, allowing the real essence of the man to surface.

She could do it; she felt certain of it! His caustic remarks never upset her; annoyed her sometimes, certainly, but for the most part she found his acerbic tongue highly diverting. Yes, she mused, she most certainly could sweeten the masterful Marcus Ravenhurst's vinegary disposition, and...

Releasing her breath in an almost imperceptible gasp, Sarah brought her wayward thoughts to heel sharply. What on earth was she thinking of? Marry Marcus Ravenhurst...? Why, it was unthinkable! Ludicrous! Besides, he would never take to wife someone so beneath his own station in life. Only the daughter of a duke or marquis would be good enough for him. Added to which, she didn't even like the man...did she?

Dressed in another borrowed gown, a pale blue dimity this time, with a high neck ending in a tiny frill, and long sleeves buttoned at the wrists, Sarah went into the room where they had dined the evening before to find her guardian sitting alone at the table, consuming a hearty breakfast. He acknowledged her with a nod, and then politely enquired whether she had slept well.

After responding that she had, which wasn't strictly true, but rather better than admitting that thoughts of him had kept her awake until the early hours, she proceeded to place several wafer-thin slices of ham on her plate and pour herself coffee; but each time she raised her eyes from the food on her plate, it was to discover her guardian staring at her in a rather disconcerting and quite unreadable way.

She tried her best to ignore him, and carried on eating in silence, but after several more minutes of this continued scrutiny she found herself asking, rather testily, "What on earth is the matter with you now? I know more often than not you're in a churlish mood in the mornings, but must you keep staring at me as though— as though I'd a smut on my nose?"

His lips twitched in response to the waspish tone. "You've no smut, but you do have two or three rather pretty freckles. No, no! Don't rip up at me, you little shrew!" he went on hurriedly when she looked about to do just that. "Instead, tell me if you've a riding habit amongst those borrowed clothes of my cousin's?"

She was rather taken aback by the unexpected enquiry. "I'm not certain. Why?"

"You can hardly go riding without one."

"I can hardly go riding without a horse, either, come to that," she parried, sweetly sarcastic. "And as I do not possess a mount, the question of whether or not I can lay my hands on a habit is completely irrelevant, wouldn't you say?"

Leaning back in his chair, he regarded her from beneath hooded lids. "Remind me to beat you some time."

He saw the slender shoulders shaking with suppressed laughter, and could not prevent a twitching smile himself. "You really are the most provoking little witch at times, Sarah Pennington," he informed her with gentle censure. "Now, do you think we could possibly continue this conversation with a little less flippancy? Can you ride, child? If not, would you like me to teach you?"

For a moment Sarah regarded him in astonishment, then quickly lowered her eyes. If she had needed more proof of Harriet Fairchild's artfulness, she had been given it now. His cousin had never written to him requesting a mount for his ward, or if she had, the money had been squandered elsewhere. Sooner or later he was going to discover the full extent of his cousin's chicanery, but she had absolutely no intention of turning informer.

After quickly searching her mind for a suitable response, she said, "Yes, I do ride, sir, but I'm a little out of practice, I'm afraid." Which was true enough, as she had not been in the saddle since staying at her friend Clarissa's home in Devonshire during the previous summer.

"Never mind that," he replied dismissively, rising from the table. "I'll see what cattle my uncle's got in his stable. He's bound to have something suitable for a lady to ride. We'll soon have you up to scratch. Meet me outside in an hour. And if you cannot lay your hands on a habit, wear that deplorable grey gown of yours. It won't matter a whit if that gets ruined. In fact, it'll be a blessing if it does!" was his parting shot on closing the door.

Sarah was too excited at the prospect of riding again to concern herself over that completely unnecessary gibe. She did not linger long over her breakfast, and hurriedly made her way back up the stairs, but stopped outside the Dowager's room.

Her guardian might be quite mannerless at times, but she was not prepared to allow his shortcomings to rub off on her. She was a guest in his grandmother's house, and it was only polite to enquire if there was anything required of her before setting off on her ride.

Buddle answered the summons, admitting Sarah with a modicum of warmth in those almost black eyes which, had Sarah but known it, meant that the highly discerning middle-aged servant had made her assessment of Ravenhurst's ward and had already awarded the young person the stamp of approval.

The Dowager, still abed and propped up against a mound of frothy white pillows, was sipping a cup of sweet hot chocolate.

"Good-morning, child. I trust you slept well?"

"Quite well, thank you, ma'am." Sarah came to stand beside the elaborately carved four-poster bed. "Your grandson has kindly offered to take me riding this morning, but I wondered if there was any service I might perform for you before I leave?"

"My dear, you are not here to dance attendance upon me," her ladyship responded gently, yet firmly. "You are a guest in my house and, as such, may do precisely as you wish. Besides," she went on, her grey eyes twinkling with wicked amusement as she cast them briefly in her formidable abigail's direction, "Buddle might become jealous if I conferred her privileged duties on to another."

"Ha! Privileged, indeed!" Buddle scoffed before turning a much friendlier countenance on to Sarah. "You'll be needing a habit, miss. I believe there is one hanging in the wardrobe in the spare bedchamber.

Hardly ever been worn, as I recall. I'll go and fetch it and bring it along to your room.''

''Yes, that is something else we must attend to when we go shopping later, Sarah,'' the Dowager remarked as Buddle went out. ''We'll order a habit made, and a few other gowns, but I'm sure you would much prefer to wait a while for the bulk of your new clothes, and deck yourself out in the latest fashions when we go to London.''

''We?'' Sarah echoed, lips twitching. There seemed to be much the Dowager had decided upon since the evening before. ''Are you proposing to act as my duenna, ma'am?''

''Yes, my dear, I rather think I shall.'' Her ladyship, looking for all the world like a very contented cat, patted the bed, and Sarah dutifully sat herself down on the edge.

''I haven't been to London for some years—not since your godmother passed away, so it's high time I bestirred myself and did a little socialising whilst I'm still able to get about reasonably well. I shall enjoy visiting my old friends. I had considered asking Henrietta to chaperon you, as she is bringing Sophia out this year, but I think you'll find it more amusing with me.''

Sarah frowned slightly. ''I'm sorry, ma'am, but I do not perfectly understand. Who is Henrietta?''

''She is the Countess of Styne, my dear, my son Henry's wife. And Sophia is their eldest daughter. Their eldest son, Bertram, is up at Oxford. The boy's an impertinent nincompoop, but harmless enough. And I shall not bore you with details of the four other children who are all still in the nursery and all equally silly.''

''I look forward to meeting them,'' Sarah responded politely, though slightly unsteadily.

''They are due home at the end of the week, so I don't

expect it will be long before I receive a visit from them,'' the Dowager remarked with scant enthusiasm. ''Henrietta's a wigeon, but a kind-hearted soul. I expect you'll like her—most people do. But I don't relish the prospect of spending several weeks under the same roof as my daughter-in-law. I'll have a word with Ravenhurst. I'm sure he'll grant us the use of his town house in Berkeley Square for the duration of the Season.''

The Dowager glanced across the room at the clock as she placed her empty cup on the bedside table. ''You run along now, my dear. You don't want to keep my grandson waiting. And don't be late back from your ride. I want to leave for Devizes directly after luncheon.''

Buddle was awaiting her in the bedchamber, and it took Sarah no time at all to change into the stylish gold-coloured habit, and to have her hair neatly confined in a snood before a beaver hat, dyed the exact same shade as the habit, was placed at a jaunty angle on her head. From somewhere Buddle had acquired a pair of black gloves and a riding crop, and as Sarah emerged from the house, she felt for the first time in her life quite the young lady of fashion.

She found to her surprise that the stableyard was deserted, and so decided to fill the time while awaiting her guardian's arrival by inspecting the exterior of what was to be her dwelling place for the next few weeks.

The late February sun was doing its best to brighten the setting, picking out the pinkish hues in the Dower House's grey stone and striving to cast its rays into those numerous shadowy areas of what could only be described as a very neglected, overgrown garden, but it was battling against overwhelming odds. Sarah cast a frowning glance up at the tall trees. Even now, still bared of their greenery, those stately beeches and elms managed to make their presence felt by blocking out most of that much-needed light.

She had noticed the evening before that Clegg had gone about lighting the candles very early because the rooms on the ground floor were so gloomy. It was such a shame, really, Sarah thought, looking along the front aspect of the fine Elizabethan building.

It was a charming house, not large, but elegantly appointed and very comfortable. Two or three industrious men would soon have the gardens in order, and if a few of those trees were felled the light could filter into the rooms, making them much more cheerful.

The sound of hoofbeats reached her ears, and she turned to see Ravenhurst, astride a large bay and leading another mount, disappear under the archway. Picking up her skirts, she hurried along the path to the stables to catch him in the act of dismounting.

"Ah, so there you are!" His expression was one of approval as he watched her approach. "I was just about to go searching for you. I cannot tell you how relieved I am to discover you're a female who can be on time!"

"I came out a few minutes ago. I've been taking a look at the garden."

His expression changed dramatically. "It's damned disgraceful!" he declared, not mincing words. "I've already told the Dowager she ought to have these confounded trees chopped down, but she won't listen."

Sarah could not prevent a smile at this. "And what would you say, sir, if people tried to tell you what you should do with the gardens at Ravenhurst?"

"Tell 'em to mind their own business!"

"Precisely! You are very like your grandmother, you know."

"Hornet!" he responded, but far from nastily, as he helped her into the saddle.

It took Marcus a few minutes only to satisfy himself that his ward was a very competent rider. She sat the hack gracefully and had good light hands.

"I wish I'd sorted you out something with a bit more spirit, child," he remarked, casting her sluggish mount a frowning glance, "but I thought it wisest to be cautious as you gave me the impression that you ride infrequently. Which I find very strange," he went on matter-of-factly, "considering I received a letter from my cousin requesting funds to purchase a horse for you, as riding was one of your favourite pastimes. And I have been paying stabling costs for almost a year."

Sarah kept her gaze firmly fixed between her horse's ears, but instinctively knew her guardian was staring at her. Only honesty would serve, now. Ravenhurst was no fool, and had probably worked out for himself where her allowance had been going.

"As soon as I came to know you a little, I knew you would never have quibbled over furnishing me with a mount," she said at length.

"Where has your allowance been going, Sarah? Gaming?"

"I think so." She heard him muttering something under his breath, and found herself coming to Mrs Fairchild's defence. "You mustn't think I have been ill-used, sir. Your cousin was always very kind to me."

"Kind!" he ejaculated. "I'll give her kind when I see her! Squandering your allowance on her own pleasures, whilst you went about in clothes fitted only for a servant. No wonder the confounded woman very nearly swooned when I turned up unexpectedly! She realised the game was up!"

Knowing that in his present mood it would be a waste of breath trying to make him view his cousin in a less derogatory light, Sarah encouraged him to vent all that pent-up condemnation on a different source by quite deliberately asking how Mrs Stanton had taken her daughter's elopement. It had the desired effect.

"And well may you ask, my girl!" The dark brows snapped together. "What the devil do you mean by getting yourself involved in that disgraceful affair?"

"Clarissa has always been my closest friend, sir," she answered, far from cowed by his staunch disapproval of her actions. "And I'm very fond of James, too. I couldn't bear to see them made unhappy because of the selfish caprice of their respective fathers who, I might add, before a silly difference of opinion, actively encouraged their children's close friendship."

She turned her head to look at him, and he could not mistake the flicker of combined sadness and regret in her eyes. "Was Mrs Stanton very angry with me?"

He quickly discovered he was not proof against that look, and didn't hesitate to reassure her. "No. In fact, I gained the distinct impression that she was more disturbed by your sudden flight than her daughter's."

"I knew it!" Sarah exclaimed triumphantly, her aquamarine eyes sparkling again. "I always thought that deep down Mrs Stanton was not happy with the state of affairs. She thinks a great deal of James, so I guessed she was far from opposed to the match."

"Be that as it may, my girl!" he countered, his disapproval returning. "You ought not to have become involved. I well expect to receive a visit from your friend's father after my blood!"

"Oh, I shouldn't worry, if I were you," she said dismissively. "He's a blustering, bad-tempered individual at times but, believe me, you're more than a match for him, sir.'' Sarah, the perfection of her forehead suddenly marred by a deep frown of concern, kept her eyes firmly fixed between her mount's ears, and so missed the look of almost comical outrage on her guardian's face. ''I think it most unlikely that Mr Stanton will seek you out. No, he's far more likely to go after Clarissa and James.''

A tiny sigh escaped her. ''I cannot help worrying about them, sir. James said it would take five or six days to reach the border. But, of course, he wasn't making allowances for a deterioration in the weather.''

Once again he found sympathy coming to the fore. ''Then you can stop worrying, child!'' he ordered with a kind of rough gentleness. ''Before we left the inn yesterday, I learned from the magistrate that only the southern counties were affected by snow. No doubt your friends had a very tedious, but quite uneventful, journey to Scotland. And who knows, they might at this very moment be standing before that infamous anvil!''

He cast her a reassuring smile. ''If it will ease your mind, I shall try to discover the outcome when I collect my greys from Bath in a few days' time.''

He then changed the subject and, as they continued their ride, pointed out various features of interest on his uncle's vast estate. When the huge Restoration mansion came into view, he caused more than one amused chuckle to rise in Sarah's throat by his scathing condemnation of the imposing ancestral home. He stigmatised the building as a great draughty barn of a place.

It was his considered opinion that the addition of the two new wings during the previous century had ruined what little architectural beauty the house had ever possessed; and as if that were not bad enough, his great-grandfather, apparently terrified of a fire breaking out, had instigated the construction of a new kitchen area, which was only accessible through miles of corridor. Consequently, by the time meals arrived at the dining-room they were always cold.

Secretly, Sarah, too, thought it rather an unprepossessing structure with little to commend it, but was far too well-bred to comment. The park, on the other hand was very much to her taste. With the exception of a small area near the eastern boundary, the landscape was quite beautiful with its sweeping lawns, rippling streams and large clumps of majestic trees.

She frowned as they began to skirt the overgrown area. "Why has this part been allowed to develop into a wilderness, sir?"

"A couple of centuries ago a woman accused of being a witch was dragged here by some of the villagers. Before she drowned, she was heard to put a curse on this place."

He raised his eyes heavenwards. "Complete nonsense, of course! Still, I suppose there's some justification for the superstition," he added fair-mindedly. "An ancestor met his death near this very spot, and my uncle came perilously close to drowning here himself when he was a youth. There's a good-sized lake hidden behind that wall of overgrown shrubs and brambles. If you like, we'll try to find a way through and I'll show it to you."

Possessing an inquisitive rather than a fanciful nature, Sarah did not hesitate. After tethering their horses to the branch of a tree, they forged a way through the shrubbery, Sarah finding the brambles' wickedly clawing thorns more threatening than any supposed curse. When they did eventually arrive at the lakeside, she looked about her in dismay at the sheer neglect of what once must have been an idyllic spot.

Taking a hold of one slender gloved hand, Marcus led the way along the overgrown path round the water's edge. "You can't deny, Sarah, it's an eerie place. Listen to that high-pitched wailing! The witch, I suspect."

"That's the wind," she scoffed.

"You think so? Well, you may be right. But what about those ghostly forms rising from the lake?"

"Mist. And you know it." She detected the slight movement of broad shoulders shaking with suppressed laughter. "You can stop trying to frighten me because you won't succeed! Tell me, instead, what that building is just ahead?"

"It's the old boat-house. Not used now, of course. Since my uncle's unfortunate experience, no one ever comes here."

"Well, someone most certainly does," Sarah countered as they arrived at the stone-built structure. A raised wooden platform had been constructed along the front wall, from which one gained access to a rather rickety-looking jetty that reached out some distance into the lake. "And has been here quite recently, I should say," she added, staring down at the clearly visible wet foot-prints.

Ravenhurst walked across the platform to the far side of the boat-house. "Well, well, my dear! We evidently disturbed a trespasser. He's left his catch."

Sarah looked down at the four large fish lying in the grass. "A poacher?"

"More than likely. He must have seen or heard us approaching, and made himself scarce." He scanned the dense area of shrubs to his right. "No doubt he's watching our every move at this very moment."

"Are you going to inform your uncle when he returns?'' Sarah asked tentatively, but instinctively knew what his response would be even before he said,

"Certainly not! That lake must be teaming with fish. The Earl makes no use of them, and if some unfortunate wretch can provide himself with a decent meal, I shan't be the one to throw a rub in his way.'' There was certainly more than just a hint of devilment in the smile he cast her. "Come, let us away, so the poor fellow can collect his dinner.''

Their arrival back at the Dower House a short while later coincided with that of a very elegant travelling-carriage. Sarah watched with interest as a sparse man in his forties, dressed in a suit of severe black cloth, alighted. He then took a few rather mincing steps away from the equipage before bowing with studied elegance to Mr Ravenhurst.

"Ah, Quilp! In good time. Two pairs of my boots are in urgent need of your meticulous attention. You know your way.'' Thus disposing of his valet, Marcus then acknowledged his stable lad who had driven the carriage to Somerset before turning his gaze on to his head groom who had not, even by the slight raising of his bushy, greying brows, betrayed the fact that he had recognised Sarah.

Ravenhurst's thin lips curled into a not unappreciative smile. "I trust your journey passed without incident, Sutton. This young lady, whom you've never met before, is my ward, Miss Pennington.''

Although she had had little conversation with the groom during her stay at the Inn, only ever passing the time of day, Sarah flatly refused to partake in her guardian's rather childish and totally unnecessary game of pretence. She acknowledged the head groom with her friendly smile, asked him how he went on, and then returned to the house to change back into the dress she had been wearing earlier that morning.

When she returned downstairs, Clegg informed her that luncheon was not quite ready to be served, so she took herself off to the library and began writing a letter to Mrs Stanton.

She had felt untold relief to learn that her friend's mother bore her no ill-will. After apologising once again for the part she had played in Clarissa's elopement—which, in fact, had been woefully small—she began to relate what had befallen her since she had left Bath, which had been a mere five days, but which seemed like a lifetime ago.

She had just reached the part where Mr Ravenhurst had arrived at the inn when she was disturbed by a tapping sound, and turned her head to see the man himself standing on the other side of the window, beckoning to her with an imperious hand.

Rising from the desk, Sarah went across to open the windows, and Marcus, lifting one muscular, booted-leg over the sill, stepped into the room.

A frown of disapproval creased her brow. "Why you cannot use the door like anyone—" Sarah caught herself up abruptly as his actions struck a chord of memory. "Do that again!"

"Do what again?"

"Climb out of the window."

He regarded her suspiciously. "You're not going to close them by any chance, so that I have to walk round to the front door?"

"Of course not! Just do as I ask!"

He looked far from convinced, but obediently repeated the procedure. "Satisfied, now?"

"That's it!" Excitement brought a sparkle to her eyes. "That's what I found so odd on the night of Mr Nutley's death!"

# Chapter Eight

Marcus regarded her in frowning silence for a moment. ''What precisely struck you as odd?''

''The way that intruder climbed out of the parlour window at the inn. I knew there was something peculiar about the action at the time, but it wasn't until I watched you just now that I realised precisely what had puzzled me. Here, let me show you.''

Brushing past, Sarah sat on the window-sill. Then, gathering the folds of her skirts beneath her, she swung both legs over the ledge together. ''That is how our intruder did it, just as any female would perform the feat.''

''Are you trying to tell me that you think, now, our mysterious cloaked figure might possibly have been a woman?'' He helped her back inside, and then securely fastened the windows. ''The evidence on which to base such a judgement, if you'll forgive me saying so, child, seems rather flimsy.''

''Yes, perhaps it does,'' she conceded. ''But the intruder's actions appeared so natural, just as though he— she was accustomed to wearing skirts. If my memory serves me correctly, that window at the inn was about the same distance from the ground as this one. The intruder was wearing breeches, so why didn't he simply step over the sill as you did? I could quite easily do so if I wore breeches.''

Marcus moved across to the small table on which several decanters stood and, at Sarah's shake of the head, poured out just one glass of wine. He sipped the rich dark liquid meditatively, then said, ''Assuming you're right, and I'm far from convinced myself, who are we looking at? Your actress friend, that middle-aged spinster and the farmer's wife.''

''I think we can safely rule out the farmer's wife,'' Sarah responded with a twitching smile. ''She was, as you no doubt recall, a lady built on generous lines. Although that cloak concealed the intruder's identity, it couldn't possibly mask a person's size, at least not to that extent. Our intruder was much slimmer and rather taller, if my memory serves me correctly.''

''Could it have been the 'Divine' Dorothea, then?''

Sarah gave the question due consideration as she resumed her seat at the desk. ''It's certainly possible, yet my instinct tells me otherwise.''

''What makes you so sure that it wasn't her?''

''Because Dottie is my height, and although I saw the intruder for a few brief moments only, I feel certain she was taller than I. And then there was that letter found on the murdered servant girl. It was rather a clumsy way of trying to incriminate Dottie in Nutley's death, don't you agree?''

Tossing the contents of his glass down his throat, Marcus came across to sit himself on the edge of the desk. ''Given what we now know—yes, I do. No doubt Stubbs will not fail to check out Dottie's story when he returns to London, but I for one do not doubt the truth of it.''

He was silent for a moment, absently swinging one

well-muscled leg to and fro. "Like Dottie, that servant girl was illiterate. Even supposing the girl did come across that letter, it would have meant nothing to her. But she certainly discovered something about someone, and evidently didn't hesitate in stooping to a little blackmail. And I think whoever murdered her planted Dottie's letter on the dead girl's body."

"And you think the intruder and the person who murdered the servant girl are one and the same person? And that that person was someone staying at the inn, don't you, sir?"

"Yes, child, I do." He stared down into her troubled eyes. "Let us go through events step by step. I think you would agree that no one putting up at that inn did so by design. Taking that fact into account, it's highly unlikely that Nutley arranged to meet anyone there. Also, taking into account the state of the roads, it was impossible for our cloaked figure to have travelled very far."

"But don't forget that it was possible to walk into the village," she reminded him.

"True. And I'm sure it didn't take long for word to spread that the inn was filled with stranded travellers—easy pickings for someone willing to take a few risks, you might say. Very well, let's deal with that possibility first, and assume someone from the village did break in. His motive for doing so must have been robbery, wouldn't you say?" and he watched her nod in response. "Yet nothing was stolen."

"I know." Sarah looked up at him intently. "But Mr Nutley's appearance would have put a stop to the burglar's intentions, surely?"

"You would certainly have thought so, wouldn't you? We still cannot be sure whether Nutley's death was an accident, or not. But let's assume for argument's sake that it was. There was a scuffle between him and the intruder. Nutley slipped, possibly knocking over the chair that we found upturned, hit his head on the settle and broke his neck. The noise woke you. How much time elapsed, after you had woken, before you entered the parlour?''

She shrugged. ''Perhaps five minutes, not much more.''

''And yet our villager, bent on a little petty theft, was still there.'' The look he cast her was openly sceptical. ''Theft is one thing—being accused of murder is quite another. Had our intruder been some petty thief, I feel certain he would have departed, instanter!''

Sarah chewed these particulars over for a few moments and quickly came to the same conclusion. ''So why did our intruder remain, sir?''

''That's exactly the point! Why, my dear Sarah? Petty theft certainly wasn't the reason. Nutley had a purse in his pocket containing several sovereigns, there was a timepiece attached to his waistcoat and he was wearing a gold signet ring. All could have been quite easily filched in the time it took for you to get downstairs.''

''How very odd!'' Sarah's brows drew together in a puzzled frown. ''What on earth was our cloaked figure doing, then, during that time?''

''I doubt foolishly trying to revive Nutley.'' Marcus moved across to the decanters once more to refill his glass. ''Let us leave that for now and move on to yet another very interesting fact—the quite deliberate drugging of that rum punch. Nutley's intention, I feel fairly certain, was not to drug everyone. If that were the case, he would have tried harder to coax both you and me into accepting a glass. But he didn't… Why?''

Sarah gazed up into his intelligent dark eyes as he resumed his former position on the desk. "I suppose it might have aroused suspicion had he done so."

"Very true...or," he continued after the briefest of pauses, "it was of little importance to him whether we imbibed or not because his intended victim had already accepted a glass."

He watched her lovely, expressive face closely and knew the instant enlightenment had dawned.

"Of course! Mr Stubbs!"

"Clever girl!" he remarked approvingly. "Nutley was sharing a bedchamber with the Runner, and it's my belief that some time during that day he got wind of Stubbs's profession. But ask yourself this, Sarah—why should this knowledge bother him? Why should he want Stubbs drugged, dead to the world?"

Her puzzled frown returned. "Well, we can be fairly certain that it wasn't because he had arranged to meet someone at the inn and didn't want Stubbs to witness that meeting. So, perhaps, he had something to hide? Something in his possession that he was terrified of Mr Stubbs discovering."

"Precisely! And that is what I believe took Nutley back down to the parlour. I think he was endeavouring to hide something until he was able to continue his journey. Now, nothing incriminating was found on his person, nor amongst his possessions, and Stubbs and I searched that parlour thoroughly and discovered nothing out of the way."

"So, you think our cloaked intruder took whatever it was Mr Nutley was endeavouring to hide?"

"I think he, or she, was searching for it, certainly, but without success, because you, my dear, inadvertently interrupted proceedings. Stubbs and I are positive that someone searched our rooms, possibly during the time we were interviewing you in the parlour. If our cloaked friend had found what Nutley had hidden, there would have been no need to search further.''

"You know, sir,'' Sarah said after several moments' intense thought, "the more I think about it, the more convinced I am that you are right, and that cloaked figure was amongst the guests staying at that inn. He or she must have heard Nutley leave his room that night, and followed him downstairs. Though, precisely who it was I cannot imagine. What is more, it seems he or she knew that Mr Nutley had something to hide. And if Nutley was involved in something underhanded, do you think this person might have been, well, an accomplice?''

He shrugged. "It's possible, but we can only speculate on that, child. I'm just glad we're well out of it now.'' He dismissed it from his mind, and gazed down at the letter she had been writing, one dark brow rising when he caught the name of the intended recipient. "Ha! Guilty conscience, I see!''

She cast him a disapproving frown. "You appear to have a propensity for reading other people's letters.''

"And those destined for myself!'' he countered, his frown as pronounced as her own, as he recalled clearly the contents of the letter that he had found in her writing-case. "How long did you intend keeping me in the dark as to your true identity?''

"I had every intention of informing you the day after our arrival at the inn. But you were in such a disagreeable mood at breakfast. And then finding Mr Nutley that way... Oh, I don't know! The right moment just never seemed to arise.'' She received not so much a growl in response to this as a grunt. "Well, you could just as easily have informed me that you knew who I was,'' she added in her defence.

''What? And risk your doing something bird-witted like loping off in the dead of night? Not a chance!''

She satisfied herself with casting him a look of impatience, and as Clegg entered the room a moment later to inform them that luncheon was about to be served, the topic of conversation ceased.

After they had all eaten, the Dowager was all eagerness to set off on their trip to Devizes. Mr Ravenhurst had mentioned that he might well accompany them on the shopping expedition, but Sarah, having by this time acquired a fair knowledge of his character, was not in the least surprised when he informed them quite bluntly that he had no intention of doing so, as he had one or two urgent letters he must write.

She was not very surprised, either, when he took it upon himself, in his usual high-handed manner, to organise their transport. Refusing point blank to permit his ward to travel even a short distance in what he stigmatised as her ladyship's antiquated bone-shaker of a berlin, which might easily become stuck in the inches of mud still lying on many of the minor roads after the recent thaw, he ordered his grandmother's team of handsome bays harnessed to his own well-sprung and far more comfortable carriage.

Not surprisingly, neither lady objected to these arrangements, and the short journey was achieved swiftly and without mishap.

Naturally, the small town could not offer those elegant establishments to be found in Bath, but Sarah was far from disappointed. For years she could only stare longingly at the pretty, frivolous bonnets and elegant gowns offered for sale; now, however, she could enter shops, confident in the knowledge that anything that happened to take her fancy would be hers for the asking.

She quickly discovered that the Dowager Countess of Styne was well known. No sooner had they entered the town's most fashionable shop, owned by a lady who had for a time worked under one of London's most famous modistes, than chairs were swiftly found for the distinguished customer and her young protégée. She quickly discovered, too, that her notion of an adequate wardrobe was certainly far removed from the Dowager's.

Lengths of silks, satins, muslins and velvets were brought out for inspection, whilst Sarah was pulled this way and that and her measurements taken with ruthless efficiency. Day dresses, walking dresses, pelisses and spencers were ordered to be made as quickly as possible and sent to Styne, and several lengths of material, including a very pretty turquoise silk, which the Dowager considered ideal for an evening gown, were parcelled up and placed in the carriage.

All Sarah's protestations fell on deaf ears. In the other shops the Dowager's reckless spending continued. A more than adequate supply of undergarments and nightwear was purchased before bonnets, shoes, gloves and many, many more "absolute necessities", according to the Dowager, were chosen by her with blatant disregard for cost.

When they eventually arrived back at the Dower House, Sarah could only watch in silent dismay as the servants, having to make several journeys, collected the multitude of packages from the carriage and carried them up to her room.

Marcus emerged from the library to find his ward, a look of combined anxiety and guilt on her face, and the

Dowager, a look of pleasurable satisfaction on hers, divesting themselves of cloaks and bonnets.

"What's the matter, child? Has my indomitable grandmother worn you out?"

"No such thing!" her ladyship put in before Sarah could open her mouth. "She's been all of a twitter for most of the afternoon. Can't imagine why. Unless she's worried that you'll come the ugly, Marcus, at laying out blunt for a few little necessities."

"A few little...?" Sarah placed a restraining hand on her guardian's arm as he made to follow the Dowager into the drawing-room. "Sir, I couldn't stop her," she told him, real perturbation sounding in her voice. "I tried. Truly, I did! But she just wouldn't listen."

"A family failing, I'm afraid," he responded, casually pulling her arm through his and guiding her into the room his grandmother had entered. "So don't waste your breath in trying, my child."

Sarah knew that that was his rather tactful way of telling her that he simply wasn't interested in how much money had been squandered that afternoon. He was so wealthy, of course, that the day's expenditure represented a mere drop in the ocean, but Sarah could not reconcile her conscience with such wanton extravagance.

That night, dressed in one of her new nightgowns, she sat at the small table in her room, and poured out her thoughts in the letter she had begun earlier in the day to her friend's mother.

The words flowed so easily from her pen as her reflections centred on her guardian. What a surprisingly complex creature he had turned out to be! she wrote. He bore no resemblance whatsoever to the mean-spirited tyrant of her imaginings.

And just why his cousin Harriet Fairchild held him in

such lively dread she could not imagine, because he was, for the most part, an agreeable man who could be quite touchingly thoughtful at times. The quill in her hand stilled suddenly, and she raised her eyes to stare blindly at the delicately patterned wallpaper.

Yes, why had she heard so many bad reports about Marcus Ravenhurst during her years in Bath? she wondered. Most of what she had been told was complete and utter nonsense. True, he could be very abrupt at times, and he certainly didn't suffer fools gladly, but he was far from the unfeeling monster she had been led to believe.

His appearance was against him, though, she mused. One glimpse of that heavy scowl would send the timid scurrying away even before he had opened his mouth, and she could quite understand why many a faint-hearted female might find his brusqueness a trifle off-putting. He could hardly be described as handsome, either, or of having a kindly face, but he did have a rather wonderful smile.

And there was no denying he was a fine figure of a man. Broad shouldered and muscular, he was ruggedly attractive and, therefore, must surely appeal to many members of her sex. Added to which he had many fine qualities. So, why then had he never married?

The thought, unbidden, came into her head, and she absently brushed the feathers of her quill back and forth across her chin while pondering over this rather surprising circumstance. He had no title, it was true, but he was excessively wealthy. Could it be this fact alone that had kept him a bachelor? Was he wary of being coveted only for his great wealth?

If that was the case, she could quite understand why matrimony held no appeal for him. Why, it was despicable to marry someone merely for money! Yet, she was worldly-wise enough to know that both men and women did just that.

But supposing he did meet someone who loved him for himself; what sort of husband would he make? Her lips curled into a wicked little smile. Well, he would certainly wish to rule the roost. Which was only right and proper, she decided fair-mindedly. A man ought to make the decisions, and shoulder the responsibilities.

Sadly, though, given Mr Ravenhurst's temperament, if he eventually married some milk-and-water miss who hadn't the courage to stand up to him, he would be in grave danger of degenerating into nothing more than a rather unpleasant autocrat. On the other hand, though, if he married a girl of spirit, and one who, moreover, coveted the man and not his money, she felt sure he would be a devoted husband, attentive to his wife's every need.

She felt certain, too, that he was a man capable of deeply tender feelings who, when parted from his love, would no doubt write long and affectionate letters, letters intended for her eyes alone, which she would keep safely hidden away.

Instinctively, Sarah's fingers sought the little device which opened the secret compartment in her writing case, but nothing happened. She frowned as she set aside her quill. The spring was stiff, she knew, but it seemed almost as if something was jamming it, preventing the flap from opening. She tried again, but it took several more attempts before she eventually succeeded, and the flap reluctantly opened

"What on earth...?"

Very carefully she eased the tightly wedged object out of the compartment, and laid it across her hand. For several moments it was as much as she could do to stare down at it in astonished disbelief, then, throwing on her robe, she rushed from the room, almost colliding with Buddle in her headlong flight along the passageway.

Ravenhurst, comfortably established in bed, propped against a mound of pillows, hardly had time to raise his eyes from the book he was reading, and answer the imperious tattoo, before the door was thrown wide and Sarah charged into the room.

"Great heaven's, child!" He regarded her keenly. "Whatever's the matter?"

"Oh, sir!" Breathless more from excitement than from her headlong dash along the passageway, Sarah plumped herself down on the bed, and almost threw her incredible find on to the coverlet in front of him. "Just you look at that!"

Setting aside the book, he obeyed the command, casting only the most cursory glance at the necklace before raising enquiring eyes to hers. "Well, and what of it?"

"But, sir, don't you see? It isn't mine!" she informed him in some agitation, slightly nettled by his lack of interest. "I found it wedged in the secret compartment of my writing-case."

At this his attitude changed abruptly. "Did you, now?" Spreading the necklace out, he studied it more closely. "I've seen you before," he murmured. "But where have I seen you?"

He looked back at Sarah, who was in the process of making herself more comfortable on his bed by tucking her slender feet beneath her. Her robe was unfastened, and the movement caused the material of her nightgown to pull taut, clearly revealing the tantalising outline of young, firm breasts.

He cleared his throat, made a mental note not to leave it very much longer before he made a trip to London to visit his mistress, and then forced himself to concentrate on the mystery in hand. "So, your writing-case has a hidden compartment, has it? Have you no idea how long this gaud has been in there?"

"Well, no, not really," she confessed. "You see, I don't ever use it, so I—" She broke off, her eyes narrowing. "No, wait a moment! The morning after we arrived at the inn, I was showing it to Mr Nutley, and the necklace certainly wasn't there then."

He did not respond, and after a few moments she raised her eyes to find him regarding her rather quizzically, and the reason for the look was obvious.

"Oh, no! You don't think that this was what Mr Nutley was so afraid of a certain someone discovering in his possession, and so hid it in my case?"

"That is precisely what I think, child, because I've just recalled where I've seen this necklace before... The last time I set eyes on it, it was adorning the neck of Lady Felchett."

He picked it up, studying the glinting jewels beneath the candle's glow. "I don't know, though. I'm certainly no expert, but it looks to me—" He checked on what he had been about to say when he noticed Sarah staring in unblushing fascination at his naked torso. "Something seems to be puzzling you, child?"

"Yes, it's that." She didn't hesitate to respond, pointing rather rudely at the triangular mat of dark hair covering his chest. "Are all men similarly cursed with all that hair on their bodies?"

"Cursed with...? You really are the most outrageous little baggage, Sarah!" he scolded, slightly affronted by this slur on his manliness but, far from cowed, she dissolved into laughter.

"I'm sorry," she apologised, wiping her streaming

eyes with the back of her hand, "but it came as rather a shock. You see, I've never seen a man without his clothes on before."

"Good God! I sincerely trust not!"

A further gurgle escaped her. "You know very well what I mean. I shouldn't have been surprised, though," she admitted. "I did notice when you came to my bedchamber, that time at the inn, that you had hairs at the base of your throat, but I didn't realise just how far they spread."

She watched as he, with all the modesty of an embarrassed virgin, pulled the bedcovers further up his chest, and chuckled again. "Do you never wear a nightshirt, sir? Not that I suppose there's much need," she went on, not giving him the opportunity to answer. "With all that on your person you must be warm enough."

"God in heaven!" He clapped a hand over his eyes. "What will the outrageous chit say next? And kindly move yourself—you're sitting on my feet!"

Sarah altered her position. "I think it might be best if we concentrate on the diamond necklace," she suggested with what he considered the most provocative feminine smile he had ever witnessed. "What do you intend doing with it? Are you going to return it to Lord Felchett?"

He scratched the side of his head, ruffling his dark hair into disarray. "No. I suppose I'll need to pay a visit to Bristol, and see if I cannot locate Stubbs," he responded without much enthusiasm. "I intended making a return trip to Bath in a few days, anyway. So I shall go to Bristol first, and then go on to Bath afterwards."

He could clearly read the unspoken question in her eyes. "Yes, Sarah, I fully intend to pay a visit on my swindling cousin. And I shall also call upon Mrs Stanton while I'm there, and discover if she has heard anything from your runaways.''

Sarah brightened at this. ''Oh, would you give her my letter, sir? I've nearly finished it. I'll return to my room and do so now.''

She had only just slipped her feet back on to the floor when the door was thrown wide, and the Dowager came purposefully into the room. ''What is the meaning of this?'' she demanded in outraged tones. ''Sarah, return to your room at once!''

''Yes, you run along now, child,'' Marcus urged gently before she had time to open her mouth and explain the reason for her presence in his bedchamber. ''Finish your letter, and then give it to one of the servants to bring along to me. I intend leaving early in the morning, so I'll bid you farewell now.''

The Dowager bade her a curt good-night, and then waited for the door to close behind Sarah before moving towards the bed where her far from penitent grandson regarded her with a wickedly mocking gleam in his eyes.

''What do you mean by permitting that child to visit you in your bedchamber, Marcus? Have you such scant regard for her reputation?''

''Oh, for heaven's sake!'' he responded in combined exasperation and amusement. ''What the devil did you think I was proposing to do…ravish the girl?''

She could not prevent a twitching smile at this. ''No, I did not. You have faults enough, but despoiling innocent damsels isn't one of them. But Sarah is an exceedingly pretty young woman, and—''

''Yes, I had noticed.''

''And you are a man.''

"I wouldn't be at all surprised if Sarah hasn't come to that conclusion, too."

"Marcus!" The Dowager rapped her cane on the floor. "This is no time for flippancy! Who will believe her innocent if she continues to visit you in your bedchamber?"

He regarded her for a moment in brooding silence. "Yes, you're right, of course," he admitted, rather reluctantly it seemed to her. "I'll have a word with Sarah when I get back. But in the meantime," he went on, giving her back look for look, "I won't have you scolding the child. The last thing in the world I want is for her to be afraid or embarrassed to come to me."

She assured him that she had absolutely no intention of doing so and, satisfied, he turned his attention once more to the necklace, requesting her to take a look at it, and explaining how it came to be in his possession.

"I don't care for it very much," the Dowager remarked when she had learned all. "The setting is rather heavy. Quite ugly, in fact! No doubt the Felchetts will be relieved to have it restored to them, though. Which is more than the Nutleys will experience when they learn about the goings-on. One cannot but sympathise, Marcus. It is one thing to discover your offspring is dead, and quite another to learn he was nothing more than a common thief."

"Nutley was a nincompoop, ma'am," her grandson responded, betraying his scant regard for the deceased. "I should be very surprised if his was the brain behind the robbery." And that is precisely what concerns me, he added silently.

The following morning Marcus was up early, and went out to the stableyard even before his ward had left her room. He had sent a message for Jeb's bays to be harnessed to his curricle and for his young stable lad to accompany him, and everything was in readiness for his departure.

Sutton cast a rather petulant look up at his subordinate, who was already seated in the carriage, keeping the bays well under control, before slanting a rather hopeful glance in his master's direction. "Will you be collecting the greys, sir? Cause ifen you are, I could quite easily go wi' young Ben 'ere, and save you the bother.''

Marcus could not prevent a smile as he climbed up on to the seat beside the young groom and took the reins from him. He knew Sutton must be feeling peeved at not being the one to accompany him, but this time he had far more important work for his head groom.

"I have business in Bristol first, Sutton. Then I shall go on to Bath. I don't know just how long I'll be away, but it's important you remain here. I need you to watch over my ward whilst I'm gone.''

Sutton's ears pricked up at this, and he looked up at his master in some alarm. "Lord bless me! She ain't likely to lope off again, is she, sir?''

This drew another smile from his master, but it seemed much softer this time. "No, Sutton, rest easy. Now having come to know my ward, I can safely promise you that she wouldn't do that. That isn't my Sarah's way. But I want you to accompany her whenever she ventures out of doors. Never let her go off on her own, whether on foot or horseback. I don't care what excuses you need to make, so long as you never let her out of your sight.''

There was no semblance of a smile, now, and his eyes grew flint-like as he stared down at the ground. "Guard her with your life, Sutton…I would not be best pleased if aught ever happened to my Sarah.''

## Chapter Nine

It was difficult to believe that within the space of less than two weeks there could be such a marked change in the weather. But so it was. February with its biting-cold winds and snowstorms was well and truly a thing of the past. March had arrived, bringing with it pleasant days of mild sunshine and almost cloudless skies, though the nights continued to be cold and there was always a light covering of hoar-frost by morning.

Spring seemed to have arrived, surprisingly, quite early. Everywhere the light greenish hues of new growth were to be seen, and Sarah, having always been an avid walker, ventured out of doors much more often. Her strolls around the Dowager's garden, however, soon began to pall. Like Ravenhurst, she found the overgrown grounds rather depressing, and decided to venture further afield.

The previous day she had walked across the Earl's vast estate and had spent a very pleasant afternoon exploring the home wood; and today she had decided to inspect the pretty village that she had passed through on the day her guardian had brought her to the Dower House.

She had almost reached the main driveway leading to the big house when she became aware of the sound of heavy footsteps, and turned to see Sutton striding purposefully in her direction. Since Mr Ravenhurst's departure, six days before, Sutton had ridden out with her each morning, and she most certainly didn't object to his company.

The groom made a cheerful companion, and his rather dry sense of humour never failed to amuse her. Apart from this, he knew the county well, and had shown her some of the more pleasant rides, and had escorted her to several places of interest round about.

She had been rather surprised, though, suddenly to come across him in the home wood the day before. Her eyes narrowed suspiciously. Yes, that encounter might well have been purely accidental. But for it to happen twice in as many days was just too much of a coincidence!

"Well, well, Sutton," she greeted him as he reached her side. "What a surprise! I expect, like me, you decided on the spur of the moment to enjoy this rather pleasant afternoon sunshine and go out for a walk."

"Aye, that's it, ma'am!" He made a sound suspiciously like a sigh of relief. "There ain't much for me to do back at the stables with the master away."

"No, quite. You'll no doubt be pleased to return to Ravenhurst and your own domain." They reached the main driveway, and Sarah's lips curled into a wicked little smile. "Where were you thinking of walking? Up to the big house?"

As this seemed the most obvious goal, Sutton did not hesitate. "Aye, that's right, ma'am."

"In that case, I'm afraid we must part company. My destination lies in quite another direction." The expression on his face was so ludicrous that Sarah dissolved into laughter. "Oh, Sutton! You must consider me the veriest dunderhead! How long did you suppose it would take me to work out your little ploy?"

The suspicion of a blush showed beneath the weathered skin, and he looked so uncomfortably guilty, like a child caught in some mischievous prank, that Sarah took pity on him.

"Oh, come along with me. I don't mind in the least if you accompany me to the village. Though just why your master should have asked you to keep an eye on me I can't imagine." She cast him a rather thoughtful glance. "Unless, of course, he suspected that I might try to leave in his absence."

"Oh, no, miss. It weren't "cause he were afraid of owt like that," he hurriedly assured her. "And that I do know. But he did ask me to keep me eye on you, right enough," he freely admitted.

Did he, now? Sarah thought, eyes narrowing again, and it didn't take many moments before she had worked out the possible motive behind the request.

"Sutton, was anything else discovered about those unfortunate happenings before you left the inn?"

"What inn would that be, Miss Pennington?"

"Don't prevaricate!" she snapped. "I have no intention of indulging in one of your master's foolish games of pretence."

A spark of respect glinted in the groom's grey eyes. He had swiftly come to the conclusion that his master's ward was a sweet-natured filly, but she certainly didn't lack spirit. Anyone who could stand up to Mr Ravenhurst the way she did must have considerable pluck, and Sutton admired her for that. Added to which his master was clearly very fond of her. And that in itself was good enough for him!

"No, nothing, miss. "Cepting I did overhear someone complaining that someone had been in their room, going through their things, like."

"Who was complaining?"

"Can't be sure, but I reckon it were that gangling wench that put me in mind of a school-ma'am. They were in the parlour at the time…her and the magistrate, I think it were. Only just caught a snippet as I passed the door. The magistrate arranged for Nutley's body to be sent back to Oxfordshire. But apart from that," he shrugged, "nothing much else "appened. We were all allowed to leave not long after you and the master went."

"And did Mr Stubbs resume his journey with the other passengers?"

"Aye, miss, that he did. Though whether he went as far as Bristol, I couldn't say. I left the stage at Chippenham as I "ad to go and collect the master's carriage and old mincing bree—Mr Ravenhurst's valet," he amended quickly.

Sarah could not prevent a smile at this. It had not taken her very long to discover that the head groom and valet had scant regard for each other. She had heard Quilp sniff rather pointedly at mention of the groom's name; and Sutton's rather vulgar response to any mention of the valet was to spit on the ground.

It had not taken Sarah very long, either, to discover that Sutton, in particular, was touchingly devoted to his master. Ravenhurst could do no wrong in the head groom's eyes. There wasn't a better master in the land, according to Sutton, nor a more idyllic spot to be found anywhere than the Ravenhurst estate.

His master's word was law, and Sutton had not hesitated to carry out Ravenhurst's orders to the letter, though Sarah suspected that time hung heavily on the groom's hands as he had been only too eager to ride out with her in the mornings. But Ravenhurst had not commanded him to go with her whenever she ventured forth in order to keep the groom gainfully employed, nor to provide her with some genial company.

Oh, no, her guardian had done so because he feared that the mysterious cloaked figure would, by a simple process of elimination, work out who must have the diamond necklace.

By the time she had arrived back at the Dower House, after having toured the quaint little village that lay just beyond the estate's boundary wall, Sarah had still been unable to work out who Mr Nutley's possible accomplice might have been.

If, as Sutton had suggested, Miss Grimshaw had suspected that someone had been going through her belongings, and if the cloaked figure had, indeed, been a female, there was only one possible candidate. Sarah shook her head in disbelief. If Dottie Hogg turned out to be the malefactor, then she was the most accomplished actress alive. And that was something Miss Dorothea de Vine most certainly was not!

On entering the hall, Sarah was informed by the butler that the Countess of Styne, accompanied by her eldest daughter, had called, and that she was to go straight up to the Dowager's private sitting-room. Sarah had learned from Buddle the day before that the family had returned from Kent, and she was eager to make their acquaintance.

Delaying only for the time it took to remove her cloak and bonnet and to tidy her hair, Sarah entered the room to discover a rather colourless female in her mid-forties, and a rather pretty girl, with large brown eyes and a riot of dusky locks, sitting side by side on the sofa, and the Dowager in her favourite armchair, making not the least attempt to stifle a yawn.

"Ah! Sarah, my dear. Come, let me introduce you to my visitors," the Dowager said, brightening perceptively.

After the introductions were made, Sarah seated herself in the chair on the opposite side of the hearth and politely thanked the Countess for the use of her horse.

"Not at all, my dear. I ride so infrequently these days that my mare gets little enough exercise. You are most welcome to make use of her whenever you wish." The kind offer was accompanied by a warm smile. "It is rather a pity that Sophia is not fond of that form of exercise, otherwise I am sure she would have been delighted to accompany you on your rides. Unfortunately, she sustained a bad fall some years ago, and is disinclined to get back in the saddle again."

"Very understandable, ma'am," Sarah responded, ignoring the Dowager's unladylike snort of disapproval, and bestowing a smile on poor Sophia, who had grown quite pink with embarrassment at her grandmother's all-too-evident derision. "It would be unkind to force her to sit a horse if she was disinclined. Perhaps she may overcome her fears, given time."

Her sympathetic understanding earned her a warm look of approval from the kind-hearted Countess. "Mama-in-law has been telling me that you are to spend a few weeks here, and then go to London in the spring. I have been endeavouring to persuade her to stay with us in the town house for the duration of the Season. You and my daughter would be company for each other."

Sarah steadfastly refused to look in the Dowager's direction. "That is most kind of you, ma'am. But I believe my guardian is wishful for us to stay at his house in Berkeley Square."

"Perhaps he can be persuaded to change his mind."

"I shouldn't bank on that, Hetta, if I were you," the Dowager put in bluntly. "You know Ravenhurst."

"Yes, yes, I do." The Countess responded, casting a sympathetic look in Sarah's direction. "He's grown so very like his dear papa…well, in looks, at any rate," she amended.

Sarah regarded her with interest. "Does he resemble his father, ma'am? I remember dear Godmama very well, but I cannot bring to mind my guardian's father." She shrugged. "But then I was very young when I paid those visits to Ravenhurst."

"Yes, Marcus resembles his father," the Dowager confirmed. "Warren Ravenhurst could never be described as a handsome man, either. But, like his son, he had a presence. Eyes instinctively turned in his direction. Just as they do when Marcus enters a room."

"Yes, that is certainly true," the Countess agreed, flashing Sarah an unmistakable look of concern this time. "Your guardian, though, does have a rather more forceful nature than his father had."

"He certainly does have that, ma'am, but one grows accustomed. Added to which I don't let it worry me. If he tries to become too high-handed, I merely take him down a peg or two by giving him a scold."

The Dowager's eyes glinted with unholy amusement as both visitors gaped in amazement, just as if they had suddenly discovered that Sarah had descended from another planet.

"Your sympathy is quite misplaced, Hetta. I'm

pleased to say that Sarah isn't afraid of Marcus in the least. It is so very refreshing!'' She looked approvingly at her grandson's ward. ''It is Sophia's birthday next week, and the family is celebrating the occasion with a party. Remind me to have a word with Buddle. I want your new evening gown finished in good time.''

The following afternoon Sarah had to forgo her walk as Buddle, having worked hard on it for many hours, brought the gown along to Sarah's room for the first fitting. The dress needed only a few minor alterations, the abigail decided before kneeling on the carpet to pin up the hem.

From her position Sarah was unable to catch sight of her reflection in the full-length mirror, but thought the turquoise silk had made up quite beautifully, although she did consider the square neckline had been cut indecently low, but refrained from comment. She soon grew tired of looking down at Buddle's bowed head and turned her own to stare out of the window, her eyes narrowing as she caught sight of a fair-haired young man busily raking up dead leaves.

''Who's that outside in the garden, Buddle? I cannot see his face clearly, but I can tell that it certainly isn't Wilkins.''

''It's probably the new lad who came round the other morning looking for work. Wilkins could do with the help. He isn't getting any younger. The lad will be here only a few weeks, though. He's hoping to find work in London for the Season, so Clegg tells me.'' Buddle's brows snapped together suddenly. ''Will you keep still, miss! How am I supposed to get this hem straight with you fidgeting away?''

Sarah looked down again at the abigail's bent head,

and her lips curled into a fond smile. For all her snappishness and impatience the woman really was a dear. "Do you know, Buddle, you're a wonderful abigail. You arrange hair beautifully, and you're an excellent seamstress. Pity you're such a scold...and a tale-bearer," she added meaningfully.

Not once since the night she had been discovered in her guardian's bedchamber had mention been made of her presence there, a circumstance which she considered most strange. Although she had sought him out in all innocence, and nothing improper had occurred, she was fully aware that she had committed a scandalous breach of conduct by being alone with a man, guardian or not, in such intimate surroundings.

She was very well aware, also, who had alerted the Dowager to the possible dangers, and raised a quizzical brow as Buddle lifted guilty eyes to meet hers.

"Now, Miss Sarah, don't you go holding that against old Buddle. What was I supposed to do? I knew there was no harm in it, even before I learned about you finding that necklace an' all. But others might have viewed things different. You were lucky I spied you. Had it been one of the other servants seeing you slip into Master Marcus's room that way, I shudder to think of the gossip."

Sarah had never supposed that Buddle's actions had been prompted by anything other than the purest of motives, but could not resist the temptation to tease her further.

"I've learned from her ladyship that you began life with this family as nurserymaid; have learned, too, which among those many chicks placed in your capable hands was your undoubted favourite."

One finely arched brow rose again. "Whose reputation were you trying to protect, Buddle—his or mine? I can only imagine,'' she went on, suddenly finding the fingernails on her right hand of immense interest, ''that you must have feared I had gone to that room with the intention of compromising your favourite nursling.''

Buddle rose to her feet instantly, and was halfway through voicing a staunch denial when she noticed the mischievous twinkle in blue-green eyes. ''Why, you little monkey!'' she scolded, just as though Sarah had been one of her former nursery charges. ''You never thought nothing of the sort!''

''No, I never did,'' Sarah confessed, not in the least shamefaced. ''But I have frequently wondered why the Dowager didn't take me roundly to task. Do you know, Buddle, she has never said a word.''

''Ah! Well, I know why,'' she responded, forgetting to be cross. ''Master Marcus told her in no uncertain terms that she wasn't to do so.''

''Did he, really? Well, was that not kind of him!'' Sarah frowned suddenly. ''Unless, of course, he wishes to have that privilege himself, and intends to scold me when he returns... Yes, that sounds much more likely, much more like him,'' she decided finally, and drew a surprising gurgle of laughter from the maid.

''I knew it! Knew the instant I set eyes on you that hidden behind that sweet face was the mind of a wicked minx.'' Buddle's disapproving shake of the head might have looked convincing had her thin lips not twitched slightly. ''I know what signs to look for, you see.''

Sarah's eyes glinted in response. ''Oh, I knew it would be fruitless trying to fool you. You're quite right, of course. I am utterly depraved. Quite beyond the pale, in fact!''

''Well, I wouldn't go as far as to say that,'' Buddle's

lips twitched again as she resumed her former kneeling position. "But it will be no bad thing when Master Marcus returns and takes you in hand again."

Sarah became serious, and raised troubled eyes to gaze sightlessly across the room. "Yes, I wonder what can be keeping him? It's been a week since he left."

"Aye, miss. But Master Marcus has always been one for keeping his own counsel. Mayhap he hasn't been able to locate that Bow Street Runner, or maybe other errands have kept him busy. Either way, there's no need for you to fret none. Master Marcus is quite capable of taking care of himself."

Sarah wasn't so much worried as just eager for news. No, she amended silently, she was eager for his return. The simple truth of the matter was that she was missing their bantering exchanges; missing his caustic remarks and heavy dark-browed scowls... She was, quite simply, missing him. Which was really quite silly when one came to think about it, she reflected. After all, she had known him for such a short time, and yet it seemed as if she had known him all her life. How very strange that was!

As the days passed and still no word reached them of his possible return, Sarah's discontentment increased, but she was careful not to show it. She found some relief in her continued daily rides with Sutton, and although she enjoyed the groom's company, he was no substitute for Ravenhurst.

She also derived much pleasure in the evenings when she would sit with the Dowager, either reading aloud to her or playing cards; and she, at least, looked forward to the regular afternoon visits made by the Countess and her eldest daughter, both of whom she considered friendly and charming; but no matter how much satisfaction she attained from these varied interludes, she began to feel increasingly that there was something fundamentally missing from her life.

As the second week drew to a close and there was still no word from Ravenhurst, Sarah had resigned herself to attending Sophia's birthday celebration without the comfort of his escort.

As Buddle had warned her that she wished to create a more elaborate hairstyle for the occasion, Sarah repaired to her room in good time, and sat obediently still on the chair before the dressing-table mirror, watching in fascination as the experienced abigail's artistic fingers busily worked away. Buddle piled the golden-brown hair high on Sarah's head so that it cascaded down in a shower of long ringlets, and then intricately weaved a turquoise ribbon through the silken locks.

When at last she was permitted to stand before the full-length mirror to see the finished results, Sarah stared at her reflection with scant enthusiasm. The dress was lovely, and Buddle had added a flounce, decorating it with tiny rosebuds fashioned from the same turquoise silk.

Her arms were covered in the first pair of long evening gloves she had ever owned, and the Dowager had insisted that she wear a lovely string of pearls and matching ear-rings, which had once belonged to Sarah's godmother. Never had she been so elegantly attired. She ought she knew to feel overjoyed. But the simple fact remained that she felt anything but.

"What is it, miss?" Buddle's shrewd dark eyes had not missed the forlorn expression. "What is it that doesn't please you?"

"Oh, nothing, nothing! Everything is just perfect!" she hurriedly assured her. "The dress is beautiful, and I simply love the way you have arranged my hair."

There was a moment's silence, then, "Come, on, miss. You can tell old Buddle. What is it that you're not happy about?"

Sarah's forced smile faded. "I'm not happy about Mr Ravenhurst's continued absence," she admitted at last. "I cannot help thinking something must have happened to him."

Buddle stared deeply into the blue-green eyes for an endless moment. "You'll do," she surprised Sarah by remarking softly. "Yes, you'll do very nicely, I think.

"Now, come along, miss," she went on in her usual no-nonsense manner, "otherwise you'll be late. Let's get this shawl round you, and you'll need make do with your old cloak for the carriage drive as your new one hasn't arrived. And, miss," she added, arresting Sarah's progress to the door, "don't you go worrying your pretty head over Master Marcus no more. He'll turn up safe and sound. You see if he don't."

A little of Buddle's optimism must have rubbed off on her, for as Sarah entered her guardian's elegant carriage, awaiting them at the side entrance, she experienced a tinge of excitement at the prospect of attending Sophia's seventeenth birthday celebration which, according to the Dowager, was not likely to be a small affair.

Although she rarely had a good word to say about her eldest son, her ladyship had had to own that the Earl was far from miserly on these occasions. She had mentioned earlier in the day that musicians had been hired for the evening, and that she wouldn't be in the least surprised to discover half the county had been invited.

Sarah was unable to confirm whether this was true or not, but as they neared the mansion, only a matter of a few minutes later, she could see a long line of carriages waiting to deposit their passengers at the front entrance.

The early March evening was dry, with a starlit, cloudless sky, but there was that inevitable frosty nip in the air. None the less, with their legs covered with a fur-lined rug, and with hot bricks at their feet, the Dowager and Sarah remained comfortably warm until the carriage reached the front entrance and it was their turn to alight.

This was not Sarah's first visit to the ancestral home. She had been invited to dine twice since the family's return from Kent. The Earl, a rotund little man in his late forties, had made her feel most welcome, and the evenings had passed very pleasantly, though she had found herself unable to mask a chuckle on the first occasion when the meal had arrived at the table far from warm, and she had been reminded of her guardian's scathing condemnations.

He had been right, too, about the large, high-ceilinged rooms being draughty; but she had no fault to find with the furnishings, which managed to combine both elegance and comfort.

The ballroom, however, was not so very comfortable. Many of its windows were ill-fitting, and the large fireplace had an unfortunate tendency to billow out smoke at regular intervals. Therefore, the Countess, very wisely, had decided not to hold the party in there, but had thrown open two connecting ground-floor rooms for the occasion.

Sophia, dressed in a very pretty gown of white sarsenet, adorned with the most delicate pink rosebuds round the sleeves and neckline, stood shyly beside her parents at the entrance to the first salon. After receiving the warmest of greetings from the kindly host and hostess, Sarah complimented Sophia on her lovely gown before following the Dowager into the room where chairs had been placed all along the walls.

They had only just seated themselves when a tall, rather handsome young man, sporting a dazzling waistcoat embroidered with bright crimson poppies, approached them. He bore too strong a resemblance to his younger brothers and sisters for Sarah not to know, instantly, who he was, even before he said,

"Grandmama! What a pleasure it is to see you looking so well!"

"Bah! Jackanapes!" was the Dowager's rather charming response, and her grandson's finely chiselled lips twitched as he winked rather cheekily in Sarah's direction.

"Now, now, ma'am, you know you don't mean that. You like me, really, you know you do. Not as well as you like Cousin Marcus, but I come a close second."

Her ladyship gave vent to one of her unladylike snorts, but there was a decidedly appreciative gleam in her eyes as she said, "If you have not already guessed, Sarah, this impertinent young chub is the Honourable Bertram Stapleton, the Earl's son and heir. Bertram, this is Ravenhurst's ward, Miss Sarah Pennington."

His bow was a study in elegance. "Would you do me the honour, Miss Pennington, of standing up with me for the next set of country dances?"

Because she had frequently practised with her friend Clarissa, Sarah knew the steps to most country dances, and did not hesitate to accept the invitation.

"I cannot tell you, sir," she remarked as they made their way towards the wide open doors leading to the salon where people were already forming sets for the next dance, "how refreshing it is to discover someone who isn't afraid of the Dowager. The other members of your family seem almost terrified of her. Poor Sophia never dares to open her mouth when in the Dowager's presence, and even your father appears to be somewhat in awe of her."

"Yes, madness, ain't it?" He raised his eyes heavenwards. "The only way to deal with the old lady is to stand up to her, give as good as you get. Cousin Marcus told me that years ago."

Sarah decided she liked Sophia's elder brother. He seemed a friendly young man with pleasant, easy-going manners, and she found herself saying, "Yes, and he's another many seem in awe of."

He slanted a quizzical glance. "Are you?"

"It would be a little unpleasant if I were, considering I am his ward. But, no," she admitted. "No, I'm not in the least afraid of him."

"Pleased to hear it! Marcus is a great gun. Pulled me out of a scrape or two, I can tell you." His glance down at her this time was almost apologetic. "It wasn't until I arrived yesterday that I was aware of your existence, Miss Pennington. I cannot recall my cousin ever mentioning that he had a ward."

Far from offended, Sarah admired his honesty. "I suspect, sir, that that was because he had forgotten himself." Her eyes danced with wicked amusement. "How very glad I am, now, that I took it upon myself to leave Bath, and put him to the trouble of scouring the country in search of me. I can safely promise you that he won't forget my existence again in a hurry."

The Dowager, following their progress into the other room, saw her grandson suddenly throw back his head and roar with laughter. She was not in the least surprised that Sarah had captured his interest so soon. She was a lovely girl whose rather wicked sense of humour would appeal to Bertram. Her grandson was, the Dowager secretly thought, a charming rascal, both handsome and good-natured, but rather too young yet to pose any real threat.

She continued to watch them, a satisfied smile curling her lips, as Sarah performed the dance's intricate steps with effortless grace. As the evening wore on her charge returned to her side from time to time, but Sarah was in great demand. Many of the young men, and some not so young, requested her as a partner, and so she spent much of the time on the dance floor, leaving the Dowager quite happily conversing with her numerous acquaintances.

The evening was almost half over when she became aware of a large dark shape looming at her side, and broke off her conversation with her daughter-in-law to turn her head.

"Ha! So, you've returned at last, have you? And high time, too!"

# *Chapter Ten*

Marcus gazed down at his grandmother in his usual lazy affectionate way. ''The warmth of your greeting, ma'am, never ceases to affect me deeply.''

''Ha! When has there ever been need for wordy sentiment between you and me, Marcus?'' Her tone was indifferent, but the look in her eyes as she cast them over his tall figure, immaculately attired in satin knee-smalls and a long-tailed coat of black cloth, was anything but apathetic. His bearing was always impressive, but in full evening garb he looked magnificent. ''How long have you been back?''

''Only long enough for me to freshen up, change and come here.'' He turned to his aunt, who was gazing up at him with the customary mixture of admiration and awe which he always managed to instil in her. ''I hope you will overlook my late arrival, ma'am, and my arrogant presumption that I might descend upon you without invitation.''

''Oh, no, no! Not at all,'' she hurriedly assured him, slightly breathless in her confusion. She had grown accustomed over the years to a man whose conversation was frequently blunt to the point of rudeness, and never in her wildest imaginings had she believed him capable of such courteous charm. "You are always most welcome, Ravenhurst. You should know that."

"Your graciousness, madam, is only just matched by your excellent taste in dress," he responded, which had the effect of sending her quite pink with pleasure, and even caused his grandmother to blink several times. "As always, your appearance is faultless."

"Well, you've certainly made her day," the Dowager remarked a few minutes later when her daughter-in-law, still with a suspicion of a gratified glow in her cheeks, moved away to mingle with her other guests.

"I have never rated my aunt's intelligence very high. But you will need to go a very long way to find a woman with better dress sense. She is always immaculately groomed. I believe in giving credit where it's due, ma'am." His eyes scanned the salon. "Where's my ward?"

"She's in the other room, dancing. The poor child must be quite exhausted. She's hardly sat down all evening. Which is something I wish you would do, Marcus. I am getting a crick in my neck looking up at you all the time."

He obeyed automatically, seating himself in the chair his aunt had just vacated, while his dark eyes continued to scrutinise the dancers in the other room. "Is that her?" he enquired, suddenly frowning. "The one in the bluish-coloured dress?"

"Of course it is!" The Dowager cast him an impatient glance. "Don't tell me you've forgotten what the poor child looks like already?"

"Of course I haven't forgotten! But her hair has been arranged differently. And what the devil do you mean by letting her wear such an indecent gown?"

"Indecent?" she echoed, rather taken aback by the unjustified criticism. "It's nothing of the sort! It is cut no lower than most of the other gowns the young ladies are wearing. Besides, Sarah has nothing of which to be ashamed. She has a charming figure. Quite delightful, in fact!"

"I can see that!" he retorted. "And so can every other man in the room!"

The Dowager refused to comment further, for it had suddenly dawned on her what lay at the root of his ill-humoured remarks. She smiled to herself as she watched the dancers leave the floor, and knew by the undisguised delight that suddenly sprang into a pair of aquarmarine-coloured eyes the instant Sarah had caught sight of her guardian.

"Oh, sir! It is so very good to see you again!" Almost running the last few steps towards him, she held her hands outstretched and, standing up, he took them eagerly in his own.

"And it is good to see you again, my child. I do not need to ask if you are well. Your delightful colour informs me clearly enough."

He then dispensed with the services of the young man who had kindly restored Sarah to the Dowager Countess by casting him a slight smile, and then turned his attention back to his ward.

Having nearly attained the age of two-and-thirty, he was certainly no stranger to feminine charms. He had seen many beauties over the years, many lovelier than Sarah, but he had never glimpsed a figure to better hers. Slender yet shapely, she was perfectly proportioned. He allowed his gaze to wander over the slim waist and hips before raising his eyes to dwell for an appreciative moment on the delightful swell of the firm young breasts.

Sarah had received numerous compliments on her appearance that night, and countless admiring glances from the many gentlemen present, but Ravenhurst's swift appraisal had felt more like a soft caress, causing a pleasurable tingling sensation to feather its way over her skin, and bringing added colour to her cheeks.

When, however, he did finally raise his eyes to meet hers, she was unable to tell whether he approved of her appearance or not, nor was she able to account for the strangely disturbing intensity in their dark fathomless depths.

"Why not ask your ward to dance?"

The Dowager's suggestion broke the mesmeric hold of that ardent gaze, and Sarah looked down at her, and then rather shyly back at her guardian in hopeful expectation, but he disappointed her by saying in his usual blunt way,

"Because I never dance, as you very well know. I leave all that prancing about to the young nincompoops. And talking of which," he added, noticing someone heading in their direction, "who's this tailor's dummy about to descend on us?"

Sarah glanced round. "You know very well who it is. And don't you dare to say anything rude to him, sir!" she ordered in an undertone. "He thinks very highly of you, and he has been very kind to me this evening."

"By all that's wonderful!" Bertram gave his cousin an affectionate slap on the back. "So you made it after all, Marcus!"

"As you see. But what the duece are you doing here?"

"Came down for m'sister's birthday. What do you think?"

"Came down?" One dark brow rose suspiciously. "Or sent down?"

"Now, now, cuz! You know I don't get into scrapes any longer. Well, none that I'm admitting to, at any rate." He noticed those dark, intelligent eyes move fleetingly to the bright red poppies adorning his waistcoat, and puffed his chest out rather proudly. "What do you think of it, Marcus? Wonderful, ain't it?"

"Believe me, young man, I should take the greatest delight in telling you exactly what I think of it," he responded with feeling. "Unfortunately, though, I have been forbidden."

"Do not take any notice, Bertram," Sarah hurriedly intervened before the young man was foolish enough to prompt further. "The musicians are striking up, and I have promised you this dance."

She whisked him on to the dance floor with unseemly haste, and soon afterwards noticed her guardian escorting the Dowager into the room set out for cards, where most of the older people present had sought refuge well away from the the younger and more boisterous guests.

She was impatient to discover what had been decided with regard to the diamond necklace, but as she had promised to take supper with Bertram, and as Ravenhurst spent the remainder of the evening in conversation with many of the other people present, most of whom were known to him, she was unable to broach the subject until the evening had drawn to a close and they had climbed into the carriage awaiting to take them the short distance back to the Dower House.

She looked across at him eagerly. "Now that we're alone, sir," she said, with sublime disregard for the lady seated beside her, "you must tell me what happened in Bristol. I'm simply bursting with curiosity."

"Bursting...? Bursting! What sort of language is that for a young lady, may I ask!" the Dowager admonished crossly. "Why, if such a word had ever fallen from my lips when I was your age, I would have been soundly whipped."

Marcus caught the mischievous twinkle in the lovely blue-green eyes before Sarah cast a look of mock censure at the Dowager. "Now, ma'am, that is a shocking untruth," she admonished, mimicking her ladyship's disapproving tone to a nicety. "And well you know it! No one would ever have dared to do such a thing to you."

The Dowager gave a shout of laughter before wrapping Sarah across the knuckles with her fan, and then turning to her grandson, whose dark eyes were alight with amusement. "You see how incorrigible the chit is, Ravenhurst. You have been away far too long."

"Yes, far, far too long," Sarah agreed. "What happened in Bristol, sir?"

Leaning back against the plush velvet squabs, he regarded her indulgently. "Not very much, child. It took me several days to locate Stubbs's whereabouts, and only did so because I had the great good fortune to run in to your friend Captain Carter."

"Oh, is he still in Bristol, sir?"

"Not now, no. The delay on the road caused him to miss his boat. He has departed for the Peninsula now, however. But whilst he was kicking his heels in the city, he offered his services to the Runner. Stubbs, as I believe I mentioned once before, was sent to Bristol for the sole purpose of keeping watch on certain premises owned by a man suspected of dealing in stolen goods.

"However, being a conscientious individual, Stubbs wanted to check the information given to him by our stranded fellow-travellers. You will no doubt be pleased to learn that he never for one moment suspected Carter of being responsible for either Nutley's death or the servant girl's, and didn't hesitate, therefore, to make use of him. He set him to keep watch on those premises I mentioned, whilst he went about verifying the information he had been given by the other stagecoach passengers.''

''And did all the stories turn out to be true?'' she prompted eagerly when he fell silent.

''All but one, yes. You'll no doubt also be relieved to hear that the 'Divine' Dorothea does have a mother living in Bristol. She is residing with her at present. A couple of days after they had arrived, Stubbs followed her when she left her mother's house, and saw her enter a theatre, presumably looking for work.

''The clerk's story also turned out to be authentic. He lives and works in the city. But I'm afraid of the Grimshaw woman there is no sign. Her sister's address turned out to be a church, of all things!''

Sarah frowned, remembering clearly what Sutton had disclosed. If Miss Grimshaw had, indeed, suspected that her belongings had been searched, then she was hardly likely to turn out to be the cloaked intruder. But why had she deliberately given Mr Stubbs false information? There seemed no good reason for having done so unless, of course, she had something to hide.

''How very odd!'' she murmured.

''Quite!'' he agreed laconically. ''Well, as you have probably gathered, all this was discovered before I turned up with the Felchett diamonds. Which really did start things moving. Stubbs wanted to return here with me, but felt he couldn't leave his post. So he sent an express to London, and whilst he was awaiting reinforcements, I went on to Bath, leaving the—er—diamonds in his safekeeping.''

He refrained from mentioning that he hadn't remained long in that city, and had taken the opportunity to travel to London to pay a much-needed visit to his mistress. The night of unbridled passion had certainly assuaged his bodily needs, but that was all. His heart and mind had been quite otherwhere, and he had left the house the following morning feeling strangely hollow inside, and experiencing not the least desire to spend a further night in the arms of his skilful light o' love.

"Did you call in to see your cousin?"

Sarah's tentatively spoken enquiry drew him out of his reverie. "I had a word or two, certainly."

She eyed him gravely. "Yes, I can imagine."

"Sarah, surely you didn't expect Marcus to permit all his cousin's underhandedness to go unpunished?" the Dowager put in in her grandson's defence. "Why, the deceitful, conniving wretch has been fleecing him for years!"

Sarah wasn't in the least surprised to discover that the Dowager was in full possession of the facts, although she herself had never breathed a word. She did consider any actions her guardian had taken completely justified in the circumstances, but the fact remained that she could not help feeling sorry for Mrs Fairchild, for the woman had been neither cruel nor even mildly unkind to the little orphaned girl placed in her charge.

"Yes, you're both right, of course," she conceded at last. "It's just that…"

"I did not turn her out on to the streets, Sarah, if that is what concerns you," he assured her, much to her intense relief. "But I have made it abundantly clear that, if she chooses to remain in that house, she will pay me rent, and at the going rate. If she falls behind with her payments, then I have left her in no doubt whatsoever that she will be evicted. And I shall suffer no qualms in doing so, either.

"But rest easy, child," he added, casting her a rather crooked smile. "I know for a fact that she was left adequate funds by her husband to live quite comfortably. If, however, she wishes to indulge in her particular vice, then I'm afraid she will need to find another source of income to cover the expenses, for she will get not a penny more from me."

Silently, she was forced to admit that he had been really most lenient, and looked at him approvingly before asking him if he had also found the time to call on Mrs Stanton.

"Certainly. And you will be overjoyed to learn, no doubt, that the runaways were successful in their endeavours, and that Mrs Clarissa Fenshaw, as she is now, has been restored to the bosom of her family, for the time being at least." He smiled at her exuberant expression. "I have brought letters from both Clarissa and her mother, which will no doubt explain events far better than I ever could."

"I must say, Sarah," the Dowager remarked after listening quietly to her grandson's tidings in increasing dismay, "you're a dear sweet girl, but it would appear you have a propensity for becoming involved with the most unsavoury characters—runaway couples, jewel thieves…and murderers, no less! I should imagine you find the peace and quiet at the Dower House quite a refreshing change."

No sooner had she spoken than the carriage pulled up in the stableyard. Without waiting for the groom, Ravenhurst jumped out, and had only just let down the steps when the elderly butler, carrying a lantern, emerged from the house.

"Oh, Master Marcus, sir!" Clegg, looking decidedly distraught, hurried across to the carriage. "Thank heaven's you've returned! I was on the point of sending a message up to the big house to bring you back."

"Why? What's happened?"

"We've had a break-in, sir. And poor Mr Quilp has been attacked. We've laid him on the sofa in the drawing-room, and I've already sent for the doctor."

"Attend to your mistress!" Ravenhurst commanded, and then went striding into the house without another word

"Well, well! It would seem I spoke too soon, child," her ladyship remarked as she stepped down from the carriage. "It would appear that the gods have ordained that you won't be experiencing peace and quiet whilst you reside with me. How very enlivening!"

Clegg, raising the lantern aloft, saw them safely across the few feet of yard and into the house. They paused briefly by the drawing-room door, saw that not only Ravenhurst but Buddle, too, was attending the injured Quilp, who was now, thankfully, sitting up on the sofa, holding a cloth to his head.

As neither of them felt they could be of any help, and might possibly be in the way, they went straight upstairs to the Dowager's private sitting-room where a fire still burned welcomingly on the hearth. At her ladyship's request, Sarah poured out two glasses of Madeira, and then sat herself in the chair opposite and stared down into the glowing flames.

It would be comforting to think that the break-in had been perpetrated by some opportunist thief, but Sarah could not delude herself. Foolishly, she had believed that, once the diamond necklace had been handed over to the authorities, the unfortunate affair would be at an end. How wrong could anyone be! Thankfully, though, her guardian had not been so simple-minded, and that was precisely why he had taken the precaution of ordering Sutton to watch over her in his absence.

She closed her eyes, recalling vividly the look in Ravenhurst's when Clegg had given him the unfortunate tidings. There had been such a strange mixture of anger and foreboding in their dark depths. Two people had died and another had been injured because of that wretched necklace! But why? Robbery, as Ravenhurst had pointed out, was one thing; murder quite another.

What on earth was so significant about that particular diamond necklace? she wondered. Surely there was more to it than just a simple case of robbery and greed? More importantly, how many more people would suffer before the mystery was finally solved?

A heartfelt sigh escaped her as she raised her eyes to gaze across at the Dowager. "It would seem, ma'am, that I have, unwittingly, brought trouble to your house. It might have been better had I never come here."

"Nonsense, child!" her ladyship responded, realising at once what had prompted the suggestion. "Who is to say it wasn't some local rascal who, learning that there was to be a party at the mansion, thought to try his luck at a few houses in the vicinity.

"Not that I have much here worth stealing, you understand," she went on matter-of-factly. "There's my jewellery, of course, and a bit of silver. But not much else. I must ask Clegg to check and see just what is missing." She sipped her wine, and a contented smile hovered about her mouth as she savoured its taste. "I must say I prefer this to the champagne served earlier. Never could stomach the stuff myself. Weak and insipid, I call it!"

It was quite evident that the Dowager did not wish to discuss further what had occurred in their absence, and so Sarah followed her lead.

"It was a lovely party, ma'am, didn't you think so?"

"Yes, most enjoyable. Although I've never held my daughter-in-law in high esteem, I have to own she is a very gracious hostess." A wicked cackle of amusement escaped her. "Ravenhurst sent her quite pink with pleasure this evening. You are a very good influence on him, my dear."

Sarah was not given the opportunity to enquire what she meant, for the door opened and the man himself entered the room to inform them that the doctor had arrived, and to assure them that Quilp, thankfully, was not too badly hurt. He then went on to warn them that they would shortly be disturbed by the sounds of hammering as he had ordered the broken window in the library boarded up until a new piece of glass could be installed.

"Thank you, Marcus, for seeing to everything. You are always to be relied upon." The Dowager finished the contents of her glass and rose to her feet. "Well, it has been a long evening and I'm rather tired, so I shall bid you both good-night. No doubt Clegg will present me with an inventory of exactly what is missing in the morning."

Sarah watched her guardian close the door behind his grandmother, and then walk across to the table on which the decanters stood. He lacked none of his natural athletic grace, and yet she detected a suppressed tension in those fluid movements as he seated himself opposite in the Dowager's favourite chair.

"Nothing has been taken from the house, has it, sir?"

He looked at her for a moment above the rim of his

glass before tossing the contents down his throat in one large swallow. "No," he said at length.

"No, I didn't think so."

"Don't jump to conclusions, child. One cannot rule out the possibility that it was some local bent on a little petty theft. It is not an infrequent occurrence, after all." He placed his empty glass down on to the table before looking directly across at her again. "And do not forget the intruder was disturbed only a matter of minutes after he had gained unlawful entry. Which would hardly have given him time to relieve my grandmother of any of her belongings, now would it?"

Sarah chewed these remarks over in silence for several moments, and had to own that his suggestions were not unreasonable, but she remained sceptical and asked him to explain exactly what had occurred.

All the servants with the exception of the valet, it transpired, had congregated in the kitchen to enjoy a late supper. Quilp, having a fastidious nature, had insisted upon tidying his master's bedchamber before joining them. He had been descending the stairs when he had thought he detected the sound of breaking glass and, suspecting the footman of dropping a decanter whilst helping himself to its contents, had gone into the library to investigate.

The only light in the room had come from the fire which, apparently, had still been burning quite brightly in the grate. Even so, he had seen no one. The next instant, he had been struck from behind.

"Apart from the table, which had been overturned," he went on to inform her after a thoughtful pause, "no doubt by Quilp himself when he fell, and the broken window, everything seems to be in order."

"So it might well have been an opportunist thief, but,

personally, I do not think so." She held his eyes with her own. "And neither do you."

He did not attempt to deny it, and said, taking her completely by surprise, "We'll discuss this evening's incident, and our views on the matter, with Stubbs in the morning."

"Mr Stubbs?" She was startled. "Did you bring him back with you?"

"Yes. I made a return trip to Bristol to collect him. He's putting up at the village inn. I deposited him there earlier before I came here."

"Then you both must think that an attempt will be made to retrieve the necklace, if this evening's fiasco was not, indeed, the first attempt to do so."

His mouth set in a grim, straight line. "One person has already been murdered, possibly two. And tonight there might easily have been a third fatality... Yes, child, I do think that this night's occurrence was perpetrated by our mysterious cloaked figure," he admitted at last. "Furthermore, I fear that whoever it is will not stop now."

"But why, sir? Why?" she demanded urgently. "What is so important about that particular necklace that someone is prepared to commit murder just to get their hands on it?"

"I have asked myself that very same question," he admitted. "And with perhaps more reason than you have had for doing so," he finished rather cryptically.

# *Chapter Eleven*

❦

A hundred years before all the people inhabiting that tiny village nestling in the hollow just beyond the estate's boundary wall had had some connection with Styne. There was not a family living there that did not have at least one member working on the vast estate, either in the house or gardens; in the stables, or on the land itself. Generations had lived and died there without so much as travelling the merest five miles from home.

Over the years the tiny community had thrived, attracting outsiders. A blacksmith from Devizes had purchased some land off the previous Earl and had built his forge on the outskirts of the village, serving the community itself and people from miles around; and the inevitable inn had been erected where the men could relax and enjoy a tankard of ale after a hard day's toil.

The improvement in the roads during the second half of the previous century had inevitably brought changes. Where once everyone had known everyone else, now, many strangers came into their midst, either putting up at the inn, or merely passing through the village on their travels. It was quite a common sight to see sporting carriages of all descriptions bowling along the main street.

Consequently, when Sarah and Mr Ravenhurst, seated side by side in his curricle, entered the peaceful community, they aroused little interest, attracting no more than a fleeting glance from an elderly woman busily working in her front garden, and from the group of children playing happily together in the road.

Like most of the other buildings, the inn had white-washed cob walls and a charming low thatched roof. At this time of the morning there were few, if any, customers. Marcus brought his curricle to a halt in the stable yard, and the sound of wheels on cobble stones so early in the day brought the innkeeper's inquisitive son out of a side door to investigate. He took immediate charge of the equipage, allowing the Dowager's grandson, whom he recognised instantly, to alight.

Sarah, who was looking perfectly charming in one of her new outfits, a pale blue walking dress and matching pelisse, and a very becoming bonnet lined with blue silk and with a matching silk ribbon tied in a coquettish bow beneath her chin, gratefully accepted her guardian's helping hand to alight. It never crossed her mind to demur when he tucked her arm through his, even though she was acutely aware of the latent rippling strength beneath the faultless sleeve of his blue superfine coat.

The instant she entered the inn the sweet smell of lavender, mixed with tobacco and spirits, assailed her nostrils, reminding her vividly of The Traveller's Rest. Here, too, the landlady seemed an industrious person, for already the wooden tables had been polished to a looking-glass shine and the floors swept clean.

As soon as her eyes had grown accustomed to the dimness, Sarah could see that the inn was deserted except for one customer, sitting at the table in the corner, casting his grey eyes over a copy of the *Morning Post*.

After ordering two tankards of ale, and a glass of wine for Sarah, Marcus wasted no time in apprising Mr Stubbs with details of the previous night's incident. The Runner listened intently, but from time to time would cast his eyes in Sarah's direction, a look in their shrewd depths that was hard to interpret.

"Well, sir, it would appear that it has happened rather sooner than either of us had expected," Mr Stubbs remarked after learning all. "The wretch certainly didn't waste much time. It would be a grave mistake to underestimate her."

"Her?" Sarah echoed. "Oh! Did Mr Ravenhurst inform you that I had come to the conclusion that the intruder that night at The Traveller's Rest was a female?"

"He did, Miss Pennington. And may I say it was an excellent piece of deduction. However, I already knew we were looking for both a man and a woman in connection with a series of robberies that took place last year."

"Really?" Sarah's eyes began to twinkle as a rather amusing thought struck her. "Did you never suspect that I might be that woman? After all, I did discover Mr Nutley's body."

"In my line of work, one needs to question the authenticity of everyone. But one also, in time, becomes a fairly shrewd judge of character. And Mr Ravenhurst was sensible enough not to waste any time in apprising me of your true identity, and the reason why he had found himself at that inn."

Sarah cast her guardian a reproachful glance, and he reciprocated with a rather mocking one.

"Yes, I don't doubt you would have preferred I remained silent. Knowing you as I do, I feel certain you would have derived a deal of wicked amusement had you been carted back to Bow Street by Mr Stubbs."

"Oh, I wouldn't go as far as to say that. But I would certainly have enjoyed putting you to the trouble of journeying to the capital in order to rescue me."

Sarah could not prevent a chuckle at the look of exasperation on her guardian's face, but then became serious again as a thought struck her. "You said you were looking for both a man and a woman in connection with certain robberies, Mr Stubbs. Did you know all along that Mr Nutley was the thief? Were you following him?"

"Oh, no, miss. It were pure coincidence we were both passengers on that particular stage coach." Leaning back in his chair, he regarded her for a moment in silence, then said, "Do you recall that morning when we were all in the parlour, Nutley included, and Mr Ravenhurst here mentions, quite innocent-like, that several items of jewellery had gone missing in recent months, and wondered whether it were the work of the same person or persons?"

"Yes, yes, I do, Mr Stubbs. I remember it quite clearly."

"Well, he weren't far wrong. We at Bow Street had suspected for some time that at least two people were involved in the thefts. In each case a large party had been held at the house. Sometimes the jewellery wasn't discovered missing until days later. But in every case a recently employed maidservant would take exception to being questioned, and would soon afterwards leave in high dudgeon.

"During a London Season, miss, most of the large houses employ extra help. Most get staff from reputable agencies, but not always. And folk are so careless. You wouldn't believe it! Often they don't even bother to check references.

"It were the same in the case of the Felchett diamonds. Local girls, at least they were thought to be all local, had been hired for the occasion. The following day, after the diamonds had been discovered missing, one of the women took umbrage at being questioned, and upped and left."

"But surely she was searched before being allowed to leave?"

"Yes, miss, she were. But the family assured us that nothing was discovered on her, nor amongst her belongings. Each robbery were the same."

Sarah drew her brows together in profound thought. "So, unless the searches were not thorough enough, the stolen items must have been handed over to someone else."

"Precisely, Sarah!" Marcus concurred. "Not another servant, however, but someone above suspicion... One of the guests attending the party, perhaps?"

"And was Mr Nutley among the guests at these parties?"

"He certainly was, miss," Stubbs answered. "But there were a dozen or more names that kept cropping up. Mr Ravenhurst were at three of 'em."

"But what about the maidservant?" she enquired, resisting the temptation to goad her guardian on this very interesting circumstance. "Surely you managed to get an accurate description of her?"

"Lord bless you, miss!" The Runner looked genuinely amused. "In two cases she has black hair. In the others, seemingly, fair or brown. She were a Londoner, a Northerner or a West Country lass. She were described as a 'andsome wench—sometimes quite plain. The only things that never varied were height and build. She were taller than average for a woman, and of slim build.''

Sarah fell silent, digesting what she had learned. The woman was evidently an expert at disguise. An actress, perhaps…? Yes, she might well have been just that at one time, and had evidently been putting her considerable talents to a more profitable use during the past twelve months. And Dottie Hogg was an actress, of course. But Dottie was not tall, nor did she have a particularly slim build.

No, only one person putting up at that inn fitted that description. An image of the middle-aged spinster appeared before her mind's eye. That greying hair could have been a wig, and the dark circles round the eyes and the sallow complexion might easily have been effected by artificial means. She recalled, too, the way Miss Grimshaw had run with such agility down those stairs, just as though she had been years younger.

And how very cunning the woman had been, too! She had quite deliberately kept herself to herself as much as possible, and had remained in her room for fear, perhaps, that someone discerning enough just might penetrate the disguise.

''I think you've perhaps worked out for yourself who Nutley's accomplice must have been,'' Mr Stubbs remarked after watching her expressive face closely. ''But, as I mentioned a while back, I didn't take a seat on that stage coach in order to follow Nutley. One of those stolen items of jewellery had turned up in Bristol, and I were being sent to that city to keep watch on a certain pawnbroker's shop that we at Bow Street had been getting some rather disturbing reports about.''

He paused to take a large swallow from his tankard. ''Nutley told me he were travelling to the West Country to visit an aunt, and until his death, and the subsequent events, I had no reason to disbelieve him, nor to think he was involved in the robberies.''

"But after his death, did you begin to suspect Miss Grimshaw, or whatever her real name is, of being his accomplice?''

"Oh, aye, miss, I suspected her right enough, but I couldn't go arresting her just 'cause she 'appens to be quite a tall wench.''

"One cannot go about accusing people and carting them off to Bow Street without good reason, Sarah,'' Marcus put in gently, amused by the look of frustration on her face. "Citizens do have their rights. If Stubbs had been able to discover her in possession of the necklace, then that might have been a different matter, but he knew it would avail him nothing to search either her, or her room.

"Remember what I told you,'' he reminded her. "Both Stubbs and I were convinced someone had searched our rooms. It was obvious that Grimshaw couldn't have been in possession of the diamonds.''

She looked at her guardian intently. "And did you suspect her all along?''

"No, I didn't. Our friend, here, kept his own counsel. I had made it clear right from the start that the only person I was concerned about was you. I really did not want to become involved, Sarah, in something that was, after all, none of my affair. But your discovering that confounded necklace has changed all that. When I eventually succeeded in locating Stubbs's whereabouts in Bristol, I did, then, insist upon knowing all the details.''

His expression was suddenly very grim. "And there's little point in trying to delude ourselves. We all feel fairly sure that she'll come after that necklace again. The trouble is, if I passed the confounded woman in the street, I'm certain I shouldn't recognise her. The only time I saw her was on the evening she arrived at the inn, and that bonnet she was wearing at the time hid most of her face.''

''And the only occasion I got a close look at her was when I interviewed her.'' There was a faint rasping sound as the Runner stroked his chin thoughtfully. ''The dratted wench is so good at changing her appearance, though. I still can't be certain that even I'll recognise her again.''

''You might not be able to, Mr Stubbs. But I'm fairly confident that I should.'' Both men looked at her sharply. ''You see, I spoke to her twice. On the second occasion she came to my room. I recall thinking at the time that there was more behind that visit of hers than mere solicitude. I realise, now, that she had sought me out for the sole purpose of ascertaining whether I had recognised her the night before. I had not and, therefore, didn't hesitate to admit to it.

''If my memory serves me correctly, I believe I also gave her the impression that I thought the cloaked intruder was a man. Which, of course, is precisely what I did think at the time.''

''Then that, Miss Pennington, is what saved you.'' The Runner looked gravely across the table at her. ''I had thought for some months that we were dealing merely with a pair of harmless thieves. One of them was most certainly just that, but the other is a very different proposition. She has murdered once…and I think she wouldn't hesitate to do so again.''

He moved his head slightly to stare directly into a pair of dark brown eyes betraying deep concern. ''Well, sir, it's up to you. As you know I was hoping for more time, but in the circumstances I think it might be best if we do what you suggested.''

"Which is?" Sarah prompted when both men remained silent.

"Remove you to Ravenhurst, where I can better protect you," her guardian answered softly, "and the necklace will, of course, be returned to its rightful owner."

"No!" Both men were startled by the vehemence in her voice. "I will not hide away like some frightened child for weeks, possibly months."

Marcus's sigh was audible. "Sarah, you don't understand the peril you're in."

"On the contrary, I understand perfectly." Sarah began to twist the strings of her reticule absently round the fingers of her left hand. "Naturally, if you are concerned for your grandmother's safety," she went on after a moment's thought, "then I shall go. But don't ask me to do so for my own sake."

She looked across at the Runner again. "Returning that necklace to its rightful owner might well put an end to the affair. On the other hand, though, it might not. Added to which, don't you think we owe it to that servant girl, and possibly Nutley, too, to bring this woman to justice?"

There was more than a hint of respect in both men's eyes, but in Marcus's it was compounded with grave concern and something else, too—something so deeply disturbing in its intensity that Sarah was startled by it.

"Well, sir?" Stubbs prompted, drawing those unsettling dark eyes on to him. "What do you say?"

Sarah waited with bated breath, knowing full well that, if her guardian insisted that she be removed to Ravenhurst, she would be unable to prevent it, and almost sighed with relief when he said,

"I say, as no doubt Captain Brin Carter would phrase it, we stand and fight."

A faint smile of understanding touched the corners of the Runner's mouth. From the first moment he had set eyes on Mr Ravenhurst at The Traveller's Rest, he had respected his no-nonsense attitude, and had quickly grown to respect his judgment, too. Unlike Sarah, he had interpreted that look in those dark eyes and knew just how much that decision must have cost him to make.

He gave nothing away, however, as he said in his usual businesslike manner, "Very well, sir. Firstly, we must try and discover if there have been any strangers about in recent days. I've already had a word with the landlord, and he assures me that no one, apart from myself, has put up at this inn in the past three weeks.

"I'll wander down to the smithy later, and hire a horse. I don't want to spread my profession abroad, but it might be worthwhile having a chat with the blacksmith. It's a fair bet he'd notice anyone not local hanging about the place."

"And I shall not delay in paying a visit on my uncle, and discover if he has hired any new staff of late."

Sarah gave a visible start. "Good gracious! I'd forgotten about that. Your grandmother hired someone to help Wilkins in the garden."

"Did she, now? Right, I'll look into that first." Marcus tossed the contents of his tankard down his throat, and rose to his feet. "I'll get back to you today, Stubbs, if I learn anything of significance."

Throughout the short journey back to the Dower House, Ravenhurst maintained a flow of inconsequential chatter that masked quite beautifully the almost unbearable anxiety he was experiencing over his ward's safety. Even now, the temptation to spirit her away to Ravenhurst, where he could place complete reliance on his trusted servants to watch over her every minute of the day, remained a highly tempting solution to his immediate problems. But deep down he knew that Sarah had been right. Even supposing the necklace was returned to Lord Felchett without delay, there was no guarantee that that would bring an end to the affair.

The Grimshaw woman had already committed murder, therefore, it was not beyond the realms of possibility that she might try to extract some petty form of revenge for having been thwarted. A sigh escaped him. How could he expect Sarah to live for weeks, possibly months, forever looking over her shoulder, watching, waiting for that harridan to strike? Of course he could not. It was unthinkable! Inhuman! Yes, he reiterated silently, Sarah had been right: the woman had to be caught and brought to justice.

As soon as they had arrived back at the Dower House, he suggested that Sarah change into her riding habit and meet him again in the stableyard in half an hour, and they could ride over to see his uncle together. He then wasted no time in going in search of his grandmother's newest employee. There was not a soul to be seen in the garden, which he noticed was beginning to look much tidier, but he did eventually run the old gardener to earth, busily at work in the potting shed.

"Why, Mr Ravenhurst, sir!" Wilkins grinned broadly as Marcus entered the gardener's private domain. "Ain't often I sees you about the grounds."

Marcus would never have dreamt of hurting the old man's feelings by informing him that he avoided entering whenever possible what was probably the worst maintained and most depressing garden he had ever had the misfortune to see. Wilkins had worked loyally for the family all his life; and it was hardly his fault that the Dowager stubbornly refused to have some of the trees chopped down, which would not only make his job much easier, but would instantly make the grounds much pleasanter.

So, he merely made some light response, and then wasted no time in asking where the young assistant was to be found.

"Wish I knew, sir. Sent the lad up to the big 'ouse first thing this morning with the barrow to pick up a few bits and pieces, and ain't set eyes on 'im since." He raised his hat to run a grimy hand over his balding pate. "Eh, sir, you don't think he'd owt to do with the break-in last night, do 'ee? Heard all about it when I arrived this morning."

"That's what I am endeavouring to find out." He looked at the gardener sharply. "What do you know about the lad, Wilkins? Where's he from?"

"Over Devizes way, I reckon he said. Came strolling into the garden a week or so back, asking if there be any work going up at the big 'ouse. Told 'im I reckoned not, as the family were away at the time. We got to talking, and 'ee seemed a nice enough young fellow, so I tells 'im I'd ask if 'er ladyship would take 'im on for a few weeks as I could do with the 'elp.

"Seemingly, that were all 'ee wanted as 'ee were 'oping to work as a footman or the like in Lunnon. Which would suit 'im better, I'm thinking." He shook his head. "Never seen 'ands blister up so easy. Only got to pick up a shovel an' the poor lad's suffering."

Marcus's eyes narrowed. "So, he hasn't done much hard manual work?"

"Ha! Wouldn't o' said so, sir. Got 'ands as soft as a woman's, so the lad 'as."

"Has he, now…? How very interesting!" The sinister smile that curled his thin-lipped mouth sent a frisson of fear to scud its way down the length of the old man's slightly twisted spine. "Where does he bed down for the night?"

"Wi' me, sir, in the cottage. Lad didn't 'ave nowhere else to stay." Wilkins cast his mistress's grim-faced grandson a sidelong glance. "The lad's a good worker, sir," he added in his underling's defence. "Look 'ow much better the garden be looking. And he be right 'andy in the cottage. Cleaned it up right fine!"

But Marcus's expression did not alter. "What did you do after finishing work yesterday?"

"Went back to the cottage, 'ad a bite to eat and then wandered down to the inn."

"Did the lad go with you?"

"Aye, sir. That he did, but he didn't stay long. Said he weren't feeling too good. Didn't even finish is ale, now I come to think on it."

"What time did you leave the inn?"

"About nine, or thereabouts. The lad were fast asleep when I got back. And he were still there, tucked up in bed, as snug as yer like, when I gets up this morning."

Marcus realised, even if the old gardener did not, that this proved nothing. The lad, if indeed he was a lad, could quite easily have waited until Wilkins was asleep, slipped back here and returned to the cottage without the old man being any the wiser.

If anything, his expression was grimmer than ever as he returned to the Dower House to change his clothes, but when he met Sarah in the stableyard a short time later, he looked for all the world as though he hadn't a care, his face a perfect mask of sublime unconcern.

For her part Sarah, too, was doing her level best to

put a brave face on it all. From that moment at the inn, earlier, when Mr Ravenhurst had freely admitted that he hadn't wanted to become involved, she had suffered pangs of conscience. And the simple truth of the matter was that he would not be involved at all but for her.

Common sense told her that she could not be held responsible for the actions of others, but at the same time she was very well aware that, had she remained in Bath with her guardian's cousin, the lives of those residing at the Dower House would not now be in peril.

Her depressing thoughts were for a moment set aside when she entered the stableyard, and was surprised to discover only the big bay that Mr Ravenhurst had commandeered from his uncle's stable saddled and tethered to the post.

"Oh! Did her ladyship request the return of her mare?"

"No. But I asked Sutton to take her back. I have something rather more suitable for a lady of your ability to ride." Ravenhurst nodded to his groom, who disappeared into the stable, and emerged again moments later leading a lovely dapple-grey mare. "I thought it time you had your own mount," he told her, smiling at the look of combined astonishment and delight on her face.

"Oh, thank you," she said huskily, the lump that had suddenly lodged itself in her throat making speech difficult. "She's beautiful!" Sarah introduced herself to the mare very gently, talking softly while stroking the sleek neck. "Where did you find her?"

"When I discovered your flight from Bath, I called in at The King's Head to hire a fresh team of horses. The landlord there used to work for my family. I noticed this lovely lady in one of the stalls. Jeb mentioned that the owner was wishful to sell her, so when I returned there last week, I made an offer for her, and brought her back with me yesterday. Now,'' he went on, leading the mare to the mounting block, ''let's put her through her paces.''

Sarah quickly discovered that the horse was a gentle-mannered creature, but thankfully far from sluggish. She was delighted with her, and for a short while she managed to forget that fearful cloud under which she now lived, but cruel reality returned all too quickly as her guardian, after an extended canter across the park, headed towards the mansion, and she recalled the reason behind their visit.

As they rode into the stableyard, they discovered Bertram in the process of mounting his horse.

''Hello there!'' he greeted cheerfully. ''I was just about to ride over to see you all.'' His pleasant smile faded. ''Heard all about the break-in. Do you know what was stolen?''

''Nothing, thankfully.'' Marcus dismounted, and handed the reins over to a waiting groom. ''As you intend paying a call, perhaps you would be good enough to escort my ward back?'' He turned to Sarah. ''There's no reason for you to remain, my dear. Tell Clegg that I won't be home for luncheon. I'll eat with Stubbs at the inn.''

Sarah did not object, for Bertram was an amusing rascal, and the journey back to the Dower House was very pleasant and over far too quickly as far as she was concerned. They learned from Clegg that the Dowager was in her private sitting-room and, after passing on her guardian's message, Sarah went straight up to the room, without changing her clothes, to discover the Dowager seated at the escritoire, engrossed in writing a letter.

''I have brought you a visitor, ma'am,'' she informed

her brightly. "And I apologise for coming to you without first changing out of my habit."

"Do not trouble yourself over that, my dear. I do not object to the smell of the stables." Placing down the pen, the Dowager turned to see who it was Sarah had with her. "Oh, it's only you, Bertram."

By his cheerful expression it was apparent that he was completely undaunted by his grandmother's total lack of warmth. "Yes, it is I. And a bottle of Madeira purloined from my father's cellar. Thought you might like it."

Her ladyship's attitude changed abruptly. "My boy, you rise further in my estimation each time I see you! Open it up, and let's sample a glass!"

Although the day was dry and bright, and quite warm for the time of year, the Dowager always had a good fire burning in the grate, even on the warmest summer's day. She settled herself in the chair by the hearth, and bestowed a rare smile of approval on her grandson as she sampled the wine.

"I'm not sorry you came now, my boy," she remarked handsomely. "Though I'm sure it wasn't just to bring me a bottle of wine."

"No. I've come to take my leave of you, ma'am. I'm returning to Oxford this afternoon."

She shook her head. "My poor old brain must be going soft, for I feel sure your mama told me you were staying until the end of next week."

"And so I was, until I learned that she's invited her eldest brother to stay. Uncle Horace will be arriving late this afternoon. And I fully intend to be well away from the place before he gets here."

The Dowager's wicked cackle echoed round the room. "Can't say I blame you, Bertram! Who wants to sit down to a sermon each mealtime?"

"Is your uncle a cleric?"

"Not just a cleric, Sarah, my dear. A bishop, no less!" He rolled his eyes in a very disrespectful way. "And the most prosy old bore who ever drew breath! I'll probably come down again at the end of the month when I'm certain he'll have left. Will you still be here then, Sarah?"

"No, she won't," the Dowager put in before Sarah could reply. "I'm taking her to London, and we need to arrive before the Season begins, so that we have plenty of time to add substantially to her wardrobe," she added with a meaningful glance at her future charge.

"Is Cousin Marcus escorting you?" There was more than just a hint of devilment in Bertram's wickedly glinting eyes. "I shouldn't worry too much about finding Sarah a suitable husband, ma'am, if I were you. You'll have no trouble there. Why, I might even marry her myself! I think we'd suit admirably," he remarked handsomely, and earned himself a flashing look of annoyance from his grandmother, but he was not deterred.

"I think your time will be better employed in finding Marcus a suitable wife. He ain't getting any younger, you know. And he ain't every woman's idea of a suitable spouse, rich as he is."

"I shall take leave to inform you, you impertinent young jackanapes, that your cousin is not on the look out for a suitable wife, because he has already found himself the ideal mate," the Dowager retorted in defence of her favourite grandchild. Then, realising she had been goaded into a foolish indiscretion, added, "It so happens he—er—informed me a few weeks ago that he was considering offering for Bamford's eldest gel."

Bertram was highly delighted with the unexpected news; Sarah was anything but. It felt almost as if an iron band had been clasped about her, and was slowly tightening, causing the most excruciating pain in a certain region beneath her ribcage.

Throughout the remainder of Bertram's visit and, later, when she sat down to luncheon with just the Dowager for company, she was able to maintain a reasonable flow of light-hearted conversation, but it was an effort. She felt anything but light-hearted, and as soon as she was able, she sought the solitude of her bedchamber.

She couldn't deny that the Dowager's disclosure had come as a bitter blow, both painful and totally unexpected. But why should this be? she wondered, sitting herself on the edge of the bed, and trying desperately to make some sense out of her wildly conflicting and surprisingly agonising thoughts. Her guardian would very soon attain the age of two-and-thirty. It really was high time he was thinking seriously about settling down.

He was a very wealthy man, and it was only natural that he would want his own offspring, children begot from a legal union, to inherit the Ravenhurst fortune. And there was no doubt in her mind that he would make a wonderful father, strict when necessary, but loving and devoted too. No matter what the world at large said of him, she knew that behind that hard, cynical exterior lay a deeply caring and very considerate man. But he was also, she reminded herself, extremely astute.

No, she reflected sombrely. He would never contemplate marriage without very serious consideration. The woman he had chosen must, therefore, have complied with all his ideals. She was no doubt a female of unimpeachable birth, a lady of grace and charm whose faultless manners and good breeding made her the perfect mistress for that lovely house at Ravenhurst. Sarah closed her eyes against the painful image of that oh, so faultless and, no doubt, very beautiful woman.

She ought, she knew, to feel overjoyed that her surprisingly kind and thoughtful guardian had at long last found the woman with whom he wished to spend the rest of his life. But the simple fact was that she hated the mere thought of his marrying.

A heartfelt sigh escaped her. She was, of course, simply suffering the reactions of an over-indulged child who had learned that its pampered existence would soon be coming to an end. Not since before her mother's sad demise had she experienced that comfortable feeling that comes from knowing there is someone close by who really cares about one's well-being.

For a brief time she had sampled the joys of a certain someone's undivided attention, and she was honest enough to admit that she resented bitterly the prospect of that certain someone bestowing his thoughtful considerations on another. Yes, that was why she felt so miserably depressed, so hollow inside, she decided, trying desperately hard to convince herself that there couldn't possibly be any more to it than that.

Well, this childishness must stop! she told herself bracingly, rising from the bed, and going across to the door. She had always prided herself on being a level-headed young woman. And she must continue to behave like one!

The Dowager, she knew, had retired after luncheon to the small downstairs parlour where the sun's rays did manage to penetrate the wall of trees and filter into that west-facing room. She would join her there, and they could discuss plans for their removal to the capital, and talk about the heady delights awaiting them in the forthcoming London Season.

Sarah was halfway down the stairs when the front door opened, and her guardian stepped into the hall. She stopped dead in her tracks, as though held by some intangible force, and watched him place his hat and gloves on to the table. As if sensing he was being watched, he looked up suddenly, and that wonderful smile reached his eyes.

His reaction at seeing her seemed so natural, so wonderfully spontaneous, that Sarah could only stare back down at him in wonder, in disbelief, almost, as the true state of her feelings hit her with such frightening clarity that it was as much as she could do to stop herself from gasping.

Then, without giving him the opportunity to address her, she swung round on her heels, and fled back up the stairs to her room, unable to believe, not wanting to believe the state of her own heart. It was all too new, all too frighteningly incredible to be true!

For a few moments she remained with her back firmly pressed against the door, trying desperately to listen for the sound of his footsteps above the deafening pounding in her ears. When she considered enough time had elapsed for him to have reached his bedchamber, she flew across to her wardrobe to collect her cloak. Thankfully, she saw no one lurking in the hall as she crept back down the stairs, and she hurried across to the front door and let herself quietly out of the house.

Both the small parlour and her guardian's bedchamber were situated at the rear of the building. If her guardian was not still in his room, then the chances were he would have joined his grandmother downstairs. Which would be a blessing if he had. The last thing in the world she wanted was for a pair of sharp, dark eyes to catch sight of her.

So, Sarah hurried along the path at the front of the house that led to the large and rather overgrown shrubbery, and hid herself behind the dense foliage of a large clump of rhododendrons.

After a few minutes, when she saw no one coming along the path in pursuit, and felt fairly confident that she had not been spotted from the house, she began to relax a little: her breathing became slightly less erratic, and the all-too-betraying flush of colour that had mounted her cheeks from the moment she had made that startling discovery slowly began to fade. But she still felt unequal to facing him.

No, not yet, she told herself as she forged her way further into the dense area of shrubs. It was too soon, and he, the astute devil, would know instantly that there was something wrong. A shudder ran through her. She couldn't bear his knowing the state of her feelings, for if he for one moment suspected, it would lead to constraint, embarrassment, even, and the camaraderie that had existed between them right from that first night at The Traveller's Rest would be gone forever.

But when had it happened? More importantly, how had it happened? Even now she found it difficult to accept the simple truth that she loved him, and yet it had to be true, otherwise why should she feel the most intense dislike for this unknown female whom he had chosen for his future wife? Added to which, she couldn't deny that she was consumed with jealousy, virulent and agonisingly painful. And where there was no love, of course, there could be no jealousy.

Her lips trembled into a wry smile. How on earth could she have allowed herself to do such a foolish thing as to fall in love with that overbearing and frequently irritating man? After all, when had there ever been aught of the ardent lover in him throughout his dealings with her? True, he had kissed her once, but that had been merely to punish her. Why, he behaved towards her more like some strict uncle, forever scolding, than a gentleman wishing to fix his interests.

And therein lay the crux of the matter. His only interest in her was that of a concerned guardian, nothing more, nothing less. He liked her well enough. She did not doubt, either, that he found her attractive. She was definitely to his taste…as he was to hers… But his heart, unlike hers, belonged to another.

A sudden sound behind her brought her out of her despondent thoughts with a start, and she swung round, praying that her guardian had not, after all, seen her go out into the garden, and chosen to follow her. She just couldn't bring herself to face him yet. It was too soon—far, far too soon. She needed more time to get her emotions under control, to come to terms with the almost unbelievable state of her own heart.

Her eyes scanned the length of the overgrown path, and for a few moments she saw nothing at all, but then she detected the movement of foliage, and watched in horrified silence as a shadowy figure stepped out on to the path.

"Oh, my God!" she croaked, from a rapidly constricting throat. "It's you!"

# Chapter Twelve

"It is, indeed, Mrs Armstrong." A far from unpleasant smile curled the attractive mouth. "Or should I say, Miss Pennington."

Quite surprisingly, Sarah suddenly felt very calm, mistress of her emotions once more, as she looked the woman over from head to foot. It was quite remarkable—there was no denying that it really was the most marvellous disguise. Anyone, Mr Stubbs, her guardian included, would never have suspected for a moment that the person standing before her now wasn't, indeed, a youth.

With short-cropped fair hair, and with her slender figure clad in workman's rough clothes, the woman bore little resemblance to that dithering middle-aged spinster who had resided for a time at The Traveller's Rest. Only those ice-blue eyes, so cold and calculating, remained the same. And Sarah hadn't forgotten those eyes.

For a moment or two she allowed her gaze to waver as she glanced fleetingly at the lethally formed piece of metal clasped in the slender fingers. "Is there really any necessity for that?"

"I sincerely trust not, Miss Pennington." The educated voice, too, was far from unpleasant. "Believe me, I have no desire to harm you, but I most certainly shall if you do not do exactly as I say." She gestured with the pistol. "Now, we shall leave this deplorable wilderness that I have been forced to work in these past days. And no more talking for the present, if you please."

It took Sarah a moment only to come to the conclusion that little would be gained by crying out for help. Even supposing someone did happen to hear, she felt fairly certain she would be lying on the ground with a piece of lead shot in her long before any help arrived. So, she decided, for the time being at least, it was in her own best interests to do exactly as she was told.

Without a word, and yet so very conscious of that pistol pointing directly at her back, she turned and ventured deeper into the shrubbery. It was far from easy trying to forge a way through the tangled mat of branches, which snared at her hair, dislodging most of the pins, but eventually, looking very dishevelled, she came out on the far side where a rough wooden fence separated the Dowager's garden from the parkland.

Ordered to climb the fence, and then to keep as far as possible to those clumps of trees dotting the landscape, she continued to lead the way across the open stretch of land towards the wood.

Her young eyes, ever watchful, scanned the rich green acres in the hope of seeing one of his lordship's many estate workers, but, sadly, she detected no other human soul. Only sheep and cows, feeding on the lush pastureland, turned inquisitive eyes in their direction, but soon lost interest and lowered their heads again to continue grazing.

Once they had entered the relative privacy of the wood, Sarah sensed the woman behind her relax slightly, though her abductor still made no attempt to speak, except to tell her in which direction to walk.

Keeping well away from the main tracks, where the gamekeeper might well be found patrolling, they headed in an easterly direction, but it was not until they had reached that part of the estate that had been left to deteriorate into a wilderness that Sarah had some inclination of where their destination might possibly be.

She had long since realised, of course, that she was being used as a means to attain the Felchett diamonds. Just how her abductor intended going about this, however, defeated her completely, for she suspected that the necklace, by this time, had been taken to London, and was probably safely locked away in a drawer somewhere at Bow Street.

All things considered, it might be wisest in the circumstances, she decided, her eyes narrowing assessingly, as the stonebuilt boat-house came into view, to allow this woman to believe that the necklace was still at hand.

"Be kind enough, Miss Pennington, to remove that wooden bar from across the door and place it against the wall," her abductor said politely, stepping back a pace to enable Sarah to carry out this feat, which was no easy task as the wood happened to be a stout piece of oak and far from light.

She then gestured to Sarah to go inside and, without giving her the chance to take stock of the dim and musty-smelling interior, ordered her to sit on a pile of empty, evil-smelling sacks, and then promptly bound her hands with a strong piece of cord before tethering her like an animal to a stout metal ring fixed into the wall above Sarah's head.

"I apologise for all this melodrama," the woman remarked with a wry smile. "I think there's little chance you'll escape when I leave and secure the door. The bars at the window are pretty stout as well. But one cannot be too careful. I hope you are not so very uncomfortable?"

"Not at all," Sarah responded with equal politeness as she studied her abductor, who had seated herself on a wooden box placed a few feet away. She made a strikingly handsome youth, and was, no doubt, an exceedingly pretty woman when dressed appropriately. She was not in her flush of youth. Nearing thirty, Sarah judged. Her features were regular, although there was a rather aristocratic line to her nose, and her hair was a soft, pretty shade of blonde.

"You are taking stock of your abductor, Miss Pennington," she remarked after watching Sarah closely for a few moments. "No doubt so that you will be able to give a detailed description to your friend from Bow Street."

Sarah was unable to prevent a smile at this. "With your undoubted talents I rather think that would be a complete waste of time." She held the woman's gaze steadily. "But may I be permitted to know your real name?"

One slender shoulder rose in an indifferent shrug. "I don't see why not. It is Grant, Miss Pennington. Miss Isabella Grant."

Sarah sighed as she looked down at the musty-smelling sacks beneath her. The woman had committed murder, and yet, now, having come face to face with her again, she could not find it within herself to hate her, or dislike her, even.

"What do you intend doing with me, Miss Grant?" she asked, raising her head to stare into those calculating blue eyes once again. Then, after a moment's deliberation, added, "I think you ought to know that I am no longer in possession of the diamonds."

"I don't doubt that for a moment." A glimmer of something resembling respect added a sparkle to those ice-blue eyes. "I was far from certain that you had the necklace, of course, even though I had managed to search everyone's room but yours back at that inn.

"But as soon as I saw Stubbs last night, I knew for sure that at one time it must have been amongst your possessions. Unlike me, you are an upstanding citizen. Upon discovering the necklace, you handed it over to your guardian who, in turn, wasted no time in making contact with the Runner."

Sarah digested this in silence before a thought struck her. "But how on earth did you know where to find me? And how did you know Mr Ravenhurst was my guardian?"

"As soon as I discovered you and Ravenhurst had left the inn, I made an excuse to see the magistrate. Stubbs wasn't with him at the time, but he had conveniently left all his notes on the table. The magistrate left me alone for a few minutes, and that was all it took for me to glean the necessary information. Ravenhurst very obligingly had even informed Stubbs where he intended taking you."

She frowned suddenly. "Now, may I ask you a question? Out of pure interest, where did you find the necklace?"

"It was in the secret compartment of my writing-case," Sarah did not hesitate to tell her. "I presume Mr Nutley must have placed it there."

For a moment her blue eyes seemed to take on a far-away look, then she smiled. "Of course! The case was on the table in the parlour. Well, well, well! I should never have credited Nutley with such ingenuity. He truly was a halfwitted buffoon, you know, Miss Pennington. I should never have become involved with him, but—'' she shrugged again ''—for a time our liaison proved worthwhile.

''But that is neither here nor there. As I was saying— I saw Stubbs last night at the village inn. He didn't see me, or didn't recognise me, one or the other. Pity your guardian brought him back. It forced my hand, somewhat.''

''So, it was you who broke into the Dower House last night.'' Sarah looked across at her gravely. ''Do not underestimate Mr Stubbs or my guardian. They are not fools.''

''I realise that, Miss Pennington. It was foolish of me to have broken in last night in the slim hope that Ravenhurst had retained possession of the necklace, but as you know I was foiled in the attempt, and have only succeeded in alerting Stubbs and your guardian to the fact that I am, indeed, in the locale.'' She waved her hand airily as though this fact was only of minor importance. ''But the trinket I covet far outweighs any possible danger...I must have that necklace!''

There was no mistaking the determination in the voice, and Sarah experienced a strange sense of satisfaction knowing that she had not been merely fanciful when she had suspected as much. That particular necklace meant everything to this woman, much, much more than just its material value. She was consumed with curiosity and was unable to curb it. ''Why, Miss Grant... Isabella? Why does that particular necklace mean so much to you?''

''Oh, it's a long story, my dear,'' she responded, her

mouth twisting into a bitter smile, but the enquiring look remained fixed in Sarah's eyes, and after a moment's indecision Isabella relented. "Well, and why shouldn't I tell you? It can do no harm, after all, and it will help to pass the time. I don't intend leaving here until it begins to grow dark."

She rose to her feet and went over to the window to stare out between the iron bars at the rippling grey water beyond. "I have never learnt to swim, Sarah, have you?"

"No, I haven't."

"Then we have something in common… But that is all, I suspect." Thrusting hands into her pockets, and standing with feet slightly apart, she looked every inch the swaggering youth. "You see before you the result of my poor mother's one foolish indiscretion, her one night of all-consuming passion. She was the only child of a country parson. Like you, she was sweet-natured, virtuous and very lovely.

"My grandfather lived close to a large estate, not unlike this one. He and his daughter were frequent guests at the house. On one occasion when they were invited to dine there, my mother met a young man of noble birth who was staying with the family. He charmed her and, foolishly believing him to be in love with her, she gave herself to him."

Her bitter laugh was mirthless. "The following day she discovered he had left without even so much as a note of farewell. Once my grandfather learned of my mother's unfortunate condition, he sent her to stay with his sister in Bristol. My mother died giving birth to me."

Sarah, her eyes now filled with compassion, looked up at Isabella, who continued to stare resolutely out of the grimy window at the fading light. There had been no bitterness in her voice as she had related her mother's sad story. If anything, she had sounded quite matter-of-fact about it all, but then, Sarah reminded herself, it must be difficult to feel any sense of loss at all for someone you have never known. Isabella began to speak again, and she forced herself to listen.

"Needless to say, I did not enjoy a happy childhood. My great-aunt was a self-righteous, narrow-minded creature who never allowed me to forget for one moment my mother's shame. But she did educate me, and well enough for me to obtain a position as governess with a well-to-do family residing on the outskirts of Bristol. Before I had been with them a month, I was violated by the master of the house."

Sarah's gasp of anguish seemed to hang in the air for endless moments.

"Yes, Sarah. I was raped. I doubt you have any real notion of what that means... And I hope to God you are never forced to find out!"

Isabella's sudden shout of laughter was a hollow sound that echoed round the cold stone walls. "My grandfather never wanted anything to do with me. I was an embarrassment, you see—a blot on his stainless reputation. My father was and still is, for that matter, a womanising wastrel, who cares for nothing and for no one... And my first employer initiated me so tenderly into the gentle art of lovemaking. It is little wonder, is it not, that I have scant regard for the male sex?"

"No, it isn't any wonder," Sarah agreed sombrely when Isabella fell silent. "What did you do? You didn't stay with the family, surely?"

"Oh, no, my dear. I sought refuge again with my oh, so very loving aunt. Needless to say, she didn't believe my side of the story. She happened to be a friend of the family, and was firmly convinced I had encouraged her friend's husband to be unfaithful to his wife. She refused to take me back, so I joined a band of travelling actors.

"From childhood I had always been fascinated by the theatre. The world of make-believe is far more pleasant than cruel reality. And I was a good actress, a natural, even though I do say so myself, but being fairly tall, I was always given male roles to play. Which suited me very well. I think I should have been a boy. My life, I'm sure, would certainly have been less...traumatic."

Sarah felt her sympathy coming to the fore once again, but concentrated her thoughts on the matter in hand by asking Isabella what made her turn to a life of crime.

"The theatre is not all joy, I assure you. But I shan't sully innocent ears by relating some of the more lurid aspects of an actress's life. Suffice it to say that, after eight years of travelling from place to place, I had had my fill. Besides—" she shrugged "—I was becoming a little too old to continue playing youths of sixteen and seventeen. So, I began to wonder how else I could make use of my undoubted talents."

"How did you meet Mr Nutley?"

"I met him when our little company was giving a private performance at a large house in London. We talked for a while, and it became obvious that he was tired of trying to exist on the paltry allowance his father made him. He seemed an ideal choice at the time. He was invited everywhere, and he was certainly more than willing to make some easy money."

Drawing her fair brows together in a deep frown, she shook her head. "But it was foolish of me to have taken him as a partner. He was greedy, you see, and impatient to get his hands on the money."

"So you started robbing the wealthy?" Sarah prompted when once again Isabella fell silent.

"Yes. I attained a position as a maid in different households. Sometimes I would work a week, maybe two, and then on the evening when a large party was being held, and the staff were fully occupied, I would steal the various items, and give them to Nutley that night, or the following day when he would call to thank his hostess for the pleasant evening.

"A week or so later I would take our ill-gotten gains to Bristol, hand them over to a certain gentleman I know, and deposit the money I received in the bank, to be shared between Nutley and myself at some later date. But as I mentioned before, he was eager to get his hands on the money. I warned him that if he started throwing brass about, people would wonder where it had come from and get suspicious. But he wouldn't listen.

"So, I made a bargain with him. If he helped me steal the Felchett diamonds, he could have all the money in that account of ours. He agreed, but insisted on retaining the diamonds and accompanying me to Bristol."

"Did—did you kill him?" Sarah asked tentatively, and almost found herself sighing with relief when Isabella, a moment later, shook her head.

"No, I didn't kill him. We managed to get a few moments alone together at that inn, and he told me that he suspected Stubbs of being a Bow Street Runner. I asked him to hand the diamonds over to me, but he wouldn't. He said he would hide them somewhere safe until we were able to continue the journey to Bristol, and so I gave him that little concoction he put into the punch. But as I have already told you, he was a fool. I could never trust him to do anything right."

Again she shook her head as though at some private

thought. "The close confines of that inn posed problems, though. I didn't want anyone to see me wandering about at that time of night, so I dressed in masculine attire and waited. I heard Nutley leave his room, and after a few minutes followed him down the stairs, but I waited too long, Miss Pennington. He flatly refused to tell me where he had hidden the necklace.

"I became angry, and took a step towards him. I must have startled him. He stepped back, fell over the chair, and hit his head on the settle. It was whilst I was searching for the necklace that you came down. I heard you in the coffee-room, and had only just enough time to open the windows before you came into the parlour. I went straight round to the back of the inn, climbed on to the lean-to roof, and managed to open my bedroom window and get back inside."

"And the servant girl, Isabella…did you kill her?"

Isabella turned her head and looked down at her. "Yes, I did," she admitted, her voice emotionless, but Sarah could not mistake the flicker of regret in the blue eyes. "It was never my intention to do so…it was never my intention to harm anyone. But the nosy little strumpet had been poking about my room. I believe I told you that, when we met for the first time at the head of the stairs, remember?

"She had opened the box where I keep my make-up and wigs, and knew I wasn't quite what I seemed. As soon as she had learned that Nutley had died, she came to me. Threatened to tell the Runner what she had seen in my room. The walls in that inn were paper-thin, and I was afraid our conversation might be overheard, so I managed to persuade her to meet me that night."

Everything slotted so neatly into place, and Sarah might have believed Isabella nothing more than a victim of circumstance except for one or two rather damning facts. "You said you never meant to harm anyone," she reminded her. "But you had one of the kitchen knives with you, Isabella, when you went to meet Rose. And you also planted a letter belonging to Dottie on the dead girl in a rather callous bid to implicate her."

Isabella made not the least attempt to deny it. "I saw the knife lying on the table when I returned my tray to the kitchen that evening. Truly, I meant only to frighten her, but I realised as soon as we met outside that I could never trust the conniving little harpy. Sooner or later she would have talked, no matter how much I paid her.

"And as for the letter…" There was a touch of malice in her smile this time. "I went along the passageway, intending to search Dottie's room, as a matter of fact, when I saw that letter beneath the door." She gave a shout of laughter. "If my memory serves me correctly she was—er—rather occupied with the dashing Captain at the time. But then, she always was a flighty piece."

This struck a cord of memory and Sarah, thrusting aside the embarrassingly vivid memory of that bedroom scene, said, "Dottie mentioned once that she thought she recognised you. You did know her, then?"

"Oh, yes. We worked together some years ago in Bristol. Then I went off touring with the company. Can't recall what she did. She certainly didn't come with us." Isabella moved away from the window, and was silent while she busied herself with lighting a candle set on one of the crates.

Then she turned to look at Sarah again. "I'm afraid I must leave you now as I have certain arrangements to make. Wilkins assures me that no one ever comes here, and I must confess I have been here on several occasions and have never caught sight of a soul. You'll be safe enough for now, but I shall need to make arrangements so that I can hide you somewhere else early in the morning.''

She frowned heavily. ''That confounded Runner turning up out of the blue has caused me a great deal of trouble! It had never been my intention to abduct you, Sarah. But,'' she shrugged, ''one must learn to be adaptable.''

''What makes you so sure the necklace is still here? All this might be a complete waste of time,'' Sarah suggested, but Isabella shook her head.

''If your guardian hasn't retained possession of it, then you can be sure that Stubbs has it. He no doubt thought to use it in an attempt to draw me out into the open.'' She picked up the candle and placed it on the crate nearest to Sarah. ''I'll return as soon as I can with some food, but I'm afraid it won't be for some little time, so I'll leave you the candle.''

''Isabella,'' Sarah said softly, arresting the woman's progress to the door, ''don't do this. You'll be caught. They will hang you.''

The woman's laughter held a note of recklessness. ''Well, as my dear aunt was so fond of telling me, I was born to be hanged. But not in this country, my dear. I have a fancy to try my luck in the New World.''

''Then go, Isabella!'' she urged. ''Go now while you still have the chance! The necklace cannot be that important to you.''

There suddenly seemed fire in those ice-blue eyes. ''Oh, but it is, Sarah,'' she countered, her voice throbbing with emotion. ''It means everything to me... Had Lord Felchett been an honourable man, had he married my mother, those diamonds would eventually have been mine. They are mine by right!''

* * *

As soon as he had changed his clothes, Marcus took himself off to the library, and began to compose a long letter to his secretary. It had never been his intention to stay away from Ravenhurst for this length of time. Even had he stuck to his original plan and gone to the Bamfords, he would have remained with them for a week at most.

But, of course, Sarah had changed all that. And he certainly had no intention of leaving her now. In a week or two he would escort her to London. But would she be any safer there? He paused in the act of dipping his quill into the standish, his dark brows snapping together. No, confound it, she wouldn't! There could be no peace of mind until that Grimshaw woman had been caught and placed safely behind bars.

Thoughts of his ward continued to break his concentration, and it was quite some time before he had completed his task. After sealing the letter with a wafer, he left the library and went across the hall to the parlour, and was surprised to discover his grandmother the sole occupant of the room.

"Where's Sarah?"

The Dowager glanced up from her embroidery. "I've no idea. I haven't seen her since luncheon. I thought she was with you."

"Perhaps she's still in her room, then." He sat himself down, and absently began to tap the arm of the sofa with his fingertips. "When I came back earlier, she gave me a most peculiar look, and then shot up the stairs. It really was most odd. She looked at me just as though I were a complete stranger."

"You do tend to have that effect on people, Marcus. I expect you said something beastly and upset the poor child."

He cast her a glance of exasperation. "I'll have you know I never so much as opened my mouth. Still—" he shrugged "—I expect it's nothing. Women do tend to take queer turns at times, as you know."

"No, I'm afraid I don't know, Marcus. You'll need to explain yourself."

"You know very well what I mean!" he retorted. "Females tend to behave oddly at a—er—certain time each month."

The Dowager placed her embroidery on her lap, and looked directly across at him. "If that is your rather indelicate way of trying to ascertain whether Sarah is suffering from her monthly, then I can tell you with absolute certainty that she is not. That was over days ago. But if the poor child seems not quite herself...well, it's hardly surprising in the circumstances, now is it?"

Before going to see Stubbs that morning, he had taken the Dowager into his confidence, admitting freely that he suspected the break-in the previous night had been perpetrated by none other than Nutley's accomplice, after the Felchett diamonds. Her ladyship had betrayed not the least sign of surprise, nor dismay. Her only comment, in fact, had been to agree wholeheartedly with him when he had suggested that Sarah be removed to Ravenhurst for her own safety.

A ghost of a smile hovered about his mouth. "By the by, Sarah refuses to leave. I tried to persuade her, but she won't run away."

"A pity, but I cannot say I'm surprised, Marcus. It's in the child's blood, after all. Her father was a courageous man, and her mother was most certainly no shrinking violet."

They were interrupted by Clegg, who entered to light the candles. When he had completed his task, the Dowager requested him to ask Buddle to go up to Sarah's room and check that all was well. Five minutes later the maid came in, her expression grave.

"Miss Sarah isn't there, my lady, and her cloak's missing from the wardrobe." She cast anxious eyes across at her mistress's grandson. "I know on fine days she's in the habit of going out for a walk with Sutton, so I checked. But he hasn't seen her, not since this morning."

"It's probably nothing, Marcus," the Dowager suggested, but not very convincingly. "Sarah may have wanted to be by herself, that is all." Out of the corner of her eye she caught sight of her butler hovering, uncertainly, behind Buddle. "Yes, Clegg. What is it this time?"

He came forward, a note in his hand. "I have just found this pushed under the door. It's for you, sir."

The Dowager watched her grandson pale visibly as he cast his eyes over the single sheet, and nodded dismissal to her servants before saying, "That woman has Sarah, hasn't she?" He did not respond, but then he really didn't need to, for his grim expression was answer enough. "We must get every able-bodied man on the estate out searching for her," she suggested in some urgency, but surprisingly he shook his head.

"No, we can't do that. Here, read it for yourself."

Although the Dowager's eyesight was not good, the letter was written in a neat hand, and after a few moments she was able to focus sufficiently to read:

I have your ward, Ravenhurst. She is unharmed and shall remain so providing you make no attempt to locate her whereabouts. You know what I want in exchange for her safe return. I shall contact you again tomorrow with further instructions.

The Dowager looked across at her grandson, who had gone over to stare sightlessly out of the window. "Do— do you think she will harm her?"

"She has committed murder once, I'm sure she's quite capable of doing so again."

"Oh, Marcus, no!" The Dowager had been reared to consider any display of the weaker emotions quite vulgar. Not since the death of Ravenhurst's mother had tears been seen in her grey eyes, but they were clearly visible now. "You must hand over the necklace," she urged him. "You have no choice."

"I fully intend to." His voice was impassive, but the look of cold fury in his eyes as he turned away from the window almost made her gasp. "And if she has harmed so much as one hair on my little Sarah's head, I will kill that woman with my bare hands." He went across to the door, but turned back to add, "I must contact Stubbs and tell him what has occurred. For the time being, ma'am, I should be obliged if you keep your own counsel."

Half an hour later Marcus, his expression as grim and as darkly threatening as a thunder cloud, rode into the inn yard. He was suffering agony over Sarah's well-being; but resentment at his inability to do anything positive to aid her only fuelled his rage. Throughout his adult life he had always been resolute, making decisions swiftly when necessary, no matter how unpalatable they had happened to be; and yet here he was, still, frustratingly in two minds.

If he sent men out searching for his ward, as his grandmother had suggested, he might well be placing

Sarah in yet more danger. On the other hand, though, once that woman had the necklace in her possession, Sarah would be of no further use to her, would be a liability, in fact. Could he really trust a woman who had killed before to keep her word, and not harm Sarah? It was a risk he was not prepared to take.

And yet, where did he begin searching? Sarah might be anywhere: here in this very village, or miles away by now. He ground his teeth in vexation. The situation seemed hopeless!

As he entered the inn he suffered a further setback when the landlord informed him that Stubbs had ridden out of the village on a hired horse that afternoon, and had not as yet returned.

"Did he say where he was going?"

"No, sir, that he didn't." The landlord scratched his head. "I mind that he mentioned he'd be back for supper, though. So p'raps he won't be too long."

"Very well. I'll have a tankard of ale whilst I'm waiting."

Marcus sat himself at a corner table, his mind deep in sombre thought. He was vaguely aware that the tap was becoming crowded with locals, refreshing themselves after a hard day's toil, but it wasn't until the room suddenly echoed with hoots of raucous laughter that he ceased his contemplation of the logs burning brightly on the hearth, and gazed about the inn. Unfortunately, his sharp eyes caught no sign of Stubbs. It appeared he was in for a long wait.

Tossing the dregs of the tankard down his throat, he went across to the counter for a refill. "What's all the commotion about?" he asked, after noting the amused expressions on several faces.

"Oh, it be only old Saul 'ere, spinning one of 'is yarns," the landlord answered."

"I tell 'ee I seen it!" vowed a near-toothless individual in a rough homespun jacket, and battered, misshapen black hat. "Seen it wi' me own eyes, I did. And 'eard it too. Oh, m'lord," he said, fixing his myopic gaze on Ravenhurst, "the scream it were fearful, so it were. Like the cry of something un'uman."

"Pay 'im no mind, sir," the landlord advised. "He always be in 'ere telling some tale. Reckons he saw the old witch up at the boat-house on your uncle's land."

The hand raising the tankard to Marcus's lips checked in mid-air, and his eyes narrowed fractionally. "So, you heard someone scream. When was this?" He caught the warning glance the landlord cast in the old man's direction. "Come on, man! I'm not interested in what you were doing on my uncle's land. But I want to know if you genuinely saw or heard someone near that boat-house."

"It were 'bout an hour ago, sir," the old man said after a moment's indecision. He stared fixedly down into his empty tankard. "Sometimes I takes a short cut across 'is lordship's land. Weren't doing no 'arm."

"And you're certain you heard a woman scream?"

"It were the witch, sir! 'Orrible wailing it were. And I saw 'er ghostly shadow through the window. All bent and twisted she were. Weren't 'uman!"

Marcus was far from convinced. The old man looked just the type to say anything to gain a bit of attention, but on the other hand the boat-house would be an ideal place to hide someone. No one local, he cast a shrewd glance in the old man's direction, except perhaps someone engaged in an unlawful pursuit, would ever venture there.

Demanding pen and paper, he returned to his table. The landlord's writing materials left much to be desired. The single sheet he brought was decidedly grubby and dog-eared, the ink bore a strong resemblance to thick mud and the quill was in urgent need of sharpening. Nevertheless, Marcus managed to pen a note which was reasonably legible. He then folded the letter carefully and tucked the note he had received from Sarah's abductor inside before taking it over to the counter.

"It is imperative that you give this to Mr Stubbs the instant he returns, understand?" He handed the folded sheet over to the landlord, watched him place it for safety upon a shelf, and then turned to the old man who was regarding him rather suspiciously. Taking a handful of coins from his pocket, he tossed them down on the counter. "Buy yourself another drink. And if I should discover this witch of yours, you shall be rewarded with the finest supper, fish or otherwise, money can buy!"

The old man watched Ravenhurst leave, not quite knowing what to make of him. If the Earl's nephew chose to go on a witch-hunt, that was his business. At least, he mused, he would be getting a decent supper at the end of it. Because he had seen her. As large as life, all bent double and swaying from side to side, and with hair all wild and tangled... Of a certainty he'd seen her!

# *Chapter Thirteen*

The flame flickered yet again, casting weird shapes across the cold greystone walls. The candle would soon gutter, and then the only light would come from that, Sarah thought, staring up between the bars at the window at that bright crescent shape in the cloudless late evening sky. She shivered, but with her hands confined she was unable to draw her grey cloak more tightly about her.

As soon as the sun had gone down the temperature had dropped like a stone, and yet she tried desperately not to think of the comforting warmth of the Dowager's sitting-room, or of the pheasant pie that was to have been served for dinner that evening. She doubted very much if that delicacy had been sampled by anyone. Hidden beneath the Dowager's prickly exterior was a sweet old lady who would have had little, if any, appetite. And her guardian…?

Sarah blinked back the threatening tears. Poor Ravenhurst must be out of his mind with worry. Right from that very first evening when they had dined together at The Traveller's Rest, he had taken such good care of her, attentive to her every need. Dear God! What a fool she had been to go out into the garden alone! But she had done so, and it was entirely her own fault that she was now suffering the consequences of her own folly.

She gave herself a mental shake. Despondency certainly wouldn't aid her cause. Perhaps she ought to try again to free herself from her bonds? she thought, but then dismissed the idea. Her wrists still felt raw after her last attempt. And what a complete waste of effort that had turned out to be! She had succeeded in getting to her feet, but try as she might she could not pull the metal ring from the wall, and had screamed out in frustration.

The memory of her fruitless efforts drew a reluctant smile from her. She would scream her head off if she thought there was the remotest possibility of someone hearing her, but she doubted a search would be instigated until morning. By which time, of course, there was every chance she would have been removed from Styne.

The depressing realisation had just filtered across her mind when she thought she detected a sound outside, and turned her eyes towards the door. Yes—yes, there it was again! It was definitely a footstep. Isabella, no doubt, returning with some food. Well, that was something, at least! She was absolutely famished!

She heard the heavy piece of oak being removed from its confining metal brackets, and then the creaking sound of the rusty hinges as the door swung open. The inevitable pistol barrel came into view first. Isabella, evidently, was remaining cautious, no doubt fearing that her prisoner just might have released herself from her bonds, and was lurking, ready to attack.

Some hope! Sarah mused, glancing heavenwards. Then she realised that the dark shape filling the aperture was too large to be that of a woman. It couldn't possibly be…? Her heart seemed to turn a somersault. Yes, yes, it was!

A strange little sound somewhere between a sob and a squeal of joy escaped her, and then she heard that beloved deep masculine voice.

"Ah! So the witch does exist, after all. And, I might add, looking every inch the evil crone with her hair all wild and tangled."

"Oh, sir!" Sarah was too deliriously happy to see him to pay any heed to his insults. Nor could she prevent an errant tear from escaping as she watched his approach. "How on earth did you know I was here?"

"I hadn't a clue where to start looking for you, my darling." Placing his pistol down on the wooden crate nearby, Marcus knelt down in front of her and began to undo the cord. "It was whilst I was waiting at the inn for Stubbs to put in an appearance that I learned from our poacher friend that he had seen and heard someone, or—er—something, in the boat-house. He was firmly convinced it was the witch.

"And I must say," he added, casting a wry glance at her grime-streaked face, and tussled brown locks, "you do resemble one."

"And you wouldn't be looking at your best, either, if you had done battle with your grandmother's shrub-bery!" she retorted, her spirit returning, but couldn't prevent a tender little smile as she distinctly heard the half-smothered oath as he grappled with a particularly stubborn knot. "You are like a knight of old, sir, riding *ventre à terre* to rescue the damsel in distress."

"Loath though I am to disillusion you, my child, but I left my fiery steed back at the inn, and walked. As I was ordered not to go searching for you, I thought I'd be less likely to be seen if I came to the exceedingly foolish damsel's rescue on foot."

As Sarah had cursed herself more than once for going

out alone into the garden, she did not waste her breath trying to account for her actions. The criticism was entirely justified, after all. Instead, she asked him when he had heard from Isabella.

"Is that her name?" He untied the last knot, and was silent for a moment as he examined her sore wrists. "I received a note from her shortly before we were due to dine. Which reminds me. I haven't eaten, and I'm slightly peckish."

"You're not the only one! Oh, do let's hurry, sir," she urged. "Isabella said she would return."

"Has returned," a rather smugly sounding voice corrected.

A gasp rose in her throat, but everything happened so quickly that Sarah hardly had time to move. She saw Ravenhurst reach for his pistol, saw the sudden flash of light from the doorway before the deafening report echoed round the stone building and her guardian slumped down on to his knees, gripping his left arm just above the elbow. Then Isabella, with lightning speed, had his pistol in her hand and was levelling it at his head.

"No!" Sarah screamed. Scrambling to her feet, she placed herself between the pistol and her guardian without a thought for her own safety. "You'll not shoot him again, Isabella. That I swear!"

"Get out of the way, Sarah!" Ravenhurst ordered in a far-from-gentle way, but she ignored him, and took a step towards Isabella to avoid his outstretched hand.

"I mean it, Isabella. You'll need to shoot me first."

Ice-blue eyes looked deeply into Sarah's. "Yes, I really do believe you mean that. Well, well, well! What have we here?" She sounded genuinely amused. "You're a lucky man, Ravenhurst. But a rather foolish one, too, for I did warn you not to go searching for her."

The look he cast her, as he rose slowly to his feet, betrayed his utter contempt. His arm throbbed painfully, and already he could feel the stickiness of blood oozing between the fingers of his right hand as he held the wounded portion of flesh. "You'll need me to get the diamonds."

"Stay just where you are!" Isabella commanded, levelling the pistol threateningly as he made to take a step round Sarah. "Although I would dislike very much to hurt your ward, I would think nothing of putting a period to your existence. You don't imagine for a moment that I would foolishly trust you. I'm not so gullible.

"You will get the necklace when I have Sarah safely hidden in some other place. She will be returned to you, unharmed, when you have handed over the necklace. Now—" she slowly backed away from them "—stay perfectly still, both of you."

Sarah didn't need telling twice, and she prayed that the man standing beside her wouldn't foolishly make another sudden move, for the pistol clasped in those slender fingers was still levelled in his direction. Hardly daring to breathe, Sarah watched her bend to pick up something lying by the wall, and caught it deftly as it was hurled in her direction.

Then Isabella disappeared into the night, the door was slammed shut, and she almost sighed with relief when she heard the scraping sound of the wooden bar being fitted firmly into place.

"If I do not end by flaying your rear, my girl, it will be no thanks to you!" Marcus ground out when the sound of Isabella's footsteps had died away. "You have the crass stupidity to go out walking by yourself and, not satisfied with that lunacy, you then place yourself in front of a maniac brandishing a loaded pistol!"

Totally unmoved by the threat, and the scathing condemnation of her actions, Sarah set the small sack which Isabella had hurled at her on the wooden crate, and then persuaded her still seething guardian to remove his cloak so that she could take a look at his injured arm.

Tossing the cloak on top of the crate, he sat himself upon it. He felt more than one stab of pain as Sarah eased him gently out of his jacket, but he was gratified to note, as she rolled up his shirt sleeve, that she did not flinch at the sight of blood.

"I was fairly confident that she would not attempt to shoot me," Sarah remarked after inspecting the wound, which thankfully was little more than a deep scratch, "but quite certain that she would not hesitate to shoot you again. She doesn't like men, you see."

"No, I don't see!" he snapped, far from appeased; then promptly forgot his anger as Sarah, unexpectedly, raised the hem of her dress and tore a strip off her underskirt, and he was afforded a tantalising glimpse of a neat ankle.

Sarah delved into the sack, wondering if it contained anything that might help clean her guardian's wound, and drew out a small flask. "I wonder what's in this?"

He took it from her, deftly flicked off the lid and raised the flask to one thin nostril. "Brandy," he informed her, only to have the flask snatched from his fingers moments later as he was about to place it to his lips.

"In that case I'll have it. James Fenshaw told me that soldiers in Spain use this to clean wounds when they can get hold of it. At least," she amended, pouring it liberally over his upper arm, "I think he said brandy."

"Here, don't waste it all, woman!" he ordered, snatching the flask back and taking a large swallow before she could reach for it again. "Ahh, that's better! It'll do more good inside than out."

He took no heed whatsoever of the disapproving look she cast him, and so Sarah concentrated on making a pad with her clean handkerchief, and wrapping the wound up deftly with the piece of material torn from her petticoats.

"Does that feel any easier?" she asked, rolling down his shirt sleeve, and helping him back into his jacket.

"Much. You make a capital little nurse, my darling," he informed her, using the endearment for the second time, she noticed, and was glad the dimness concealed the pleasurable glow that rose in her cheeks.

Being a level-headed young woman, however, she tried not to read too much into those sweet words, and went back over to the small sack to see what other goodies it contained. Luckily, Isabella had had the forethought to bring more candles, together with a bottle of wine, a wholesome loaf of bread and a good wedge of cheese, and Sarah quickly lit a fresh candle from the remnants of the old before it finally went out.

Holding the new candle aloft, she gazed about their makeshift prison, and noticed something lying near the door. "How thoughtful of Isabella!" she exclaimed, bending to pick up the item. "She's brought us a blanket."

His jaw dropping perceptibly, Marcus gazed across at her as though she had taken leave of her senses. "Thoughtful...? Thoughtful! I'll give her thoughtful when I get my hands on her!"

The look in his dark eyes boded ill for their captor as he stalked across to the door. It was securely fastened by the wooden bar and did not so much as creak when he put his full weight behind it. He then went over to the window, but here again the metal bars were solidly in place, and he knew that it would be a complete waste of time and energy trying to prise one loose. It looked as though their only chance of escape lay firmly in the hands of the Runner.

He threw himself down on the pile of sacks, and sniffed suddenly, his threatening expression being replaced by one of distaste. "Phew! What is that revolting stench?"

"I expect it's those sacks you can smell. One gets accustomed to it after a while."

"Does one?" He looked far from convinced. "Well, I'll take your word for that. What else did the darling creature see fit to provide us with?"

Sarah collected the food and wine and joined him on the pile of old sacking. While she busied herself breaking two goodly chunks off the loaf and dividing the wedge of cheese, Marcus picked up the wine, drew the cork out with his teeth and spat it on the dirt floor before offering her the bottle first. Sarah found that she was thirsty and swallowed the rich red liquid with gusto.

"Here, steady on, child!" He snatched the bottle from her. "I don't want you tipsy. And have a thought for your bodily functions, for heaven's sake! There aren't too many places to hide in here when the time comes for you to relieve yourself."

Sarah paused in the act of biting into her chunk of bread. "Must you be so vulgar! I was just beginning to enjoy this candlelit supper, and now you've gone and ruined it." She betrayed more than just peevishness in the look she cast him. "Though I suppose it's hardly a new experience for you."

"And what, precisely, is that supposed to mean?" he

enquired, after taking a drink himself and wiping the back of his hand across his mouth.

Flatly refusing to admit that she had felt a twinge of jealousy at the thought of the many times he must have enjoyed an intimate meal with only his mistress for company, Sarah merely shrugged and began to eat the wholesome fare, but after a while broke the silence that had grown between them by saying, "Isabella wouldn't have hurt me, you know. It's only men she dislikes."

"Yes, so you've mentioned before."

"And it's quite understandable really."

She then went on to relate the woman's rather sorry life history, but the look on his face informed her clearly enough that he was far from sympathetic, even before he said, "Others have suffered equally, Sarah, and have not resorted to murder."

"I know," she agreed softly, brushing the crumbs from her skirt, "but I cannot help wishing, now, that I'd never given you that necklace. For all I care, Isabella is welcome to the wretched thing!"

"My sentiments exactly!" he astounded her by divulging. "If I hadn't given it to Stubbs, I would have willingly handed it over to her already."

"She won't rest until she has it, sir. She considers it hers by right. She told me she is Lord Felchett's illegitimate child."

This ignited a spark of interest, and his brows rose. "Is she, by gad? Well, I can't in all honesty say I saw any resemblance, but then, I was hardly looking for it." He reached for his cloak and the blanket, and began to spread them over their legs. "Let's hope Stubbs doesn't delay too long bringing it here."

"Is it still in his possession then, sir?" Sarah was astounded, even though she recalled Isabella saying that this was possibly the case. "I thought he wouldn't have hesitated in returning such a valuable item to Bow Street."

The look in his eyes was decidedly guarded. "Stubbs suspected that she would make an attempt to get her hands on it again, and so retained possession of it to—er—flush her out, as it were. Now, let's try and get some sleep. With any luck it won't be too long before Stubbs comes to our rescue."

Sarah made to move a little way away, but was pulled roughly back against him, her head forced down on to his broad chest and firmly held there.

He felt her slender body stiffen, and could well imagine that that lovely face of hers had already stained to an embarrassed shade of deep crimson. Undoubtedly, this was the first time she had ever lain stretched out beside a man, and the knowledge brought a gleam of satisfaction to brighten his eyes.

"We'll keep each other warm this way," he remarked in an attempt to assure her she had nothing to fear. "We've little enough coverings, and it's beginning to get damned chilly." As though to add credence to his words he shivered. "There'll be a frost before morning."

Sarah dared not move, hardly dared even to breathe. The latent strength in that hard muscular frame both frightened and aroused, causing her pulse rate to soar and awakening that strangely disturbing yearning deep within.

If the feel of his fully clad body could have such a devastating effect on her, how would she react if that image she had had of them lying together naked, their limbs seductively entwined, ever became a reality? She was powerless to prevent a little shiver of sensual pleasure running through her at the mere thought.

Misunderstanding completely the reason for the convulsive movement, Marcus removed his hand from her head, and pulled the blanket further up about her shoulders. The simple action brought her back down to earth with a jolt, and she did not know whether she felt reassured, or utterly disenchanted: perhaps a little of both.

No matter what her own private fantasies might be, her practical guardian was holding her this way for one reason only, and although it was grossly improper, it did make sense to give each other warmth if they could. So, she wriggled into a more comfortable position, moulding her slender body close to his, and was ordered in no uncertain terms to stop fidgeting. She could not forbear a smile; scolding was, after all, so much a part of his nature.

For a while she lay there listening to the steady pounding of his heart but, lulled by the steady rise and fall of his chest, and the comforting stroking of her hair, it wasn't long before her eyelids grew too heavy to keep open.

By the sudden deepening of her breathing Marcus knew the instant she had fallen asleep, but continued absently to caress the soft golden-brown locks. It had been a mistake to force her so close to him; he realised that now. He could clearly feel the soft roundness of her breasts through the thin material of his shirt and the warmth of her slender legs nestling against his own, and experienced that inevitable stirring deep in his loins.

He was a virile man, and not accustomed to curbing his very natural male desires. A string of experienced mistresses over the years had satisfied his needs whenever the mood had taken him; but he had never felt for one of them, nor indeed any other human soul, the tender emotions he experienced for this young woman.

Without conscious thought he raised his other hand to trace the sweet curve of her jaw, and Sarah stirred slightly, murmuring in her sleep. Yes, he could quite easily raise that lovely face and awaken her with softly coaxing kisses. He was experienced enough as a lover not to frighten her with urgent passion, but to arouse her with gentle caresses until she willingly gave herself to him.

Yes, it would be so delightfully easy, so intoxicatingly pleasurable to do so, too, but he knew he must not. Certainly not at the time, but soon afterwards she might regret what had taken place between them; might possibly become resentful, especially when the inevitable happened and they were forced to marry. And that, he reminded himself, far from concerned at this very real possibility, might well prove to be the outcome of this night's escapade if Stubbs didn't hurry and put in an appearance.

Sarah was the first to wake the following morning. For a few moments she was a little disconcerted to discover her head not resting on the accustomed softness of a comfortable pillow, but on what felt something very like a hard stone wall. Then memory returned, and she carefully raised herself so as not to disturb her guardian, who appeared to be resting, still, in the arms of Morpheus.

Her lips curled into a tender little smile. How different he looked when asleep, and yet the high-bridged aristocratic nose was just the same, as was that square determined chin; but the deep clefts on either side of his mouth seemed less pronounced, as were the tiny lines at the corners of his eyes.

Suddenly his eyes were open, staring fixedly up at her. "Ah! So you're awake at last. You sleep as one dead, Sarah. I was beginning to get cramp."

Not the most loverlike words from a man who had held her in his arms all night, she thought wryly. But how typical of him! She edged away a little, and turned her head to stare at the early morning light filtering through the grimy window.

"Mr Stubbs never turned up, then?" she remarked absently.

"Oh, he popped in for half an hour or so, but the sound of your snoring soon sent him away again."

The fulminating glance she cast him before scrambling to her feet brought a deep rumble of masculine laughter to echo round the cold greystone walls.

"I am not an aggressive person by nature, sir, but there have been many occasions when I have experienced an almost overwhelming desire to box your ears soundly. Never more so than now!"

Raising his good arm, he rested his head on his hand, and gazed up at her with the most wickedly masculine smile she had ever seen. "In that case I shall take leave to inform you, young woman, that you are a very disrespectful ward."

"And I shall take leave to inform you," she countered, "that from the beginning of our acquaintanceship, I have never considered myself your ward. Nor have I ever looked upon you as a guardian, for that matter."

"No? How very interesting!" The look he cast her was openly challenging. "How do you look upon me, Sarah?"

As my love...my life, her heart answered. She turned

away lest he should glimpse the truth mirrored in her eyes, and said, in quite a remarkable interpretation of a frosty middle-aged spinster, "I look upon you as possibly the most irritating man I have ever had the misfortune to encounter."

He chuckled at this. "Never mind, my darling. You'll grow accustomed to my little foibles in time."

He made to rise, checking perceptively at a noise outside. Sarah, who had heard it too, looked back at him, but remained silent at the warning look in his eyes. She turned her attention to the door. Could it possibly be Mr Stubbs at last? Her hopes plummeted when the door opened, and she glimpsed that, now, all-too-familiar pistol clasped in slender fingers before Isabella came slowly forward.

"I trust you passed a not-too-uncomfortable night?" The smile she cast Ravenhurst was not pleasant, enmity clearly visible in her eyes. "Sarah, if you would be good enough to come over here to me, we shall be on our way."

"Enough of this tomfoolery!" Marcus ground out before Sarah had taken more than a pace or two towards the door. "Take me, and let Sarah get you the diamonds."

"Thank you for the offer," Isabella responded, her eyes never wavering from his face for a second as she gestured Sarah to approach, "but I think I'll stick to my original choice. Not only am I certain that Sarah would never willingly harm me, as you most assuredly would given half the chance, but I rather think that her company is more to my taste."

Sarah noted the look of disgust flit across his features, and hurried forward before he could even think of trying to overpower Isabella. Her wrist was snatched, and the pistol was placed to her temple, and yet, strangely, she experienced no fear whatsoever for her own safety, only for the man's standing several feet away.

"Don't even think of moving, Ravenhurst," she warned, pulling Sarah back and out of the door.

Once outside, Isabella released her hold to toss a folded piece of paper down on the boat-house floor, and then slammed the door closed in what seemed almost a triumphant gesture while signalling to Sarah to pick up the wooden bar.

She did not hesitate. The last thing in the world she wanted was for Ravenhurst to come charging out, and receive another bullet. He might not be so lucky next time. She bent, about to pick up the heavy piece of oak when she saw a sudden movement out of the corner of her eye.

Mr Stubbs seemed to appear from nowhere. The next instant he was cursing loudly as he grappled with Isabella for the weapon. Although they were both of a similar height, the Runner was far stronger; but Isabella, with a strength generated by stubborn determination, fought like a wildcat to retain a hold on the pistol. They swayed this way and that, almost toppling over at one point, then retrieving their balance.

Had Sarah not been witnessing it with her own eyes, she would never have believed it possible for a mere woman to put up such resistance. Two pairs of arms rose in the air, and then swung in a wide arc down again. There was a sudden deafening report, the boat-house door flew open and Ravenhurst came hurtling out, almost knocking into her as she watched Mr Stubbs fall to the ground, his face contorted in agony as he gripped his leg.

With lightning speed, Isabella ran part of the way

along the jetty and drew out a second pistol from her jacket pocket to hold Ravenhurst once again at bay. She either did not notice, or was simply unconcerned that Sarah had gone to the Runner's aid.

Ripping yet a further strip off her already depleted undergarment, Sarah attempted to staunch the flow of blood pouring from the badly injured knee. She was vaguely aware that a conversation of sorts was taking place between Ravenhurst and Isabella, but so concerned was she over Mr Stubbs's welfare that she took little heed of just what was being said.

The remnant of petticoat was soon sodden, and blood oozed between her fingers. She raised deeply troubled eyes to Mr Stubbs's face, and saw him make a gesture with his own.

The silent message was discernible enough. Altering her position slightly in an attempt to hide her actions from the ever-alert Isabella, Sarah felt in the pocket of the Runner's jacket. Her fingers came into contact with cold metal, and something else, too.

Very slowly, she eased both pistol and necklace out, handing the pistol to the Runner before rising slowly to her feet. Ignoring his gesture for her to step aside, she turned and walked slowly towards the jetty, coming to a halt beside her tall guardian.

"Here, Isabella, this is what you want." She held out the necklace in the hand coated in the Runner's blood, and felt heartily sickened by the unmistakable flash of triumphant delight in the woman's eyes. "Here, then, take it! More than enough blood has been spilled already over the wretched thing," and with that she hurled the necklace away from her in a gesture of revulsion, as though to handle it further would infect her with the same malignant obsession.

The sparkling stones, glinting with all the colours of the rainbow, seemed to hang suspended in the frosty morning air for such a long time. Isabella leaned against the wooden rail, her arm and fingers stretching out in a frenzied attempt to grasp the precious trophy.

There was the sudden sound of splintering wood, followed by a terrified, high-pitched scream as Isabella tumbled over the edge. And the last thing Sarah saw as she rushed forward were Isabella's fingers, still clasping the necklace, disappear beneath the murky grey waters.

''Oh, my God!'' She turned imploring eyes up to Ravenhurst. ''She cannot swim, sir...she cannot swim!''

He seemed to hesitate, but only for a moment. His cloak and jacket were tossed on to the jetty, quickly followed by his boots; then he dived into the lake. Sarah waited, her heart pounding against her ribcage, her eyes frantically scanning the surface of the water for what seemed an interminable length of time, but what was possibly no more than two or three minutes. Then she saw bubbles rising to the surface, and Ravenhurst's head, blessedly, appear above the water.

His fingers blue with cold, he held on to the jetty with difficulty. ''God, it's freezing down there,'' he gasped, trying desperately to catch his breath, ''and as black as pitch. I can't see a blasted thing!''

He took a deep breath, and looked as though he was about to submerge again, but Sarah, kneeling down, reached out and held on to his arm firmly, as though her very life depended upon it.

''No, sir! Please don't try again! It's hopeless, and maybe it's better this way... Perhaps it was the only way.''

Then she promptly dissolved into tears.

## Chapter Fourteen

Setting aside the book, which had failed completely to capture her interest, Sarah went across to the window and stared down into the garden. It was set to be yet another dry, bright day. Everywhere looked quite normal, quite tranquil. It just didn't seem right somehow. Surely there ought to be something, anything, to betray the tragic happenings of a few hours earlier?

Isabella's triumphant expression as she had reached out and grasped that most coveted of objects flashed once again before Sarah's mind's eye, as it had so many times that morning. She shook her head in disbelief. Three people had been injured, and three others had died, including Isabella herself… And all because of that cursed gaud! Was it really worth all that carnage?

She gave an almost imperceptible shake of her head. Of course, it was not…at least, not to her. But to Isabella, of course, it had meant everything. To her, no price would have been too high…and she had paid the ultimate price: her own life.

Sarah closed her eyes, trying desperately to blot out the memory, but it would not leave her; perhaps it never would. But she remembered other things too: the way

Ravenhurst had clambered on to the jetty, and had taken her in his arms, comforting her until all tears had been spent. Then, gentle understanding thrust aside by the domineering aspect of his character, he had insisted on being the one to summon help, leaving Sarah to do what she could for Mr Stubbs.

It had seemed to take no time at all before several of the Earl's men had arrived, bearing a stretcher. Sutton, appearing with her mare, had escorted her back; and no sooner had she set foot inside the Dower House than Buddle, at her most dictatorial, had whisked her upstairs, where a hip-bath, already brought up from the nether regions, had been awaiting her.

It had been bliss to soak in that rose-scented water and rid herself of the unpleasant odour off those evil-smelling sacks, which had clung to her like a second skin. Some time later Buddle had returned, bearing a breakfast tray, and had informed her that the doctor had arrived and that Mr Stubbs had had the bullet removed from his knee and was now resting comfortably in the guest bedchamber.

That at least was something, Sarah supposed, releasing her breath in a tiny sigh. But how long would poor Mr Stubbs be laid up? And, more importantly, would he ever be able to return to Bow Street if the injury left him a cripple? She shook her head in disbelief. Who would have believed it possible that putting up at such an innocuous-looking place as The Traveller's Rest would have resulted in such very grave consequences for so many people?

She felt even she would never be the same person again. When she had left Bath, believing the life of a governess would eventually be her lot, she had experienced at least some hopes for the future, but she experienced no such pleasurable expectations now. She had met Ravenhurst again and, incredible though it was, had fallen in love with him.

But it would not be too long now, a wickedly taunting voice reminded her, before she would see the only man she had ever loved, the only man she could ever love, married to someone else... No, her life most certainly would never be the same again.

The bedchamber door opening broke into her deeply depressing reverie. She did not need to turn her head to see who had entered: the loud tut-tutting reverberating off the walls informed her clearly enough.

"I don't know, Miss Sarah. You haven't eaten a morsel of that food I brought you."

"I wasn't hungry."

Buddle drew her disapproving gaze away from the untouched tray, and fixed it on Sarah's slender back. Her eyes softened at once. "Come over here, miss, and let me see to your hair."

Like an automaton, Sarah moved across to the dressing table, and sat herself down on the chair. Buddle piled the silky brown locks high on Sarah's head, her expert fingers working quickly, but from time to time her eyes would stray to the mirror to look at the reflection of the forlorn little face.

"It probably won't make you feel any better, miss, but his lordship's men managed to fish the body out of the lake. All twisted among the weeds it were, with the diamond necklace still clutched in the fingers. But at least she'll be buried proper, now. And she won't be placed in a pauper's grave, neither. Master Marcus has seen to all that. She's to be buried in the churchyard, and no one any the wiser. They'll just think the poor woman drowned in the lake."

''That was kind of him to arrange that.''

There was a further long silence, then Buddle said, ''And poor Mr Stubbs is still sleeping like a baby. Mind, the doctor gave him that much laudanum he'll probably sleep the day through.''

''It might not be a bad thing if he does.''

''No doubt you'll be taking luncheon with the others, miss. Her ladyship and Master Marcus are in the downstairs parlour now, if you would care to join them.''

''No. I think I'll remain up here. I'm not very good company at the moment.''

Buddle's eyes narrowed as she pinned an errant curl into place. There was more behind all this apathy than reaction to the events of yesterday evening and this morning; Buddle felt certain of it. Time for a little harmless deception, she decided, casting her eyes ceilingwards in a brief request to the Almighty for forgiveness.

''Well, that's a pity, because I was hoping you'd take a look at Master Marcus. I passed him in the hall a while back, and it might have been my imagination, but he looked a little flushed to me.''

Sarah's eyes rose from their contemplation of the lacy covering on the dressing table and met those of Buddle's in the mirror. ''Didn't the doctor take a look at his arm?''

''Oh, yes, he did that, miss. Said the wound was good and clean, and put a fresh dressing on it, but…'' Buddle shook her head, looking genuinely perturbed. ''I've known many a light wound turn very nasty, the patient becomes feverish, and then…''

Sarah was on her feet in an instant. ''I'll go down and take a look at him.'' As she went over to the door, she missed the satisfied smile curling a pair of thin lips.

"And if I think it's necessary, we'll summon the doctor back at once."

Sarah entered the parlour a minute or two later to find the Dowager sitting in the chair by the fire, busily plying her needle, and her guardian lounging on the sofa, appearing perfectly composed. He looked up as she entered, and rose at once. They moved slowly towards each other, each scrutinising the other's face.

"You are looking a little pale, child," he remarked, grasping her hand and guiding her over to the other chair by the fire. "Perhaps you should return to your room and try to rest."

And you are looking...fine, she thought, deciding Buddle must have been imagining things after all.

"If the roses have faded from her cheeks, Marcus, it's hardly surprising after what she has been through." A hint of respect gleamed in the Dowager's grey eyes. "I saw you so briefly this morning, child. I'm afraid Buddle is the most wickedly overbearing creature alive, hauling you upstairs that way. But if it's any consolation, she only ever bullies people she likes."

Sarah couldn't prevent a slight smile at this intelligence, and turned to look across at her guardian, who had seated himself on the sofa again, and who looked back at her with such a depth of warmth in his dark eyes that if she had been pale earlier, she felt very certain that that was no longer the case.

"It—it was very kind of you to arrange Isabella's funeral, sir," she remarked shyly.

"I didn't do it for her, Sarah. I did it for you. I knew you would fret if she was placed in a pauper's grave. Very few know of the circumstances surrounding her death, and it shall remain so. As far as the local inhabitants are concerned, a woman merely drowned in the lake.'' His lips twisted into a wry smile. ''Yet another fatality to substantiate that wretched curse.''

''And it is certainly more than the woman deserves,'' the Dowager remarked. ''Yes, I know of her life history, child. Marcus has just been telling me all about it,'' she went on as she received an unmistakable look of reproach from a pair of blue-green eyes. ''But it doesn't alter the fact that she was a murderess, and perhaps it is only justice after all that she died for what is little more than a piece of trumpery.''

Sarah caught the frowning glance her guardian cast in his grandmother's direction, and looked at him sharply. ''What does her ladyship mean, sir?''

He appeared slightly discomforted, but responded promptly enough with, ''The necklace was quite a remarkable imitation of the original. When you brought it along to my room, I was not perfectly satisfied that it was genuine, so when I went to Bristol I had a reputable jeweller take a look at it, and he confirmed it was paste.''

''I do not perfectly understand you, sir.'' Sarah drew her brows together, genuinely puzzled. ''Are you trying to say that at some point after it was stolen someone switched the genuine article with a forgery? If so, where in heaven's name is the real necklace?''

''No, child, I'm not suggesting that at all.'' He couldn't prevent a smile at her continued bewilderment. ''It's my belief that, some time in the past, Felchett himself had a copy made and sold the original to pay off his mounting debts. He's always been a gamester, always been heavily in debt, but whilst his wife was seen wearing that valuable necklace, he managed to fool his creditors into believing that he still had funds.

''That, I would imagine, was the reason behind his anger when a stir was caused over the necklace's disappearance. Any expert would have seen at once that it was a forgery. And he certainly didn't want any scandal attached to his name, especially not having just arranged his son's very advantageous marriage to a wealthy Cit's daughter.''

Somehow, the knowledge that the necklace was nothing but a worthless imitation seemed to make everything so very much worse: the loss of life; poor Mr Stubbs lying upstairs, his career as a Runner probably at an end. Sarah looked gravely across at her guardian, her eyes mirroring her concern. ''What will happen to Mr Stubbs, sir, if he doesn't make a full recovery?''

''It's too early to tell whether he will or not, but there's no denying his knee is badly damaged. In a week or two when he's stronger, I'll arrange for him to be taken to London to see my private physician.'' He cast her a reassuring smile. ''Don't worry, child, I have no intention of abandoning him to his fate. He came to our aid. Rather later than I had hoped, but that was hardly his fault.''

The look of concern in Sarah's eyes was replaced by one of interest. Evidently, much had passed between Mr Stubbs and her guardian before the injured man had succumbed to the effects of the laudanum. She was curious to hear the Runner's side of the story, and didn't hesitate to ask.

''When I had luncheon with Stubbs yesterday, I informed him of the disappearance of my grandmother's under-gardener, and of my suspicions that he might not be a youth. Stubbs guessed that, if the gardener was the woman he was seeking, she would have put up at an inn not too far away.

''After I had left him, he hired a horse, and began visiting the villages round about. At a place about five miles from here, he struck lucky. The landlord of the inn had let a room to a lady, and had been paid to keep it until her return. Once the landlord discovered Stubbs was a Runner, he didn't hesitate to show him the room, and sure enough, tucked away at the bottom of the wardrobe was the damning evidence—a box containing wigs and make-up.''

''I wonder if she was proposing to take me there?''

''As to that, child, we'll never know. The note she threw on the boat-house floor merely informed me where to leave the necklace for her collection. However, to continue: Stubbs informed the local magistrate, and a round-the-clock watch was arranged to be placed on the inn. It was getting late by this time, so Stubbs dined there, and then set off on his journey back here.''

His lips twitched. ''Unfortunately his mount decided to cast a shoe, and poor Stubbs was forced to walk the best part of the way back. It was very late by the time he arrived at the village. Our landlord, roused from his bed by Stubbs's thunderous knocking, completely forgot about the letter I had written.

''Fortunately, the landlady, an early riser, was up before daybreak, spotted the note on the shelf and, thankfully, didn't waste any time in taking it up to Stubbs. And it was while he was making his way through the home wood that he had the great good fortune to spot Isabella and followed... The rest you know.''

''Well, that is all very interesting, I'm sure,'' the Dowager remarked, breaking the short silence that followed her grandson's disclosures. ''But we have far more important matters to discuss... Your marriage for a start.''

A spasm of pain ran through her, and Sarah lowered

her eyes, thereby missing the angry glance Marcus shot at his grandmother.

"Yes, it's all very well you looking at me like that," the Dowager continued, completely unruffled by her grandson's scowling disapproval. "But you know yourself that Sarah cannot possibly remain unmarried now."

The surprising mention of her name brought Sarah's head up sharply. She glanced from her guardian's angry countenance to her ladyship's smugly satisfied one. "W-what are you talking about, ma'am?" she asked, taken aback somewhat. "I am not going to be married."

"My dear child, you cannot possibly spend all night alone with a man and remain single. Why, it's unthinkable!"

"B-but I didn't spend all night alone with a man. I spent it with my guardian."

The Dowager gave a cackle of wicked laughter at the look of outrage on her grandson's face, but Sarah, not quite realising just what she had said, rose to her feet in some confusion, and continued to look at them both in dismay. "But nothing improper occurred, ma'am, I assure you."

"I do not need your assurances over that, child," the Dowager responded, still smiling wickedly. "I am certain Marcus behaved like a perfect gentleman. But no matter what you may think, he is very much a man, and a marriage between you must be arranged without delay."

"No!"

Sarah's staunch refusal echoed round the small room with devastating clarity, bringing Marcus to his feet. He cast a brief glance at the determined set of her lovely features and then turned to his grandmother in no little annoyance.

"Would you kindly leave us, ma'am?" His tone was clipped, making it abundantly obvious that he was more than just a little nettled over her interference. "Kindly allow me to do my proposing in my own way."

"Oh, very well, Marcus." Setting her embroidery aside, the Dowager begrudgingly rose to her feet. "But for heaven's sake don't be afraid to put it to the touch! You've been shilly-shallying long enough."

Annoyed though he was, Marcus was powerless to prevent a grudging smile of admiration from curling his lips as he watched the door close behind his grandmother. She had probably known from the day he had brought Sarah to this house that his feelings for his ward went rather deeper than those of just an attentive guardian.

His smile turned rueful. Not that he had ever seen himself in that light. Right from that very first night at The Traveller's Rest he had been attracted to Sarah, and not only physically: her wit and intelligence had appealed to him too. Never before had he experienced such an overwhelming desire to protect; to cherish.

Discovering her true identity had certainly been a setback—no, much more than that, a bitter blow; but he had taken comfort in the knowledge that the constraints placed upon him as her guardian were, blessedly, for a limited period only.

He had been fully prepared to indulge her with a London Season; he had owed her that much, at least, for all those joyless years she had endured in Bath. He might possibly have derived much pleasure himself from squiring her through the social whirl; and would certainly have attained much satisfaction from keeping all would-be suitors at bay.

In June, once she had attained her majority, of course,

his guardianship would, thankfully, be at an end. Freed of encumbrance, he would then have been in a position to further his own interests, and woo her in earnest. Sadly, though, that delightful prospect had now been denied him; the events of yesterday had effectively destroyed all his well-meaning intentions and carefully made plans.

A deep sigh of regret escaped him. The Dowager had meant well, but she had probably quite unwittingly done more harm than good. Sarah, he felt sure, was still brooding over the events of the morning. It was hardly the most appropriate time to declare himself…but what choice had he now?

He turned to look at her. She was staring fixedly down at the brightly patterned carpet, as though to look at him were abhorrent to her. But he knew this wasn't so. She liked him well enough… But was liking enough?

"I'm sorry it had to happen this way," he said softly, his voice sounding diffident, totally unlike his own, even to his own ears, "but you must realise that we have little—"

"I realise nothing, sir!" she cut in sharply. He was right: her emotions were raw, and this on top of the battering they had received during the past twenty-four hours was almost more than she could bear.

She stormed over to the window, fighting to control the hot tears of biting anger that threatened at what she deemed a most unflattering proposal. She was being offered the one thing in the world she most desired, and yet she was being offered nothing at all.

If he loved her—yes—then it would be perfect, utter bliss to accept; but he was offering her the protection of his name no doubt out of some misguided sense of chivalry and obligation… And for what? What had he done after all? Nothing! Well, she wouldn't permit it to happen!

"I believe the acknowledged mode is to thank the gentleman for his kind offer, but unfortunately I find myself unable to accept." In a desperate attempt to appear politely composed, she had tried to keep her voice level, unemotional, but had only succeeded in sounding haughty, disdainful almost, and his eyes narrowed. "After all, there is no need for such drastic measures. We have done nothing of which we need be ashamed. Nothing improper occurred between us."

"I don't need reminding about that, my girl!" he ground out, both hurt and annoyed by what he took for indifference on her part. "But I damned well wish it had, then you wouldn't be standing there now spouting out this flummery at me!"

Astonished by his vehemence, Sarah swung round and regarded that beloved scowling countenance uncertainly for a moment before an almost hysterical gurgle of laughter rose in her throat. "Why, Mr Ravenhurst! I could almost believe you wish to marry me."

"But of course I wish to marry you, you foolish creature! Why the devil else would I be asking you?"

For a few moments it was as much as Sarah could do to gape across at him, while trying desperately to suppress the surge of exhilaration coursing through her. He had sounded so convincing, as though he genuinely meant it... But how could that be? What of this other woman he wished to marry? Surely he was not prepared to thrust her aside without so much as a second thought like some worn out shoe?

No, he wouldn't do that; she felt certain of it. His disposition was far from fickle. He was not the kind of man to transfer his affections from one woman to another with callous disregard for anyone's feelings but his own. So, could the Dowager have been mistaken? Might it just be possible that his affections were not already engaged?

She watched him move with less than his usual athletic grace over to the decanters and reach for the brandy. She wanted nothing more than to believe that he truly wished her to be his wife and was not merely offering her the protection of his name, and yet a nagging doubt remained.

"It is kind of you to say that, sir," she responded, managing to keep the hard lump which was trying desperately to lodge itself in her throat at bay. "But I understood from the Dowager that you were as good as betrothed already to a certain lady whose name I'm afraid I cannot recall."

The hand raising the glass to his lips checked for a moment as he turned his head to look at her, his expression unreadable, then he tossed the contents down his throat in one large swallow. "So, she told you that, did she? Confound the woman!"

Sarah was not quite certain at whom this curse was directed, but she suspected it was at the poor Dowager. She watched him reach for the decanter again, his hand not quite steady. "You do not deny it?" she prompted when he remained silent.

"No, it's true enough." The contents of the second glass went the way of the first: down his throat in one swallow. "There was a time when I foolishly considered marrying Celia Bamford. Thankfully, though, I never got round to asking her. You saw to that."

Sarah felt as though she were on a see-saw, one moment her hopes plummeting, only to soar the next.

"How—how did I manage to do that?"

"It was while I was journeying to her parents' home in Somerset that I suddenly took it into my head to pay a call on you. I'll admit, I wasn't best pleased at the time to discover you'd absconded." Sarah watched in fascination as a tender little smile curled his lips. "But since, I've blessed you every waking moment. Your actions stopped me from making the biggest mistake I could ever have possibly made."

Placing his glass back down on the tray, he turned to face her squarely. "Look, Sarah, you and I get along very well... Come, couldn't you stomach me as a husband?" His voice, now, was like a caress: gentle; coaxing. "I'd never hurt you, you know that. You could have anything you wanted—carriages, jewels, fine dresses... Anything you asked for would be yours. But I would want children, Sarah. I would try to be patient, give you time to come to..."

He caught the tiny sound like that of a suppressed sob, and saw the tears glinting on her lashes. He took an uncertain step towards her, wanting desperately to take her in his arms, and to assure her that everything would turn out fine, but checked himself. He didn't doubt the depths of his own feelings, only hers.

"Oh, confound it!" he cursed. "I'm no damned good at this sort of thing. If you cannot bear the thought of me as a husband, then say so. I can't...won't have it forced upon you!"

Sinking her small white teeth into her bottom lip in an attempt to stop it trembling, Sarah watched him stalk across the room to stare down at the brightly burning coals on the hearth. Her spirits had soared to such dizzy heights, she felt as if she were floating on a cloud of pure happiness. He loved her. Against all the odds he loved her…and more. He loved her so much that he would not force her into marriage.

Once again she found herself having to do battle with that stubborn lump before she could manage in a voice barely more than whisper, "I think I ought to make it perfectly clear right from the start, sir, that you cannot buy me. I want neither carriages, nor jewels…I only want…you."

For a moment it seemed as though he had not heard, then very slowly he turned his head, and what he saw mirrored in those lovely blue-green eyes sent him striding wordlessly towards her.

With hands not quite steady, betraying the fact that he was still labouring under deep emotional strain, he took a hold of her upper arms and stared down at her intently, his dark eyes searching, devouring each lovely feature in turn. "Do you mean that, my sweet Sarah? Do—do you mean you really care for me?"

She managed to raise one arm, and stroked his cheek with gentle fingers. "Didn't you know? Didn't you even suspect?" she murmured before his mouth came down to cover hers in a kiss so full of loving tenderness that had there been any doubts left in her mind of the depth of his feelings for her they would have been instantly swept away.

"I felt sure you liked me," he murmured, burying his face in her soft curls. "But I never dared to hope that…"

"That I could ever have been foolish enough to fall in love with such an arrogant, overbearing creature," she couldn't resist teasing. "Yes, it quite amazes me, I can tell you. But I recall my dear mother telling me years ago that women are not always sensible when it comes to matters of the heart."

There was little gentleness in him this time. Moulding her body to his so that she was frighteningly aware of every hard sinewy muscle in that powerful frame, he captured her mouth with a possessive hunger that left her lips slightly swollen, her senses reeling and her mind in little doubt of his very ardent desire for her.

"I think we had better sit down," he suggested, rather breathless himself from the passionate exchange. "I managed to contain myself last night, but much more of this…well, I cannot promise to continue behaving like a gentleman. I'm only flesh and blood when all's said and done."

She laughed at his rueful expression as he drew her down beside him on the sofa, and looked down at the shapely hand still retaining a gentle hold on her own. "When did you fall in love with me?" she asked shyly, resting her head against the comforting strength of his broad shoulder.

"I'm not perfectly sure, my darling." His lips curled into a warm, reminiscent smile. "I cannot say that I'm a believer in love at first sight, and yet…I knew for certain when I kissed you in the barn, remember?"

"Oh, yes. I remember," she responded softly, smiling herself at the memory. "I thought you had done so to punish me."

"No, not to punish you, Sarah. I was merely trying to show you how dangerous it was to be alone with a man. And all I succeeded in doing was proving to myself that I had fallen in love for the first time in my life." He dropped a kiss into her hair, and then, placing his hands on her shoulders, held her away from him so that he could look down at her enchantingly lovely face. "And, of course, I was not best pleased over your obvious regard for the young Captain?"

She found this rather surprising confession extremely gratifying, but didn't hesitate to reassure him. ''I certainly liked Captain Carter, but I was never in the least danger of losing my heart to him. And he is certainly far from ready to form a lasting attachment. That is most definitely for the future.'' She frowned suddenly as yet another memory returned. ''But you won't forget to write to him, will you, sir? You promised you would.''

''No, I shan't forget. And my name is Marcus, by the way.'' He pulled her back into the crook of his arm. ''Now, when will you marry me, you abominable girl?''

''Whenever you like, Marcus,'' she replied, finding his name came quite easily to her lips.

''Do you want to be married in London, or somewhere quiet?''

''I think I should prefer a quiet wedding.''

''And so should I, my darling. I'll leave for the capital in a day or two. I promised Stubbs I'd take that wretched necklace to Bow Street. Whilst I'm in London I'll obtain a special licence, and then we can be married as soon afterwards as you like.''

''Tomorrow wouldn't be too soon for me,'' she responded and was rewarded for her good sense with a further demonstration of his masculine passion.

''Nor me, my love.'' His mouth remained hovering above her sweetly parted lips, but before he could experience the considerable pleasure of kissing her again, the door opened.

''Good God!'' He bestowed one of those famed, heavy scowls upon the intruder. ''You've barely given us time to get acquainted.''

The Dowager, completely unmoved as always by her grandson's black looks, focused her attention on Sarah, noting the flushed cheeks and brightly sparkling eyes, not to mention the decidedly swollen lips. "By the look of your future wife, I should say I've been away decidedly too long already!" She turned to her butler, still hovering by the door. "Clegg, bring up a bottle of champagne from the cellar. I do believe we have something worth celebrating!"

"We do, indeed," Marcus concurred, quickly setting aside his resentment at the interruption.

"And Sarah and I will need to put our heads together and work out the wedding arrangements." The Dowager resumed her seat by the fire, looking a picture of blissful contentment. "Have you decided where in London you intend holding the ceremony?"

"We've decided on a quiet wedding," her grandson informed her.

She looked mildly disappointed at this, but brightened almost at once. "Yes, that might be best. I dare say Sarah wouldn't care for hundreds of strangers milling round her on her wedding day." She smiled warmly at the loving couple, who seemed to be experiencing the greatest difficulty in keeping their eyes off each other. "Will you hold the wedding at Ravenhurst?"

This drew Marcus's attention. "No, I think we'll be married from here, if you don't object. Then, afterwards, I shall take Sarah to Ravenhurst." He looked at his intended with that wonderful smile that had won her heart. "Unfortunately, my love, with that Corsican upstart still reigning supreme on the continent, a honeymoon abroad is out of the question. So I suggest we spend a few quiet weeks together at Ravenhurst, and then go to London."

This sounded perfect, but before Sarah could voice her wholehearted approval to the scheme, the door opened again and Buddle entered.

Her shrewd dark eyes took in the situation in a trice,

and a suspicion of a satisfied smile hovered about her lips as she looked across at her mistress. "There's a footman here from the big house. His lordship's compliments…and would you, Master Marcus and Miss Sarah care to join the family for dinner this evening?"

"No, we would not!" the Dowager snapped. "My son only wants to ferret out what has been going on."

"He knows already," her grandson countered. "I explained everything to him this morning. No matter what your opinion of your son may be, ma'am, you cannot deny that he is extremely discreet, as, too, is Aunt Henrietta." An arresting look suddenly took possession of his features. "Wait a moment! Isn't my aunt's estimable brother staying with them?"

"Yes, he is. And that's even more reason for not accepting," the Dowager muttered. "Who wants to sit down to dinner with that prosy old bore?"

"I most certainly do!" He turned to Sarah with all the excitement of a schoolboy. "The Countess's brother is a bishop. I can obtain a special licence from him. We will be married tomorrow!"

"What!" The Dowager looked across at her grandson as though he had taken leave of his senses. "You must be mad! We cannot possibly arrange everything in so short a time. Surely you want all the family and your friends to be present?"

"No, not particularly," he responded with brutal honesty. "Of course I shall invite the Earl and Countess. But we can hold a big gathering to celebrate our marriage when we're in London."

"Shabby!" The Dowager beat a tattoo on the carpet with her ebony stick, her usual method of informing people that she was vexed. "And you Ravenhurst of Ravenhurst! Shabby, that's what I call it!"

"But, ma'am, it would suit me very well," Sarah assured her and then, diplomatic to the last, added, "And when we do go to London, you could join us there. I couldn't possibly arrange such a big party without your help. I would need you to advise me on who to invite, and to help me organise everything."

This suggestion seemed to placate the outraged Dowager somewhat. "Yes, yes, I think I could be of help to you, child," she agreed, betraying more than just a little enthusiasm for the scheme; then her brows snapped together again. "But that doesn't alter the fact that the ceremony itself would still be a paltry affair."

She fixed her staunchly disapproving gaze on her grandson. "And you haven't given any thought to poor Sarah," she remarked in a last valiant attempt to make him see reason. "She hasn't anything in the least suitable to wear for such an occasion. Though I don't suppose for a moment that it would bother you one iota if the poor girl turned up for her own wedding dressed only in her shift!"

He resisted the temptation to respond to this highly provocative suggestion, though Sarah noticed the wicked gleam that sprang into his eyes before he turned them towards Buddle, who was still standing silently by the door, waiting for a positive answer to pass on to his lordship's footman, and who had a suspicion of a wicked twinkle in her eyes, too.

"Buddle, you most admirable of creatures! I'm relying on you to come up with something suitable for my future bride to wear on her wedding day."

"Well, sir, there's the cream silk gown and matching bonnet. If I furbish them up a bit, I think they would serve very nicely."

"You traitorous wretch!" The Dowager waved her

ebony stick threateningly. "You dare to encourage them in this folly and…and I shall turn you off!"

Buddle thrust her scrawny bosom out to its farthest limits. "Master Marcus, sir…I'll do it on that score alone!"

\* \* \* \* \*

*Don't miss the conclusion of Anne Ashley's Regency duet in Volume 2 of the The Regency Lords & Ladies Collection, available in August 2005.*

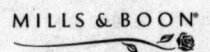

# MILLS & BOON®

## The *Regency*
# LORDS & LADIES
## COLLECTION

*Two glittering Regency
love affairs in every book*

REG/L&L/LIST

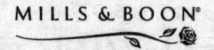

# MILLS & BOON®

# The Regency

## LORDS & LADIES
### COLLECTION

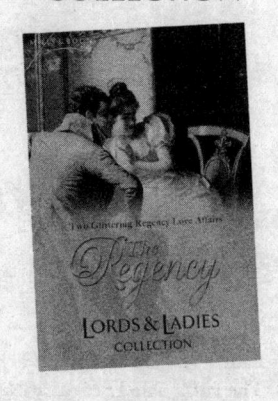

*Two glittering Regency love affairs*

**BOOK TWO:**

My Lady's Prisoner *by Ann Elizabeth Cree*
&
Miss Harcourt's Dilemma *by Anne Ashley*

**Available from 5th August 2005**

*Available at most branches of WH Smith, Tesco, ASDA, Martins, Borders, Eason, Sainsbury's and all good paperback bookshops.*

**Narrated with the simplicity and unabashed honesty of a child's perspective, *Me & Emma* is a vivid portrayal of the heartbreaking loss of innocence, an indomitable spirit and incredible courage.**

ISBN 0-7783-0084-6

In many ways, Carrie Parker is like any other eight-year-old—playing make-believe, dreading school, dreaming of faraway places. But even her naively hopeful mind can't shut out the terrible realities of home or help her to protect her younger sister, Emma. Carrie is determined to keep Emma safe from a life of neglect and abuse at the hands of their drunken stepfather, Richard—abuse their momma can't seem to see, let alone stop.

***On sale 15th July 2005***